Solow

Transatlantic
Blues

Transatlantic Blues

~~~~~~

Wilfrid Sheed

HR

A Henry Robbins Book

E. P. DUTTON | NEW YORK

Library of Congress Cataloging in Publication Data

Sheed, Wilfrid.
    Transatlantic blues.

    "A Henry Robbins book."
    I. Title.
PZ4.S5385Tr 1978 [PR6069.H396] 823'.9'14 77-24629
ISBN: 0-525-22226-X

Published simultaneously in Canada by Clarke, Irwin & Company
Limited, Toronto and Vancouver
10 9 8 7 6 5 4 3

To Miriam
and about time

Transatlantic
Blues

1

~~~~~~

"You want to hear a good confession, Mac?" Chatworth leaned against the armrest breathing a stream of friendly booze. Friendly so far, anyway: we'll see how this chap shapes up.

"I don't think so," said the fellow in the window seat. "No."

"Ah, come on, it'll be an experience for you. A real old-fashioned Catholic confession. How many of those do you get to hear?"

"I'm not qualified. I'm not in orders," said the man fatuously. Not shaping up too well. Some sort of a limey bastard. My confession's not good enough for him.

"It's OK. We're over the Atlantic. Anything goes up here. The pilot can marry us, if worse comes to worst. Come on, now. 'Bless me, Father, for I have sinned.' "

"Please, I'd rather not." Naked terror now. Can't take it, eh? A little of the old mumbo jumbo. Turn you into a peasant lady with whiskers.

"It has been ten years to the day since my last confession."

"No!" The man bucked against his seat belt. "Absolutely not! Stewardess!"

"All right, all right." Pendrid Chatworth stood up. No seat belt for him. Question of faith. "You don't know balls about the priesthood of the laity, do you sir?" He swayed gracefully over his doubled-up neighbor. "Fashion me a people. Then we'll see."

There was only one other passenger in first class. Worldly looking fellow, not the priestly type at all. Then again, the original twelve Apostles were said to be a real mess. So. Let Grace do its mysterious work in this flabby citizen.

"Father, I want to make my Easter duties."

"Sure, sure, go right ahead. The guys at Beth Emmanuel will get a charge out of it."

"No, no. You mustn't tell them. Seal of the confessional. Not a word to the boys at Beth Emmanuel."

"OK, if you say so." The man had an offensively humorous face. Many sins of humor in that face. "You know you talk funny," said the man. "What are you, British or super-rich American?"

"That's one of my sins. Linguistic disloyalty. We'll get to that later. This has to be done in order." He sank a knee to the carpet. "Bless me, Father, for I have sinned."

"Don't mention it." His partner beamed.

"Please."

"Well, what am I supposed to say?"

"Just mumble something in your own faith."

"OK. Sholom Aleichem bar mitzvah oi veh . . ."

Chatworth thought seriously of giving up. A believing Jew would have been terrific, the best, but this joker—OK, God writes straight with crooked lines, so why can't I? "To begin with, I'm a very successful man," said Chatworth.

"That's not confessing, that's boasting."

"Shut up," Chatworth snarled. "You don't know shit, do you?"

"That's no way to talk to your confessor."

"Fuck you, you secular pig. You had a great religion once. What'd you do with it? Boiled it down to make wisecracks."

I must say, the man was the soul of politeness. "I consider this confession closed," he said. "And watch that slobbering mouth of yours, my son. I might be obliged to perform a penance on it."

Not bad, not bad. Chatworth shook hands on that and barged out into the aisle. How about tourist? That's where Christ would be, down among the poor. Chatworth pushed through the curtain.

"Can I help you, sir?" The stewardess tried to intercept him.

"I don't know. Can you?" He looked at her in fuzzy surmise. "No, you're a woman. Wouldn't be canonical."

She floundered. The kid has no footwork at all, can't handle the fast stuff. "Can I take your coat, sir? It's awfully warm in here."

"I'll be the judge of that," he said.

Chatworth slumped into the nearest aisle seat as if he belonged there. He scratched his nose and looked preoccupied. You had to use cunning in these cases. The girl hovered for a minute, obviously untrained in this kind of work. Lovely legs, just like old Diana's, but that's not our mission tonight. Then she almost broke into a run and disappeared in the rear of the plane. She wouldn't be back for a long time. "Sir," he whispered to a wraith by the window. "I know this is peculiar. But I'm afraid of airplanes, and they've got the seat belt sign on. So just in case we crash, would you mind hearing my confession?"

"Say, aren't you Monty Chatworth?"

Chatworth flinched: if you think that's a silly name, you should hear what *he* thinks of it.

"Pendrid, actually. Yes."

"I watch you all the time on the TV. I didn't know you were Catholic."

"I'm not. I mean, no, not for a long time. I just want to make a confession, that's all."

"You do, huh?" Chatworth had never seen such a stupid expression. Was that a bar to a valid sacrament?

Afraid not. "Have you tried psychoanalysis?" said the cretin.

Oh, no! "You don't know *shit* do you?" Chatworth began to shout, and ended in a whisper. If he got too mad, repentance would fly out the window. And besides, the fellow knew who he was. Dignity was the watchword. "Excuse me, but how could you say anything so commonplace, Father?"

"Guilt?" croaked the man.

"Fuck guilt," said Chatworth. "It's not like that at all."

He made a few more calls down the aisle: one fellow wanted to pray with him as the plane went down—an unspeakably vulgar suggestion, worthy of the new Church. No, not fair. Nothing could be that bad. Another man, a Negro from Martinique, took him off guard. "I am a Catholic myself, sir, and I have never in my life heard such blasphemy." Chatworth wanted to cry at this. He reached for the Negro's hand. Was there a ring somewhere he could kiss? This was the real thing. Better even than a vengeful Jew. The Negro said, "I am shaking your hand because I am a Christian as well as a Catholic. Otherwise, I would break it finger by finger." Attaboy and Alleluia.

"I'd still be in the Church if there were more Catholics like you," Chatworth said ardently, his eyes suddenly brimming.

"You're quite mad," said the Negro. "Have you tried psychiatry?"

Ah, they all let you down eventually. Still, the man was right about blasphemy. The first dark hint of sobriety was beginning to show. If he returned to his seat now, it would be holy hell in there. The drunkenness would beat and squeeze its way out by inches through the top of his head.

4

And every thought it passed would be bitter enough to vomit, if only thoughts *could* be vomited. He had to keep going, hanging on to his drunkenness till he passed out in his hotel room, God willing.

He found one last empty seat and talked to a man who pretended to be asleep, telling him a long rambling tale with some sins in it. He remembered confessing like this the last time in Rome during the Vatican Council. He had searched the whole city for a confessor who didn't speak English, and had poured out his dirty heart. And when it was done, he knelt in the dark and waited for that impossible lift of the soul that comes with God's forgiveness. But instead, he heard his own voice in its worst transatlantic whine, saying, "What kind of game is this for a grown man to be playing? God gave you a tongue to be understood." That was his electronic voice, known and admired by many, loathed by himself: fluty, ingratiating, with vowels bought from a pimp in a checked coat who also forged passports. He only heard it like that when he was in trouble.

That was his last Kosher confession. He knew he couldn't make an honest one ever again, though he might try, as tonight, to creep up on it with drunken stealth. Already the electronic voice was testing, tapping the mike, suffering preliminary feedback. So, even though his audience was asleep now for sure, with lips puttering vehemently, Chatworth didn't tell everything he knew.

Pendrid "Monty" Chatworth would have enough to do in London over the Easter weekend and it shouldn't be too hard to forget the plane ride (though it was a pip, was it not?), or the whole bloody evening. There were those who dressed as women when drunk, and those who asked to be flogged. In his way he had done both. Well, busy busy. The limousine was waiting and he climbed in thinking Work. Appointments. Tapes with the P.M. and Sir Larry.

Two problems about this. Jet-lag insomnia was the first.

He could feel it coming in advance. The natives were sleepy, it was past their bedtime, and there'd be no one to talk to: just some furry-tongued fool keeping the hotel bar open, and a distasteful waiter serving him. The other problem was London fever, something incomprehensible to a real Englishman. Chatworth felt like a schoolboy again driving through the dark sprawl. Addison Court, Addison Gardens, Addison Crescent, *Gloucester* Court, Gloucester Mews—huge city with a tiny heart. He cursed the smug size of it. That's the reason he had been unfaithful to it and had lost his heart to New York, that flashy little thing. Fat, slatternly, dolorous London still sat here: come back to me when you're tired.

That isn't a sin, you fool. You can't be unfaithful to draft beer and red buses. The hell you can't. That's the first sin, the daddy of them all. And he'd consummated it earlier this very night in New York, before witnesses.

There *was* a man in the bar, doing a crossword, so probably not too far gone. Foreign office sort of fellow, waiting for late night cable no doubt. Chatworth took an adjacent armchair and counted off two minutes and said, "Ennui?"

"Too many letters," said the man.

"It's good to be back in London."

"Ah, you must be an American."

Very nice. Of course he was an American now. The moment he stepped off the plane he became the other country. His natural condition was foreignness. Even his damn religion was imported. He bought a couple of double whiskeys and another couple. Put the old brain to sleep once and for all. It still felt like a neon strip, but the London fog would roll in shortly.

"Am I keeping you up?" he asked the man with the puzzle.

"Not at all. I only sleep about one night in three, and I'm not sure that it's really sleep at all, you know." Good God, what had brought this on? "I mean I dream that I'm lying in bed, if you know what I mean."

Most boring thing one had ever heard. The consul here was basically shallow. All surface. Could probably keep a secret, though. "I say, would you think I was cracked if I asked you to hear my confession?" He hadn't meant to say it. No guilt-sodden pervert ever felt smaller.

"Not at all. Ex-priest are you?"

"God no, nothing like that."

"No? Ah well. I only wish I could do it properly, in a chasuble and a black box."

Chatworth was instantly suspicious. Was this guy drunk or something? Chasuble and a dark box indeed. Cut the crap now. Chatworth decided to skip the opening gambit and get to the meat and potatoes. "I've been untrue to everything I believed as a boy. Ah, that's growing up you say. I'll argue the point some other time. But the next batch, the mature convictions—that's something else, no?"

The consul was already nodding and muttering expertly. Chatworth cocked an ear. He suddenly realized the son-of-a-bitch was talking Latin.

"Are you Catholic?" he asked sharply.

A quick shake. "No, no. You were saying, my son?"

Shit, the guy was a *real* pervert. He was enjoying it. The consul looked round with bright eyes to confirm. "Proceed, my son," he said. "You're making an excellent confession."

"I'm going to bed."

"A humble, *scrumptious* confession."

Chatworth barged out of the bar, leaving the consul smiling and nodding to himself. I know his type. Christ—I *am* his type.

Chatworth did not go to bed, not in this pillow-chewing rage, but phoned the car service; and when the limousine showed up at the door, he gave an address miles out in the country, far enough to keep them driving for hours. "Goddamn English," he muttered. "God*damn* English."

They pulled up finally at an old churchyard, call it Stoke

7

Poges. To protect the innocent. The driver wasn't going to be surprised by anything. He obviously gave the Eucharist to any passenger who demanded it. "Will you be long, sir?"

"Yes. Quite possibly. Just keep the lights on so I can see my way in."

The high beams of the Rolls lit the tombstones, and he read them carefully as he stumbled past. Snotty bastards—think you're better than I am, don't you? You think being dead is everything.

The door was mercifully open . . . Christ, what a smelly religion! As the car lights followed him loyally, flecking the pews, the whiff of the stone said Papist not Protestant. Roman Catholic churches still stank up a storm, in an odorless world. I'm home, gentlemen. What do you make of that? Too Yankee, you say. An Englishman would only come in here for the brass rubbings.

He groped his way to a confessional, and wondered for a crazy instant if it was occupied. Haunted anyway. As he knelt on the extra-hard wood, which seemed to kneel back at him, he could swear he heard breathing behind the grille and could sense a head being inclined. Real enough, or anyway the best you could do for reality these days. And the ghost would be a good listener. Not one of your "slam bam thank you ma'am" confessors so common in the new Church.

He told his story at opulent length, and it took a bitter turn as he sobered up; and then he began making fun of it, and it dried up completely. What the hell are you doing here, Chatworth? Damned embarrassing. Hope nobody recognized me. He crept out quickly into the daylight and past the scornful tombstones.

The driver was sleeping confidently, his lights still blazing. Chatworth had to shake him awake. "Fascinating brass rubbings in there," he said.

"That so, sir?"

"Yes. Sorry."

2

~~~~~~~~~~~~~~~~~~~~~~~~~~~~~~~~~

Did any of that really happen or is that you fancifying again, boss? I like to tell stories about Chatworth. It makes him seem almost real.

All that is known for sure is that the alleged Chatworth left New York three nights ago, to tape his last shows for this season or his first shows for next, depending on whether you use a Gregorian calendar, and is now safely back in his sanitarium, a 747 jet. Seat belts, stripped walls, sealed exits, it generally suits him very well. At least, it's all the sanitarium he has time for in his busy rounds. But that night, he may possibly have tried to escape in some modest way. He is not available for comment.

I am, up to a point, Monty Chatworth myself, but that does not mean I am always available for comment. Even to you, my little tape recorder. I will not be held accountable for all the babble that goes into this machine.

Right now I am working on my style. And a style that comes in a million electronic particles is not always itself. Ask Donald Duck, ask anybody. After the first time you've

9

seen your face speaking Japanese or Swahili, and have heard your voice rumbling over a picture of the Queen, the king's horses can't put you together again. It is simply up to me, Mephisto the Incredible, to ride herd over this crazy ensemble, this mechanical menagerie, and see that it works: see above all that it remains *different.* Chatworth's very existence depends on his not seeming to belong on television at all, a form of lunacy in itself, you might say—quite rightly, being an exceptionally bright audience tonight.

Not only is Chatworth TV's Amazing Thinking Man who speaks in little bite-sized paragraphs, he is cursed with a special sound, which disappears in a twinkling if he listens to other people too long. He is a compulsive mimic—not by birth but from terror: the poor little tyke remembers a time when a wrong vowel could fetch him a thick lip—and if his famous slipped-accent slipped any further, he'd be done for. So—he talks for the sake of talking, watching the sound, hearing the style, keeping this twentieth-century miracle on the road.

Gibble, gabble, testing. What shall we talk about today, Monty? Well, I thought I'd talk about lights, Tom Fred Bob, which are, as you know, my natural element. Light and heat, the home of the stars. And yet, a funny thing happened to me the other night which I thought might amuse you, Sam Dick Obadiah, especially. Now, you might suppose that any darn fool could trip up to a platform, curtsy, and receive a prize (a third consecutive New Testament for excellence in religious studies, while the crowd sneers). To be sure, an amateur might tug at his collar a bit, blink, gargle, and blubber at the lights. But a pro will simply become himself.

Yet, the lights at this year's Emmy awards hit me like Lucifer, as if I'd never seen light before. It was like some super spirit containing a million smaller ones. The whole country had rolled itself into a sun beaming down on Chatworth.

Adjusting my eyes professionally to the glare, I fell completely apart. I reached for the famous modesty and it wasn't there. Instead, the little screen in my head shows replays of Chatworth, preening uncontrollably in his dinner jacket. "This is not so much an award for me" (the hell it isn't) "as for what my colleagues and I have been trying to do" (whatever that may be). I deflect the rays off myself and onto my cameramen, only to have them come bouncing back stronger than ever. What glory to be able to thank others: co-workers, my foot; without my light they are extinguished.

Five was it? Six? A record anyway for a public affairs show. Hot damn. This is the country I want to impress, not that other one, and its approval is now pouring out of the slot like gold. After the first three awards, I start sending up assistant producers and groups of two or three rosy little men to accept for me. Only to be praised by them, too. "And of course—Monty Chatworth. The one and only. The conscience of television. Mr. Literacy." The applause begins again, as I am seen from a fresh angle: Chatworth, the modest team-worker, sitting right now with his sound crew on this night of nights. I had stopped going up there myself at just the right moment. Naturally.

Later, I shake hands with all of them and walk to my dressing room alone. The sterling fellows scatter like moths. Friendship in this business is a pure affectation. I learned that on the way up, when celebrities used to practice their friendliness on my talk show and their surliness afterwards. It is the friendship of fishes in a tank, swimming now together and now separately, as their interests dictate. How can you really be close to a Screen Credit? Dine with this assistant grip and you upset that one. Win a prize and you upset everyone. In replay, one of this year's losers smiles, touches my elbow; he wants to be known as the best loser in history. I realize he is trying to break my arm.

Still, tonight was the night, was it not? I reached blindly for the Chivas Regal. My plane wouldn't leave for three hours and I decided to celebrate by myself. Twenty minutes on, I remembered too late that the Devil himself devised such celebrations to crown his gifts, on the seventh day of Creation, while the Lord was relaxing with the funnies. At first it was delirious. You don't have to be self-effacing by yourself. Everything goes. Praise flooded my pores. I'm good, goddamnit. America the impregnable: impregnably crass, shrewd, and indifferent; I've beaten you, you bastard. Let vanity be unconfined.

I am not much of a drinker, mainly because of my schedule. Chatworth can never appear drunk on television or in public places, where gossip writers hatch from one celebrity and crawl to the next. He must also keep up his sleep or Mother Network will be angry. So when he drinks it is with the slobbering wildness of a man who lives by rules. With so many outer clocks, he forgets to wind his inner one. Then he writes little sentences about it. That's the shame of it—he writes his own material.

That night I was living dangerously, because I was flying to London on a public airplane. But what the hell—could I or could I not walk on water, huh? What was that the man said? Conscience of television. Jesus Christ. Suddenly I could hear laughter all the way from Chatworth Manor to the graveyard in Yonkers. "Pendrid, you *swore* you would never take this business seriously." A chorus of women joins in, a noxious mixture of the Supremes and the Luton Girls' choir. "Chatworth's got a conscience, oh baby baby, Chatworth's got a conscience, a-going to St. Ives."

Living dangerously. Decidedly so. *However.* Let us consider. People who travel first class do not watch television; right? In particular, no sane person spends his last expensive hours in New York watching Emmy awards. And besides, I have never made a real fool of myself in public. Don't I get one on the house? And finally, I'm never too drunk to perform. Even at Oxford, I could always weave past the bobbies, looking remote and statesmanlike. "Sorry, scuse, so sorry" —that's how it'll go tonight. When all words have fled, I can always mumble "scuse" like an ambassador with his teeth missing.

But first I must raise my spirits again even for that. Where had all the praise gone? Each drink had picked up a little bit of it and run it around the sewers of my bloodstream till it looked like orange peel. I am at least a competent professional? You and Mickey Mouse both. First among my peers, anyway. Hah! Did you see some of your peers tonight? The one with the belly button almost beat you. Lucky there was no one there who could wiggle his ears. Conquer America— God what a shoddy ambition. Still, I'd rather be a conscience than a belly button, wouldn't you? *Shit*. Why did I have to *grin* like that? Coast to coast?

Enough. Time to go. Call for the jolly old limousine and hit the road, Mac. Fresh air and bounce bounce. Do world of good. Feel better in a jiffy.

"Congratulations, Mr. Chatworth. You were great."

"Night. 'Kyou. Night." Night who? George for old England, Herbie for America. Or other way?

I glided, with enormous dignity, past the man who locks up.

"Could you sign this for my daughter?"

Signature? Hopeless. One of first things to go. "Other time. Sorry. 'Kyou, George?"

I climbed into the limousine, but fresh air and bounce bounce turned out to be the last nail in my coffin. The next thing that happened was on an airplane, and I have no comment to make on that, except to say that it was probably taken out of context and blown out of all proportion.

We are now passing over the Azores, my spiritual home. I shall be buried there some day under a huge cruciform credit card.

Who are you, anyway? Introduce yourself. You say your name is Sony? What kind of damn fool name is that? A Japanese war baby, I'll warrant.

I am talking, ladies and gentlemen, to my tape recorder, a handsome little devil and my closest companion now that the serious women have left. Who else is there? If I confide in a regular human, I'm at his mercy. Women in particular sell the magazine rights the day they meet you. In fact, celebrities may soon have to give up women altogether, and take to bestiality, if they haven't already. At least Sony here can have his tongue removed at night, and his memory erased.

Why confession? What is all this Catholic madness? Beats me. Like everyone else, I thought I'd left the old Church the moment it came of age; it wasn't a gentleman's church or even a cad's church anymore, so there was certainly no place in it for me. I certainly wasn't going to confess to a guy in a sports shirt, even if he was hiding it under something. Vatican II was like gypsies moving out of a store front. They might as well never have been there. Suddenly the Tabernacle was just a piece of furniture, an empty chest of drawers, and my spiritual life was a cheap hotel room, just like yours, average businessman, and yours, Mr. small policyholder. My contract expressly forbids any mention of religion and my contract knows you better than a lover.

Yet here I was, a born-again atheist, with the glare and smoke of King Panavision's flash bulbs still on me, craving absolution like a child. And not just absolution: I wanted the whole murderous exchange—abasement, scouring and gutting, and peace at any price. Picture an old man sitting on a swing in an empty playground, waiting for something to happen; picture the same old man giving up and dosing himself with castor oil and going to bed without his supper. That was me.

Because frankly, I hated confession more than anything else the gypsies did to us. It was tough enough keeping up appearances in my crazy home and school, without having to bluff God the Son on Saturday nights. The only good part was bouncing down the steps afterwards knowing I'd gotten away with it one more time. I had exposed myself and I had not been damned; I would be punished, of course, but not annihilated.

Spiritual flashing. The box was the one place where I could fling open my overcoat and reveal my soul. It wasn't my idea —the Church absolutely insisted on it. "Take it off, take it all off." Until, like a shy girl doing a striptease in an icehouse, I stood shaking before the impresario himself. And the Big Fellow would nod his blue jowls and grunt, "OK, kid—I've seen worse. Next, please."

Ah, these similes. There are no similes for confession. Believe me, I have tried them all—women and shrinks and death by drowning in the squishy arms of booze, and they couldn't get me to take off my spiritual coat. Especially not shrinks: having talked to God, I wasn't going to be fobbed off with some Park Avenue earth creature. They could none of them convince me as the gypsies had that *I must not lie to them.* And without that iron law, the magic won't work.

I even found that the next best thing, confessing to women, was a very different sport from confessing to Father Pilsudski or Father Murphy or the other stone-faced judges of the week. I guess I told some truth to Diana at Oxford and some more to Maureen in California—in fact I became quite the slatternly truthteller for a while—but that truth was only a codpiece, a seductive device. Try pulling that stuff on Father Spoletti and you were dead. Any attempt to make yourself sound good or interesting, or anything but subhuman, was met with waves of contempt. That was the price you paid for peace. But what peace!

Am I alone in missing this? Or is there a market out there? I don't just mean for Catholics, but for peak-earning audiences everywhere. S and M for the spirit.

Spinning back to America, the home of problem-solving,

let us briefly review the commercial possibilities. Maybe I can unleash it for the fall season. The nondenominational confession to go with your exorcism kit. Then I can open a string of confessionals across the country, like Fred Astaire dance studios, where you can speak your piece to genuine Monty Chatworth priests who miss *their* end of it—being the ears and mouth of God for a night.

Maybe I'll spring it on the network and see if they salute. Unfortunately, the things that really made it sing are banned by my contract: the real whips and chains not only contravene the First Amendment but are in terrible taste. Maybe we could bring back the great staging, the upended coffin with someone like Vincent Price inside, growling in Latin. But that was just tourist stuff anyway. The real terror of penance would have been the same in a hospital room on a bright sunny day. Standing naked before your Maker is the same all over.

But who would go through that crazy experience for less than hellfire? And who would take that shit from anyone less than God? And those are just the two things no sponsor will touch. Simulated, sure—but soft-core humiliation is no humiliation at all. I tried an est session once to see if it brought back that old feeling, and it was like having a tired Catskills comic flail me with newspapers. Who cared? There were no sins anymore, so there was nothing for him to get at, except my embarrassment, that old thing. Father Mulcahy could hit a lot harder than that with a single yawn.

You know something, Chatworth? It's not really funny. The old Church may have blown out through Pope John's windows, but I can't joke about it yet. The gypsies left that curse behind and it sticks. Besides, confession was a real experience, like sex. The rollercoaster terror, the blasted heath, and the healing voice—it has to exist somewhere. I don't want the other stuff back, just that. It was unfair to make one sacrament so real, in that sea of dreams.

Are we nearly there yet? That goggle-eyed bastard over

16

there is fairly busting to talk to me the moment I put my machine down. He'll ask me if I'm taping a show. Hah! Little does he know—I'm taping that rich stuff that doesn't go into my shows, the Chatworth reserves.

Well, just to wrap up today's episode: The Church of Rome, ever old and ever new, where the very rich rub shoulders with the clergy—that's one for you, Priscilla—and all sins are forgiven except one, which is for us to know and you to find out. All right—just tell me this. Is it something you do around the house? No, not especially. In bed? Yes and no. Is it pride? Is it winning Emmies? How many times? Four, five. But Lord, I missed out on Special Effects.

Could that really be it? I remember the night they voted me broadcaster of the year in the Fresno area, and I went around apologizing to perfect strangers; and after the eighth-grade yearbook named me the fastest altar boy in New Jersey, I felt rotten for a week. But that was all in fun. This latest outburst could be serious. In the appearance racket you can't afford to show your face like that; after 10,000 letters of sympathy, I'd be through.

What do we do, Tonto? For the busy man who doesn't have time for a midlife crisis? I just want to tell the public I'm a fraud, that's all. Being Chatworth all the time is like trying to keep a straight face in church. Talking to you helps a little, as long as you keep your distance. It takes me back to the old radio days when I spoke to myself in different voices to pass the time, and set out seriously on the road to disintegration.

So what do you say, Father Sony? I've long admired your work among your people. Please to hear humble confession? What the hell, we've talked about everything else. And it's either you or goggle eyes here.

What's that you say? "Give me a boy until he's twenty-five." Ah, of course, you're a Jesuit. Which means as usual that you're right and the Church is wrong? Ah so. Children can commit sins, adults can't. They've already committed

17

their sin, their bones are set; they can only live it out. And if Jesuits don't believe that, the hell with them.

Circling pattern is right. That fellow will go mad if he doesn't talk to me soon. Is he a reporter? If so, they're making them awfully fat these days. Then again, anything that moves is a potential reporter this year.

Look intense. Babble, man. Give us a guest editorial, Monty. Time for our wisdom exercises. "It could be, Walter, that the only confessor left for twentieth-century man is sitting right here on my lap. Yes, the humble tape recorder: a talking machine with no one at the other end. You will notice [smile] that its little mouthpiece looks sort of like a confessional grille and it is dressed in black. [Smile fades] Perhaps now that we have arrogantly dismissed our other gods and sent them packing, our troubled hearts can still find something to say to the only two gods that remain: ourselves and our technology. Think about it."

On second thought, you think about it while I make my getaway. Tonight's sermonette will be gummed for you by the Dali Nusbaum from troubled Hoboken. I'll see the rest of you in the funny papers.

3

~~~~~~

Take hotel rooms. They are really just becalmed airplanes, are they not? Two ways of saying *you haven't landed, you have no home.* A thousand dubious men and women have slept in that very bed in there; for a hundred bucks anybody can have it. And the same goes for the armchair. All my furniture whores around like that. It'll support Hitler or St. Francis if the price is right.

Well, if you must live like this, New York is the place to do it. They even put fresh paper round the toilet seat to make it seem like a virgin again every day. And if you can't have a real old family bog, what's wrong with a Hostess Twinkie? Americans are so good at being homeless, they must practice it at home. Surely you can understand that, you bastard son of a missionary. You're pretty confused yourself, you know that, Sony? Born of Know-how out of Trade Agreement. You probably even have some Buddhist parts, you sneak.

"Forgive me, Father, for I have traveled." Chasing my soul like a ball of fur from country to country—surely that can't be right. Whiplashed perpetually by jet lag, Chatworth is always tired, always alert. Bath water only complicates both conditions, and makes Father Sony here cry like a baby. Yeah, New York still has the power to make me feel good. The Golden City still lurks here behind the scrim of garbage and rage. Even the bathtubs are crisp and encouraging, compared with the dank caverns of my childhood. You could float a duck at Chatworth Manor and never see it again; and even in our London house there were pockets of cold water around your middle while the steam lashed your feet.

You want to hear about that stuff, Sony? Christ, you'll listen to anything. But that's priests for you: they can't say, "Get out, you bore me"; they can't hire bouncers. OK, "My Life—a Confession." Or rather, a symphony in embarrassment.

Where to begin? Spying my reflection in a shop window at the age of eight and realizing like a cat that it was not just another cat in there but a friend, possibly even a hero. This was even more important than learning to tie my shoelaces at six or paddling in the Serpentine at about three, other snapshots of mastery. This was pure Me, doing nothing at all: red blazer and school cap, a jaunty ribbon of underpants showing at the waist in imitation of some forgotten idol, a definite style. Like the cat, I wanted to reach out a paw and touch. Vanity. My jewel. I wear it in my sock at all times and it bites like a scorpion.

But it was not just vanity. I satirize myself, a Catholic vice. It was also good to know that I gave off a reflection at all, and that the reflection looked more or less like other people, like schoolboys, like William in my favorite *William* books.

There were no other people yet—I'll introduce them as they come along. My mother was an elaborate corset I'd once glimpsed when she thought I was sleeping; and she was an audience when I showed off, a large, vague applause sign. My father was a mustache and tobacco combination; a sandy sort of man. My sister was a lordly, very English voice saying,

20

"Buzz off, you little horror." The rest were Irish maids of all kinds: laughers, cuffers, singers, ugly beautiful women. I remember rolling on the floor looking up a dress at wonderland. Little fellow's only six, he means no harm. Little do they know. For a few seconds, I wallowed in the future before I was scooped out. But outside of that sneak preview, I was rather a slow developer.

The only thing that rivaled myself in interest was the coming of World War II. That would be super. The barrage balloons against a blue London sky (the summer of '39 was a beauty) looked like ads for a coming circus. Inside the shop window, once I got my mind off that fascinating face, was a panoply of war toys: miniature Hawker Hurricanes and Blenheim bombers, the latest in tanks and field guns, and the deluxe of the day, the H.M.S. *Rodney,* to complete my collection of capital ships. All my pocket money went into armaments. At home my room was zoned into air strips, deep-water ports, and a front line somewhere in France: the Somme, the Marne, I assumed we'd fight at all the same places again, like a series of football stadiums. Presiding over all this, my father's cap and bayonet from World War I, hanging above the bed.

It was an answer of sorts to my mother's room, which was crammed with holy pictures, knickknacks, bones of saint. World War II was my first religious commitment, and, of course, my first betrayal. Wartime propaganda was cranking up and it was perfectly designed for an eight-year-old. No one was too small to tote a sandbag or douse an incendiary bomb. We had exhilarating drills at school, charging down fire escapes and flinging ourselves to the cellar floor; even digging a trench and wrestling contentedly in it. The face on the shop window was cannon fodder: gallantly missing in action, Group Captain Chatworth. Enough said.

My fear that the war might somehow be avoided at the last minute was triumphantly laid to rest that Sunday morning in September. There were long faces on the grownups of course, for the sake of form. But I could tell they were as happy as larks inside. The pastor said, "Well, it's a relief, isn't it?" and we all trooped down the street like late-night revelers: old people, young people, all in this together. I also remember the street as gray and empty except for us. Is that possible? My Irish mother was as excited as anybody, crying great boisterous tears. Although she hated the small group of Protestants that ran England, she loved the Crown, which she thought of as basically Catholic, and the real English people. My father, whose moods (except for irritation) I never bothered to analyze—didn't think he had moods, didn't care—stroked his mustache and said, "I'll be needing that hat, Pen."

Ah, yes. Air raid warden. Me trotting at his side looking for chinks of light. In hog heaven . . . God knows the English later made fun of this period, and then with that wonderful derision of theirs made fun of the next period too, the serious one, and of everything any good about themselves; but I missed the evolution of these jokes and do not really understand them now, though I make them with ease. I secretly still admire Mrs. Miniver. But then she was the last thing I saw.

Because that winter my father announced we were pulling out and going to America. I was outraged and desolate at losing my war. Worse still, we didn't just get up and go, but had to wait around for papers and clearances, while I felt like a guest in a doorway, not fully able to enjoy my war anymore. The sinking of the *Graf Spee* was terrific of course and we followed it like cricket in the newspaper hoardings: the three gritty little English ships tormenting the bully—wasn't that what the Sceptered Isle was finally all about? I wondered if the incident mightn't help to end the war just like that, since we'd clearly demonstrated command of the seas: if I couldn't be here, I didn't *want* any war. Beware a boy with no sense of proportion.

The war stalled again as though waiting for me to leave.

I was sent to stay with an obscure aunt while my father wrestled with the bureaucrats. My schoolmates said goodbye solemnly; they were going to obscure aunts of their own. Despite all our drills, we were being scattered and got rid of. Formby, who brought my attention to tits, a phenomenon I hadn't really taken in before; Ruggles, the class favorite (no reason that I could see), who said, "I'll miss you, Chatworth" (well, I guess that was the reason); Satterthwaite of the flat feet; and so on, like an old regiment breaking up. I see them now in First War khaki singing "Blighty" in soft voices.

At my aunt's I met some actual soldiers who were billeted on her place, and one of them showed me how to assemble a rifle and present arms; also how to goose-step and give orders in German. Name of Lynch; undoubtedly killed in action, with that attitude. He had a skinny, humorous face and black crinkly hair; I remember him perfectly. I used to think about him sometimes when I had trouble with Irish-Americans over the limey war.

Next memory, trainloads and trainloads of troops, on newsreels and in real life, with one man always grinning with a front tooth missing, waving V for victory or thumbs up, and bellowing, "We're going to hang out the washing on the Siegfried line." Another joke now. Goddamn limeys make a joke of God himself. How could I keep the faith when they didn't? I know it was childish, but those men on the train believed it didn't they? Or was it a gag even then? Why didn't someone keep me informed?

Stop bleating, Chatworth. You made up World War II out of the whole cloth. How much of it did I really see? I'm not being new French novel about this. In that atmosphere it was child's play to hallucinate. For instance, I could swear I saw the boys coming back from Dunkirk, with that gap-toothed Tommy still out in front, but I couldn't have. Newsreels, and dozens of trips to the aforesaid *Mrs. Miniver,* have come between me and the facts. Likewise, the war at sea now consists of men bobbing up and down in the water making cups of tea. My wartime England is really an MGM lot, ghastly with good cheer. I was in America when I saw *In Which We Serve,* and my lip trembled pugnaciously over it, and later over just about any plucky cockney that Hollywood could dredge up. Such sentimentality is paid for later with a cold heart. A whore's progress. I believed everything once, felt everything. But baby look at me now.

They took Chatworth away eventually, leaving behind his *Wonder Book of the Army* and his maps with the pins in. He believes there was a slight disturbance dockside when they took away his gas mask, which he'd thought was his for life: a flailing tantrum in fact, with father puffing mildly on pipe and mother laughing, damn her, a sure-fire cure. Father points pipe at man with huge baby face. "That's an American." Good Lord.

Chatworth was bad company on the trip out. For one thing, he openly craved a torpedoing. At night he sat by his porthole craning for enemy submarines, damn near praying for them in fact . . . "if that be Thy wish."

Meanwhile, the convoy wallowed along like a troop of circus elephants, all safe and smug. Chatworth cursed aloud. He had a high, embarrassing voice in those days and didn't hesitate to use it in the ship's dining room, denouncing deserters and slackers and sundry rats who left England at a time of need.

"Daddy, *make* him shut up," said his sister, Priscilla. "The sound is so dreadful."

"He'll subside eventually, I daresay," said Daddy.

Argh! Time for a hair-pulling contest. Meanwhile, father here, "But Daddy, *how* can you leave England at a time like this? Haven't you got an old commission or something?"

"Hush, Pendrid. I'm a spy," said Mr. Chatworth, and the people at the next table laughed.

I still recoil whenever I hear little English boys talking. "But Daddy." I resented my father all the way over, not only for being a traitor, but for making me one, too, and finally for making a joke of the whole thing. Meanwhile, my mother said incessant rosaries to keep off the very torpedoes I yearned for. France fell about then, slimy little frogs, and England stood alone.

In such a state, I was in no mood for America. The famous skyline could certainly do with a good bombing. Yes. Glorious. Those big buildings splitting like firecrackers, bleeding fire; terrified mobs pouring down the streets as German fighters strafed them—well, a bit severe that. I decided to stick to the buildings and let the civilians go, with a good lesson.

The children were much too soft and fat. That was the first thing I noticed. A striped T-shirt with chocolate running down it seemed to be the uniform. By George, these people could use a war. And then, quite disjunct from that, an inferno of legs pounding along Fourteenth Street, couldn't take that in at all, and a hotel room with buses whining below and strange cries of "Pull it in Mac" and "Fucking Jersey drivers," and being interviewed by an English actress for the wireless.

When was that? I dimly remember a studio full of smarmy little refugees, busily buttering up their new hosts. "I think America is super. Ice cream popsicles and the World's Fair. Super!" whinnied one of these horrors.

I edged my way up grimly and let the actress have it. "I think it's pretty rotten, if you ask me."

She had a fixed smile under the make-up which looked quite menacing close up. "Surely you don't mean that, sonny. This great country has opened its heart to you."

"I wouldn't know about that," I said stiffly. "I do know that my own country is fighting for its life while theirs is sitting back stuffing itself." I felt triumphant. I shouldered my way past the little snivelers, feeling like a film star myself.

In the taxi, my father said, "I do think you might try a little manners over here. Just a suggestion."

"Suppose I don't take it," I said defiantly. This was, after all, a moral issue.

"I recommend that you take it."

I am getting a clearer picture of him about now. A lackadaisical man, who only showed animation when somebody entered or left the Catholic Church, and then not much. "So soandso's Roming it, is he? Good, good. I thought we'd get the old heathen eventually." But in vagueness is strength. To my surprise, I did not answer back again. I didn't try manners, but my rudeness became a little less spectacular, i.e., I didn't broadcast it over the BBC anymore.

I continued to give it to those in close range, however. This included my new hosts, the Snodgrasses of Larchmont, and their son, incredibly named Elmer. The least I could do for the war effort was make these people uncomfortable, and I never missed a chance. "What d'you suppose it costs to light this place?" I said at the Rye amusement park. "I can think of some far better uses for the money."

A Chatworth sampler. A small boy with a hint of buck teeth deployed smugly in a rosy mouth. He was especially hard on the amusement park, because he was tempted to enjoy it. "None for me," he said at the hot-dog stand. "You could feed a regiment just with what you people waste." Yet, the bright lights were tempting as sin and the barbaric noises in the night; there was a *texture* to American life that made him sick at first but which excited him, too, and made him want to laugh and shout, "Well all right, then!" Instead he said, "These people have absolutely no taste, have they, Daddy?"

"Between ourselves, no," said Daddy.

Mr. Chatworth just showed up for weekends. Between times, he pottered about in the import-export business, feathering his nest while the bombs fell. One of the reasons I'm still confused about my father is that I went on believing this for years, only learning at University that he was a spy after all, working for the man called Sinister, and that our delay in leaving England was occupied in strategy sessions. I find this hard to forgive.

"Quite frankly, I'm ashamed of my father," I told Elmer, who was—give the little twit his due—a good listener.

"How come they let him out of England?" Christ, Chatworth, you had it right there. Elmer gave you the big fat clue on a platter with an apple in its mouth.

"I daresay he pulled strings. He knows bags of important people. I say, what are all those funny-looking flags doing on your wall?"

"They're college football teams."

"I see. Dartmouth. Brown. Harvard. Are those your favorites?"

"Not especially. They're just for decoration."

"I see. Just for decoration." Amused smile. "Football teams."

Dear God, I can't stand much more of this. No depth analysis ever hurt more than a history of embarrassment. And yet our plucky little limey lad was not the worst you'll see of me. He was only doing his duty, and the Snodgrasses appeared to be impressed. "I love your boy's spirit," said Mr. Snodgrass. This was nice of him because we'd just had a disgraceful row—in fact if I tell you that one maybe I'll be let off the rest. Just finish this martini here and absolve myself and be on my way.

Props. Book-lined study, chessboard, soft-voiced man in tweed jacket and corduroys. Bert Snodgrass had known my father at Oxford and was, I now realize, a quintessential Rhodes scholar: absolutely average in looks, mind, and bodily hygiene. He had just beaten me at chess, because I refused to take a handicap. Score one for John Bull.

"I suppose this was originally a war game," I said, and Bert Snodgrass agreed that this must be so. He told me all he knew about chess. Unfortunately, I detested idle conversation, and particularly did not want to hear about the Ming dynasty right now.

"That's very nice," I said. "Of course, if England and America ever went to war, we'd blockade you and starve you to death in no time."

Snodgrass seemed to consider this carefully. "I suppose you would," he said. "The retreat from Dunkirk was an excellent use of defensive knights."

I stood up. *"Retreat?"* I said. "Retreat? Dunkirk was a dazzling success."

"Well, of course, in its way. But it was still a retreat."

"I will not have Dunkirk called a retreat."

"All right, then, a masterly withdrawal. Look, Butch," yes, he called me Butch, "we all admire your pluck enormously . . ."

"My pluck has nothing to do with it," I snarled. "We're talking about facts."

"It isn't easy being a refugee."

"Refugee!" I screamed. "I am not a refugee!" I raised my fists and glared.

With my parents, it would have stopped right there. But there was something in Snodgrass's face, a half smile, almost of encouragement, a softness, that demanded more. I marched over to the stool he was sitting on and said, "Will you or won't you take that back?"

"Look, Butch. There's nothing wrong with being a refugee."

OK, I tried to hit him in the face. I'd been trapped into it. Now let's get out of this room right away. And out of the house too and into the yard where the lightning bugs are going full blast and the crickets are gunning their engines and the air is like a steam bath: an aggressive American night.

There to cry tears of rage into the grass. Embarrassment had made its first shy appearance. It would move in with its trunks and birdcages later.

Quick progress report on the other faces in my life as we begin to circle. Sister becoming, I realize, what passes for good-looking. Growing breasts, unless my eyes deceive me. Learns pig Latin and taunts me in it, before I grasp key. "Little toad" becomes "itlay oadtay," as I recall. Also jeers at my haberdashery and gives much thought to her own. Surprises me one day by embracing me and kissing me on the lips, then running off. I can make nothing of this.

Mother still very concerned about war. More patriotic than my father it seems. Very strange for a girl called O'Grady. She listens to all available news bulletins as the Battle of Britain hots up, and backs me to the hilt in my John Bull attitudes. Encourages me to sing "Knees Up Mother Brown" on all occasions.

So we say farewell to the Snodgrasses. Before we left, I picked a fight with the luckless Elmer and left him half-strangled on the lawn. I really hadn't meant anything like that and I got panicky as I ran to fetch the nearest Snodgrass. "I think I've killed him. I didn't mean it," I chaffered. Ann, or Mom (loathsome word), ran past me grimly and ministered to her purple-faced son. Up to then she'd been rather plasticly kind to me, but she was ice cold now and for the rest of my stay. Elmer recovered in no time, but he treated me like a dangerous animal from then on. Bert Snodgrass remained technically friendly, but there was nothing inside it anymore. And the last time he said, "Butch is a real little fighter," he didn't smile.

To hell with them. They were soft people. I had every excuse. I came from a bulldog race that was fighting for its life. I had no time for softness or anything else American. I was nine years old. Now let's, for Godsake, change the subject.

4

~~~~~~~~~~~~~~~~~~~~~~~~~~~~~~~~~~~~~

I don't know if it's a coincidence, but last night's show went uncommonly well. I hit, don't you agree, just the old unassuming note that can be such a strain when you don't feel up to it. When Harry mentioned the Emmy awards, I suddenly saw nothing but Snodgrasses out there and my own rotten little self, and my grimace was a classic.

So. I believe there are athletes who won't change their socks during a winning streak, and confession can't be any smellier than that. It won't be easy to confess on a plane from New York to L.A. You can't feel guilty on the way to California unless you've gained weight. But then, some Saturdays were like that. One had to confess anyway, for practice, so one dredged up little lies and rages. The sacrament still worked; you felt just as rotten and relieved. Let me see what I can find appropriate to California. Is liking Los Angeles a sin in itself? Not strictly? I'm beginning to worry about you, Sony: you don't know a sin when you hear one.

Every year, rightly considered, contains all the horrors you need, so I'll just keep going straight. The next period concerns Chatworth and Power, as we watch our war-torn brat attempting to take on a whole continent with rib-tickling results. But first, a thought from our underwriting grant.

The world is full of books about sensitive boys finding themselves, but we never hear from the others—the insensitive boys who don't find themselves. That was me, the real majority. What becomes of those snout-nosed bullies who terrorized you or those salacious dwarfs who beckoned you to the bushes? They disappear into adulthood and tell no tales. Yet, we are the ones you need to know about. Who cares about the sensitive ones, besides themselves? If there were so many of them, where does all the trouble come from?

They lie, that's what it is. Ja. They lie about their own vileness. Der little people are even more guilty dan der leaders . . .

"Excuse me, sir."

Oh, good grief. I'm not safe even when I'm talking to myself.

"Aren't you Monty Chatworth?"

"No, no. I'm his idiot brother Pendrid." As Monty I would have to be nice to him. As Pendrid I'm on my own. "I'm going to be Eva Braun in the school play."

He grins with delight. You can't insult a member of the public. He lopes back across the aisle with his anecdote, and will even protect me now from the other passengers. Good old Towser.

Where was I? Well, "Monty," as all you groupies know, is my *nom de telly.* After raging at "Pendrid" for years, I let them talk me into "Monty"—but by then it could have been Bozo the Clown. The first faltering steps in dog shit are the most instructive. So let us return to the boy in the shop window, that statuette of Pride, and see what became of him.

I might have been sensitive if it hadn't been for the war effort. My parents had signed me up for a Catholic boarding school—full, naturally, of Irish boys; and you can be sure

31

that the confrontation between John Bull and the Micks will be every bit as gripping as the death of Little Nell. But for a while I thought I had everything going for me. I was a rabid Catholic in the making, a Fred Astaire among altar boys, which guaranteed me protection from the fuzz—the priests who ran the place. I also had, my sister tells me, a certain insinuating charm (her word was "slimy," but let it pass) of a kind that has since inflated like a goiter and endeared me to millions. And I was, till then, quite without fear, having never met anything to be afraid of. Fearless boys are a lordly minority in any school, and it was great while it lasted. Anyway, it took all this and more to keep me from being killed in the first week.

Chatworth playing football in the dusk with a rolled sock for a ball. Depression, you know. The field is a long hilly lawn, murky at the edges. You run until you're tackled, then drop the sock. Big sleepy boy called O'Brien tackles Chatworth too roughly for his taste. "Hey guys, a fight." Chatworth is hauling at O'Brien's knees, which turn out to be tree trunks, damned awkward, but O'Brien goes down eventually, laughing, and Chatworth clambers onto him like a bird. O'Brien still laughing, unbelieving. "OK, kid, OK." He tries to remove Chatworth, but finds himself briefly pinned. Chatworth is fighting like a tiger. An Englishman can lick ten of these people.

O'Brien rolls him over at last. "Say, you're pretty strong," he says. Gets up, rubs at grass stains. Crowd disperses. Chatworth tackles him again. Jesus. This time O'Brien trusses him up and pins him good. "What's the matter with you, kid?"

Chatworth breathes defiance.

"Look, if I get up, can I trust you not to do it again?" Shakes head. "No."

O'Brien digs his knees uncertainly into Chatworth's biceps. A gentle boy, nothing to fear. "I can't, huh?"

"Absolutely not."

Impasse. O'Brien doesn't want to kill him, but it seems it will take that. Visions of Dunkirk. The crowd watches, confused. They've never seen the like. O'Brien digs harder. "Say Uncle," he says.

"Say what?"

"Say Uncle."

"Why should I say that?"

"It means you win."

"But you don't win, you know."

Almost time to go inside now. O'Brien's knees tremble. Poor bugger, I don't blame him.

"Why don't *you* say Uncle?" says Chatworth.

O'Brien stares unbelieving. Then grins. Everybody laughs, a warm comforting laugh. "You've got a lot of guts, kid. OK, Uncle."

Chatworth gets up stiffly, walks to house through what he takes to be a respectful crowd. Chatworth has left his calling card. Made in England. O'Brien says, "Stop picking on us big kids, do you hear?" More laughter. Oh God, spare us such triumphs.

It won me my first audience; and like all my audiences, it was based on a misunderstanding. I was obviously quite mad, but I had guts. So my work was cut out. A couple of days later, I picked a fight with an Italian kid called Ponzo. O'Brien and I and some others had been having a bull session in Ponzo's room without the host's invitation, and Ponzo came in and yelled, "Fungoo, everybody out!" The others complied amiably but I sat tight, "until you ask me politely."

Ponzo pushed and I pushed back. "You're crazy," said Ponzo. He probably didn't want to go ninety-eight rounds with a maniac over such an issue. "You better be gone when I get back," he said, starting out no doubt on a twenty-mile hike.

O'Brien, my patron, said, "I'm backing this kid against the whole Italian army." He put his arm around me and we left Ponzo's room together.

It was my mission now to start foolish fights. Strange, what the Lord calls us to. I had never been much of a fighter. But with O'Brien betting me against the field, I could only raise the ante myself. And for a while it was quite a cozy arrangement, with my opponents usually backing off in mock fear. "Don't hit me, Sir Winston. I ain't tangling with old Sir Winston here." By selecting the biggest boys, I guaranteed that I would never get hit. Eccentricity was my meal ticket, and I laid it on with a thick brush.

I've often wondered where my parents found that school (Mother swears she can't remember). The boys ranged from awesomely stupid to bright-but-lazy, and so did the monks. I was started off in the fifth grade, where they were still struggling with reading, was promoted the same day to the sixth grade, where they were still struggling with reading, and finally, two days later, found myself becalmed in the seventh grade, where the struggle had ceased. Each class seemed exactly like the others, except the boys got bigger. We studied the same texts, mostly to do with the War of Independence (of which I had not previously heard), the capitals of the forty-eight states, and some other jaw-breaking material.

"Potty education system," I said in a noisy aside; ruminating out loud was my new thing.

"I'll bet you've got a great one back in England, huh?" said my roommate, Tim O'Connor.

"Well it's a sight better than this one, I can tell you."

Picture now a bedroom full of boys, some entering, some leaving, the light fading, the room sometimes empty, then full again, little Sir Winston holding court like Socrates for these young baboons.

"That war of yours, you know, the one you're so in love with, was just a minor skirmish for us. I gather we were engaged in something rather more important on the continent."

"Is that a fact?"

34

"Yes. And the killing thing about it is that most of your chaps were English anyway, weren't they? Your Washingtons and Jeffersons and so forth. They spoke more like me than like you, you know."

"I'd never thought of that."

"Now as to this present war, the one you chaps are avoiding so carefully, the first thing to understand is our Suez lifeline." I followed the war punctiliously in those days and knew where all the arrows pointed. Of course, these Yahoos barely knew there *was* an African campaign.

"You know, if our chaps fail, you people will be next. I hear the Germans are developing long-range bombers that can make New York and back in an afternoon. And, of course, they won't even have to do that. They'll have Jamaica and Trinidad by then and [pause for gravity to sink in] I wouldn't be a bit surprised if they have Canada as well."

"Gosh. I hope you chaps don't fail."

Did that make me suspicious? I can't remember.

"Don't worry," said a solemn, rat-faced boy called Muldoon. "If there are any more at home like Sir Winston here, they won't fail."

Stray laughter in the halls, the word "chaps" echoing, oh I had warning enough. But their interest was so sincere that I dismissed the faint bleeps. Meantime, I decided to carry my forays into the classroom. The name "Cecil" came up, God knows why, in our reading, and I put up my hand to correct the reader's pronunciation. "That's supposed to be 'Sissel,' you know."

The teacher, one of our very dumbest, said, "Over here you'll find we say 'See-sil,' Pen."

"Well, that's just wrong," I said flatly.

"Maybe, but that's the way we say it."

I decided to let it go—you can't fight on every front. But alas, when my own turn came to read, the damn name came up again, and not only that—the name next to it was Ralph.

"Sis-sel and Rafe," I said stoutly. And then to be helpful,

"Look here it's an English book, isn't it? And these are English characters, aren't they? So they have to be pronounced the English way."

Father Cornelius seemed to be at a loss. He just kept saying, "Say 'Seesil' and everything will be OK," with a silly fixed grin. Finally, he made me stand out in the corridor, which was no punishment at all. I was still seething proudly out there when the class broke up.

"You really hung in there, kid," said Muldoon. "You showed me something today."

"Matter of principle," I said stiffly.

Tell me I parody myself. Tell me that Muldoon didn't laugh as he turned the corner. Tell me anything.

Anyway, Muldoon told the story again that night to some other guys, until even Chatworth was embarrassed. "It was nothing," I said.

"Raw courage is nothing?" said Muldoon incredulously. "Boy, I wouldn't stick my neck out for 'Ralph' if I was over there. I'd say 'Rafe' and 'Sissel,' yes *ma'am.*"

The talk turned quickly to sex, where I was lost. "Won't you take it in your hand, Mrs. Murphy?" said Muldoon. "It weighs but a quarter of a pound. It has hair on its neck like a turkey, and it spits when you shake it up and down." I knew of no such phenomenon. My friends grinned greasily and said, "Hoo boy!" and "Mm *mmmm,*" and my own member stiffened inexplicably. But I was too proud to ask why.

My knowledge of sex and of life lost a year that one never quite makes up. My English pals had been just about to discover what Mrs. Murphy was up to—they were baying all around it—and the Americans had probably discovered it last summer. But I did swallow enough pride to ask my roommate, O'Connor, some offhand questions, as if I just wanted to brush up on some details.

"You don't *know?*" he said. O'Connor paused and frowned. "Well don't come to me, Winnie. 'If you corrupt the least of my little ones'—I can't remember what happens to you if you do that, but I know it ain't good."

It only occurred to me years later that O'Connor knew no more than I did, and that his peculiar laughter at dirty jokes came as much from unease as lust. Anyway, sex and I were competing for public attention (as we still are), and after a while I would yank the conversation back to something solid like postwar recovery until an oaf like Ponzo would clap his arm and shout, "Fungoo!"

The Italian kids had nothing to say about war that year, so they forged ahead with sex, while the Irish panted to keep up. This might even explain why Ponzo had the good sense not to fight with me that day: he had glimpsed a higher good than scuffling with maddened little boys. Anyway, this brings us to our one Jewish kid—and if anyone can tell me what he was doing at St. Boniface, I'm still waiting. One thing he did was change my life, but he could hardly have been sent just for that.

Morton Green was a quiet, studious kid, and hence something of a man of mystery in our hearty establishment. Picture him hovering on the edges, watching, as I describe another corner of this pigsty. The football field. Our coach, a German monk who thought he was Knute Rockne. "Show me a good loser and I'll show you a quitter," he would grunt at the squad. Actually, we lost all the time, so we developed some excellent losers. Our Saturday nights were voluptuously wretched as the players scuffed the ground with their feet and refused to answer questions: performing prodigies of bad losing. Suddenly, Father Walburger would set his jaw up there at the head table and narrow his tiny blue eyes, totally wrapped up in his dream, and begin then and there drawing diagrams for next week's game on the tablecloth while the rest of us ate. Later, there would be a team meeting with the squad trooping in grimly, only to emerge clapping their hands and shouting, "Let's go get 'em," although the next game was a week away.

Green and I watched all this, both of us too small to play, but I at least dead eager to, as soon as I could figure out the bally game. I was quickly caught up in Father Walburger's dream and never missed a practice. He had put in some complicated systems based on the Notre Dame shift which were totally beyond our personnel, even when there was no enemy to run against. "OK, ladies," shouted Walburger, who'd heard of Rockne's scathing sense of humor. "Come on, girls."

I thought he was neat, and I asked Green if he didn't agree. Green paused a moment, and then said, "I think he's a fucking Nazi."

I don't know why I was so shocked. I hated Germans with every fiber. But Green had interrupted my emotional flow. I had to act quickly. My reputation for irrational rage had to be honored. Chatworth pushed Green viciously in the chest and he toppled, mostly from surprise—no knockdown. He got up slowly, picked up his books, and walked away.

A hundred novelists have since told me what he was thinking. To me it was just another Chatworth triumph. Later, I told O'Connor about it and he said, "I guess Jews don't like to fight."

"Is Green Jewish?"

"Are you kidding?"

I knew about Jews and didn't know. Just as I knew about sex and didn't know. For instance, when O'Connor told me that Green had "done something" to the school dog, Ninian, I knew exactly what he meant, and knew that it was deeply disgusting; yet, I didn't know beans about intercourse. And I knew it was just like a Jew to do a thing like that, whatever a Jew was. I have tried flushing out this particular cesspool several times, but the fetid material just stirs sluggishly and comes to rest as it was.

O'Connor seemed to have no animus against Green, but my own indignation must have amused him, because after that he began feeding me Green anecdotes, concerning various farm animals (O'Connor's imagination was not limitless) and even the school matron. "The filthy little swine," I would mutter, and slam the pillow with my fist. "The unspeakable little rat."

"It's got something to do with circumcision, I believe," O'Connor said cautiously. "They have to have it all the time."

The magic It. I have since realized from remembered appearances that O'Connor was as circumcised as anyone and didn't know it, and so was I. But at the time it seemed like more Devil's work. I took to punching Green in the arm for retribution every time I saw him, at first under the "two for flinching" rubric, but later just for living. He never fought back. Circumcision had sapped the beggar's courage. "Take that for Ninian," I said. "And that for the cows and pigs."

What strange gentile curse was this? I don't really know anything about Green. I do know that Ninian was a male Doberman who would have torn him to pieces at the first unseemly advance.

I guess Green was just trying to creep through the school year without incident. Fat chance with mad Sir Winston around. Bullies don't write memoirs, so let's say I wasn't a bully. I was just misled by O'Connor. Yet O'Connor himself was polite to Green. I look now for some expression of approval or otherwise on the chorus of Irish boys, but I see none. I look for a signal, "Hit the Jew." But all I can see is my own face, red and brutal as a Regency rake after his third bottle, pounding away on poor Green: no one creeps through Chatworth's world without incident.

Put Green back on the sidelines a moment. He doubtless expected no less at St. Boniface and felt lucky to get off with a lightweight bully like me whose punches, I later learned, couldn't hurt a kitten. As for me, my only insight into bullying is that it's a habit you slip into like picking your nose. Banal? That is correct. Anyway, it was never more than a hobby: my real passion that fall was football. Father Walburger must have noticed that I was the only lay observer at practice every day, and finally he called me over, so that his own role might be fulfilled: "Hey, half-pint. Come and show these oxes how the Notre Dame shift works." Thus did Rockne discover the Gipper, and Father Walburger a third-string quarterback. I had long since memorized the plays, and was crisp as lettuce in the huddles. "Shift left on three. O'Brien off tackle." Slap the palms. Bark the numbers. Take my little dance steps and fling myself at some puzzled giant. "Ja, you can learn a lot from little Chatworth here. Size isn't everything."

The hell it isn't. I'd have traded all my fighting spirit for twenty pounds, and so would Walburger. Still, he liked me as a mascot and even tickled my stomach under my jersey one day after a workout. "You don't mind do you?" he said a little anxiously. "It's all in fun."

Why should I mind a thing like that? Oh ja, ja, now I know. The fat, shaved head, the gleaming glasses. Disgusting. Still, there was really nothing to it.

As the scores ran up relentlessly against us every week, Walburger would put me in the games for a few minutes, as a peace offering I guess. It was always 48–0 and the afternoon was eternally dark and cold. I would run off a few innocuous plays—in those days the quarterback seldom if ever handled the ball, so all I had to do was say shift left or right and go into my little routine. Afterwards I would swagger off the field with the veterans. O'Brien would clap my butt and Walburger would fling an arm around me, and I didn't give a shit what the score was.

Others did, however. After we had lost the last game by some prodigious figure to a school which had installed the newfangled T-formation, a fight broke out—among our own men, naturally. Historians puzzling over the poor showing of the St. Boniface team in 1940 may find this suggestive. Maloney accused O'Donnell of dogging it, which God knows was true of all of us, but Maloney was the fattest. The two squared off under the goal posts in modified bare-knuckle championship style, and a natural ring formed around them. The other team glanced back, as it might be at a knitting contest, and kept heading for their bus. But St. Boniface was starved for a little aggression of its own and an electric thrill ran from shoulder to shoulder. Shouts in the gloaming. "Come on. Lead with the left, the *left*. Ah shit." A roar went up with each punch, and a sustained roar for the combos. Then a sort of sigh as the victim extricated himself and squared off freshly.

For all my swagger, I had never seen a real fight before, and was at first unmistakably frightened by it. Reality always has me at a disadvantage, its texture being so different from my dreams. For the first few minutes these two wanted to kill each other, I could swear, and the air picked up the animal charge.

Then came the long holding-on part, with anger spent; the two pecking grimly at each other, wondering why they were doing this; each unwilling to quit, but too weak to win. They still had their shoulder pads on and could hardly keep their arms up. A sadness came over the crowd now; the good part was over. But no one knew an honorable way to end it. A sort of eternity. Maloney (or O'Donnell): "You ready to quit?" O'Donnell (or Maloney): "Fuck you." And a desperate volley of punches. One nosebleed by now, two thick lips, three swollen eyes, I can't count anymore. Maloney, a plump guy, looking like hamburger. O'Donnell, like a corpse. Very dark now, faces a blur of pulp. Come on, come on.

Finally, our fullback and my personal patron, O'Brien, who could have broken either one of them over his knee, stepped in. "OK, that's enough." A sigh from the crowd. They wanted a result.

Maloney looked up at O'Brien blearily. "I can lick the bum. Give me five minutes."

"You couldn't lick him in five days."

Well, there was no arguing with O'Brien. They gave each

41

other one last glare and began to walk away. "Com'ere" said O'Brien. "I want you both to shake hands."

"Who're you, God or somebody?" muttered O'Donnell, but after a moment he stuck out a bloody paw, and Maloney stuck out another, and the deed was done.

They stalked out separately through the crowd, which opened obediently as for royalty. They'd shown the magic quality, guts. I already knew that most guys would go any distance to avoid this kind of bloodletting—knew it and had profited from it. The crowd began to buzz up the hill that led to school, keeping a respectful distance behind the heroes, satisfied, I guess, that the football season had ended OK after all.

I don't know what got into Chatworth at this point. Maybe the thirdstring quarterback wanted in on the glory. If courage was the coin, his pockets were jingling.

He spotted Morton Green and belted him in the face. Green held his mouth and looked at him. There was no end to this thing, was there? Chatworth would never stop. So Green took a deep breath and ran at Chatworth and beat the shit out of him. Now let's get *out* of here.

Not so fast, of course.

Look, I'm in a hurry. On the air in two hours and all that. Can't it wait?

Just a few routine questions, sir. They'll improve your show. We won't be detaining you for long.

Oh, very well. (Slumps back in chair)

First, did Chatworth fight bravely and well himself? Had he any regrets about that?

Chatworth (mumbles, pretends to be drunk): 'Fraid not. Didn't fight bravely and well. No.

Did he fight at all?

Christ, *no*. Now leave me alone.

Was he afraid?

No. (Chatworth brightens slightly.) I don't think so.

What was it then?

Embarrassment.

Explain.

My crown was too big for me. I told you I wasn't any fighter. Besides he was the same size I was. I had no excuse anymore.

Did you make one anyway?

Christ, yes (buries head in hands). I said I had a cold.

How did the crowd take that?

They were amused. They said, "Sir Winston isn't feeling quite himself tonight." And "Poor chap can't fight with a cold, you know." And "We'll have to call off the war for tea." They being mostly Muldoon, who'd set me up for this and led them now like a cheerleader.

O'Brien?

Disappointed. Shook his head and walked away. Christ, that hurts. I'd lost my first sponsor. Are you still there?

Just a jiffy, sir. What about Green?

Pleased as punch. Obscene grin. The Irish kids carried him shoulder high. I can see their faces now, big as balloons and jovial. Great kidders. The football players held Green up there and somebody stuck the ball in his hands. Like Christ on Palm Sunday. I'd given them a *real* end to their season. Later we will see O'Donnell and Maloney scrubbed and shiny and not looking half bad. And they will want to hear the whole story again.

And you said Uncle?

(Croaks) I said, "Uncle till next time."

Was there a next time?

(Whispers) No.

Well, that'll do for now. I'm not sure I accept the bit about not being afraid. We may have to come back to that. It's a little too much to say, isn't it, sir? "I was afraid." Yet the whole confession may be void without it.

I don't have to confess to a policeman at all. Why aren't you a priest tonight?

Hurray for Hollywood! Priest shows are out this year,

police shows are in. So meet Officer Sony, unflappable London bobby. Anyway, you did Green a favor, you know, if that's any comfort. He never looked back. Now it's not material, but I do wish you'd answer one question for my own satisfaction. How do you generally justify the incident in your own mind?

That the Jew was right and I was wrong and I knew it.

(Laughs) That's a good one, sir. (Pause) Well, I'll be on my way now, and you'll want to be thinking about tonight's performance, I expect.

Oh God, yes. "Monty Chatworth's guests tonight include . . ." I only hope there isn't a Jew among them. I'd probably bust him right in the mouth. Or hide under the desk. Has anyone else ever been physically intimidated by a Jew? Why not? Anyway, don't give me the Jew as eternal victim. They can always lick their weight in Chatworths. The galling thing is that they're outsiders, too, and they're so much better at it than I am. I've been a Jew all my life in that sense, and never got the hang of it. That night Green and I changed places and I became the school Jew. Mort grabbed my vacancy on the elite, and if he wanted to read poetry and sneer at football from then on, why no one could see anything wrong with that.

I heard that, sir. Very valuable testimony indeed . . . Well, ta ta. Confession is good for the soul, isn't it?

Well, yes. I actually feel a little better now. But don't go thinking we've come to the real poison yet. For that we'll need to invent more than an MGM bobby wobbling off on his bike. For that we'll need to invent the frigging Pope. Or failing that, Barry Fitzgerald.

5

Good enough for Los Angeles, but not here. Playing it now in my Jersey hideaway, with the banging Atlantic in the background, it sounds desolately cute. But then Chatworth can be desolately cute, can't he? That's the problem I try to remedy on these little retreats.

Because I *was* serious once, I distinctly remember it. Was it that year or the next?

What did a boy of ten going on eleven really make of all this? I look at the occasional children on my show and see nothing but shallow smartness and routine heartlessness. But they are old to themselves, older than they've ever been before. So suppose we picture Pendrid Chatworth as a little man instead, a homunculus, to get a fix on him. In fact, let's make them all old men, as old as they felt. Again and again I put on my knickers and return blinking to the scene; I drain my martini and lunge at Green. Then I'm unclear. I can feel the cold earth as Green pinions me and see the circus faces around me, but I can't remember what I was thinking. Except that I'm abroad, I have no business here. Yes, the foreignness, that's the thing.

Well. A tale told by a midget is more to my taste anyway. Most children bore me, even when there's an adult along to interpret. I can't take all that sensibility unaccompanied by intelligence. It's a damn menace.

For the next few months, the little man must have been unhappy; therefore, I have no regrets. Bad times do not belong in a confessional. Winter, credit down to zero. Free at last from anyone's expectations. A real grownup would have cut his throat, I suppose, but I didn't understand the situation well enough. The obliging O'Connor continued to listen respectfully to my war commentaries and to giggle at my English comic songs. "Some like football, some like darts, some like knitting and the simpler arts," I warbled.

"I didn't know the British had a sense of humor."

"You bet. Look here. One chap says, 'Have you seen Aunt Bessie's chest?' and the other one says, 'I beg your pardon?' "

"I never knew that."

It was OK, nothing had happened. The kids ignored me, except for the stray snigger. "That Green is a heckuva fighter, isn't he, Chatworth?" said Muldoon, fanning his joke in.

No answer.

"Isn't he, Chatworth."

"I guess so."

Muldoon, who wears glasses and is a sissy in his own right, goes underground. The boys could go home for weekends if we wanted, which gave a jerky shunting quality to St. Boniface social life, as one's status might be pushed back or forward in one's absence. It also gave Muldoon his chance to operate, because he never went home at all. Perhaps he wanted to keep an eye on school politics, or perhaps his home was as nasty as he was. For whatever unpleasant reason, he and his big brother, Pat the enforcer, were always around, forming the only power group we had.

I, contrariwise, spent most of my home weekends at those English war movies I mentioned earlier, grimly determined (a new specter) not to lose my English accent. Since I couldn't hear my own voice, this wasn't so easy. I'm afraid Chatworth made rather a display of himself in Philadelphia by standing during "God Save the King"—was that little round of applause ironic? Never mind. Duty was duty.

"How do you like your new school, sonny?" asked the chorus of old ladies in our village.

"Mediocre."

"My. Where did you learn a word like that?"

"At a proper school. In England."

So you see, I hadn't learned much yet. And I can't say my father helped. He was sickeningly polite to American faces: "I marvel at your autumn colors—or should I say fall? A *much* better word, by the way." But behind their backs, his tongue forked Englishly. To hear him tell it, the American language was a debased form of grunting, the eating habits were infantile ("I actually saw a grown man drinking milk. Extraordinary."), and the political system wouldn't have met the needs of a band of gorillas.

I quickly got in trouble by passing some of this on to the chorus of old ladies. "Daddy says American tea bags are obscene," or some such crusher.

I had never seen the old man ruffled before—his hair actually stood up in back, as from a maddened gesture. When he got me outside he said, "Pendrid, you're getting older and you really must learn about manners."

"But you *did* say tea bags were obscene."

"I suppose I did. I must be more careful. But Pen, I said it to *you,* not to them."

"Hmmph."

"Look Pendrid, you do want to help the war effort, don't you? Well, offending Americans is *not* the way to go about it."

"I can't see that any good is served by hypocrisy."

"You must simply take my word for it," said my father.

As to that, I considered myself as good a judge as he. I,

47

after all, had mixed with the people. "Isn't he cute?" said the old ladies. The village we lived in was made of old ladies; they come at me now in a body, one and indivisible.

"My schoolmates?" say I. "Well, they're nice enough chaps, but most of them are intellectually contemptible."

"Isn't he marvelous? They must have a wonderful education over there."

Yes, ma'am. I'd show them an education all right. Fast on the feet, down on the toes. Sir Winston flashes his form: rears back and lets fly.

"I'd say mine was adequate. French at seven, Latin at nine, and so forth. But I fancy one could do much better at numerous establishments."

No, no, I didn't say that. My gift for mimicry is renowned, but I never said those things. I'll tell you who said them. It was Muldoon, perched on the school steps with a claque of rowdies, waiting for me one dark Sunday night. I remember the long trudge up the drive, the slight pinch of homesickness, the balloon faces looming suddenly—blown up again with Irish mischief.

Muldoon must have spent the weekend like a ward politician, because half the school was out there as if posing for a group picture. And Chatworth, knee-deep in snow, still wearing shorts in a world of knickers, finds himself facing a kangaroo court. Light behind them, more like hanging judges, though I see their faces when it suits me. Muldoon states his case.

"Hey Pen——drid. Showed the white feather did we? Bit of a disgrace to the regiment, what?"

"Is that supposed to be English? They don't talk like that, you know."

"Don't they, you know? Frightfully sorry. How do they talk, then?"

"Like me."

"Oh. Like *you*. You mean, 'I've got a most fearful cold, old chap. Can't possibly fight today. Mater says positively no fisticuffs.' "

At first I thought they were kidding. "You'll never get it right, Muldoon," I said, and picked up my suitcase.

"Won't I, old chap? I say that's a bit of a blow, isn't it chaps?"

"Quite. Ripping," said Murphy, a complete ass.

"I guess you have to have buck teeth," said Muldoon. "And you have to like to pick on little guys." The fun had faded and I realized my socks were wet. "The way you guys used to pick on Ireland all those years."

What the hell? I swear I'd never heard of this. "What's that about Ireland?"

"Yeah, until they drove the limeys out, the way Green drove you out. Hey, that's a good name. I never thought of that. Green, you're an Irishman."

Yeah, Green was there, smirking with the best of them. I looked for a friendly face, someone who'd appreciate my comebacks if I could think of any. But in the dark of that year, I could see only cruel Oriental grins. "Are you there, O'Connor?" I said.

Yeah, he was there all right. Faithful O'Connor, my roomy. "My parents told me about the famine," he said solemnly.

The kangaroo court broke up for the time being. O'Connor moved about our room afterwards in stiff silence, as if he owed that much to the potato famine, but he wasn't the problem. Muldoon was; and for the rest of the winter, whenever he could find a quorum, the court would suddenly assemble, in the gym, by the lake, anywhere. And I would be subjected to a killer dose of John Paul Jones, Bunker Hill, and running through it all the cowardice and stupidity of the British. A Kafka character would have snapped in no time. I didn't understand the questions, and I wasn't allowed to answer them anyway. For instance, "I hear you guys fought in bright red coats. *Very* smart."

"Good enough to beat the Irish," I sniffled.

Two in the arm from Murphy for that. "We was starving," he said. I was fighting two countries and losing to both.

49

"If Ireland ever fights England I'm going to join the Irish Air Force and bomb the shit out of you," said Muldoon.

"Perhaps they can find an opening for you in the German Air Force," I said.

But wit without courage was worse than no wit at all. Two in the arm from big Pat Muldoon. "I resent that," he said. "My brother is not a Nazi."

The only answer was to sock Muldoon, but I was afraid of bringing on one of those scenes: a tapestry of Chatworth at bay, the school forming a silent ring, Chatworth frozen in his foreignness; everything silent except for the plop of mitten on chin; snow falling softly. Ghastly. So Chatworth, after all that fuss, fails to fight for his country.

Yet, if you suppose that Chatworth was downcast, you don't know your man. It was a new world to be coped with, the world of cowardice, but I would make my way in it pugnaciously. A complete change of character? Child's play at that age. Meanwhile, at home I was miraculously my old self. My father was seldom around, owing to the demands of his iniquitous import-export business (I later learned that he was inspecting cargo ships for possible espionage), and the old man's visits annoyed me slightly. I felt like a deposed regent. For a pair of otherwise genteel people, my parents made love like the Ace Moving Company on a heavy assignment, and of course I knew, didn't know, what they were up to next door.

For the rest, my mother listened to every news broadcast going, until one could fairly hear the bombs exploding outside. British pluck was the thing that year. Tales of unspeakable courage and good cheer. Blown off a lavatory reading Jane Austen, by George. Magically, I would forget Muldoon and picture myself lugging cups of tea along the underground platform with a cheerful word for the wounded, slipping an occasional cigarette into a plaster cast. "Thanks, chum." That was where I belonged, among my own people.

Nevertheless, by February I was unmistakably bored by the broadcasts. I even hoped that Mother would miss one now and then. But that was only in my heart.

"Can't you turn that junk off?" a voice chirps. "I'm sure they can fight their silly war without your un*divided* attention."

That was my sister, a harridan by now in a funny sweatshirt. (It couldn't have said, "Kiss me, I'm British," could it? Ah, the distortions of memory.) Anyway, pigtails, curlers, mouth painted like a savage. Chatworth rounded on her.

"Isn't it enough that you've adopted their vile customs? Do you have to forget your own heritage completely?"

"Go suck a lemon," said Priscilla of Hollywood.

"Children, don't bicker," said my mother.

I pulled my chair sternly closer. I would listen to the damn news if it killed me. Months of unparalleled boredom lay ahead. My sister left the room giggling, free.

March, April. Weekends spent at home to avoid Muldoon, only to wind up with Gabriel Heatter. "*Can't* you say something to Priscilla?" My envy is now ungovernable. If I must listen, so must she.

"She doesn't have to listen to it if it doesn't concern her," yawned my father, who never yawned unintentionally.

"But she's turning into an *American.*"

"Ah well. There's a lot of that going about."

So the ghastly charade continued. My sister was talking by now with a godawful Anglo-American accent which she broadened in all directions for my benefit. "How goes the war, old man? Jackson? Solid? 'Ow you say in your country?"

I frowned. "I don't find that funny at this particular time."

"No? Well, thank God one of us is taking it seriously."

She capered off down the stairs, out the door, always going somewhere. Her life seemed so full. She talked of divine boys in the village, though I never saw any. A few pimply louts, maybe. And her room was plastered with pictures of Errol

Flynn, giving an effect of teeming activity. "You stick to your Winston Churchill," she said. "One of us has to keep the faith."

I have since discovered that those years were as lonely for her as they were for me, and that her village was as empty as mine. She went to a local school where if you didn't talk about divine boys you didn't talk about anything. She strove tearfully to keep up. She hated the boys. She hated America. She told me all this years later in England, where she now lives stubbornly.

Obviously a pompous ass for a brother was just the thing she needed to help her through those years, no? "It's all right. You were fun to have around," she says. Priscilla remembers me, oddly, as a merry little fellow. She says I saw the joke and used to do a funny imitation of George VI's speech defect. She lies, of course.

Well—maybe once or twice, to fend off teasing. No more than that. I knew the English had a marvelous sense of humor and could laugh at themselves. Wasn't that what we were fighting for?

Actually, I must have brought it back from school where the boys had unearthed the dogma that the English had no sense of humor at all and were deviling me with that. So I laughed at the King and at Churchill and at anyone else they wanted, just to prove I could. And Muldoon said, "What kind of scum laughs at his own leaders?" Bang bang. Two in the arm for being a traitor.

This was intolerable. Bullying in its later stages gets slovenly: Muldoon had forgotten the point. "Churchill saved your ass," he said, "and you're making fun of him three thousand miles away in Uncle Sam's backyard." I was reaching the same situation as Green, where I would *have* to fight back. Soon.

But it was never the right moment. I was tossed in a blanket on St. Patrick's Day by two Italians, as I screamed, "I'm as Irish as any of you. My mother's an O'Grady."

"Fungoo," said Ponzo.

"It's funny—you don't *talk* Irish," said Muldoon.

It was always the audience that paralyzed me, the fear of making an irreversible ass of myself. For the same silly reason, though, I never cried or admitted pain. Stoicism is easier than it looks. Years later, I searched out Jimmy Muldoon, by now a skinny insurance man with five kids, who seemed nervous to see me, and he said, "Yeah, we were afraid we were going to kill you. I guess we were impressed."

I did my best to gloat. *Well, you're really impressed now, aren't you, Muldoon, with your piddling layaway plans? No fear like the fear of celebrity.* Muldoon, who was in town for a convention, didn't know how I'd found him or what I wanted. His eyes danced like flies behind his rimless glasses. *Kiss my toe, there's a good man. I made it, didn't I? And how are things in Altoona?* I sent him two tickets to my show to rub it in all the way. He left sniveling uncertainly.

But it wasn't the same: I wanted the kid in knickers, not this broken hulk, or family man. I actually had just one last chance to square things with the real Muldoon in that very year of 1941. Circumstances and spring weather had pushed me into courage. Little Jimmy liked to swim, and I found him down by the lake one brilliant June day, while everyone else was off watching the fatuous sport of baseball. He looked nervous then, too, because he didn't have his gang with him and he was just a little guy in a bathing suit, blinking his weak eyes at me. I suddenly realized he'd avoided being alone with me up to now. Muldoons have to make their way through school, just like jocks, just like Brains, and his secret was never to be alone. Ah, sweet day, let me pause and enjoy this a minute. The moment when power shifts. Every bird in the Northern Hemisphere is singing, the water shivers on his knobby little torso. The lake is no longer a mud slick but a glowing bowl, a sultan's caldron, with me stirring.

"How's it going, Pen?"

Not a word. Chatworth is ten feet tall now and doesn't need words.

"You ever get weather like this in England?" He starts to

dry himself. "You know something? I can't stand baseball, either. What do you play over there?"

We play war. I step up smartly and hover there a second until he straightens, six inches away. No unfair advantages for Chatworth. Then I push him daintily back in the lake.

He swims around a minute or two as if this were a great idea, glad I'd thought of it, then cautiously swims back to the bank. I'm waiting. As he starts to hike up I lean gently on his shoulders and down he goes again in a blubber of mud. Both silent now. He swims alongside and I trot urbanely to keep pace. Picture a monocle and a pencil-thin mustache and a puff of white handkerchief in a blue blazer and you've got it. Where is my audience *now?* I step on his hand. He grabs at my ankle. I dance away.

What's all this doing in a confession? You'll pay for this senile gloating, Chatworth. A grown man cackling over his footwork of yesteryear. All right. Enough. The time passed.

Never fear, we'll salvage some embarrassment from the scene. Muldoon, looking like a drowned rat, stands in the water up to his waist and says, "Whaddya want, Chatworth?" Not as scared as I'd like him to be. If he gets out we might still have that fight in front of the whole school and I'm not sure I want that. Not at all sure. And I can't keep him in forever. He rolls over now, understanding this, and floats on his back. Suddenly I am *his* prisoner. I had so hoped to find another coward, and had really counted on Muldoon. He watches me slyly. Maybe he is a coward. How much am I willing to pay to find out?

Chatworth looks desperately nonchalant, folds his arms, yawns. Chatworth isn't fooling anyone. Muldoon stands up again. "I repeat. *Whaddya want Chatworth?*"

Now, here is the bad part, Father. Looking back, I *know* I had the guy. He was shivering and scared shitless, and he would have come out of that water on any terms. But there was still Muldoon's army to reckon with and—well, let's just get on with it. I said, "Muldoon, I'm the only English kid in this school and I'm a long way from home and I'd appreciate it if you'd stop picking on me." There was a maddening throb in my voice.

Muldoon pretended to consider. His lips were turning blue and time was running out. "Well, I guess that's right," he said as if weighing his terms carefully. "It must be tough being away from your folks—"

Thin lips and death. "My folks are over here with me. It's England I miss."

"Oh?" Muldoon blinked water. The concept of missing a whole country was beyond him—as well it might be. I couldn't think of one fucking thing about England right then. "I guess it's tough," he said vaguely. Then suddenly, urgently. "You know the kidding's just in fun. You're really a popular guy, you know that?"—well, I won't horn in on Muldoon's confession. That's his cross to bear. He came unstuck for his own good reasons and crawled out and dried himself again and walked back to school, and I never had any more trouble with him.

Cowards don't leave records (except funny ones): they just disappear like bullies. So let's not say I was cowardly, just that I was shaking at every outlet, worse than after the Green fiasco. I had let my enemy off the ropes, for fear he would get me later or next week or next year; he and his brother and countless others in grinning masks. You remember my scalding tongue on television? It came and went with my sense of the lynch mob. So did my winsome charm. That was fear, deep in the bone. Fear of offending, or of starting something. A scene can easily get out of hand and then we'd be staring at each other again across the water, Muldoon and me. What the hell, a piece of empty flattery or even of base toadying is a small price to pay. Besides, they love it out there. To judge from my gratified mail, after I have soothed a Brando or some tiger in an Afro, I can't be the only man in Transatlantica who lives in fear of nameless disaster.

6

Up in the air again, scurrying across my transatlantic cage.
My life wasn't always so cramped. A few years ago I was
doing my famous specials on the world's trouble spots, and
I hadn't a care in the world. But TV burned money in those
days, and Chatworth was a luxury item. Nowadays I'm as
likely to be found standing in front of somebody else's pictures, or doing authentic-sounding voiceovers as I bang my
rickshaw. Ah, inflation. And I am condemned to shuttle
between the two countries that tear at my guts; allowed, like
an Elizabethan beggar, to linger in neither one.

OK with my little friend here. Priests are only supposed
to hear confessions in their own dioceses, and Father Sony
is in his element up here in the ether, snug in his jumbo jet,
with all the machines going. At some point in the mid-
Atlantic we are both more at home than anyone else on the
plane.

So after I sold out my country to a rat-faced sissy, what
next little man?

With Muldoon off his back, Chatworth enters a new phase. The rest of his critics lack wit and spirit. O'Connor backs off from the potato famine. Freddie Bartholomew movies are still a menace ("Hey, it's Winston up there, don't-you-know"), but a mob without its Goebbels can be handled.

The threat is still there, though, curbing and shaping like a sculptor's hammer. Chatworth is defined by threat. My mother complains to a waiter in her high English voice and I think, watch out, Mother, he'll hit you. Two in the arm, lady. "Absolute tommyrot," says my father; and I can hear the listener saying it afterwards to his friends. "Absolute tommyrot, dontchooknow." I bring Good German O'Connor home for a weekend and I'm embarrassed by everybody. (Doesn't the beggar know any words except "Swell, Mrs. Chatworth?"—and where the hell is our peanut butter, anyway?)

But this is time we're talking about now, duration. There are fewer single scenes, though the faces are clearer. England swells and recedes, always a little further out. Irishness sneaks up engagingly. Like a pimp in an occupied country, I have learned the angles of racism. I hadn't realized till now my mother's value on the open market. So by next St. Patrick's I have promoted her to a roaring Celt and myself to a full half-breed. By the next, I'll have dug up ancestors who fought with Wolfe Tone. I'll be chiding Maloney good-naturedly for not knowing about the Battle of the Boyne. I'll have routed the Italians.

It began as a survival tactic, and I won't apologize. But I couldn't leave it at that. I was very brave between fights, and no one had ever stormed the St. Boniface social register like this. I began pumping my mother about Ireland and she answered like an English tourist—the lakes of Killarney, a bunch of monasteries, the horse show. Very nice. "But what about the wonderful fighting spirit?" I said.

"Well, and a lot of good it did them," she says, slipping

57

into a slight Irish accent under the pressure of my obsession.

"Well, and didn't it keep them going for hundreds of years now?"

It is not true that we broke into a jig at that point with me playing the pipes and all. My mother was really quite apathetic. "There's good and bad in all countries," she said. "Blood? I gave a pint last week and I daresay it'll work as well in a Negro as in anyone else. It's just like petrol, really."

"Why did we all leave?"

She finally breaks under Chatworth's grilling. "Because Ireland is so dreadfully dull, I suppose."

Hopelessly weak-kneed, I decide. Doesn't know who she is. Bumbles through life. At some point bumbles to England and bumbles into Father. What am I now, thirteen? Why are they still keeping things from me? "Father, how did you meet Mother?" Speak up now man, and don't say "I don't remember."

My father is going through a strange period. He tells me that my mother was a bareback rider in a Liverpool circus —which I take to be his way of saying that I bore him. He is probably worried about the sinking of the *Normandie* in New York harbor, which is his beat. But I assume he is thinking about the price of wool, and I rage.

"I didn't know Mother could ride," I say bitterly.

"Ah well. That's it, you see," he trails off vaguely.

"Father, how Irish am I?"

"As much as you like, I suppose. It's a rum thing to want to be, I must say."

He is like a daffy peer in an English movie. I am ashamed of him. I know everyone in town does imitations of him behind my back. Mother is weak; Father is mad; I have no one to turn to. I will have to be Irish on my own and in spite of them.

Who were these people that I disown so lightly? I hear tears in the next room that I didn't hear then. It seems my mother's best friend was killed in the Blitz with her two children. I didn't take this in. While I was trading her Irish blood on the status exchange, she was crying over *English* people who happened to be dead. This was on such a different plane from my own thoughts that it didn't register; it was like finding a football player among your baseball bubble-gum cards.

As for Father: a well-bred English boy can go on forever not knowing what sort of parents he has; in fact, you're lucky if you're told what the old boy does for a living. I suppose they tell each other. My mother had gold stocks in Kenya that she swears she didn't know about until her broker said they were worthless, along with her Burmese rubber and her Rangoon hemp, after the war.

So I had no idea back then that my parents had been prominent socialites before the war, in the fast Catholic set (if such be possible), and that Mother was about as Irish as the Duke of Wellington. Her family had a real Irish name and they were gibberingly staunch Catholics, to make up for whatever crime had earned them their money, but they were not the stuff of my Irish schoolmates. They had never contracted frostbite over a peat fire or fled to Boston in rags; during the famine, they probably imported their own potatoes. My mother's English face and voice fairly screamed this information but I couldn't afford to take it in while I was at St. Boniface.

My father came from an old Catholic family in the north of England, and it was their private chapel I drove to that crazy night—only to find it wouldn't hear my confession. You don't belong here, said the first Earl of Chatworth from the apse, you belong in a *studio.* Rubbishy feller from the BBC. He's not English. He's not even Cah-tholic. I sent him packing, you can be sure. The first earl dozes off triumphantly.

Why my father, the last genuine Chatworth, was sent to do his war work and end his family line in a country he loathed is one of those great bureaucratic mysteries. Perhaps they thought he was the sort of English-gentleman type the Americans go for. (In which case, they hadn't met my schoolmates.) Anyway, it meant five miserable years for both my parents. My sister, who was paying close attention under her mask, tells me that Father had volunteered for every possible branch of the service, but was turned down because of World War I complications: including extensive nerve damage, fear of the dark, night fears—a screaming carnival of disorders under the clamped lid. He chose a quiet village in Pennsylvania to keep us far away from his work. Tewksbury, Pa., was a halfway house to England, having no twentieth-century aspects whatever; and just to make sure, we kept the house teeth-chatteringly cold. It was a retreat house for Father, a place where he could reassemble his nerves. Junior, you will note, was invaluable in this.

Mother had a different problem: galloping melancholia. Our house was too big and she had to run it without servants —she who had never run a one-room flat without servants. Her grim struggles with the alien frying pan and the wily fried egg would have made the kind of hilarious book that was appearing at that time. "Moira O'Grady Chatworth goes to war." But for her it was quiet sobbing and desolate cries of "drat" and, more terrible, "God, what's the use?"

Why didn't I hear this at the time? I hear it very well now. It didn't suit my sense of greatness. Mother's gallant attempts at cheerful conversation, her efforts in some sense to "raise" me, just seemed pathetic. The boys at school all had wonderful mothers: their way with pie crust and waffles was much noted. I didn't have a mother at all, in that sense. She was just another handicap for Pendrid to shoulder. The O'Connor weekend was my Trojan horse. Mother beaming: "I've tried something new for you. Spaghetti!" "Swell, Mrs. Chatworth." And, Tiny Tim, such spaghetti! Runny, glutinous, slapping your necktie with every cold mouthful. Such laughs, we had. O'Connor blinking, keeping out the flying sauce; oh God, he can't go on. The spice—what is it, tarragon? sage?—she's poured in the whole bloody canful. "It's swell, Mrs. Chatworth." Pats scrawny stomach. "Boy, am I full."

Spare me, Ghost of Weekend Past. Did O'Connor try to raid the icebox? To find nothing in there but Crosse & Blackwell marmalade? I had hoped to keep America out of the home, but Mother had expressed an urge to meet my friends, and O'Connor seemed the most harmless. He played the part with glazed earnestness and later on was always deeply respectful about my parents. "How's your mom?" became his litany. All right—I knew what he was saying to the others.

Ah, the crosses I had to bear. My father's fatuous joking, his *gentleness*—well, by St. Boniface standards the man was simply a fruit. Every manjack at school had a father who fished and fixed cars and mended roofs. Gad, the activity in those homes: Dad up there nailing, Mom rolling out the pie crust, Junior pounding his mitt into the funny papers. Well —it was all awful and American, of course; but still—my parents . . .

They were a whole lot easier to cut loose than my country. I didn't owe them a thing. They had done nothing to prepare me for America, and even now their way of life plumpened me for mockery. I could see now that my father's anti-Americanism had actually poisoned my chances here. "It's really a great country," he said on December seventh as I packed my little bag for school, but by then it was too late. Rafe and Green and Muldoon had already happened. I had fought for his point of view and been routed.

Our homunculus ceases altogether to think. America has entered the war, to his hysterical delight. His father notwithstanding, Chatworth's heart almost bursts over the Pearl Harbor bombing. The famous American fleet, out to tea that day. Ha ha! There'll be no more jokes about England now. (There he's wrong.) He must be careful not to gloat. Again the whole school seems to be waiting for him, that December

61

evening. "We're in this together, now, Sir Winston." The idiot Murphy claps my back. "We're gonna bail you out now, Winnie." I am pummeled randomly, happily. "Let's go *get* 'em, Winston."

"We were there first, you know," the old Sir Winston murmurs, down to a whisper by now.

"I know, I know. You were great."

"I thought you chaps would never get here," I say quietly. "Welcome on board. We've saved a little bit of war for you." Tojo has bailed me out.

My patriotism flared anew. I couldn't become an American now. The cachet of being there first was too good to pass up. Of course, their brute numbers might be useful, but our soldiers were better disciplined and had a much keener sense of humor. I would keep this to myself, for the most part.

My Irish fantasy proved a useful way station in my flight from identity. I would not become an American, but it couldn't hurt to become a little more Irish. I still believed that my mother's people had fought for freedom in the bogs instead, as I now suspect, of selling out first thing to the British, and I thought it made a useful point to show them that an Englishman could also be an Irishman. It was a shoulder-to-shoulder thing, terribly World War II.

A useful point to those goons! Please, not while I'm drinking. These first-class stewardesses are a menace, patroling the aisles with giggle juice. In fact, drinking and confession never did mix. I remember a Saturday night at Oxford when I couldn't stop laughing over masturbation. Anyway, let's say my Irish fling at least made a better fraud of me. Our Scene: St. Paddy's Day, 1944. A boy's bedroom lined with shamrock. By now I am the worst Irish bore you ever met. For instance, " 'Mother Machree' is *not* an Irish song."

"It isn't, huh?"

"And neither is 'Galway Bay.' "

"You're kidding." O'Connor is nonplused. "That's too bad," he says at last.

"You want to hear a *real* Irish song?"

"I guess so," he says uncertainly. He is spared my war strategy briefings now, but can hardly duck his own culture. So I give him "Young Roddy McCorley." And I give him "The Croppy Boy." None too certain of the tunes, because I got them from a library book and am not the world's strongest a cappella singer. Still, the feeling is there and the gritty authenticity.

"That's it, huh?"

"Yup."

"I still like 'Galway Bay.' "

A warning shot; O'Connor is getting uppity. Warning royally ignored by Chatworth. More boys enter to hear the parade on the radio and to provide a quorum for Chatworth's embarrassment. Did Oedipus suspect something was wrong every time the chorus of old men rolled up? "Of course, you know," our hero starts right in, "that the real Irish don't celebrate St. Patrick's at all."

"Is that a fact?"

"Yup. They even close the pubs."

There is a pause, while Chatworth sings along with "O'Donnell Abou." "That's one of the few real songs you'll hear today," he tells them. He points out an amusing anomaly concerning Princely O'Neil, one of the song's heroes: to wit, that he was actually an Ulsterman—yet "O'Donnell Abou" is never sung in the North, because it's anti-English. Curious, what?

Another pause. O'Connor picks at his sock. Feigns embarrassment. Did I tell you he was sly? "Look, Winston," he says at last. "The guys have asked me to say something." He looks around for support. What guys? "Yeah, they got together last night and they said, 'You're his friend, O'Connor. He'll listen to you. *You* tell him!' So they drafted a statement and it goes like this. 'We the undersigned Micks Wops and Ginzos don't give a shit how Irish you are. You are still a limey prick to us. (signed) The friendly sons of Mother Machree.' "

"Excuse me." My martini drips like rain from the man's sleeve.

I have been joined by another fan. Hold on a minute. *"Monty Chatworth?"*

"Yes and no." Meanwhile, what are you doing in my seat? Have expense-account executives no pride anymore?

That's better. He picked a bad moment to horn in. The rage comes back when I think of that scene as if it had never left.

What happened next is that an imperious roar went up from the kids in the room and I had no choice but to join in, almost breaking my throat. I am one of the boys now and know a joke when I hear one. I laugh in cold dry spasms. I determine that from now on my fraudulence will be light as French pastry. I will not bore people with it.

"That was a pretty good gag," I tell O'Connor later. "Did you think it up yourself, or did the boys really get together?"

O'Connor looks at me, calculating. He is, as I say, sly. He needs a crowd. I dominate him, one on one. "I made it up," he finally says. I salute his courage now. I wonder if it figures on *his* tapes.

7

~~~~~~

Even an airplane lunch can trigger meditation, or intellectual burping. Thus, if it is true that you meet everyone you're going to meet by the age of twelve, then Muldoon was my basic enemy and O'Connor was the spoils for which we fought—the public. In fact, I still use O'Connor to model for the man in the street, the one in a million whose courage, loyalty, spite, seem exquisitely balanced at average, unmoved by anything higher or lower—and hence a mystery to the likes of me. In my version he came from Nutley, New Jersey, served in Korea, returned to Nutley, by God, with a tale to tell about the bathing in Tokyo, and subsided into real estate. But I may do him an injustice. It could be Rutherford, New Jersey.

Still, O'Connor could be as full of surprises as the real public, and this faceless wonder influenced me in two significant fields, sex and religion, as much as anyone I've met: in the former, simply by flapping in front of me like a sail, but in the latter—well, that's one of my vintage sins, small and sturdy, and guaranteed to make me feel unworthy even in the pygmy palace, or BBC building, where we're about to conclude our Third World Revisited series, part XII, on the related problems of hunger and starvation.

My chronology is hazy, for its own good reasons. Saints live outside time. But it seems to be spring and the religious dimension has just entered my life.

Not, you can be sure, a sensitive youth finding God, but a lout finding a role. Up to now my spiritual life had been a series of hot flashes. Sweet feelings in church as a child. I fancy I remember my own baptism—shafts of light on the priest's surplice, ruddy monsignors (my mother's side is chock-a-block with middle-level clergy), beaming relatives: the salt on my tongue tastes like sugar. Then, ardent prayers for things I want. "Puh-lease, God, sir." My mother grants them surreptitiously to make me believe, or so I suspect. Next, currying favor with Father Wolfgang by that sensational altar boy work: dazzling footwork with the Book, fast hands with the cruets; and to top it, a trip-hammer delivery of Latin, gaining three precious minutes on breakfast. Widely appreciated. Wolfgang is a chainsmoker himself and he wants that first cigarette, so he races me and we come off like Gilbert and Sullivan patter singers.

Then suddenly I'm Irish, which adds a head-banging quality to my Catholicism. It is my new patriotism. I carry my Sunday missal high through our deserted village. "I'm a Catholic, if anyone wants to know." The birds sing and the dogs bark. St. Pendrid has a way with animals. I make lists of famous Catholics. Fight, team, fight. The kids at school must think I'm nuts, but their hands are tied. Catholicism is Irish, and they can't make fun of it. Yet.

Being as I'm now an Irish Catholic, I have of course a great devotion to the Blessed Virgin. I search my mind now to see what I could have meant by this. Practically nothing is known of this admirable woman, yet I was in a fever of love, for the blue gown and the birdsong. (What birdsong? *I don't know.*) I even wrote some poems to her which O'Connor discovered; and if they'd been about anyone else, he would have bust a gut laughing. But the Virgin was sort of Irish too, so he never said a word.

The Virgin also meant purity, which smacked right away of clean restaurants and the safety of daylight. I have still not constructed the sex act from the jokes I hear; in fact, my picture of it is a weird amalgam of activities, all of which are needed to account for the ghostly bangings in my parents' room. But I am more conscious than ever of the murk of these discussions, a crotch-scratching, sweating, burrowing fug, heavy as stale smoke. The Virgin would surely not approve of this. I am maddened by not knowing what they're talking about, and frightened by the sense of sniggering conspiracy. I am outside again.

"Do you confess to that stuff?" I ask O'Connor.

"What stuff?"

"Those jokes."

"I guess I should, huh?"

"I think they're foul."

"I guess they are."

"So why do you go along with them?"

Ah, poor O'Connor. Locked in with a madman. He has no answer, of course. You can't argue with the Blessed Mother.

"They're not even funny." I drive it home uncertainly, not having understood a one of them.

"That's right," says O'Connor, having understood little more.

Yet the next time Ponzo came round with a hot one, O'Connor listened and began to giggle as usual, with only an apologetic glance at me. We had agreed that Ponzo was disgusting—but what can you do?

"Whatsamatter Winston, don't you get it?" said Ponzo.

"Sure I get it," Chatworth said grimly. "I just don't think it's funny."

"You don't? Muldoon pissed himself over it."

"Yeah, he would."

67

"Chatworth doesn't like that kind of joke," said O'Connor.

"He doesn't?" Ponzo was nonplused. "What's wrong with it?"

"He says it's an insult to the Blessed Virgin." I hadn't meant that for general consumption, but now I had to stand by it.

"Yeah? Listen, I wouldn't want to do that." Ponzo began to back out of our room, as if he'd seen a vision. "I'm sorry, kid, I didn't know you felt like that. Jesus."

A bad day for me. Because a year later, when I was burning to hear them, I still couldn't get a dirty joke out of Ponzo, or anyone else. By then, my goddamn purity was a byword.

It was not just the Ponzo incident that did it. About the same time a wave of goosing broke over the school. Guys would reach for each other's nuts and then run off laughing like maniacs. The first time it happened to me, it was like an electric shock. I slapped wildly at the hand behind me—what could it possibly want? The worst of it was, the feeling was not unpleasant. No getting round it. It was *merry*. I even wanted to grab back, but my assailant was gone in a shriek of laughter.

Mother of God, what was this? I had never heard such behavior discussed, but I knew a sin when I felt one. I also knew, didn't know, all about homosexuality. Some part of the soul must walk the streets of nighttown from infancy on, knowing what it knows. I was surprised by almost everything in those days, yet deep down I was surprised by nothing.

I made it clear that I wanted no part of such games, and thanks to the curious delicacy of these boys, I got my wish: again with mixed feelings. Again I am outside, though apparently by choice. A lonely saint. I can still see a roomful of merry fellows with the murk high. They are talking poontang as hard as ever, the goosing has not deflected their tastes. I press my nose to the invisible glass. Let me in. It isn't just murk in there, I see that now, but laughter and friendship. Impurity and fellowship are indissoluble partners. I enter. Maloney is finishing a story. "Isn't that right, O'Connor?" he says suddenly, and grabs O'Connor's balls. A wail of laughter, as O'Connor strikes back.

They see Chatworth and the laughter stops. Not a word is said, no obvious signal given. What has O'Connor told them? The miserable little priest stands dithering. "Don't mind me," he says. "We were leaving anyway," says Maloney. They know it is wrong to do this stuff, but maybe they can make up for it by respecting my virtue. As surrogate for the Blessed Mother, I'm good for some quick spiritual points.

Winston the fighter, Pendrid the prude—what did they think they were dealing with? Only with what I gave them, I suppose, as I defined myself this way and that. They would live through the H-bomb and the space program in the same spirit; when the new Ice Age comes and the world splits in two, they will get used to it. By the age of twelve, I had met the public.

Yet Winston and the prude were real aspects of me, and I had no business letting them die. Little Pendrid and his scruples was a joyless little fart. Yet I miss his earnestness. And his blessed freedom from humor, that killer of dreams. And I can't altogether call him joyless, can I? His heart sometimes burst with happiness over his phantom lady in blue.

Never you mind. Little Chatworth would betray the lady in blue, and the gentleman in red, and all the woolly folks long before he met you, Father. Vanity was the termite as usual: I was getting on pretty good with the guys by now— partly because they'd never seen anything like me and partly because I'm congenitally charming. Even when I was trying to be obnoxious, some part of me was buttering them up. Besides, I was a handsome little chap and don't let anyone tell you that doesn't help, even in marine boot camp. A handsome man who isn't *too* stuck on himself will always have friends.

There was at least one other prude in the school, called Foley, but he never spoke or washed his socks, so he was no competition. I was the debonair prude, and as I say, it made the guys feel better to have one friend like that: it showed they had another side. I was getting a little bored with it myself, as uneasy moilings occurred in my own lower front —but vanity could still beat sex in a fair fight. So we talked sexlessly about the war and about Roosevelt and they got a chance to act like little priests too, before going off in a roar of goosing and poontang.

Pendrid the prude would perhaps have died a natural death; but the God of embarrassment had other plans for him. The agent was once again the mild, rudderless O'Connor, who flung into our room one night bawling his eyes out and in need of help. "Whatsamatter? You hurt yourself?" He shakes his head, sits on the bed shivering. "Did someone beat you up?" Shakes, shivers. Every question whips up a fresh storm of tears. I rack my brain for explanations. "You *sure* nobody beat you up?" Waaagh! "Well, I'm glad you're OK." I give up and he sits on in catatonic silence.

"Look. Can I get you something?" It's lights-out time and Father Wolfgang will soon be making his grouchy, nicotine-poisoned rounds. O'Connor hasn't moved. "You want to see a doctor? Did you get bad news from home?"

Hopeless. My questions have exhausted my experience of tragedy. He finally undresses and gets into his pajamas and lies groaning in the dark. Wolfgang opens the door, a blow-torch of booze and smoke, and slams it shut. O'Connor gets himself a glass of water to replace his tears. Sits by window, staring out. Dark night of the soul for fair. I wonder how his middle-aged soul remembers it? Finally, just as I'm dozing off, the bugger tells me his story. Or tries to. "Ponzo," he starts, and then "Ponzo . . . did," and then "Ponzo did . . . something *terrible,*" et cetera. He isn't boring me, though. I suddenly realize that I might be getting the information I crave.

"Yes, yes. Go on." I try to keep the exultation out of my voice. After all, the bugger is suffering.

O'Connor exerted all his weaselly literary powers that night to keep the point at bay—how he happened to *be* in Ponzo's room, what he'd had for dinner, the most piercing analysis of an evening I've ever heard. My new information was coming at a cost. His voice sounded strange now in the dark. It was like a younger guy, a child, talking to his mother. I was almost asleep again when he blurted out the last bit. It seems that Ponzo had put his penis in O'Connor's mouth and urinated. That was all.

These things shock you once and that's that. My young self is nowhere more hidden from me than at this moment, and I can only offer clumsy adult equivalents for the cataclysm that shook me like loose glass. Nausea, fear, excitement, little words like that. Also a serious desire to kill Ponzo in his vileness, and to nurse O'Connor back to health. I picture myself rushing to and fro frantically, fluffing O'Connor's pillows, looking for weapons, opening and shutting windows. I probably just lay there.

"I'm going to tell Father Herman." I know I said that. My world was swimming and only by being a pillar of righteousness could I hope to steady it.

"No." O'Connor sounded panicky. "Don't do that."

"Why not?"

"You'll get the guys in trouble."

The guys indeed. It dawned on me slowly that Ponzo was smaller than O'Connor. How did his penis get into O'Connor's mouth in the first place? A delicate question to raise; but necessary.

"He's stronger than he looks," said O'Connor, anticipating.

"Yeah? I saw Muldoon pin him in three seconds flat. *Muldoon.*"

"Well, that's different. Italians go crazy when they want something like *you* know. They have the strength of ten men."

"Uh huh." I tried to sound skeptical, though I wasn't really. It sounded possible.

"Well, he tricked me," said O'Connor. "And that's the truth."

He pretended to sleep. The subject had already been trivialized beyond repair, but my wrath was up and roaring.

"There's a lot of filth in this place," I said.

"I agree," muttered O'Connor.

"I don't want you hanging out with that crowd anymore."

"Don't worry, boy. I won't. Not after tonight."

"And maybe," a thought struck me, "some of the filth is in ourselves."

"You could be right."

"I'm not perfect myself, you know. I'm human. I know what it is to be tempted."

Wild.

"Yeah," I continued. "You have to take real steps to avoid that stuff. I don't just mean Ponzo and those guys, but the evil in ourselves. Right?"

"Right." O'Connor was beat right down.

"What would you say," and I scarcely believe this part myself, "to a nightly rosary?"

"OK, sure. That'd be swell."

There was a silence. "Well?" I said. "Let's go."

"What, *now?*" O'Connor was drugged, sleepy.

"Sure, why not? When you don't feel like it is the best time to do it. On your knees, now." Chatworth's spiritual authority was enormous. He could not have commanded a chicken with physical force anymore, but he had something mightier. "The first sorrowful mystery," he intoned in a firm clear voice. And O'Connor, fogged and humiliated by Ponzo's trick, mumbled his part obediently. It might have been an episode in the life of a saint ("his power over others was

72

extraordinary even at an early age") except, of course, that Chatworth was just passing through.

The next morning, Chatworth woke up and said, "I'm still going to see Father Herman."

O'Connor, bleary, said, "What about?"

"About that abominable thing you told me last night."

"Oh. Yeah."

"Only just for your sake, I'll leave out the names."

O'Connor was out of answers. He just stared at me like the Martian I was. Was it after this that he got even by way of that limey prick gag? If so, Othello himself would have called it quits with that one. But I'm not sure. There was no shape or plot to O'Connor's life, just one little thing after another.

After lunch, I went to see Father Herman, the headmaster. Beat me and stone me for this next bit. I can't get absolution anywhere, so I'll just have to fry in hell for it. Let us commence.

Herman was always nice to me. He was an affable, red-headed man, probably drawn by lot to run the school—the Carpathians are a strange order—and he was nice to most people. But I was also a star pupil, I guess (although it was hard to tell with such Neanderthal schoolwork), and an English boy added cachet to his moth-eaten establishment. (Where did my parents *find* this place? But I wander.) His office suggested golf clubs, farm equipment, a jar of chewing tobacco. He was the gentlest of these gentle priests. He took my news gravely but calmly. Could it be that he'd heard of such things before? I stumbled over the coup de grâce, not sure what word to use for the male member. Herman seemed, incredibly, slightly amused.

So much for the piercing insight of kids. I couldn't tell humor from embarrassment on the simplest adult face. In a school of that quality, at the tag end of the Depression, Herman could not afford to lose a single breathing boy—either through expulsion or whatever scandal I might kick up at home. He must calm me or perish.

73

"That's too bad," he said when I finished. "Yes, that really is too bad."

"Well, what are you going to do about it?" I demanded.

He tapped his fingertips together. "I don't know. I'll have to think it over."

Incredible. Think it over!

Stung, bitter, *right*, Chatworth exploded and out came names. My story wasn't interesting enough, huh? Want a little spice, do you? Naming Ponzo and his friends was a sort of pleasure. But when I got to O'Connor, I gagged. "You're not going to expel them, are you?" I croaked.

Herman, in memory, is purple, wheezing with suppressed laughter. Thought you could surprise a monk with a tale like that? Not really. He is just a salmon-pink businessman who cannot afford to lose customers. "I don't think that will be necessary. Maybe a little rearranging of roommates and a bit more spirituality for all of us, eh?"

I didn't tell him then about O'Connor and the nightly rosaries, did I? I hope to God I didn't. Saints are supposed to keep those things under their hats. I am getting up to go. "You were right to come to me," Herman says. Irony? I don't know.

The school shows its usual blank face. Nobody knows or cares about its two-bit Judas. I go straight to the chapel and pray before the chalk-and-blue statue of Herself. I have broken a promise and I am truly sorry. But I was trying to do the right thing. I really was. God's work. Mary's work. I am also a sniveling little turd and my adult self sneaks up and delivers a mighty kick that sends little Chatworth spinning across the pews and into the aisle.

The man in front peeps at me between the seats. Hello there. Nice fan. I'm ready for you now. My indignation over the Ponzo outrage just leaked away, and with it much of my baby-fat superiority. The penis in the mouth seemed just silly, possibly funny, and Ponzo was just a happy-go-lucky

Italian kid who'd try anything for a laugh. (I later learned he was the son of a Mafia big shot and is probably a junior godfather by now.) O'Connor is safe and sound in Nutley or Rutherford, handling his kids' drug problems with his usual surefooted finesse. All that remains is my own pimply sin. The rest is gone like that year's leaves.

O'Connor and I tried the rosary a couple of times, until one night he began doing his part in a deep bass voice.

"What do you think you're doing, O'Connor?"

"Frog in my throat."

Then he did the next bit in falsetto.

"Come on, shape up," I say weakly.

Then he does Jimmy Durante and I break up completely and giggle like a fool. "For Pete's sake, that's blasphemy, O'Connor," I splutter.

"Whatsamatter, I always talk like that. Umbriago, stop da music."

When we resume, I still can't stop laughing, and finally I give up and do an Eleanor Roosevelt Hail Mary and a Bill Stern glory-be. And after that we abandoned the rosary.

8

We're coming to you tonight from the Petrol Room of the Inflation Arms, London, where cultured Arabs break furniture with their teeth and crap in the fireplace. Otherwise, you couldn't ask for a nicer bunch.

Now that you've wrapped up world hunger, you say you need a woman? Waiter, send up a woman. What kind of a woman does sir want? Will it be rags or furs tonight? It doesn't matter. Just send one with about twenty thousand miles on her. A loyal creature with a life of her own, who'll wait right here while I race around the globe doing good. A fiercely intelligent woman who won't see through me immediately. A forties mind in a seventies body. And step on it.

Impossible. Lisa, for instance, was loyal but airsick. Also, a Spanish accent was the last thing I needed in my linguistic monkey barrel. If you don't mind, I'd rather not talk about Lisa right now. "You can't make a baby in a hotel room," she said. "Maybe in a bus station, but never in a Hilton," and that was that. "Maybe that's why you like hotel rooms," she added.

And while we're on the subject, I don't want to talk about Maureen either. She would be down in the lobby in a sleeping bag protesting something. I don't want to talk about any of my crazy women. They're all either insoluble problems or just another mirror. And I detest mirrors. I browsed my fill off real ones at an early age, before the female kind arose. At thirteen or so, sex was moving in its props and equipment but it had no place to go but me.

"Coolly she appraised herself and rather approved what she saw. From slim tapering waist, to pert little rosebud breasts, to alabaster thighs, to oh my God, oh Jesus, bring me some water quick" . . . it wasn't quite that bad. Chatworth was more sidelong about it; he liked to take himself by surprise. One afternoon he catches a dazzling smile that hasn't been there before. He watches until it fades like paint. Who knows, it may come in handy someday.

"You like looking at yourself?" says O'Connor.

"No." I lie.

"Then you must love to punish yourself."

It's true. For a few weeks, I cannot get over my new face. When I lock myself in the bathroom, it is not for the usual reason: it is to reassure myself that the face is still there and good for another fifty years. There is no trace of the homunculus. The little boy who left England with blood in his eye is quite dead. He would no doubt cry over what has taken his place. He would probably rush out and buy a goose for Tiny Tim, as if that ever solved anything. All right, kid—I'm pretty ashamed of you too. Evil-minded little prig.

Ah, I don't know. He did his best. He loved God and country. Didn't smoke or drink. I've given him corrupt motives just to get even. I've made fun of him because I can't stand his damned innocence. Please accept an old man's apology.

A fashion note as we leave him. He is wearing knickers by now, something he swore he would never do. The old ladies cluck over his courage, wearing short pants in snowdrifts, there'll always be an England won't there Mabel; but the Irish kids laugh inanely as usual. Laughter is a menacing sound in those days that might come from anywhere; he threads his way among it like a rat in a maze. Some movie is shown at school featuring rear admirals on the bridge in long white shorts, and the school rocks with mysterious glee. The homunculus, kicking off his chrysalis, is embarrassed for his people. "Shorts are jolly practical in hot weather," he reasons. "Are they, old bean? Yerss. I suppose they must be, what?" Now, thirteen and ex-Irish, he learns from their laughter that shorts are funny. He begins to see the joke himself.

So Chatworth sheds his shorts, not a matter of really crucial principle, and his one-piece underwear too, which had his friends really rolling. "Hey, its got a trap door, guys. How d'you work it, Winston? You press a button and it flies open or what?" solemnly asked. Every joke attracts its own fanatics—in this case a fellow called Gilhouley, who'd never bothered me before, but who suddenly swipes a pair of my "coms" (limey for combinations) and parades around in a derby and a monocle from the nonfunctioning drama department, saying, "What, what?" and "My word, that is a good one." He puts his face right next to Chatworth's and says, "Frightfully sorry, old chum, but have you seen my underwear? I can't seem to get to the bottom of it." Since nothing else seems to set Gilhouley off, and this sets him off to madness, Chatworth decides to let the underwear go, before the mob picks it up and makes it this season's Chatworth gag. His mother complains about this, and says he's too easily swayed by others, so he ends up in a silly argument with *her* about it.

It will have been noted that Chatworth also does American imitations now. This is not his fault. He is cursed with

78

a quick ear, and is confident he will get back to limey when the time comes.

Meanwhile, my father groans, a pitiful lowing sound, over my atrocious Americanisms, though he doesn't seem to mind Priscilla's. At home, I cannot help being English. It is like an officers' club in Rangoon, so English you could be living inside a teapot. My father takes to reminiscing ferociously. He forgets my age and tells me about punting at Oxford and mad dashes to London in Puffy's roadster and turning up at tutorials next morning in his evening clothes. The road is lined with Kentish strawberries, Devonshire cream, Somerset apples. There is always food about. When he gets back to Oxford, the tutor is reclining on the sofa, toying with a leg of duck *en gelée*. ("A messy business, duck. Try to remember that, Chatworth.") My father dangles a bottle of champagne from the night before. "Ah. You're the chap from Fortnum's," says the tutor, reaching out a hand for the champers. Meanwhile, the gramophone plays "Yes, We Have No Bananas" over and over. A sneeze goes off in the next room and a tremulous girl in beads peeps in.

"I'm so sorry. Champagne always makes me sneeze."

"Ah, Miss Rogers. Mastered our Herodotus, have we?"

Since I only took in about one word out of three, I remember it all rather strangely. For instance, between Candlemas and St. Swithin's, my father always went grouse hunting with future prime ministers, hip-deep in grouse, only to return to the most fabulous breakfasts. "Ah yes, the breakfasts, the breakfasts," he burbles, as we bite into our Wonder Bread toast. "Sides of flange and haunches of grimmon and silver Scotch crampons gleaming fresh from the river"—my father seems to hover over the sideboard of memory for an eternity, eyes afire. "And, of course, that was our light meal," he adds.

I see how such a one could hate America, with its fifty-seven varieties and its twenty-eight flavors of sugar substitute; and during the long vacations his indignation slips back under my own skin. Reluctantly I enter his world, and be-

79

come an Edwardian dandy, complete with side whiskers. It is either that or a pouting American teen-ager, pouting in a vacuum. Our village is so lonesome that there is no one to be American with. Priscilla goes around with a girl friend so lame-brained that I fear I'll be put off women for life if I listen to her.

So Father it is. At thirteen I am already an emotional whore and want him to like me, because there's nobody else around. At least that's how it starts. As I watch and listen he draws closer, enters. He is there still. When his euphoria waxes truly frantic, Father even begins to remember his public school with pleasure. Exquisitely talented boys scribbling verses to each other in Latin before marching arm in arm to the Somme to be wiped out in a body. A sad thought, but again there is food to set things right. Cider flows in torrents between the cakes and sweetmeats and fresh country eggs. And marmalade—was there ever such marmalade? So, an old soldier dying in torment, dribbling the little bit of water he is allowed, dreams of banquets. But we are jumping the gun. At the time he was cool and amused. "Fearful little gluttons in a starving world," he says. "Of course it had to end." I suppose I remember the food so well because of what happened when we returned to England in 1946. My father would have given his soul for an American hamburger by then. But there wasn't so much as a fledge of widgeon.

He sits forever in the shade, sipping his tea ironically. "Yes, a whole generation was wiped out, and I came within a whisker myself."

As I begin to reconstruct it, father must have left his public school in 1916, had his sticky time of it in the trenches (gas, frostbite, friends dead in the mud—all the usual sort of thing), and returned to Oxford with a bandage round his head in—now this doesn't make any sense—1922? Where was he in between? Those years seem to have disappeared. And there was no bandage round his head either, to judge from the photographs. He turned up at Balliol spanking new, and keen as mustard, just in time for the Varsity Drag and the dash to Brighton, and possibly even the tipsy flight to Paris. Wasn't he a bit old for that? *Where had he been?*

Too late to ask him now, and mother professes not to know. Failing memory is her ally and she claims it in draftfuls. It seems they met at Oxford, and he was a marvelous dancer, and so, naturally, they danced nonstop for fifteen years, pausing only to deliver Priscilla and me to our Irish nannies. Until, of course, this beastliness with Hitler. That was the version I scratched together from their small talk. My mother still has an album of old snapshots from the *Tatler* and such, and I study it furiously for clues. Both parents seem to have spent their lives changing from tweeds to evening clothes and swapping light banter with Lord and Lady Fang of Houndsditch. My father's face is invariably friendly and expressionless, as if the dog show and the hunt ball were all one to him; my mother is simultaneously animated and sad. "Let's not talk about the past, dear. It's so morbid," she says now.

I worry about those missing years because they may explain something missing in me. How did they patch up my father and make him seem like new after the trenches? In what strange country house did they teach these shock victims their dance steps and their talk? "Remember always to mention the Devonshire cream, old chap, and the breakfasts. Above all, the breakfasts." My father the zombie stirs, and a small light goes on—quite enough for an English gentleman. "Now remember, Chatworth, if you *do* the right things —dance till dawn, pour champagne over future prime ministers (you'll know who they are), and so forth—nobody will ask if there's anyone at home upstairs. Get the picture?"

This collage of bad RAF movies is as real as half my real memories. The instructor taps the board with his riding crop. "You see, chaps, you'll all be *better* English gentlemen for this. If you had any actual memories, any souls, you might make mistakes. Now that you've had all that blown out by

Jerry, we can produce a class of gentlemen that the world has never *seen* before." No, no. I love him. There was no such school. "Oh yes, and we'll find a girl for you when the time comes. Vivacious and a little unsure of herself should be the ticket, Chatworth. She watches your movements closely, like an uncertain dance partner. Goes along with everything. And then a daughter, a toy for you both, bright but shallow, quite taken in by your replica of a live man. And a son. My God, yes, a son . . ."

Believe me, there is no truth in this. But if there were—well, we have little Pendrid here, doggedly absorbing his father's fake memories of an England that never was, memories grafted onto an empty brain in a rehabilitation center somewhere in Cornwall. "Your son will meet the following specifications. By ten, he must be a super-patriot ready to die under Kitchener, ready to fight to the last breath for the Royal Exhibition—we'll need him in case Jerry decides to come back. Standard intelligence will do: enough to run the country, but not one ounce more. He will need self-esteem bordering on the stuffy—which means virtually no powers of self-analysis. And, above all, *he must not be taken out of the country.* If for some reason he *has* to be, board him at an embassy. Or failing that, make your own house as like an embassy as possible. *Keep him away from the natives.*"

One last question. "Catholic, Chatworth? No problems at all. Just the type we want. This is a little complicated, but get as much of it as you can." The glassy-eyed veterans, in their battle fatigues and plaster casts, roll about wretchedly. "You see, men, as you go through the motions at Oxford and so forth, it may be observed from time to time that you are not really enjoying yourselves much. This is inevitable, because in fact you are not. But it doesn't matter a jot if you're RC, because English Catholics are presumed to have a secret life elsewhere. They approach this world with something called 'the law of measure,' which means they may play with it politely, or even with a certain tolerant gusto, but they know it isn't important. And this means that they need show *no real feelings at all.*" The instructor (in full military regalia from the Khartoum offensive) lowers his monocle. "They are nature's gentlemen," he says quietly.

I have to clown to keep from crying out. Khartoum offensive, indeed. My father must have summoned his wits for this last big lesson, because he never veered from it. Whether he was taking me to Mass or the circus, or even, finally, dying in pain, the glass around him never broke. I never saw a real feeling except irritation, which even machines are subject to.

Of course, I lie. To get even. Father's life was his feeling, a seamless act of considerateness. For instance, I am thirteen and sick, nothing serious, but a high fever and, I later learn, a polio scare. I feel his hand. "Pendrid, I insist that you get better." He has flown from Washington, bumping VIPs right and left, because the wartime trains are so slow. He sits with me all night, as if I were dying beside him in a trench. No feelings. Play in your own vomit if you must, Chatworth, but don't say silly things like that.

The fact is I can't stand his damn goodness. I must scrawl filth on it right away. Why didn't it help me more? Why didn't he *say something?*

So I leave him, a waxwork. In the kind of crazy country house that frightened me as a child they have put him together and even programmed his virtues. It's the least I can do. Having betrayed him and his Church and his family, and above all his smug integrity, I can't afford to believe he was real. Father, forgive me for all this. But you had no right to be so much better than I.

9

Back to my milk run. Pointed toward New York, I no longer see those things. I only remember listening politely to my father in the summer of 1944, as one listens to some old fool in pantaloons telling how he circumnavigated the globe. But my real business at the time was right here, in this land of beaten gold I am now approaching. Let me chant you a pastorale. The penitential rags go back in the actor's truck for now. Get out of my room, you smelly priest.

Actually, most people probably don't need confession at all—there's enough humiliation in real life. You have to be a pretty exceptional person to have to kick your own teeth like this. No, seriously, there's so much praise for any celebrity to process, like Christmas mail: women propose to even the dingiest of us in ungovernable quantities; their lives are cruelly empty, it seems—goatlike husbands, swinish children (I don't know what they expected)—except for their hour with me or Johnny or Mo. During that hour they apparently sit before their sets scarcely breathing, gushing forth more love than Mary Magdalene on her best day, soaking our faces in it; prior to tottering off more dead than alive to croak out what's left of it on atrocious note paper.

Well, I'm used to it, most of the time. I understand it's not me they love, but something I know how to do, a technique. And I know that they are tough cookies, deep down, who ride roughshod over their husbands, using me as a weapon, and who gut their wretched children with lovesick demands. I have no illusion that if I stepped out of the magic box I wouldn't get the same treatment from them; I *have* had the same treatment. My old friend Lisa used to write to David Frost.

Nevertheless, it *is* love, twisted and leprous as the best. And it even fortifies me. Until the cup runs over and I have to vomit the love out. So. These confessions are simply ways of clearing my stomach for more love. Praise tastes passing sour as it leaves; the lies lose their candy flavor and reveal their strychnine base. Those people don't love me; they are sending me their sickness. I know them. There is no love in them.

My fault, then, for taking them seriously: for reading my own mail and lighting up, even with irony, whenever a woman offers me her body, and for not recognizing the affront to her husband that the offer is meant for. It's unprofessional and I'll do no more of it. I'll cut my ration of praise to the bone. Oh God, easily said. A man can drown in the amount I get after every broadcast. And I still *hear* it, unlike the others, every last whisper.

Anyway, Father Sony looks bored and resentful today. Gorging and then confessing is frowned on by the authorities; you are supposed to mend your ways, as well, and I can't afford to do that. He will not give me absolution until I write to each of my fans as follows: "You, Winnie Porter of Ridgefield, Conn.—go back to your husband Fred immediately. He is a fairly good man, just as I am a fairly good man. There is nothing else around. If I were really the God you're looking for, why the hell should I choose *you*. But I'm not. And neither is Fred. I'm just a guy who broke away from his quaint Victorian family, made his way laughing and crying to the top, and is now on his way to receive the Witherspoon award for integrity in broadcasting."

It never rains but it pours these damn awards. This one spooks me a little. It sounds like an old man's award, a virtual obituary. I don't need to work on my modesty today, but on my confidence, its friendly rival.

So. On with the dithyramb. I am in Cape May, New Jersey, 1944, strolling the boardwalk with a springy step and a furtive eye for the girls. For a boarding-school boy, these developments take place in his absence, so to speak, and in jerks. I have finished eighth grade at St. Boniface, whatever that means (a piece of wilted cardboard with my name spelled wrong) and have completed another year that the school has tacked on meaninglessly, and I will just have to keep going there until the war ends. My father seems to have run out of educational ideas. There is a feeling in the school that this is the summer something happens. Next year's pecking order will be established by who tells the best story in September. So I prowl the boardwalk, sniffing popcorn and looking for I don't know what. Sailors stroll by bearing pandas and leis from the rifle range; girls cling to them patriotically. Chatworth catches his reflection in the funhouse mirror. Even distended lengthways or sideways, that is some kind of face.

He goes back to his hotel more than half in love with himself. Chatworth still has his crotchets, mind you. He believes he dislikes American swing music and confides this tactfully to a gentle splayfooted boy at his hotel. The guy has his door open and Chatworth, Lord of the Summer, has sauntered in.

"What do you see in them?" he says over the blare of Harry James.

"Mm-mm," says the boy, one Bobby Winninger of Germantown.

"Well. I mean they're so soupy, aren't they?"

Winninger is big, slow, and has rimless glasses. Remarks seem to slow down and die as they pass through him. His wall is papered with masters of swing. Can you do that in hotels? Who is this Winninger anyway?

"And all the songs are about love. With all the things there are in the world to write about, why does it always have to be about love?"

"Love is a universal emotion," says Winninger at last. "Love is the greatest thing," he adds.

"Yeah, well, maybe. But I could see someone getting tired of it."

Winninger furrows. "You see, this music is originally for dancing, and dancing is an activity for girls and boys, and girls and boys often feel a certain way about each other when they dance."

Chatworth knew this, all right. This hulking pedant was only confirming what his scrotum had long since learned. "And when they feel this way," Winninger lumbered on, "they want music that says, 'Well all right, Jack.' Or as the poet says, 'If music be the food of love, it's solid with me.'"

Yes, yes. Solid indeed. Chatworth could picture the girls with their skirts flying and their white legs splaying and chewing each other on the dance floor, and he sensed that this music served a purpose, though he continued to call it soupy out of principle. Americans were potty about love; he'd been saying it for years, and in those days it seemed like a betrayal to change his mind about anything at all. So he listened disapprovingly to Winninger's Dorsey records till Chatworth's mother got alarmed and came looking for him.

"Incredible stuff," he told her later. "You can't really call it music, of course."

"Why did you stay so long?"

"Interesting chap. Has some weird theories about music." Winninger's theories about music were mostly to the effect that it was sexual foreplay, whatever that was. "Love makes the world go round, and music is its handmaid. Do you read me, gate?" These theories didn't bear repeating to his mother.

Absolute rubbish, of course. Winninger was built for the study, not the dance floor. The shine on his glasses when he talked about the real meaning of Benny Goodman's clarinet or of the phrase "hot licks" was that of a mad professor circling a tadpole. Chatworth didn't follow a word of it, of course, but it was a soothing kind of gibberish, like leafing through corset ads and reading about tummy paneling and thigh control. Strangely comforting.

"You wouldn't say all that about Bach or Beethoven, would you?" he said the next day.

"Sure I would. What do you think the *Moonlight* Sonata is all about?"

"Dunno. Moonlight?"

Winninger adjusted his glasses. The chap was a riot. "The moon happens to be a highly erotic symbol. It affects the tides and the human mind, and by extension the tides within us. Also, it enables one to see the beloved," he winked.

"Also it rhymes with June."

"Well, June is a midsummer month. Life is bursting all around us," said the big fellow. "It may not be a coincidence that the human mouth makes the same sound for both concepts."

Groovy. Super. What's the Chinese for June? I tried my father's voice in my head and my sister's, to get the right note of amusement. Anyway, Winninger was too priceless, a German professor transposed intact, like the Cloisters.

Or was he? Unfortunately, I was at the age where even the *Encyclopaedia Britannica* can set one's knees trembling, and Winninger's lumpish slide lectures began gradually to get to me. In that slow mind, everyone sucked and scraped and blew to one end. The sounds of the night were a symphony of humping and mankind was no exception; his song was like

88

the rubbing of a cricket's legs. Every jingle became a sexual steam bath. "Pepsi Cola hits the spot"—well we all know what that means, don't we? "Twelve full ounces, that's a lot." Wise up, kid, and suck along. It makes the world go round. Winninger's fat, sleepy face sent out damp waves of sexuality. He wasn't priceless at all: he was a bloody menace.

Priscilla was the one who came to find me that day, late for dinner again. "Keep your hands off her, Winninger," I almost shouted. At the very least, I expected him to tell her about the real meaning of the slide trombone, and for Priscilla to wither him with a wisecrack. I was embarrassed for both of them. But they were both very polite and mature and talked about, oh, the kind of people who came to Cape May, Tidewater Virginians and what not, very heavy stuff; they were both older than I and made me feel it. I wandered out into the corridor, raging ambiguously, and when Priscilla joined me a minute later, I snapped: "Isn't he the kind of American you hate? Big fat face. No sense of humor . . ."

"He seemed rather nice."

"You're kidding, Priscilla—you! I've heard you talk about Americans like him. I guess he can speak three words a minute if he really pushes, and two of the words would be 'er.' "

"He seemed quite intelligent. And he wants to take me to the movies."

"*Intelligent.* Oh no! Do you realize that that idiot thinks all music is sexual?" I had done it again: blurted the unspeakable.

"Does he now?" said Priscilla, and gave me a ravishing smile. "Maybe he'll take me to a musical, then," she said.

So much for saving my sister. Priscilla's life at the time was largely devoted to tormenting me, and she would have gone apartment hunting with King Kong to embarrass me. She did go to the movies with Winninger and it must have been one of the dullest evenings in the history of dullness, but later she told me, with shining eyes, "He's pretty good. Yes. You might even say he's extremely good. But what I'm looking for right now is a fully licensed sex maniac."

She was looking, I guess, for company. She was too quick-clever and British for most boys and had to settle for these slow, self-important ones who didn't recognize the problem. A Bob Winninger was the best she could get if she wanted to have an escort and make it look as if she were doing something with her summer. (I would like to do something useful with this information, but they're all gone.)

"Don't judge a book by its cover," she warbled. "In a taxicab, you'd be surprised."

"You're kidding. What do you really do with him?"

"A bit of this and a bit of that. You'll know in a few years. Or else, you won't."

Under the prod of her teasing, I wanted once again to storm into his room and tell him to leave my sister alone. But the big fat fellow just sat there solemnly all day as innocent as a priest. (Or did I, in fact, storm in? And did he say, "I'm not doing anything she doesn't want, kid." No. The fact that I remember this perfectly doesn't mean it happened.)

In my head, *everything* happened. Bear in mind that Priscilla's was the first nipple I'd seen and the first bush, and she was sacred. No one must touch those things, let alone a fat slob with a mind like a heavy tractor. She must become a nun. Give herself to God. And even He better keep his hands to Himself. (This didn't mean I necessarily liked her.)

In this inflamed condition, I met a little girl from Wilkes-Barre, and thank God for that, I suppose, because heaven knows what embarrassment I had been barreling toward. Maybe the Big Bang itself. Betty Lou Burch was plump and "cute," with a solemn trusting gaze and what I take now to be a nervous smile. I love her still, however flabby and dull-eyed she may be, however many letters she writes to Johnny Carson begging for escape. She had a summer of impossible glory at the age of twelve.

Betty Lou used to sit in the lobby by herself, hands and ankles folded neatly, and peep at me; and one day I went over and said gruffly, "You wanna go for a walk?" I was driven to it. My sister had just finished telling me, "He moves surprisingly well for a big man"—how sadly she got her kicks that summer—and I was blinded by visions of fat hands groping, and after that of endless greasy nightclub owners to come, mauling my crazy sister, and I had to do something.

Betty Lou nodded—she seldom did more than that—and silently we strode out toward the beach and walked the sands for hours, and I loved her feverishly because I had to. I walked tall for a little fellow, a throbbing blob of willpower, and my Brunhilde matched me stride for stride. I can still see Betty Lou in a white dress against an impossible sunset (impossible because we were facing south), or cheerleading in sticky Kodachrome and tangoing under a blue moon, because she was all of love; I have added nothing since. The seasons change as we walk, leaves fall and dogwoods bloom. I find myself murmuring Winninger's bloody songs. We are an old couple now, yet marvelously fresh and unlined. We've come through!

"Maybe we better be getting back," said the little girl, hitching at her shorts. Who are you? Oh yes. Betty Lou Something. I nodded. We wheeled around silently, a scrawny boy in a T-shirt and his plump little blonde child, and straggled back hand in hand. The band in the distance was unmistakably Tommy Dorsey's and my sister could go to hell in her own way.

We repeated this the next day and every other day, and like most pastorals, there wasn't much to it. Her sweetest words were, "You're weird" and "I never met anyone like you in Wilkes-Barre." While as for the adoring gaze that warmed me to yeast, it was really the only gaze she had and she applied it to everything.

Yet, she seemed to enjoy my company in some way. Was it my conversation?

"Growing up is frightening," I remember saying. "It's like a rollercoaster. You've got to have trust in the Maker." Pause. Is she supposed to say something? "It's scary. But like you say."

At times I was strong and quiet. At others laconically pithy. "You've gotta ride with it, Betty, wherever it takes you." I don't suppose there was any single famous movie star who wasn't pressed into service. And Betty Lou smiled on them all impartially as she trudged along.

On her last night there, she gave me her address in Wilkes-Barre. Her father was a minor union official and she wasn't accustomed to vacationing at Cape May. In fact, if I couldn't make it to Wilkes-Barre, I would never see her again. I kissed her expertly, plumbing the depth of my resources, and she kissed back. Sensationally. I was taken off-stride. For a first kiss, that was a hell of a job.

We sat on the sand with our arms round each other, and her breath was as warm as her unchanging gaze. She wanted to go on and I did my best. She had logged a lot of hours with a weirdo for just this moment. We clung together for some time, not knowing (I not knowing) what to do next. The movies always dissolved at that point. It is definitely not true that I said, "We'd better not go any further. I'm a Catholic."

The next day I saw Betty Lou and her mother off on the train and I was rich with sorrow. The fact that I would never see her again added enormously. I walked back along the empty platform, crushing her address in my pocket, then smoothing it. I needed no belted raincoat for this. Her face at the window was lost in smoke, but I knew it was tear-drenched. And that evening I walked the sands by myself, my heart bursting proudly. Threw a stone, shook my head, resumed walking. The game of life takes funny bounces, my friend.

It was enough to float me through our last two weeks at Cape May. If she'd stayed I'd have been stuck, but her absence was sublime. I was asked by the hotel hearties to perform in the local amateur contest, and I realized how much I had changed. Two years ago I had sung "Underneath the Spreading Chestnut Tree" and "The Siegfried Line" in a heavy cockney accent and had won five dollars in war stamps. A little buck-toothed English boy catering to apes. This year I gave them a stiff "no."

Sorrow and loss were a marvelous new mansion to play in. And the pleasure was doubled when my sister broke off with Winninger. "You were right about him. You were right about Americans," she said, granting me a wisdom she needed *somebody* to have around here.

I must have looked blank—which was known to happen around then. "He's a rat," she said shortly, giving up on my wisdom. From which I deduced that the big earthworm had made his move. And what a move it must have been. "Honey, it's what we're here for. It's all there is," I imagine him wheezing. "Three doctors out of four agree it's good for your wind." Poor Priscilla.

So we both had our great sorrows that August and I only hope hers was as much fun as mine. Probably not. Right after that, she and a friend at the hotel named Margot got picked up by a couple of sailors on the boardwalk and she told me, "Ugh, was that flat. Honestly, they were so young, and they were *much* scareder than we were, and absolutely *nothing* happened. We wound up drinking chocolate ice cream sodas and talking about their hometowns." I couldn't tell if she really minded that much; she was quite the phony at sixteen. "Fancy, this country being defended by boys with pimples," she said.

My mother was horrified nevertheless and tried to get her to promise not to do it again.

"But Mummy. Don't we owe them something after all they've done?"

"You can always bake biscuits for them."

"You're joking and you're not making a terribly good job

93

of it," Priscilla muttered below Mother's established hearing level, and then louder, "Look, Mummy, they're young and lonely and they want female company. Is there anything wrong with that? It's only—natural," she glanced at me guiltily. Winninger had left his paw marks on her mind.

"There's lots of female company around to give them whatever it is they want. Let them get it from American girls."

Priscilla left the room in a rare rage, slamming and stomping. "Talk to your father," called my mother. "He's coming down for the weekend."

I guess she did, because there was more stomping and slamming in the next room. I couldn't hear a word, but I imagine the waxwork saying, "Yes, let them stick to their own kind" and "I know about soldiers, my dear." Meanwhile, father working the military brushes, trimming the old mustache. Why do I always lie about this man? Chatworth streaked to the door in time to see Priss streaming along the corridor.

"Where you going?"

"None of your beeswax."

She and Margot tried again that very night and Uncle Sam's defenders were not so innocent this time. I came in on the end, of course, and got it all jumbled in my excitement. The story was over before it began. I know that Priss turned up at my door crying. "They said it was our patriotic duty," she started right in. "They said, 'Fuck this after a year at sea.' " She looked at me wildly. Was I the person to tell this to? Me, reeling from the word "fuck" and already out of it. "They said we were teases and pr-professional vir-virgins who had led them on and w-wasted their shore leave."

Mad visions drenched me, I was helpless. It was *me* they had threatened; it was Priscilla and *me* they were all after. "So what happened?" I croaked.

"Well, I said, rather desperately, 'How about a nice ice cream soda?' and Walt said, 'Fuck a nice ice cream soda,' and he took a bottle of whiskey out of his duffel bag and said, 'Here, drink this, chick. It'll get you in the mood,' and he jammed it against my face. Smell me, Pen. Isn't it foul? It ran all down my chin and over my dress."

I smelled, and it was indeed distilled awfulness. The crazy visions began now to smell and sweat. "Then what happened?" Did I really want to know?

Priss looked at me blankly. Was I old enough? Was it sinful to tell me? I see her now as an unbearably beautiful woman stuck with a gibbering useless little boy; or alternately as a wanton hellcat stuck with a lubricious teen-ager. Both pictures are equally clear under the boardwalk lights. "I'm not sure what happened next. I think Margot went along with them. She said, 'What the hell? It's supposed to be fun, isn't it? And there's *nothing* we can do about it.' I don't know what I said. I don't—oh God, I wish there was someone I could talk to."

She ran from the room. "Don't tell Mummy," she said.

Priscilla kept to herself for the last week, though she was as cheerful as ever when she had to be. What made her tick? I didn't even bother to wonder. My studies of the human heart were limited to one.

Years too late, I talked to her about "that rather awful summer," as she called it, and I asked her what really happened that night, and she said she couldn't remember.

Amnesia runs in our family, to the benefit of all. So ends my pastorale.

10

～～～～～～～～～～～～～～～～～～～

The last hour or so in flight is the worst, because new arrivals are meant to be fresh, and not the broken umbrellas they feel like. So let us think fresh.

Chatworth hung on to the rollercoaster and trusted the Maker. I went to church the next morning, Sunday, and offered up my whole family, and a senile peace descended. As my brain cooled, I figured out that Priscilla's sailors were probably normal enough guys with a skinful of booze and an urge to show off. Your American serviceman notoriously lacked discipline. Margot, at least, seemed none the worse for it and was seen around Cape May after that with a raft of servicemen and a smug smile. Priscilla announced that all American men were drips and that she was off sex until we got back to England—where, even now, a conga line of Spam-fed chinless tanglefoots was preparing for her, kicking to a rumba beat.

Going back to England was suddenly a real possibility, and it conditioned all of us as the Second Coming conditioned St. Paul. The Allies were already zipping through France, which was no bigger than Rhode Island or someplace, with colorful, gritty General Montgomery in the lead, smirking from his tank, followed by some GIs whose trifling assistance would be grossly exaggerated in the American press. The war in Europe would be won by fall. My own interest in military strategy had lapsed lamentably, but my father kept maps and drew arrows on them, his artificial temples throbbing; and I forced myself to follow his summaries. Priscilla's accent went into reverse and became more English than it has ever been since (she, too, had moved into MGM England, boots, brolly and all). My mother became essence of Miniver, comfy and fat of ankle as she trudged the shops. "We call it maize and you call it corn. Extraordinary!" she exulted. Our pathetic little garrison capered with glee over the speck on the horizon.

Me? Ah, me. "Isn't it wonderful, Daddy?" "Isn't it super, Mummy?" "Real *strawberries!*" God, how I strained. "The Ardennes! Just a few potty trees. Come on, Monty. Show them what for!" The fact is, I wasn't sure I wanted to go back at all.

At least, not quite yet. In the long run, of course, one wanted to go back more than anybody. When it came to bobbies and red buses, my family self was a flag-waving fool. Yet, something about America held me—something I didn't even like. For one thing, I wanted to go back to St. Boniface and share my summer wisdom with my friends and hear theirs, and not miss another development. The boys in a country grow up together whether they know it or not, and if you miss that, you just have to fake it.

Around then I had one of the few dreams I can still remember—maybe because it was a sitting-up dream in the best family armchair. Priscilla's sailors came to my room and I made friends with them immediately, so that they wouldn't kill me. The first pair consisted of a big redheaded moron and a sensitive Italian looking for love in the heart of violence. They were OK. But then, in walked a belching Irishman and a Texan and I had to start over. And then slowly the whole country passed through the room, swaggering and spitting,

97

tough, colorful, American, and I knew I couldn't make friends with all of them. And I noticed behind me on the bed my English sister, writhing, rejecting, wanting America and hating it, crying on my shoulder for help and laughing at me for an English prig; Priscilla, *the only girl I had ever seen.* That was what they wanted, not me. So, just to keep their friendship, I joined their laughing, swearing fellowship, and climbed aboard. Come on Priss, we're in this together.

The sailors faded to nose-picking nothings, watching idly. I had appeased them the only possible way. I was saving my sister for God and they respected me—for just one instant, and then, in real life, I was tearing at my clothes and trying to choke myself! My God, what a thing even to dream. Or had I dreamed it? Was that fat Negress really Priscilla? I went to confession the next evening, but I couldn't get myself to say it.

"I thought something about a girl."

"Was it grave?"

"Yes, it was grave."

"Well, we must all struggle with these things." He didn't want to hear about it. (Contrary to rumor, I seldom met a priest who gave a damn about my sex life.) I wish to God he'd choked it out of me. It might have spared me this confession.

. . . Come, come. We dramatize, don't we, Chatworth? Dr. Furman explained it, or even invented it for all I know, and I left his office perfectly happy. "Your sister probably wanted you, too," he said, "and was frustrated because you were too lee-tle. Also, der vas der incest taboo." I invent the accent, because psychiatry stories fall hopelessly flat without it. He was really a tweedy Englishman. "Two little orphans of the storm. Hansel and Gretel. Of *course* you wanted each other. Poor little tykes."

In real life, I am still trying to figure out why they're giving an integrity award to a licensed schizophrenic tonight. I have, of course, a good side, named Plunkett after Blessed Oliver, and a bad side named Snead, because it is the meanest sound in the language, but that doesn't add up to integrity, even by American standards.

I'm afraid Snead just might get out as they are handing me the award, and start dancing like a goat. Actually, the prize is for Plunkett, who had a little burst of activity himself at this very point in my story. Perhaps the memory of it will give him heart.

Having noplace else to go until Monty stormed into Berlin, I returned one last time to St. Boniface, where they gave me special classes to prepare me for England. Hah! Still reeling from the summer, I fell upon religion with terrible violence, bursting it open like a bank vault. Not serving Mass to curry favor anymore—quite the opposite: I even gave up my altar boy career because it was a vanity. I gave up piety and conspicuous churchgoing, because I wanted the real thing, Goodness itself. I didn't need to be a prude anymore. The boys, who were still wobbling cautiously through the grades beneath me, could tell whatever jokes they liked; I understood the jokes now (after some rather oblique, monkish biology lessons based on ferns), and I laughed at them and kept my eye on the distant light.

I read the lives of the saints, and for a short, dizzy spell I loved everybody and forgave everybody. As Ponzo, instantly at ease with this year's new Chatworth, recited "The Goodship Venus," a glow of pure seraphic love filled me. "You're OK, Winston," he picked it up. "You too, Frank," I said. There was only one sinner to worry about and that was me. What a load off my mind. The world's evil vanished like mist. Priscilla's sailors were just poor old humanity doing its best; God's love darting at them, missing, coming again as fresh as a new day: at these wild, crazy Americans of all races who continued to parade through my sister's room, in swelling volume.

I thought briefly of the priesthood, but decided that even that was a vanity. I would simply consort with sinners and let them know that everything was OK. No sermon, no disapproval. Just, be of good cheer. (I believe, yes I do, that my TV shows have done something like this after all. Hence my award.) I must emphasize the sincerity of my loving tolerance, because it was so outstandingly successful; my schoolmates, ever ready to accept a new Chatworth, voted me most popular boy in school. I was never happier in America.

In this mood, I was even prepared to take a new look at my mother, whose sitting room had once seemed as gloomy as a convent parlor, and then as tinny as a rummage sale. She was the last of my family to come into focus, because I was so used to the blur, and I saw that under her whore's make-up of religiosity, she was really a good woman.

"Do you really need all that stuff?" I asked gently. "Toe of St. Jude and so forth. Isn't God enough?"

Her reply was surprisingly vehement. "God is too *much.* These are the closest I can get."

Ah, such wisdom. I honestly could not tell you now whether my mother was intelligent or not—she bypassed the question. Her remarks were somehow always off the point, so that when she blundered into shrewdness one never knew whether she meant to. (She blundered into shrewdness surprisingly often, but that might have been the luck of the Irish.) That night, however, she seemed like one of those apparitions who appear to saints and tell them to ford that river or plant that tree and a monastery will spring up on the spot.

I decided then and there that she was a saint herself, and I still think so, whatever it means, and I think I'll mention her name tonight when the amalgamated muffinheads give me their gingerbread award for inner cleanliness.

Monty Chatworth sleeps in pajama tops for his own very good reasons, in an extra-large single bed. He has no plans to marry ("And make a million women unhappy," he says, twinkling) but is seen often in company of mongoloid child star Burgess Fang.

These program notes from the Hotel Purgatorio in New York are to indicate that I'm still awake and feeling rotten. The two sleeping pills I slipped in there to polish off Mother backed up on me and I've got a three-alarm headache. God, that was a disgusting performance. When the MC called me "a wit with a heart" I broke into that silly grin again and it wouldn't go away. After that I tried to be humble, but I couldn't remember how it worked and wound up smugger than ever. Even the MC seemed sickened. Ah well, drinky-poos indicated. Now, let's see. Mother. God, I met a platoon of her in England—uneducated girls hiding behind vagueness and scheming inattention, working their crazy tangents; in my mother's case, barricading herself further behind religious objects. In another case it might have been tiger skins or prehistoric teapots. Wisdom! Little did I know that peasant spirituality is terrifically upper class. And how better to win father's famous heart pacer? Shit. She couldn't compete with his brains or his style, but she could really lay on that old peasant faith, before which even Catholic lords must bend the knee.

Poor old thing. All she wanted from me was some undemanding company and maybe a helping hand around the house; and what she got was young St. Augustine himself, keen as mustard, piling on the religious hardware, digging up Coptic crosses, making even religion a challenge. And to top it off, she had to pretend to be interested.

OK, Snead, you've had your fun. I'm sorry I invented you that night in Fresno. A disc jockey needs someone to talk to, but not that badly. The last spring of the war in America was a good one for Mother and me and the Western mind in general, and even you can't spoil it now. It was much better than peace ever was. The newsreels showed tanks rolling through the spring mud and delirious Europeans flinging themselves on board, and the Chatworths were right up there in spirit, kissing and laughing. "They don't show enough of Monty," my father complained, but he didn't really mind. He was even free to enjoy America a little, now that the promised land was in view. He took us on a trip to Niagara which was, he admitted, not bad of its kind, "though excessive, of course, like everything in America." He parodied himself in his delirium. Priscilla joined him eagerly. "The Grand Canyon is fine if you like a bloody great hole, right Daddy?" Yes, yes—and the Everglades, if swamps are really your sort of thing.

One got closest to the plastic heart by joking, and Priscilla applied herself eagerly, as if she were trying to keep him alive. She loved him that year, and the air crackled with their lovemaking. I was out of it, I had no sense of humor, but I had something better. Their jokes made me smile tolerantly —that twinge of envy was nothing. Priscilla's eyes were always just a little bit anxious as she joked ("Am I pleasing you, Daddy? Is that a good one?"). On the night before we left, she startled me by saying, "Mummy is an ass, of course. I can't stand her." So, in all this bleak land, she had found nothing but my father.

I, on the other hand, had found God, and believe me he came in handy. Of course my mother was an ass, I knew it all along; but an ass is perfectly OK in the eyes of God. So is a half-dead ex-soldier with a bound volume of Bulwer-Lytton for a brain, and so is a whorish sister and even a bloody-minded little boy who'd have killed them all if it weren't for the loneliness of it all. The popularity prize at school was a final touch of irony. It was like crowning the village idiot and making him king for a day. They were paying me for all the laughs I'd given them. I didn't fool those little Irish bastards for a minute.

Never mind. Again, religion rescued me. Little St. Pendrid forgave them all. With his smug little smile, he packed his bags and departed. On the last day of school, they all, led by O'Connor, shook hands warmly, as if they had really liked him after all. Hah! Them and their smiling Irish irony. At least they'd settled scores for their damn famine. Meanwhile, a forgiving soul is untouchable. Chalk another up to The Man.

. . . Thought you'd get rid of me, eh Plunkett? That award was like blood from a maiden's throat. I won't have to go back to my coffin for days. You're lucky I didn't tear the plaque to shreds in my gleaming fangs. (Actually, I knew it would only have earned you another award for integrity, so what was the use?) Now, go on with your story. I'm not a bit sleepy. And if you don't put me to sleep soon, you know you'll be crazy by morning, don't you?

Very well. Monty has won the war at last, and our little toy saint is filling his bag with knickknacks, which includes things like long blank summer days at our Pennsylvania house, a burlesque of a country idyll as I wade through creeks and pretend to fish. I do not wish to be Huckleberry Finn, thank you very much. I read a lot, but am too proud to become the characters I read about. Still, a little of Huck goes in there, as in all American suitcases. Now what about the guy I came in with—the boy in the shop window, smiling, naming himself like Adam naming a new animal? Can I reclaim him on departure? No. The window is empty and the face has changed. I have resisted, I have held on—and suddenly I'm somebody else.

I took with me back to England a very small sliver of America, a splinter—made of a tumbledown village in Pennsylvania, some hot gloomy visits to Philadelphia, and an unlikely collection of school friends. Out of this I would eventually fashion a whole country for my memory bank. It is no wonder I sometimes get it wrong.

My America (like other people's Americas) consists of a thimble of personal experience mixed into great vats of popular culture. To wit: the kids from St. Boniface seemed to me to typify the whole sprawling continent, yet they were all out of the same pocket; they came from middle-class Catholic families that had weathered, or better than weathered, the Depression and could afford at least the lower depths of private schools. Doctors, insurance men, one or two farmers. The boys cherished the street toughness of their grandfathers, but it was an empty ritual by now. When I finally

103

stayed at O'Connor's house, I found the latest in home appliances, pop-up toasters, foam mattresses—pretty quaint now, but that house looked like a palace then, with its pink porcelain washbasins and fawns dancing on the glass shower door. The guys had nothing to be tough about anymore, and I doubt if O'Connor's kids even pretend to be tough. Yet, you would not believe the working-class generalizations I have spun from this gang, or my own tales of a slam-bang childhood. If they had really been tough, they'd have broken my legs and bent my skull out of shape.

As it is, they have only housebroken me. Nursing me with mockery and offers of friendship, they have made me one of them: a nice American Catholic boy. Or have they? I am confused on the point. There is an Englishman inside, I know it, and I try grimly to summon him up as I fly back over the Atlantic now with my terribly English father and sister who have kept the faith without trying and are fairly bursting to be home, and my mother, out of place everywhere. Yes, I'm looking forward; I flog myself into caring. Flying, at least, is exciting. Dashing from window to window to see different aspects of the Atlantic. All rather blue, actually. My father rattles on about what he'll do first and what he'll do second. Restaurants, cricket grounds, looking up old Puffy. (There is no old Puffy; it's an incredible lapse of the training school.) I listen, now, a sympathetic grownup.

"Perhaps you'd better turn back," I tell him.

"What's that?" my father looks at me blankly. "I say, Pen, do watch out. It's only an ocean. One drop of water is much like another."

"Perhaps you'd better turn back," my grown-up self repeats ominously. But my voice is killed by the engines, and by a pair of handsome teen-agers, careening off people's knees, acting like the children they were in 1940, erasing the American years.

It is a long ride, and I spend some of it working on my vowels. "Whatcher cocky?" I say to myself solemnly. "Bi' of all right, that. Blimey, crikey core stone 'er crows." By the time we land, I am a chirpy 1940 cockney all over again. *I have kept the faith.*

"Whatcher mate?" I say to the porter.

"What was that, sir?"

"I said, 'It's a bit of orl right.' "

"Yes sir, very good sir."

No. Nothing like that happened. It was more gradual. We ate our watercress sandwiches in silence. The passport man said, "Welcome home." It was raining and my father said, "At last. *Real* rain." Priscilla laughed.

The atmosphere is gentle and quiet as death. "I say," my father pipes suddenly. "I actually found a bit of watercress in my sandwich. There must be a mistake." His voice caroms around the tin shed.

"Can I help you, sir?" says a steward.

"Yes. Take a look at this monstrosity of a sandwich and let me know if you find anything."

The steward peers into it. "Yes, that's watercress all right, sir," he says.

First the rain, then the sandwiches? I don't know. I do remember my father staring at the lumpy bread and the tattered sprig with real distress. "Must be the Labour government," he said with a sharp laugh. Then he brightened, and on the muggy bus ride to London he cheerfully noted various indigenous plants, clamoring fuchsias and perennial aphasias grown only in Central Hampshire, actually, in a voice louder than usual. His years of diplomacy were over, and I became aware of a red-faced Tory gentleman I had never met before.

We checked into a small gray London hotel with an elevator for two, manned by a dotard in livery who couldn't stop it within two feet of any given landing. "I say, this is intolerable," said my father, who was squeezed in with me and a fat suitcase. "Stop the bally thing and we'll jump for it."

Was he really angry? He still did it facetiously, but with

strain. "I could swear I spotted a piece of meat on my plate," he said over supper—still working his watercress variations. "Must have the old eyes tested."

"The English haven't recovered from the war yet," said Mummy.

"Yes, yes. Of course not. Still, they could always take care of one at Willoughby's. At least the waiters had *teeth* in those days. Must be new management." And so on and on. "Two inches of bath water. Barely enough to cover the old coccyx." Priscilla laughed with effort: Daddy must be kept funny at all costs. I was frankly bored and somehow missed the note of nervous terror in his voice.

"You must remember what they've been through," Mummy persisted doughtily.

"Yes, yes. But it's no excuse for inefficiency." His forehead throbbed and his voice was louder than mine had been as a child's. "People used to know how to *do* things in England."

"But they're all away at war, you see."

"*Blast* the war." My father wiped his mouth with his napkin. An old couple glared at us in the murk of the lounge. My father looked down morosely at his coffee cup. He was lost, but I wasn't sorry for him, only embarrassed. I was used to his making a fool of me in America, but not *here*. "I suppose all the decent coffee has gone to war too," he muttered, and Priscilla laughed like a maddened animal.

I see now that my father had simply run out of instructions; he had not been programmed for postwar England. For the next few days, he molders around like a dog looking for a corner to die in, and we all go on about our business. Priscilla is already blindly in love with England and doesn't need him anymore. She thinks shabby hotels and toothless doormen are super and she awaits the dingy future with a clear eye. My mother the saint is glad to be back as one enjoys putting on a dressing gown and flip-flops; after we get our flat (don't ask Sir Pendrid how, he just lives here) she queues for fish and scraps of meat as cheerfully as any old fool, laughing ruefully when they run out of things. It seems a better life for her than the demanding pre-war social whirl that my father surprisingly appears to miss so much. And she regales us with comical queue anecdotes and killing bus-conductor yarns. "It's amazing how they've kept up their spirits after all they've been through," says she. "The wonderful cockney wit is still intact."

"I must say your experience has been more fortunate than mine," says my father. "I've never seen so many cases of shocking bad manners. Nor, come to that, do I care to be called 'ducks' by wart-infested shop girls."

"*I* think the breakdown of class distinctions is one of the grandest things the war has done." There is a glinting threat here. What grievances may be surfacing now that Father is weak and the rabble is upon us? He stares back without speaking. His position is clear. I must be mistaken—that can't be contempt in my mother's face? *This is my world now: you top people are done for,* she seems to say.

If so, does she feel free to go all the way and say stupid commonplace things in front of him? Are the street mobs that close? Before we find out, if we ever do, you'll be wanting to hear more about me I suppose? Naturally, because I'm a celebrity and these other people are merely more mirrors. Isn't that right? You want to know what the Celebrity thought about England. My parents, who are going through some grim death struggle in the kitchen, have begun to bore me frightfully. I tune them out and they leave my fifteen-year-old consciousness quietly, like poor relations, while I resume my lonely godhead, the wonder of Me.

11

~~~~~~

. . . Are you still awake, Snead?

. . . Yes, Ollie. Fresh as a daisy in fact. This is just like the old days. Your story fascinates me. All the Nembutal in China wouldn't put me out now. Since they'll be coming to get you in a few hours anyway, you might as well keep talking, brother.

So be it. Frankly, I thought the English were ridiculous. Their voices you already know about. But the crap they said in them that year! "Sorry, so sorry, sorry." If I had punched one in the mouth I'm sure he would have apologized. Or thanked me in a hail of "ta's." ("Straightened the old teeth, did we? Ta, ta very much, *ever* so much, ta.") And better still, they were all midgets. At a willowy five foot eight Chatworth towered over most of the nation. Wandering the streets like Gulliver, his pockets full of lead weights called coins, Chatworth struts.

"Hey Mac, you got any Charlie Barnett?"

The clerk in the record shop cowers. "Charlie who, sir?"

"Forget it, Jack. How about some Jimmy Lunceford? Or

the Count?" I am merciless. What has become of my loving kindness, you ask? It has become very subtle. Love is an act of will, not emotion. I wish these people well, but I don't like them. That sentimental glop I was wallowing in for a while has nothing to do with laying down one's life for one's friends, for instance. That, of course, I would do without hesitation.

My father has absentmindedly given me a huge allowance and I swagger under it like a Texas oil man. I take taxis and mild old men open the door for me as I shower them with tips. "What are these thingummies?" "Florins, sir." "Very good. Have a florin. On me." And buy yourself some new teeth.

Ah, teeth. My father eggs me on unwittingly. "The specimens of manhood one sees on the streets of London these days. Oh dear, oh dear," the old squire mutters. But I don't need him to tell me. I am Maloney and O'Brien and the rest now, incredibly toughened by America. *There is no menace here.* That is the trouble with it. The air is occasionally pierced with cries of "One lump or two?" Nothing more. Even the surly shopkeepers are like whipped dogs. "We can't do ih, we 'aven't go' ih, we can't ge' ih," they whimper. My father confirms that I am not a traitor. This is not the England I left behind.

After two weeks in London, we fan out in search of relatives. And what relatives: aunts who walk like Groucho Marx, uncles tough as schoolgirls; girl cousins built like tractors, boy cousins who lisp or stutter and roll their *r*s. The talk soon turns to the new bishop of Sudsey-on-Tees. Not quite a gentleman, perhaps. Still, he gets close to the people, I suppose. Chatworth is bored and shows it. Nobody minds, or even notices. Privacy is all. Uncle George is fearfully excited about the restoration of Chipping-Gumbo Cathedral. Aunt Mirabelle is more taken by the return of county cricket. Nobody cares. Conversation is like five people working at different hobbies.

"I see you've closed the west wing."

The west wing indeed! Eyes light up briefly. "Had to, you know. The servant shortage is dire. We've still got Simpson, but after that I simply don't know." Simpson, deaf, pouring soup on one's shoes, is the last great hope.

Chatworth imagines explaining all this to Muldoon. "Had to close the west wing, don't you know. And after that, we had to shoot poor Simpson, of course." My contempt is undisguised. I rise from the table demanding to be excused. As the door slams, I hear Aunt Mirabelle say that I'm going through a difficult age. Pah. I'm going through a wonderful age. I march outdoors in an exuberance of sulkiness. Do not suppose that all those pouting teen-agers are unhappy: some of them are ecstatic. The air out here is soft and stupid. I want to punch it. These people have all died in the war. I am alive.

Uncle George joins me, surprisingly, and we stroll, I don't know why. "I suppose you'll be going to Oxford like your pa-pah."

I shrug churlishly. "I haven't given it a thought."

"Well—it's soon to tell, I suppose."

I give him no encouragement. My pa-pah, is it? Get a load of *that*, Muldoon.

"You're very like him at your age," he babbles.

Amazing. Very like my pa-pah. Fruity toot toot.

"We were surprised when he went into trade," the old man says desperately. "Of course, he saw the way the wind was blowing. It's country solicitors that have to shut their west wings these days."

Lucky to *have* a west wing, you old fart, says Muldoon.

"I only wish you'd seen Chatworth Manor before the war," he snivels. "We thought nothing of house parties of forty or more. Then the army took over and left it a perfect shambles."

"At least you're alive," I say tersely.

"Well, that's very true. We all have to make sacrifices. One can't complain," says Uncle George, complaining. "Well, I'll be getting along. It feels like rain. I've enjoyed our chat."

One meaningless sentence after another. Go inside and tell them I'm at a difficult age, meatball. No wonder this country is in such sad shape. While millions of Englishmen were dying, Uncle George hung onto his little kingdom and whimpered. The noble war effort I've been hearing about probably consists of thousands of Uncle Georges fighting for their chicken coops. Don't blame *me*, folks.

This, by the way, is Monty Chatworth speaking, he of the integrity, who wouldn't come out against the Vietnamese War for the sake of his image. OK, I don't apologize for that —an Anglo-American has to tread carefully, and I'll accept stones from only about half a dozen living people—but I'm almost Uncle George's age now myself, and I've been known to throw tantrums over the room service in first-class hotels. George wouldn't have complained if his teeth froze in the washbasin overnight. So perhaps a man has a right to his west wing, eh? Anyway, Uncle George had been sharing his egg ration for a week with this little pig from over the water, and the above is the pig's response. Well, at least I always had integrity.

It was the same at Uncle Henry's and Aunt Maude's, where the interests were respectively renovating the choir loft at St. Cuthbert's and the preservation of game birds. Henry and Maude had closed down *both* wings and were sore as a boil about it. As for the famous English breakfast, the sideboard groaned under a load of powdered eggs, powdered milk, and all the artificial jam you could eat. My father lined up for it looking stricken, as if he were in a prisoner-of-war camp. My mother was, of course, repulsively comfy.

"This house used to be much too big," she confided through her bullhorn. "It gave me the willies."

"You've become very resourceful in America," Aunt Maude told mother as she actually made her own tea.

I didn't recognize this for satire, and thought it pathetic.

111

I didn't know that Maude despised my mother and was forever out to humiliate her.

These trips to relatives were like forced marches through enemy territory for Mother; but now her enemies were brought low, and were living like Irish peat farmers. Well, well, well. As Father sat grimacing over his sliver of powdered egg, my mother bustled out to the kitchen to see if she could lend a hand. America had been the making of her, she said. "All this class nonsense. I've quite gotten over it."

"How clever of you," purred Maude.

As for Priscilla, her fever for assimilation raged on, and she even found something to like in the sallow hermaphrodites alleged to be our cousins. Young Viscount Swithin (don't ask me; they all had different last names) had a huge collection of *castrati* records and so she went bananas over *castrati* records, squealing as if it were Frank Sinatra. Hortense raised her own pigs, including a pet one called Quentin, and Prissy became more excited about this joke than the rather phlegmatic Hortense had ever been. Prissy was determined to get a toehold here, to have a real home at last; but she hadn't captured the listlessness of the natives, who weren't even interested in their own interests. Even later, when she caught on to this, her own listlessness was horribly overdone: too much gusto underneath. Another American tragedy.

Me they all considered some kind of strange wild animal, as I laid on my American accent and my all-round toughness with a heavy hand. "What do you make of old church windows?" said Egbert, a fellow sixteen-year-old with whom I was supposed to "hit it off."

"Not too damn much."

"Pity. Elizabethan madrigals?"

"As long as they clean their rooms."

So much for hitting it off with Egbert. My companions now were Muldoon and O'Connor, and we had a fine old

112

time of it doing the stately homes. I suddenly had a comic style based on their old routines, and I was *the only one here who had it.*

So everyone got their kicks except Daddy, who kept sinking visibly. The trouble was, he couldn't blame anybody; it was all the fault of the beastly war (which he himself had shirked). When you find your homeland in senile decay, no excuse is good enough. At least, that's what I thought he thought. Now I'm not so sure. I think he felt guilty about missing the war, spy or no spy. I think his relatives, in these immensely complicated visits, were conveying resentment. I think, incredibly, that they considered him flashy.

We wound up with the Scottish branch (every family has one), and I was in the mood for something craggy and forbidding to explain my own inner toughness, but I didn't get it. Uncle Fergus was soft and hairless and damn near an albino. His kilt kept falling down around his hips, giving him the outline of an over-the-hill flapper. And his accent was about as Scottish as Anthony Eden's. Uncle Fergus, like everyone else who looked like that, was rumored to be fearfully brave. Group Commander at Dunkirk. Made tea while the bullets sang. "Oh dear, they've ruined our best pot. I *am* vexed." Stamps foot, giggles.

What good did it do? Everything had been bred out of them but courage and they could only be men at gunpoint. Perhaps seemingly sissy was just a game the rest of the time, but they played it (all but the women) with zest for twenty-four hours a day. They must like it. Even a manly coward like myself was preferable to that.

Finally, there was cousin Cynthia. Lisping, lantern-jawed Cynthia, who became (was then?) one of the great beauties of Great Britain. (I still can't see it.) She dogged me around on my lonesome walks, saying things like, "Don't you think bores should be shot?" and "Your time in America must have been super."

My surliness went down superbly with Cynthia. "You're better than all of them. I wish I had your guts. Of course, I'm a socialist," she explained.

"So?"

"Well, all these titles and things. What do they *mean?* My potty ancestor had a bigger battle-ax than your potty ancestor. And besides, he probably cheated."

My sin in that household was that I thought Cynthia was putting me on. I'd learned my lesson all too well in that way, and I believed the kid was Muldooning me. I lost a great friend.

Swimming up through the sludge that was her family, Cynthia—ah, what do I know about her family? I later did a special about the Battle of Britain, and the section on the unsung heroes of the home front was a classic, based partly on my memories of Cynthia's family.

Meanwhile, some home opinions.

Priscilla: "Pen is such a Hollywood brat. Honestly, Mummy. Can't you do something?"

Mother: "I think I like him better than his cousins, anyway. He's a man at least." (Never mind where I heard these opinions.)

Father: "Eh?" (I made this one up.)

Excuses? Well, for one thing, their famous war effort had been ridiculously oversold.

Me: "Did you suffer frightfully?" (Observe brutal imitation of that "frightfully.")

Cynthia: "Lord no. Except from boredom."

Me: "But as the bombs screamed . . . ?"

Cynthia: "What bombs? I don't recall any bombs."

No bodies on stretchers either, or gaunt nurses with lovers missing action? No. Only a sheep with third-degree burns. "The war against boredom was lost in the first year," she said. "We didn't even try. Unconditional surrender. 'Let's all see how boring we can be' was the motto. I promise you, there was not one interesting moment."

114

It didn't occur to me that she was talking about some kind of hell; nor that she might not be talking for the whole nation (in those days every passing remark was the last word on the subject). Entwistle Castle, I learned just in time for my documentary, had been turned into a hospital for shell-shock cases and calmness was enforced for medical reasons. Cynthia had talked in whispers for four years, while they brainwashed the vegetables. Quiet country walks, an occasional sing-song—nothing very different from World War I and Daddy's funny farm. Once a bomber pilot had cried himself to sleep on Cynthia's breasts; she had found him wandering in the woods, looking for his crew. I wish she'd told me that then. But people will blurt out anything for television.

Excuses not good enough? Of course not. The truth is, these people frightened me. I couldn't understand them, and there was no way I could break into their conversations. So I did the only thing I knew—the tough American thing. Still not good enough? All right. Let's see. Suppose I understood them perfectly and didn't fear them at all, but was afraid of becoming *like* them? Some truth in that. By the time I reached Scotland, I was using whole phrases of theirs—the mimic's curse; I was slipping into languor; I was becoming once again the thing that Muldoon and the guys had laughed at.

So I talked American with all my strength and blocked them out as best I could, and Cynthia thought I was super, and all the time the undertow of turbid Chatworth blood sucked at me until I was almost my old self. I even found myself thinking—all these castles and titles and things. Not bad, Chatworth. At least—not bad to have that *plus* the common touch. Will you buy that, Father? (*Say* something, Father.)

At that, I was better off than Prissy, who had seemed to be doing so famously. On the train back from Scotland, we found ourselves alone in the corridor, and she said, quickly

115

as though it was hot information, "I don't think *any* of them liked me," and she started crying. Tough it out kid, I thought, like me. She kissed me, her only friend, and ran for the toilet, where, as usual, she transformed herself into a brainless ninny.

We returned to London from our triumphs in time for me to sit for a school entrance exam. The story is quickly told. In spite of being the brightest star in St. Boniface's gap-toothed crown, at least three years ahead of my grade, I failed triumphantly in every single subject. How's that, guys, I thought? Is Sir Winston dumb enough for you? I even did an Astaire dance step on my way out of the building. It was either that or mortal embarrassment.

My father was nonplused ("But they put out a marvelous brochure," he said of St. Boniface) and in some curious way apologetic. He had planned to send me to his own old school, but he couldn't very well turn up with something like me. "This is saddening, Pendrid. Saddening." Was I actually an idiot? The possibility had to be faced. All that Irish blood Maude had warned him about. He looked closely to see if my eyes joined in the middle. "My fault I suppose for not attending. But your reports from St. Boniface were so dazzling" ... (dazzling, though I had made every effort to dumb down and be in the swim—an effort everyone else was making too, in perfect ratio).

"Well, it can't be helped. We'll just have to send you to a crammers."

Crammers, was it? Egad, not a crammers! (What was a crammers?)

I wasn't that cocky. My father's expression could still make me feel like a soup stain. Anyhow, a crammers turned out to be an outpost of Dickens territory long since strip-mined by English humorists. It was staffed by what I took to be willful eccentrics (English "characters" had been done to death in wartime propaganda, and had outlived their usefulness), who offered us successful examination results as it

116

might be an abortion or a forged passport. Jenkins's Tutorial Establishment actually bypassed education altogether. Their only texts were examination papers—all the relevant ones set in the last fifty years, with odds of repetition calculated and noted as in *The Racing Form.* "At worst, you should answer two questions brilliantly, waffle on the third, and run out of time on the fourth," Mr. Jenkins told us quite seriously. "That is all we can give you."

Old Alma Mater. The only school I ever felt at home in, with its seedy realism and its total absence of moral tone. For passing out ceremonies, no speeches, no uplift: just the piece of paper they'd promised you. "Here, boy. And don't tell anyone where you got it." The student body matched the policy brilliantly. It ranged in age from twelve to sixty and no whorehouse ever assembled a shadier cast of patrons: an Indian prince dripping in rings, a boy film star with the skin of an old man, a shabby chap from the Foreign Office who kept trying to expose himself (nobody would look), and much more. Outside of the flasher, they were all furtive as pornography customers, avoiding each other's eyes and scurrying for the exits: probably taking the wrong bus and doubling back to Westminster. Among them they were sitting for every examination in the British Empire—civil service, Oxford pass, diplomas in gardening and veterinary medicine. It made no difference to our small band of tutors. They could teach *any* examination. Within six months, I was able to pass London matriculation without knowing any of the subjects involved; and by applying Jenkins's methods later, to pass every exam that ever came my way afterwards. Hence, I remain a profoundly uneducated man. Which suits me very well.

I think I'll rest here, having come to a bright patch. Jenkins's, among its other glories, was totally un-English. It belonged to no class and occupied no niche in English society. Nobody ever said they went to Jenkins's. It left no mark, bred no character. It could have been in Singapore or

Rangoon. I was relieved for a moment from cultural pressures and the new Chatworths that regularly and dismally resulted from them. In that neutral atmosphere, I could be myself, whatever that was. I don't remember. Only a sense of buoyancy and daylight.

Not to last, of course. But let us sit down here a moment. I am, believe it or not, drenched and exhausted. I have sweated through two pairs of pajamas and it is morning. No more nasty thoughts. Snead has dozed off: I don't think he likes England. As a native American, he tends to go out of existence there. Just a last toast to Jenkins's, an old boys' reunion of one. Miraculously, they didn't even work me very hard; their incision into the flab of education was so clean, their filleting so neat, that there was really not that much work left to do. And I was not burdened with lead weights of knowledge, which would have been such a handicap in my profession—or, I fancy, in most professions.

So let's hear it for Jenkins's. I have on this tape accomplished my first ungainly return to England, more hideous, because it proved that I had learned nothing, than my arrival in America, and I have fetched up at a good place. PLEASE, NO MORE.

I am empty and ready for praise.

12

~~~~~~~~~~~~~~~~~~~~~~~~~~~~~~~~

Exhaustion, my dear and good friend. Normal people feel a breath of it every year or two, but it blows in my face constantly, and I know how to bend with it, dance with it. When Mr. Snead shows up in his little porkpie hat with eyes to match, I know it's time to put up the shutters. Snead, as you know, started life as a comic grouch, complaining about smog and such, but my wife kept feeding him lines—well, we'll get to that later. Luckily, on this last occasion I knew I had some days off and I was able to get out here to Jersey and lock Father Sony in the closet and sleep for twenty-four hours, and my voices are gone. I wonder whether Joan of Arc ever worked on radio?

You can come out now, Father. This is my retreat house and you can sleep under the wooden bed. Now be honest: do you know anyone else who comes to New Jersey to pray?

Why do I get so tired, you ask? Because being Chatworth takes it out of you, believe me. And it's Chatworth or nothing. Why does *everyone* break down in this business? Because life is so dull inside a magic lamp. Every genie likes to be out and about—anything to keep out of the lamp. So we sign up for two movies at once plus a nightclub show. We overwork, because what else is there? If I stopped for a year, I'd never be able to reassemble Chatworth's parts. His voice would go this way and his face that and he wouldn't be worth a nickel. That's the worst of these foreign models. He is, even as performers go, a highly delicate synthetic, and he needs lots of light and attention, like a talking plant. So work he must.

Unfortunately, he is getting rather too much attention right now. He seems to be in the middle of one of those insane publicity cyclones that blow up unaccountably around the mangiest of us. Since magazine sget their ideas exclusively from other magazines, it is inevitable that some two-bit singer or talk-show host will be shot up in the air every few months in a barrel of wind and noise. But no one should know better how to handle this than television's thinking man, Oxford-educated Monty Chatworth, right? Come on Monty, show these rock stars how it's done. They're country kids and they need help from an older man. *I* need help from an older man, but he died.

Anyway, with a little rest and vitamin C, it isn't too difficult, chums. Look at how badly most of the praise is written. Doesn't that tell you something? Out of town especially, they fawn on one blindly as if they wanted one to stay in Toledo forever. Big names, look at the Big Names that come to Tombstone. Why did *you* come to Tombstone, Mr. Ripper? Did a friend recommend us, or other?

And then some reporter, heavy with years, will stamp your praise onto a piece of paper, as the assembly line cranks on. Here is an oldy and goldy that I keep out here as a penance. It is drawn from my trench-coat days, when the very phrase "trouble spot" conjured up visions of Chatworth agonizing over it calmly—two reporters for the price of one plus a

120

transatlantic heart that pounds and murmurs at the same time. The BBC and NBC saved a packet on me that year.

So without more ado, here's Monty.

"The man sometimes known as the first gentleman of television," writes Amanda Twichell—and I'm not responsible for her name or her prose, "came to town last week to pick up the Walmsley Humanitarian Award, and I must say he certainly lives up to his billing. Monty must be the most unassuming man in a not very unassuming profession, and his manners are so good you can almost see your face in them. [Ms. Twichell's face should not be subjected to this sort of thing too often.]

"He says his native habitat is hotel rooms and his one piece of personal furniture is a picture of his family—featuring a pretty, bright-eyed sister, a mother who must have been a real Irish beauty, and a father who makes you do a double take: because he looks more than a bit like Monty himself, right down to the small mustache and the gentle eyes. Monty sweeps it into a drawer. 'All Englishmen look alike,' he says smiling. And the smile is twice what you get on TV: easily enough to light up Civic Center and heat a family of five.

" 'Tell me,' I say, as he lights my cigarette, plucks at the perfect crease in his pants, and sits down in one effortless motion, 'tell me how you feel about this very distinguished award?'

" 'Bloody silly, actually,' he says refreshingly. 'I mean to say, there are millions of real humanitarians in the world, aren't there? Fathers and mothers making unbelievable sacrifices every day of the year, doctors and nurses in slums, and so on. Whereas I, by way of contrast, am paid extremely well simply to call attention to these people. And yet, you see, I get the award.

" 'Why don't I turn it down? Because it's so pompous to turn down awards. There is no grubbier form of vanity. And

121

perhaps my getting it will call attention to the people who do deserve it. So instead of thanking mom and dad and my wonderful co-workers I shall thank cancer research and Oxfam and so forth. It might help a little.'

" 'Tell me, Monty, what got you into good works in the first place?'

" 'A fabulous contract,' said this rather unique guy. 'No, seriously, I'm a reporter, not a philanthropist. It just seemed that everything I reported on was a fresh source of anguish. And I felt I couldn't just say, "Well, there we are. Now we've seen the starving bodies and bloated bellies, let's return to our studio." So I began telling people how to help. In a way, it's part of reporting, isn't it?'

" 'But don't you feel some sense of personal mission too?'

"He looked embarrassed. 'That sounds awfully pretentious, doesn't it?' Chatworth shies away from compliments like a show horse before an impossible jump—because, he claims, he believes every one of them. But I repeat the question anyway. 'Well, let's just say I come from a very religious family and a very religious upbringing, and perhaps this is how it expresses itself. But don't forget, they *do* pay me for it.'

" 'Yes, but you've also taken some terrific personal risks, haven't you? Going to the front lines in the Six Day War, dodging shrapnel at the Holiday Inn in Beirut . . .'

" 'That's different. That's just my job. I have to do something for my money.'

" 'Oh come on, Monty. There must be more to it than that. You'd get paid just as much to stay home.'

"He squirmed. 'Am I being modest again? Sorry. I'm really quite fearless, deep down.'

" 'But wasn't your father a hero in World War I?'

" 'He did his job.'

" 'And isn't there some family pride involved? Or at least a sense of obligation?'

" He smiled, 'To the job, yes. You see, the sort of journal-

122

ism I'm trying to do requires live ammunition. You can't get somebody else to do the story for you. The best researcher in the world couldn't tell me what dodging shrapnel felt like. I had to find out myself. Don't call it courage, though. It's professional ambition. I do it for myself. I want to be the best TV reporter in the business. Otherwise I'd faint at the sight of blood.

" 'You see, Ms. Twichell, I'm so busy most of the time thinking about camera angles and such that fear is just a nuisance, like someone phoning at the wrong time. I want to produce news film comparable in quality to the best commercial films. And danger is just one of my studio conditions.'

" 'Didn't you ever want to be a creative director, an artist?'

"He smiled again. 'I guess that puts me in my place, doesn't it? No. I decided as a kid that my art was real life itself. I have no interest in making up stories. Interpreting what's already there is rich enough for me.'

" 'Has your transatlantic background helped you to see real life in a special way?'

"He grinned broadly. 'You might say that, yes.'

" And how come you're not married, if that isn't too personal?'

"His smile vanished like a power failure. 'I *was* married once, as you know. Like most actors and reporters (and I seem to contain the worst of both), I wasn't very good at it. You can't take your wife on a dangerous assignment, can you? One has to travel light, like a priest.'

"It seemed like a funny comparison, so I asked if he was religious and he shook his head [in one effortless motion, no doubt] and said, 'That's like asking, are you a saint? No comment. To get back to your previous question—I haven't married because I can't find a woman who really loves suitcases as much as I do; and, you know, I'm quite moody between performances. Like most actors I suppose.'

" 'I don't believe it,' I said. '*You?* The unflappable one?'

" '*That* is just one of my trade secrets. You'd never guess, would you, that I am a screaming neurotic underneath?' he said urbanely. 'One short step from the booby hatch.'

"I had no idea whether he was joking, and for just a moment I felt a little creepy as his face came closer and he grimaced hideously. Then he winked and said, 'Don't be taken in by my little horror movie. I was just practicing. Now where were we?'

"My next question was about his hobbies, but it looked kind of trivial. And before I could ask it, he was off and running again. 'The important thing, I believe, is to use the airwaves God gave us to the best advantage. It is as if He had said, "Lo, you have fouled the waters and laid waste to the land. So let me offer you my personal element, the sky, and we'll see what you can do with that. And, well, lo, we haven't done much have we? Even the air has been designated a wasteland.'

"This man, who thanks his stars he doesn't feel a sense of mission, raised his voice slightly. 'All those immortal souls, feasting on sitcoms and ketchup baths—there must be something better, don't you think? But it isn't easy, you know. Our programs have to be better than better. We must compete one on one with the zoom lens and the filter and all the things the ketchup-bath people have months to set up. We must provide film as good as Hollywood's billion-kilowatt best in the light of an occasional firebomb. And we must beat them, not just tie them, at literacy.'

" 'That's fascinating,' I said. 'But tell me, Monty, what brought you to America in the first place?'

" 'Choo choo train?' he said irritably [there is a reason for this].

" 'No, I mean my readers don't know much about zoom lenses, I'm afraid, but they do like to know where people come from. So what brought you to America?'

" 'Greed,' he said, in that delicious dry way. 'Sheer naked avarice.'

" 'But seriously.'

124

" 'I fear you're determined to believe only the best of me. Very well, then, lies it is. I came over for the challenge. Is that better? The sort of work I do would be done in England by *somebody,* if that was BBC policy, or else by nobody. Over here it's up to me. If I can sell it, they'll do it. *That's* the policy in America, and I like it.'

"Monty can talk about his profession for hours, and will if you let him. He says that his life defies human interest—that it lacks the simplest ingredients. 'Nevertheless, you must have *had* a childhood?' I ask.

" 'I don't believe in childhoods much. I don't like the past. It's usually an excuse to bully people.'

" 'But were you happy as a child?' I insisted.

" 'Sometimes. But to finish what I was saying. I came over here like a good American to escape the past, to join your marvelous melting pot. And the first thing I discovered was that if some kid started carrying on to me about his, say, Irish past, I knew two things. One, that I was dealing with a second-rate kid, and two, that I was in for a licking.'

" 'Really? The Irish?'

" 'The Poles, the Greeks, never mind. Luckily my acquaintanceship was limited.' He seemed impatient again. 'Don't get me wrong, Twichell, I love a parade in pantaloons and kilts, so long as they check their weapons. But please don't bring back the real past. There's always a history of murder in there.'

" 'Well, that's very interesting, and I know it'll give my readers something to think about,' and I really meant it. One of the things that has made this man a legend in his time is that he has not been afraid to bring intellect to TV. In fact, he has practically ordered us to think—but so charmingly that it's a pleasure. And I understand something else, and that is his unmistakable decency, which is as big as the outdoors and as small as the gesture of seeing me into my coat and calling a cab as we said good-bye."

That was some gesture. Also absolutely necessary, because she would have fallen down the elevator shaft without it. "Wha' the fuck are you talking about?" were her last words. "The Irish never hurt a fly."

But that's not my fault. She made the drinks herself, saying each time, "Don' worry about me, skipper. My little ol' tape recorder never touches a drop." Unfortunately, I thought she had clicked it off with her elbow as she reached for a glass, and I felt at liberty to be miffed. They had, after all, sent over this old bat who was way past live reporting, and who was writing for readers who died in 1940, and I had every right to get sore and throw her out. Believe me, I don't need the *Mirror* Sunday Supplement. Then, I don't know, maybe she clicked it back on again with the next swipe. Anyway there it is, a sample of the praise I get even on my bad days. The point is I also said some pretty sarcastic things that she left out completely, because her editor wasn't paying the poor woman to run celebrities out of town. And those, outside of the occasional sniper in Oshkosh, are the people who sweeten my path through life.

So how can the weakest head be turned by that stuff? Listen to it closely. Putting intellect in television indeed. By this she means those little intellectual noises of mine that are worse than no intellect at all. God's own ittybitty element—the airwaves! This is the very heart of my racket—like a dog act on the old Ed Sullivan show. Here, fresh from Bulgaria, is a man *thinking*. Shazam. And he looks so cute while he's doing it. Really stretches the mind, you know?

Finally, as for the modesty: it's like a bit of business you pick up in vaudeville playing the Palace in Sheboygan. I used to be so overwhelmed by the size of American compliments that I got flustered every time, and this looked like modesty. Hell, it happens to all Englishmen over here. And before I knew it, it became part of my routine: taking bows for my big heart and then taking bows for not taking bows. But it's true. I couldn't do it if I wasn't sincere. When the mood is right, any old praise tastes sweet, doesn't it, Ace? Christ yes, any old kind. Even Amanda Twichell's. And the flush and palpitations of pleasure do the rest.

To be fair, though, I did like the part about the zoom lens and the filter. Very informative.

So that's it, you suicidal stars of tomorrow. Humility's the word. Brush up your groveling. From Arthur Godfrey to Jack Paar, it's the coolest form of communication, perfect for one-room apartments and stuffy motel rooms. And, of course, techniques have advanced remarkably since those days. Just as the athletes get bigger, the saints get meeker, until we arrive at—Chatworth the Obscure. Brought to you by shrinking satellite. This year's Mr. Humility scored exceptionally well in the head-bowing and shit-kicking competition, and looks divine in sackcloth. But what swayed the judges most was the talent section. "There is only one sinner and that is me," he said with plums in his mouth. Isn't that something, folks? Can any of you go lower? Now before we go off the air, would you mind just groaning a little for our audience, Monty? And maybe a little smack with the bat?

Actually, I could have won that contest at fifteen with a straight face, but by sixteen I was in and out of real humility for good. England encourages a damp way of looking at things and I saw in a trice that being the only sinner in the deck was as pushy as any other claim. In fact, any sort of fuss was suspect. Being a saint isn't all roses. Suddenly I couldn't even be generous, because I would know I was being generous, and that would constitute a fuss and get me ruled off the court. I could only empty myself out and do God's will (and pretend I wasn't doing that, too). Even being empty was pushy.

The sloe-eyed sophistication of my spiritual life that first year in London would have staggered St. Theresa; or at least had her in stitches. I prayed without feeling, because feeling was bound to be false. Likewise I "did Good" (not too damn

127

much, actually) without emotion, because any emotion would lead to self-congratulation. When Prissy and her weedy new friends (don't ask me where they sprang from) talked about, oh, famine victims, I would snap, "I can see you're enjoying yourselves tremendously." They'd look chagrined (amused); Chatworth has scored (fallen on my ass). "Other peoples' suffering is great fun, isn't it?" I would say. "Especially when one has *the correct attitude* to it." They'd be speechless with guilt. "Oh come off it Pen," Priscilla would say. "What kind of attitude are *you* taking? Aren't you enjoying yourself at our expense right now?"

Quite. A saint's work is never done. Priscilla, like my mother, could stun you with these fragments of intelligence, because she usually didn't appear to be thinking at all. Embarrassment, my old friend, farted cheerfully in my face, and I realized I would have to polish my act still further. Let them enjoy their famine victims. They were probably purer at heart than I, and could do it sincerely. Chatworth's self-knowledge was not given to everyone.

On the way out, I heard one of Priscilla's weeds piping, "I think your brother's quite killing!" and "I think he's *divine.* Where did you find him?" English people didn't bother to lower their voices. I supposed this was their way of communicating, since they never said anything honest to each other's faces. Does Priscilla laugh? Or does she say, "He's all right"? Priscilla is on my side even as she leads the enemy.

For the first time I am lonely. Muldoon and O'Connor grow dimmer; there may after all be situations where they can't help me. I even see them, for a horrible moment, unable to cope with a room full of bleating Englishmen. I am on my own.

OK. I'll beat them at their own game. I'll outclever them with killingly priceless japes and then I'll sock them with some good old American wisecracks. Honestly I will. You can bet your ass. Super.

But this is yet to come. My brilliant, unparalleled London

debut will not be till the spring. Meanwhile, I must play with infinite cunning to the only audience I have: God himself. One of my finest roles.

Religion has saved me in America, when reality threatened; but England was really a much better place for it. The light was too bright in America, the churches too new, the priests had just been unwrapped. (Nobody ever accused me of consistency: I loved those American qualities as much as I hated them.) The old churches of London spoke to my blood. They were my London. As a virtuoso in humility, I reveled in their shabbiness. And as a Chatworth I was, damnit, coming home: to a tradition as sturdy as any of Muldoon's. I began in particular to haunt the Brompton Oratory at odd hours and to take confession like a drug.

"Father, I think I have spiritual pride."

"In that case, you probably haven't."

Ah, what do you know? I had long since mastered the double jackknife and the higher calculus of spiritual pride. I would still have to perform alone, even in the confessional, because no priest could go the pace with me. I peppered these long-suffering men with conundrums from the seventh mansion of the soul, and hardly listened to their humdrum responses. At that point it was still fun, because my sex life was practically nil. For one thing, I could not imagine such a thing as a sexy English girl: the very way they moved their bodies showed that sex was not a factor. And I won't even discuss their clothes. One of our cleaning girls made a maddened pass at me when we were alone in my room, but it was like being embraced by a woodpecker. By the time I had made out what she was up to, she had dashed from the room. I can still feel her cracked lips and the hand pecking at my groin. "Honey, take your time," I whispered after her jauntily. But sex here was something to be snatched in desperation raids: it did not hang lazily in the air or hum through the streets as I distinctly remembered it doing in America. It did not exist in the streets at all, except for those dark shapes in doorways which seemed to be French because they called me *cheri* as I passed. "Come up 'ere, you naughty cheri." Surely that was French?

So I had at sixteen a sort of Indian summer of prepuberty, further prolonged or embalmed by my churchgoing. Concerning which Priscilla said, "You don't have to take it *that* seriously, Pen."

"You said that about World War II as I remember," I said.

"Leave him alone," said Mother. "One can't love God too much."

"But Mummy, I *know* Pen," said Priscilla, glinting at me. "It's bogus, isn't it Pen? Come on—tell your sister."

"Perhaps it is," I said tersely.

"No perhaps about it, you old hypocrite. Old Pen loving God too much, fancy that. You know, Pen, my friends think you're absolutely divine-looking, so you don't have to do it, you know. In fact, one of them said, 'You've simply got to save that gorgeous hunk of man from the priesthood.'"

"You lie," I shouted.

"Stop it at once, Priscilla," said my mother.

"Eh?" said my father (made up again; he wasn't even there).

A sultry female argument follows, with my sister shouting that Mummy always takes my side, and Mummy calling her a "little heathen," and her saying, "Well at least I'm honest." I leave the kitchen with a certain Christian aloofness that is peculiarly my own. But once outside, I know the snake has entered my garden. *Which of her friends had said that?* I know Prissy isn't lying. Her voice is unbearable truthfulness.

I ran feverishly through her collection of weeds. A sorry gaggle of subdebs and postdebs and washed-out gentlewomen—better than the men, but that was about it. A compliment from them wasn't worth having. So, how about catching a late Benediction, old man?

I went to my room to grab a necktie. Wasn't worth having?

130

Praise even then was worth having from anyone! Even in that terrible prefab American slang, it burbled like a brook. Just by itself, with no face attached, it moaned like a breeze and winked like a diamond. I stood in a trance. I was in love with a compliment!

"So long, sexy," said my sister as I slammed out. What was she doing this for? No time to find out. I caught the bus to the Brompton Road, still desperately rehearsing my sister's friends. Of course, it was a different *kind* of good looks over here. . . . Even that did not help most of them. But perhaps there were one or two. A girl called Celia could look pretty good if viewed sympathetically. In fact, she could look sensational. Mother of God, could it be Celia?

Benediction was an interlude. Or rather, with the lush organ music and the musky Oriental smell, it was a celebration. The gold crucifix was raised—this was the best and sexiest place in London—and we sailed into the *Tantum Ergo.* God would not mind this. Benediction was, unlike the Mass, a cheerful occasion, a get-together, even a little worldly and vulgar. Grimly my spiritual sophistication made its stand. But the snake was up and roaring. I knew that if it turned out to be Celia who said that, my Indian summer was over for sure.

13

Good old New Jersey. Ever since St. Boniface days it has been the place for me to go whenever I want to feel that earthly life is overrated and that all below is vanity. And it never lets me down; in fact, earthly life seems stupendously overrated in Jersey.

Out here in the blue, in my mobile home, my jet-propelled jailhouse, my little season in the sun still rages harmlessly: three magazine features in a row, and I'm over the worst of it. In fact I'm suffering from very mild withdrawal symptoms: why can't an article appear about me *every* day? And if I'm that good, why not a Nobel Prize? I've seen it with a lot of my people: gorged and bloated with success, yet their eyes burn for more, more. Only the best of my generation? What about the last generation? Who was better?

It won't happen to Chatworth. He knows too much. And he's been to New Jersey. (What's that, Father Sony? Leave you behind in New York next time? Nonsense. Frozen batteries are good for you.)

And now the two of us are on our way back to London,

the world's most unlikely comedy team. Shall we try a little preventive confession this time? Dear old London, the home of crowds buzzing on Tyburn and of BBC cocktail parties. Why not? It was in London that I made my social debut at sixteen and it was a pippin, was it not? I also learned the English heart that year as Scott learned Antarctica, and the knowledge comes in handy to this day.

It all began with the "hunk of man" compliment. My pursuit of that led me into society like a piece of red meat dangled under my nose.

It wasn't Celia, which would have been bad enough, but a girl called Millicent Marchbank who said it. Because if it was a strain seeing beauty in Celia, it was damn near impossible with Millicent. Skinny, fashionably sunken-chested, with a sarcastic mouth—it was a workout, I tell you. Yet if she admired me enough, it could be done! "She says you look like Byron and Errol Flynn rolled into one gorgeous frame," said my fun-loving sister. So I set to work transforming this pallid drooping creature into someone worth my respect, someone —how about this?—too delicate to touch. Yes, that's the line I would have to take. Millicent couldn't stand without sagging. In fact, she looked as if she needed watering. But if I placed her by a window in the moonlight with a veil of some kind, white as a ghost from sheer good breeding, I might just swing it.

Chatworth winced when he saw the real thing and always would. This must be borne in mind in what follows. I never even liked the girl. OK?

Spring comes to Park Lane, but not to get excited, as the English used to say. You are not to imagine clouds of birds in miniskirts. I don't know where these came from—a new race must have been imported since the 1940s. What we had then were herds of plough girls decked in war surplus: ankles swollen beyond repair from bicycling, faces brick red from the cold. Still, they had broken out their summer frocks, with the faded polka dots and the crushed flowers, to greet the April sun, and as they churned along on their bikes there was a definite sense that the late war might end eventually.

Milk-fed Chatworth, with his straight bones and his white teeth, felt more than ever like a prince. Nevertheless he was a social problem, because he didn't belong anywhere. He was a schoolboy without a school, and could not explain himself. "Tell them you're down from Balliol," Millicent would tell him later and this is as good a way to introduce her as any. I followed my compliment to Priscilla's parties, and I took this stringbean's advice, only to run into a chorus of trouble.

"Down from Balliol, eh? What are you reading? Do you know Pipgras?"

One particular girl, Prudence Harmsworth, who seemed to turn up everywhere, became quickly obsessed with the Balliol connection. "I'd like you to meet Pendrid Chatworth, he's down from Balliol," she would tell everyone in sight.

"No, actually, I'm on my way *up* to Balliol," he'd say desperately.

"*Up* to Balliol? This year? On a Breckenridge?"

So his social life was based on a fraud from the beginning. In this world of smooth pink faces, it was not difficult to hide his age: but an airtight system of lies was harder to come by. Millicent seemed amused by my predicament. "Tell them you come from Tuscaloosa Tech. That sounds fearfully authentic. Or how about Noter Dame?"

"Are you sure she's the one?" I whispered to Prissy.

"Absolutely." I was glad to hear it, because to the naked eye, Millie seemed bent on my destruction. She spotted from the first my capacity for embarrassment, which she took to be deliciously American. For instance, one last time.

"I thought you said you were *down* from Balliol," says the relentless Harmsworth, almost in tears, while Millie smirks.

See Chatworth squirm. "What made you think that?" he mumbles.

"Didn't he say that, Millicent?"

134

"He told *me* it was *up* to Christ Church. What *are* we to believe, Pendrid?"

Harmsworth drifts away, hurt and baffled. What is up and what is down? But she will return.

My sister finally fixed me up head-to-head with Millie by way of a double date with Millie's brother Augustus. Prissy's taste in Englishmen has always puzzled me. In any normal country, Augustus would have passed for a screaming fag—which meant that over here he was probably a Battle of Britain pilot with palm. He was achingly droll, and totally dependent on italics. Thus "Who *is* that extra*ord*inary little man with that gar*gan*tuan woman?" And he thought it was funny to throw bread at waiters. There is a strange time lag after wars, as a nation waits for its heart to catch up, and Augustus was stuck in the middle of one. "Augustus, you're *too* much," says Millicent to this thirties mannequin. Fungoo, says Muldoon, faintly.

That very first night we were asked to leave two restaurants and each time I wanted to clap a hat over my face like a gangster; but my companions giggled loudly all the way out. "I've been thrown out of better 'joints' than this, my good man," says Augustus to a resigned maître d'. "A bordello in Singapore, to name one at random." Augustus reaches for the wrong hat, a huge derby in which his thin blonde head swims. "Come, my little chickadee," he says to Prissy. "Let us fly, my peach pit." He reaches over the hatcheck girl's head again and grabs an umbrella which he opens for Prissy. "Where am I? Borneo? Rangoon, you say? Somewhere in the veldt? You, sir," he says to a bouncer who is looming, "are a particularly fine specimen, a credit to your plucky little people." Pause. "Just a word to the wise: a bar of soap could make all the difference."

"You don't want me to call the police, do you, sir?"

"You're absolutely right. I'll drink to that." Augustus shakes hands with the bouncer. "Here, I want to give you a gift from *my* people." He puts the derby on the bouncer's head, where it perches like a thimble. "Here's your crown—and here's your blooming scepter." He hands over the umbrella, and bolts, with us bolting with him.

"Oh dear, oh dear." He stood on the sidewalk laughing mirthlessly, and Millie and Prissy were patting his back and saying "There, there" and laughing too. I managed to croak out something, I suppose, about watching for the cops; not knowing that I now belonged to a charmed class and that the world was my nursery, too, if I wanted it.

"Shall we try Churchill's?" said Augustus, suddenly bored.

"It's past Pen's bedtime," said Priscilla, and then looked horrified; it was the final kick in the head. Her tears of apology the next day would do no good. We straggled home like refugees and went to bed.

I assumed that I had seen the last of the Marchbanks. They disgusted me, and my sympathies were by now all with the bouncer, who was at least an honest working man; in fact, I wished he had mashed the hat over Gus's yellow hair and stuffed the umbrella up his ass. An American would have. The English weren't ready for democracy.

I raged at them doubly because I had failed altogether to impress them. My few interventions had been received in silence. I couldn't get my "awfully's" and "frightfully's" straight and I couldn't figure out how the English joke worked (there was no question of saying anything serious). Since they laughed at everything else in sight, I was crushed. Babies. Parasites. I didn't even *like* their damn jokes. All I could hear was the constant wheezing of Gus's machinery. Yet some quality in me, which I would like to disown right here, was already beginning to learn the jokes, master them; and they are now, as everyone knows, part of my repertoire.

Priscilla surprised me a couple of days later by saying that she and the Marchbanks were going punting, whatever that meant, and would all love me to join them.

"Oh, come on. They can't stand me and you know it," I said.

"You're *kid*ding," said Priss. "Millie thinks you're absolutely delicious. Scrummy enough to eat."

Scrummy? "She certainly keeps it under her hat," I said, adrift among idioms. "Anyway, you'll agree that her lousy brother actively detests me."

"No, no. Wrong again. Augustus thinks you're jolly good value. It just takes time to understand these people." No one had looked blanker, could have looked blanker, than Augustus, whenever I spoke. But Priss explained this. "He says that you have a dry Yankee wit. One doesn't see the point right away. Then one simply roars."

"One does?"

"Yes one does."

Well, well, well. So that was the old meal ticket, eh? The old gravy train. Dry American wit? Coming right up, ma'am. With tassels on. If I can just remember how to do it.

Thus the four of us began our Season, Augustus looking bored as ever, but no doubt roaring when he got home, and Millie concealing her admiration with Teutonic thoroughness. I couldn't go with them to the big stuff of course, the hunt balls and the like, but I was good for minor parties in Chelsea and church benefits, where brothers danced with sisters and large-boned girls tried not to lead each other. My parents didn't seem to mind if I stayed out all night as long as Priscilla was around. So we remained a team.

What was in it for the Marchbanks? I began to think that upper-class Englishmen had no real motives at all. It would be a terrible breach of form to actually *want* to do something: how then could one complain of this *dreadful* dance and those *awful* people? Only those things that were genuinely awful were ever praised, i.e., deliciously bad Westerns, gorgeously bad taste. Teen-aged sociologists can be brutal; after all, they are fighting for their lives. Easy to make fun of the limeys, eh Muldoon? Wrong again. They are making fun of themselves.

Augustus, for instance, knows that Englishmen dance badly, bobbing up and down as though an actual fox were the object; so he dances outrageously badly, until criticism is stunned. For her part Millicent, who lacks the simplest tools of seduction, has become a stage vamp. "Be kind, Pen. I bruise easily," she purrs. "Those eyes. They frighten me sometimes." Is that the supply the compliment came from?

There is no feeling in this girl. Yet Prissy insists she is more crackers about me than ever. "That's her way of expressing it. You know how it is when the English try to show emotion." The truth is, Prissy is as much at sea with these people as I am. She is bluffing. She leads roars of laughter that go nowhere. Yet could she be onto something? Millicent is quite different with her. The two of them often drop away from the general conversation and talk to each other with solemn animation. Dull stuff, from what I catch of it, but sincere. Perhaps then the aching, grinding flippancy is confined to cross-sexual encounters? Ah ha. I decide to plow on.

Millie still rather desperately molds little jokes out of my identity crisis. "My mystery man," she calls me; and I overhear her talking about my days at a logging camp in the Klondike. " 'Boots' Chatworth they called him. Don't be put off by the babyish appearance. That boy can lick his weight in bobcats. Can't you, love?" she sees me hovering. Another time, I am the youngest man to have graduated magna cum laude from Harvard, a scientific wiz ahead of my century. "Tell them about all those marvelous equations and things," she says. She is scraping bottom and she knows it, and my vein of embarrassment is about played out.

In front of the others she has a demonic fluency, but her vamping grinds to a halt when we are alone, and she is awkward as a schoolgirl. Hah, perhaps that's it. She has been at convent school all of her conscious life, and has never met

138

a man before, except through a grille. When Gus and Priss leave the table, she is all aflutter, calling people over, collecting a crowd; or failing that, bulling her way to the ladies' room.

Dancing's all right. It means she's up and doing. It's almost as good as field hockey, now that she's got the hang of it. I laugh at her. I can handle this tomato.

I concede Millicent the public arena and use the time to concentrate on my moves. Chatworth cannot yet compete with the babble of tongues; his voice is pitched wrong and he's not even sure they hear him. So I work on my cigarette lighting, door opening, eyebrow raising—a hectic schedule, it turns out. I learn how to look too bored to talk, and suspect that half of them are doing the same. I learn to dance from their mistakes. Much of the famous Chatworth style, which now seems bred in the bone, is acquired in that sweatshop in a couple of months.

Alone with Millicent, I adopt a dazzling new tactic. I, a male, am serious with her. I talk gently but firmly about her plans and dreams, until a look of terror comes into her eyes. In front of a crowd, she'd have cut me to pieces. *"Dreams,* old boy? A cottage for two somewhere in the blue—that sort of thing?" But alone, she can barely croak out, "I'm really not sure," or "Daddy doesn't believe in universities for women," before making her getaway to the ladies' room.

The more she dreads our tête-à-têtes, the more masterful I feel. As she gazes around wildly for Priscilla to rescue her, I practice smiling through locked jaws and other local tricks. I even practice not smoking before the Queen is toasted. The hours fairly race by in this fashion. She is really waiting for Jungle Boy to pounce and save her from her shyness. We have kissed good night a few times, and she has a lot to learn from the kid from Wilkes-Barre. Her lips are sealed cold and she looks at me anxiously. Did she do it all right? She is never more vulnerable, or more lovable.

I don't care how much she makes fun of me so long as I

can have those moments. As the evening draws on, her mockery grows frantic, then trails off: she knows she will have to face the Moment, the first heavy pass from Jungle Boy—and she will do at least twenty-five things wrong. It will be infinitely worse than the first fox trot at Lord Bunce's coming-out party. Yet one must press on.

I'm sorry, but I loved her in this state of fear before the kiss, with all her arrogance unraveled. In those days it didn't seem so awful to love women in this way. I tell myself I've changed since then, that I don't need that look of fear anymore, the trapped stare of someone caught in the headlights of a car, but I really don't know.

Soon enough, she came to understand that the good-night kiss was all that was going to happen, and her fear turned to relief. At least she responded now with wintry gusto, pressing my hand in a businesslike way—there, that's done. Good night, little man. I realized I would have to raise the dose or lose my status and revert to my role of unidentified schoolboy. I suppose I could have stood that. Time would have cured it. But I needed her fear, the way I'd needed Morton Green's back at St. Boniface. I'm not a bully, am I? Let me show you my philanthropy award. I needed her fear the way one wants a neat woman to unfasten her hair. I wanted her to strip off her goddamned English armor, with the cute sayings on it, and join me on the jungle floor.

There was, however, one catch to all this—outside of her own fantastic footwork at the front door. I was a Catholic and could not do such a thing lightly. I have forgotten my theological ruminations out of very shame, but I'm sure they were intense, because before I could do anything at all in those days I had to work out the explanation. In this case what it boiled down to finally was that I had to get a little bit drunk and out of control before I could administer the coup de grâce. Not as easy as you might think. "Am I out of control yet? No, damnit. 'Nother little glass of champagne. *Now* I'm out of control. Oh Jesus, I can't even stand up." The margin for innocent sin is razor thin.

Throwing up on Millicent's dress in a punt on the Thames would not seem the best way to break the ice. But it did, just like that. Places please, for a burst of romance. We are bobbing under the pussy willows, and a slight nudge of *mal de mer* has put me over the edge. No way she can stuff me into a cab this time, so she holds my poisoned head in the shambles of her lap and caresses it gently and I realize I have stumbled on just the right combination of guilt-free potency. I begin to feel woozy stirrings in the pit. Until now I have loved nothing about her *except* her fear of me. Suddenly I have something else: she is nursing me through a bout of embarrassment. No one has ever done that before—Mother, Father, the rock-voiced men in the box. "Thank you," I say, trying to kiss her through her frock, and drooling on the cotton daisies. "Made an awful ass of myself."

"That's all right." She is at ease now too. The necking contest is over. Or so she thinks.

Not so sure I like this. My headache goes spinning off in a new direction. Am I still out of control? Why not? The sin has been in the planning: utter spontaneity is the ticket now. I undo my trousers roughly with one hand, popping buttons wantonly, and paw the air around her with the other. I'll show her Jungle Boy is a beginner too. Put her at her ease.

I can still sense the thin face looking down at me. I couldn't see it then, because I was burrowing artlessly under her skirt, doing fine as far as I could tell; but I could feel her hand go stiff on the back of my neck. My own advance hand had reached something dry and wiry—was this the place? At any moment she would go hog wild, if my reading was anything to go by. My need to keep everything spontaneous in the eyes of the Lord kept me hurrying along. Rub-a-dub-dub. I mock myself. Everyone has trouble the first time. Why can I barely face this scene?

After several minutes, I saw that my reading had been a tissue of lies, and I supposed I'd just better push ahead with the next part. I looked up at her face and was surprised to see that her eyes were shut tight. Was one supposed to say something? What was the protocol? I made some sort of endearing mumble as I located my dry harsh target with my left hand and began to swarm forward. Her eyes opened— with what? Fear, contempt, *apology?* What is that look? I can't see it.

"I think you'd better put that away."

It doesn't matter how that is said, does it? I looked down at "that." The eager red-faced moron did not know that the chase was off. I have always suspected its sanity.

"I'm afraid it's not my sort of thing," she said.

Don't apologize to me, you freak. I was miserable and wet with rage. There is no sadness like unto a Catholic boy who has committed a sin with nothing to show for it.

"What is your sort of thing?" I snarled.

There is a silence, except for the lapping of water, which sounds like waves crashing now. There is no crowd to appeal to, no montage of Prissy and Augustus walking to our table laughing. The rescue team. We have chosen a spot under the willows where only a willful Peeping Tom can find us, and he wouldn't be of much help. She is trapped with me.

Now this is another thing I don't remember exactly. Was she polite, and did she say, "Are you sure you want to know? You Americans are so idealistic." (In which case I cry hoarsely, "I want the truth, damn you!") Or did she decide to cut me off brutally and be rid of me forever?

It's not important, perhaps. In both versions, what she says eventually is, "I think my sort of thing might be your sister."

Dry heaves now into the willows, but furious mental activity too. I am not thinking of Prissy as such—that will come later—but of me. Millie has been going with me so that she can be close to Prissy. So where the hell does that leave Gus?

Ohmygod—it's not possible. Not with Old Jolly Good Value here, the sometime Jungle Boy? I steady my stomach with sheer will power and look around savagely.

"And what is Gus's sort of thing?"

"I really don't know," she says vaguely. Waves a hand. "I'm not sure he has a sort of thing." Lost it in the war, no doubt. Poor chap. She looks away, as if on director's instructions. You must admit the English make jolly good actors. She adds as a sort of afterthought, "Me, perhaps."

This is too grotesque to be shocking. I presume I am open-mouthed. She feels a social obligation to talk. "I'm sorry to be so desperately Henry James about the whole thing —us corrupt Europeans taking advantage of you innocent Americans sort of thing. I'm sure that if you lusted after Priscilla you would repress it fiercely. And quite right too."

My God, how did she know? These people were so damn clever, that was the worst of it. "I'm sorry," she said again. "I suppose I've led you on. I didn't mean to. I think I really hoped something might happen between us. I thought you were rather super."

Her skirt was still hiked up. That was nice. It took real class not to yank it down primly. Maybe I ought to give it one more try. I still have one sin coming on the house. She shook her head and pulled the skirt down slowly. So damn clever.

"Here, put your head on my lap. I like that. And Pendrid? Let's be friends."

"What?" I bellowed forlornly. "Fucking no OK to that."

She shrugged. Have it your way, sonny. That's what comes of being polite to these people. "Shall I do the punting?" she says. Chatworth nods. He can't punt his hat.

14

~~~~~~~~~~~~~~~~~~~~~~~~~~~~~~~~~~~

I must warn Prissy about these people at once. Then I must change my life.

Request permission to leave this scene now and return to America. "Not so fast, Mac." You're going the wrong way. Your mind is packed for London.

This is no threadbare Kafka official blocking my way, but a streamlined FBI man with shoulders out to here. "Have you a history of syphilis or communism, sir?"

I must wait. Crouched in the back of the punt, with Millicent paddling me home. I see, through a vapor of vomit, a slick cool creature with a half smile of utter triumph. She has annihilated another brutish male.

Only now do I imagine Millicent holding back tears, but that's just my conscience having a little fun. A couple of years later she tried to kill herself, but that had nothing to do with me. I cannot take on all the sins of the universe. All I know is, she looked like Lord Runcible whipping a fuzzy-wuzzy as we punted back to the Henley boat station, and I was too hung over and miserable to look beyond this. *I* was the one with feelings around here. My imagination has since atoned for this oversight and I now see her crying for days, wasting, preparing her suicide. Thus do I scourge and flatter myself.

To repeat, I must warn Prissy about these people, and then change my life. I rush for the Brompton Oratory and pray with a comic intensity worthy of Buster Keaton. I confess at a gabble (did the priest hear a word? I hope not) and race back to my pew for some real two-fisted remorse. Yes, I have lusted after Prissy, I have taken one step in their abominable English direction: Millicent in her leering decadence has seen into my heart and recognized the germ of evil, her own little brother, in there. It's in all of us, of course. The question is, *what do you do about it, my son?* This country has chosen to cultivate it for hundreds of years. *Fleurs du mal.* Amusing little plants that kill on contact. I have come too close already.

I kneel till my knees burn. Does self-satisfaction come now or later? No, I am truly sick and frightened. These people whom I despised so recently have begun to terrify me. They find my innocence *amusing.* They consider me a pompous child in the ways of the heart. They laugh at my every move —lumberjack, Harvard man—it's all the same joke. The solemn American hick, with his Bible and his four-square penis, waiting for Miss Right. "I hope you don't think this is wrong"—*that's* the endearment I had whispered in the punt. Now I remember.

God is my strength, but oh how I hate to be laughed at. No religion can compete with my fear of that. I am already half leering at Chatworth with Millicent's leer. My virtue seems as clownish as it had at St. Boniface. Am I going to go through life playing this scene, a randy little parson blundering into boudoirs and whorehouses while the crowd roars? What's happened to my famous equilibrium, my Christ-like understanding of sinners? Just when I get used to last year's sin, they pull a new one on me and knock me on

145

my padded behind. Only when I have seen them all will I be beyond shock. That's me, now, talking into this tape.

I silently scream a last wild prayer for guidance, knowing that it's typically American to pray for guidance. "You're doing great, kid," sing the Heavenly Host. "Your mom would be proud of you," avers St. Joseph. The rancid kidding of the last few weeks has settled deep in my soul. I have graduated and am one of them. If I want to be.

Goddamn their blasphemy. They're not that good. Chatworth catapults out of the Brompton Oratory as from a locker room. Go get 'em, tiger. Warn Priscilla. Then change that life. Sisboombah.

"I don't want to see those people again," he tells her in the inevitable kitchen. It is a sunny deflating scene. Priscilla has suggested I help with the dishes, as if I were an ordinary mortal.

"That's dreary of you," she says. "Why don't you want to see them?"

"They're awful, that's all."

"This is rather sudden isn't it? You liked them all right yesterday."

"Did I? I don't remember *ever* liking them. It never came up."

"Don't be clever, Pen. Something has happened, hasn't it?"

There's a nerve-racking, limey tenderness in that last sentence; Priscilla is on their side.

"Not especially," I say briskly.

"Something with Millicent."

"No."

I am unprepared. This is some great warning I'm giving Prissy—like a dwarf waving his arms through a frosty window.

"They're just awful," I grope. "They don't take anything seriously."

"How perfectly dreadful of them."

146

"You know what I mean."

"You mean you can't keep up with their jokes and you're jealous. And you've become frightfully deep to make up for it. Is that it?"

I am furious, but I still cannot tell her the facts. Some ghastly American reticence binds me. "They're decadent," I try again.

"Whatever that means," says Prissy, angry now herself. "Well, I'm going to go on seeing them. We can always find a fourth."

"No! You won't!"

She stares at me. What look of crazy ardor does she see? My hand is on her arm, though we are not a touching family. "Don't talk like that to me," she says shakily. "Ever."

"They're bad people." I am helpless.

"Pendrid. Something has happened."

"No."

"I'm going to ask Millie."

"No. Please no."

Triumph. "All right. Then tell me yourself."

I am so anxious not to hurt her that I tell it all wrong and leave out the point. "Milly is fond of you," I wind up tamely.

"So what?"

"And Gus is fond of *her.*"

"Well, that's very natural."

Am I doomed forever to relive my mistakes? I am twelve and I have just launched my thunderbolt at Father Herman. It has fizzled. Very well. I will try harder. Shazam. I am a killer. I bow my head and tell Prissy the worst. It sets out to be a lurid account of upper-class vice, worthy of Father Donohue on his way to Sunday golf. In fact, as I pick up the round phrases of my old pastor, I realize how little it all amounts to. Like the terrible tale of Ponzo's penis, it has lost something somewhere. All I see is a small boy ranting.

I look at Priscilla. She is shaken—but by what? Who is sick around here?

Is she going to humor me? "I think they're awful," she says at last, with real panic. "I don't ever want to see them again." It is Priscilla's trademark to run from the room at such moments. As she does so, it is my turn for sickly triumph.

Later models of the Prig will be more and more sophisticated, until we arrive at the International Good Guy that you all know and like. "One of the few genuinely nice people in show business"—and why not? Nobody ever studied harder, or tried on so many styles.

The next few weeks can be filed under comic melodrama. I call this my Lord Gladstone phase, and it is best pictured in gaslight with me in a stovepipe hat. A Grand Master of niceness must sample everything, so I have a go at low life, starting with the whores in Shepherd's Market and working my way to Soho. I told myself I was looking for unclassed persons like myself, who stood as far outside this fetid society as the waifs at Jenkins's did. It is a common mistake for saints to make, to overrate whores.

But what else was there? My own family could only churn up more and more Millies for me; that's how it is at the top of the tree. The fruit gets thin. If I wanted to meet the rest of England, I'd have to do it myself, starting with this riffraff who never talked about Balliol and whose vice was strictly cash on the barrel.

What I also wanted of course was to drown my adolescent hots in a spiritually acceptable way, and so I rushed about town with my halo on fire. And these girls were infinitely accessible, almost as if they were waiting for the right sociologist to come along. There was something especially cozy about the market, with the girls chatting in pairs from early afternoon on, or passing the time of day with old customers, or just moving about like cats, with no particular purpose— I guess some sort of movement was required by law, but it

148

didn't matter what. For the lower depths, it had a comfy feel to it, like a tea shop where the door goes "ping."

At first I just watched, the way one watches pets, trying to guess what's on their minds: why they stop at this window and not that, and where those little bursts of apparent decision come from. But it wasn't *that* cozy. Several policemen indicated that I was supposed to keep moving too, that English law required an endless shuffle from everyone. I also gathered that the girls did not really like being stared at. Quite understandable. I was not going to make a social gaffe with *this* crowd, my last resort.

"You like to come upstairs, cheri?"

Ho ho. I saw the joke of the "cheri" now. French my blooming arse. A rickety cockney with pancake make-up. Bless you, my dear.

"No. I'd just like to talk to you," I say. And seeing her blank look, I hand her a ten-shilling note.

"What are you doo-in'?" She comes to life. "ere, take this back, you bloody twit." She stuffs the note in my hand. Girls up and down the market glare or look away. Chatworth has done it again.

England, you've beaten me, you sod. There is no corner of you so low and mindless that there aren't mistakes to be made. I flee the alley and the girls behind me giggle like debutantes. Or so I imagine, as I wait for my bus to Kensington and the blank looks of my parents. I am unequipped for life at any level. Worse than unequipped—my whole psyche is skewed wrong. You might as well pray, you holy fool.

Perhaps my drift from the higher spirituality began that night. I lay drenched in grief and unworthiness, yet I had nothing to confess. Clumsiness is no sin—in fact, it is rather encouraged as a token of good faith. I know in my heart that a truly successful fornication would not have left me half so repentant. So my prayer lacks theological rigor. "I'm just worthless. It's all so rotten." Sly old Chatworth, escaping

149

into vagueness. I am going to win one soon around here or bust, sin or no sin.

I gave up the market˜and decided to work Piccadilly, which seemed less clannish, more impromptu. The market was like a club, and all those strays were its members. Nobody new had appeared there in years. Now I was heading for the wide open spaces on the no. 9 bus. Jiggling, for a brief moment pleased with himself, marvelous resilience. Chatworth is a wonderful character. I need this feeling if I am to accomplish anything.

I feel like a veteran tonight. I understand these exchanges are supposed to be smooth as silk. "Not tonight, love. No hard feelings," I croon. I glide by on gabardine wings, the King of the Spivs. "'ow much?" I say suavely. "Werl—'ats a bit steep. I'll give you a quid." She steps into the light: a gargoyle.

"I'll take it," she says.

"Well, I don't know, a bit tired actually," I mutter. She grins maliciously. Well, not to worry.

"Enjoying the night air, are we, sir?" Oh Christ, a cop suaver than I.

Still, I will not be shaken. I understand the machinery now. The bobbies sweep you off the street like a snowplow, and into the girls' bed-sitters. It is not in anyone's interest that you linger on the sidewalk, forming a consumer public. But they're all really quite harmless, like my MGM figurines.

I shall have to take potluck tonight and rely on my fast vision. The girls are master manipulators of lamplight and you have to get so close to examine them that you are half-committed. "Two pounds, love." There is no flipping French spoken in this quarter, just statements as flat as a butcher's. Unfortunately, I do not have two pounds, and am forced to retreat again. Money will be a problem, I can see. Besides, *what do I want with them?*

"Going out again, Pen?" says Mother.

"Yup."

"Where do you go when you go out?"

"The flicks, usually." That would mean thirteen flicks in a row.

"You must be quite an expert in the art of cinema," says Priscilla, who has regressed for the moment to bullying flirtation: I have taken away her Marchbanks and left her with nothing. "Not to mention quite broke."

"Leave him alone," says Father. We are all quite startled when he says anything apropos. Most of his remarks are general these days, on the state of the nation or the Church. E.g., "Priest workmen indeed. As if you could get *any*one in France to work, even the bishop of Paris." More to himself than to us. But now the old clock has boomed and we are paralyzed. "Young men go out at night. It's perfectly normal. *Leave him alone,*" he says. I sidle away.

I hear his footsteps behind me. No, it is just some bank clerk on his way to a mass murder. But Father knows what I do at night. He understands. How bloody.

It is raining, a condition I barely notice anymore, except that it gets the girls into their belted raincoats, which makes their outlines even more attractive, and complicates my work. I feel my father's nudge. "Let's take this one." We'll do it together. I'll show you how I make that banging noise.

I can't tell what's rain and what's sweat. Of course, there is no father, no nudge. And I had the nerve to call the *Marchbanks* decadent. My own incestuous little family has cooked up some poisons that would send them screaming. But we don't name our poisons; and we don't even enjoy them.

Reflections on a wet pavement. My parents never allowed themselves to bicker during the war—the family was a precious relic that had to be protected at all costs; but now there is bad blood in the air, and anything that is said by the one is at least silently disapproved of by the other. A strange postwar indulgence. So on another night it might have been the other way round, with my mother bawling, "Let him

151

alone." And then *she* would have accompanied me on my walk, disapproving of this and that one, looking for a nice Irish girl, and following me up the stairs to say a rosary—oh God, forgive these thoughts. I'm not myself.

One outgrows the family, and one shrinks back into it. Priscilla spends her evenings at home now. Her next move will be, oddly enough, in the direction of the Communist party, but right now she has returned for shelter—only to find the shelter is down and my parents exhausted. Prissy is not as tough as she thought. These people over here are not playing. They are rougher than Americans.

I refuse to shrink back into the family. Tonight I will shake them off my back forever and mount the stairs alone. I pick a raincoat blindly. There are two quid squinched in my right hand and I lace my left one under the girl's arm and march her to her place of business in lockstep. For what? To talk? Don't be ridiculous.

"Would you like to talk for a moment?" I temporize. Perhaps I can convert her.

"Talk? I haven't got time for that, love." Starts to undress. Am I out of control? I am not even interested. Good lord.

"I'm paying you to talk," I say.

"Oh, you're one of the kinky ones, are you? I'm sorry, I don't do specialties."

"I'd just like you to talk for as long as you'd do the other."

"You wouldn't 'ave time to say 'Clement Atlee' in that case, love."

"Why, how long do you take to do the other?"

"Four minutes in and out. Check it with the coppers. They clock me. The original four-minute miler."

"Don't you ever take a break?"

She looks old and tired even in the muted light of her off-pink bedroom. Her breasts sag and her stomach is covered with scars. How can she work this assembly line? I want to help her, comfort her, bring a little light into her dark world and then perhaps screw her very gently. Show her

152

there are decent people out there. That wouldn't be too sinful.

"When I take a break, it's not with kids like you," she says.

"Who's it with, then?" I mimic unintentionally.

"Time's almost up, dear. I'll take the two quid, if you don't mind, plus a little something for the maid. And I hope you've had a night to remember."

I hand over the money blankly. "There's still time for a little something." She puts her hands on her mottled thighs and beckons roguishly. "I hate to short-change a customer, even a baby one."

I shake my head. "Just tell me something about yourself, how you got started . . ."

"That's it, sonny. My conversation is more precious than gold itself. Mr. Woolworth couldn't afford it. You'll see your own way out, will you, sonny?"

A tough little people. As I slump down the stairs, she calls, "Next time pick on someone your own age." I guess it is kindly meant.

I return to the family.

Here comes the London darkness now, plunging at us. I always seem to be coming in at night, so all my dreams of London are dark, with occasional thin strips of light. We worked in the dark at Jenkins's to save electricity. Our flat was dark on principle. And the whores used the dark as prop: their chalk-white faces stayed buried in it till the deed was done.

But the darkest place of all was the confessional, which with my new life had become a tunnel of horrors, part of the London underworld. It was like suddenly coming to my senses in a strange place. The priest was no longer a toy for Chatworth to play with. He was a hanging judge, silent, nodding, processing my swill. I hate more than ever to make a fool of myself, yet for this man I do it on command. Why? Because I want to make a fool of myself *officially* and knowingly and receive grace for it. I want my Millicents and my Fifis to say, "You are forgiven. Clown no more." Embarrass yourself no more. I can't ask the girls to say it, but I can almost oblige the priest to say it for them.

Afterwards I lurch through the streets like a blind beggar. Will nobody take me in? The people behind those curtains there—do you want me? I go to pubs and listen, over my half of bitter, to the speech patterns and the serpentine simplicities of the London mind. Surely I could cut a figure here? No. I've tried it. They'll tear you to pieces, boy.

I'm told that every adolescent goes through these silent months, but surely each must pass through a different country. We watch and wait; we have been dispossessed. I began to feel bitter at my parents for jerking me from country to country until I belonged nowhere. I didn't realize that they were handing me my meal ticket, worth $200,000 per and up. It was a bloody apprenticeship, but I was learning points of manners and sensibility like a botanist. I now know exactly what it takes to make an Englishman angry; I know how to make a forthright statement in American with no risk whatever, and how to skirt bad taste in two languages; I know how to make you like or dislike me at will—even (and this is like a ventriloquist drinking a glass of water while he works) when I am talking to both nations at once. God forgive me for using this knowledge.

To get myself off the streets, I join a jazz club and meet a girl called Emma, and find that I can do no wrong. Life is insanely simple after all. My encyclopedia of mistakes runneth over, and I can make no more. Besides, she is point 2 down from me on the social scale—not far enough down to cause trouble. We maneuver a meeting in her room, and wear each other out petting in the usual style of the prerevolution. Step one goes smoothly, steps two, and three, and I realize she has no brakes at all. I am like a doctor with an etherized patient. I must make my own difficulties if I want any.

Suddenly the box looms up like the Flying Dutchman. I imagine the mildest of priests going ape, losing his biretta, lunging at me, as I confess copulation.

"I'm a Catholic," I tell Emma solemnly.

"I'm High Church."

Well. That settled that. We knew exactly where we stood theologically. She got up and made some tea and we never addressed the subject directly. My thinking had—how to put it for a family audience?—deflated me: it really was like the air going out of a tire. Curious. I learned later that very evening that it would have been better to say, "We just did it, Father," than all the things I felt I had to say instead, about how far and how long and other feverish trivia. The priest didn't ask me for any of this: in fact, he seemed to be bored to distraction. English confessors just can't seem to bring their game up for impurity the way Americans can. He muttered something about considering the girl's feelings and that was that.

I hate to bore people, and I wanted to stay and impress him with my real sin, which was nothing less than confession itself. I had gotten sex and penance so hopelessly intermingled that I couldn't think of one without the other. All the time I'd been walking around and around sex and talking to it and being saintly in its presence, I'd been imagining how I would explain it later—how phrase this act, how abase myself for that—until I'd become the kind of saint who can't exist without his whorehouse.

And London is still my whorehouse. This prim ruin that I had taken for sexless fairly reeks of it by now. In my dreams I still wander the mews and markets, smelling sex; the shapes are lovely, but the smell as I get closer is cheap and used and mixed with sperm and garlic. (Can you dream smells, or is it just the idea of a smell?) Anyway, I am overwhelmingly

155

drawn to it, until the dream of confession sends me reeling away—to the next mews and the next. It is a sin I don't have to confess; I am half mad because I can't confess it. As I land now in spanking new Heathrow and wait for this year's assortment of deodorized bunnies to spot me, that London comes back to me in all its dank triumph, and I look for that magic box where I can confess it out of my system once and for all.

Well, all this is rather a lot to lay on a bored Oratorian Father, and I say nothing. He asks me to pray for him. Fat lot of good that will do.

I don't know what would have happened with Emma. I can't imagine not just going straight ahead with her. But then I can't really remember what stopped us at the bed's edge in those days. There was something, all right, that blocked one like a pane of invisible glass, but what was it? As soon ask someone what it felt like being hypnotized. Yet I treasured it, *whatever* it was, and even prayed for more of it.

Anyway, I never found out about Emma because my father pulled a fast one on all of us. Winter was coming and it threatened to be a pisser. Which meant that pipes would freeze, railway lines ice over, coal wouldn't move. The country had been miserable enough in the summer, the small promise of spring having turned to mud in the scrimy rain. People were sick of looking at each other, in their shapeless wartime clothes, yet they were forced to look at each other constantly, in one queue after another. Mother still reveled in it ghoulishly, because it made up for missing the war. But it was too much for Father.

On the day that my matriculation results arrived (flying colors, ho hum) he suddenly announced, "I want to go back to America." We barely heard it, taking it for one of his remarks-at-large. "And I *mean* to go back to America."

"What? You? America?"

"Yes, me, America."

"But you *hate* America."

156

"Do I? Is that the impression I give? Odd." He shook his head. "Perhaps I did at one time. I don't now. I think it has marvelous vitality." He said this in such a tired voice that I all but laughed. Having criticized every custom and institution on the American continent he was down to their damn vitality. Next it would be their "marvelous sort of innocence." "Anyway, I don't like what's become of this place, and I don't think it's been good for the children."

Oh my God, he knows everything. He has stripped me with one flick of the tongue. I wrench my mind over to Priscilla: what is bad about her? She has joined a local communist club where the moral tone is dizzying. Prissy has distanced herself hysterically from the Marchbanks, and her new friends neither drink nor dance nor make jokes. Humor is considered a bourgeois trick (I agree with this) and incest is quite out of the question. It is all like joining a convent.

"I didn't mind the friends you had before, the whatshisnames, Metcalfs? Marchbanks. I understand that chins have been abolished since the war among the better sort of people —but at least they *were* the better sort of people."

"David!" quoth my mother.

"Oh come off it, dear. We would all dearly like to extend this class indefinitely if we could, but it hasn't been extended yet. If anything, it's shrinking. And in the meantime, there's no point in sentimentalizing these others," he paused and drew breath, "out of some misguided sense of one's own social inferiority."

This was the cruelest dig at old O'Grady yet, a sign that England might be bad for him, too.

"Are you trying to raise a pair of snobs?" Mother fairly shouted.

"No, only one lady and one gentleman."

"And you think America's the place for it?"

"Yes, oddly enough, I do."

My mind was at war but I was too smug to know it. My mother was absolutely right, morally—and I knew something about "these others" too. I knew (having seen it all) that they could be tough and resourceful. Yet the suggestion of my own innate superiority was hard to dismiss out of hand. The result was a kind of vague excitement over the whole argument wherever-it went.

"I apologize to both of you for bringing you back," my father said gravely.

I looked at Priscilla in my goofy joy and realized that she was crying. She had never argued with my father; in fact, for this last bad year, she had been the only real friend he had, laughing at his jokes whenever she decently could and clearly and simply loving him. Now she couldn't even *frame* an argument. "I'm not going, Daddy," she blurted at last.

"Yes you are," he said quietly.

She shook her head. "I'll live with Ron."

"Ron? What Ron?"

"At the club. Ron Adams. I love him."

"Then we can't go," said Mother contentedly.

"Oh yes we can." There was iron in my father and he was happy to be using it again. "Priscilla, I'll be heartbroken if you do this, but it won't alter my plans. You are a grownup, free to make your own decisions, but so am I. Now tell me about this Ron if you please?"

"He isn't a gentleman, if that's what you mean."

Well, that was that. We sat in silent gloom.

"I'd like to meet him before you move in with him," said my father finally, "gentleman or no."

Priscilla left the room. Would she have the guts to bring a communist boyfriend around here? "You and your sort of people make me bloody sick." "Yes, I suppose we must." Father would be magisterial: he has lost an empire but found a role. The family would splinter, but about time perhaps. The question was, could Priscilla face this? Who needed whom around here?

She spent the afternoon in her room, and skipped supper.

Afterwards, as I sat on my bed thinking deep thoughts of me, she tapped on the door.

"Pen? Are you there?"

"Speaking."

She was wearing flowered pajamas, in what seemed like a conscious effort to be childish. "What should I do, Pen?"

"Well, that's up to you, isn't it?" snapped the apostle of toughness.

"Daddy doesn't want me, does he? He told me to go to blazes."

"I wouldn't say that. He told you to be an adult and make your own decision."

"Oh, be an adult. Fly to the moon. Just like that." She paused. "You know why he's doing it, don't you? For you. I can do as I choose. You're the prize."

Vanity swells like a blowfish. "I don't believe you," I murmur.

"Oh come on, Pen. You're too intelligent not to have noticed it. He adores you. He only tolerates me. Why do you think he's been so hangdog since we got back? He feels as if he's let you down. This country isn't good enough for you. So he's even willing to go back to America and face the beastly hot dogs for your sake."

"I never said I wanted to go back."

"Oh, Pen, it's perfectly obvious. Every time he says something nasty about England you chime in like gangbusters. And the way you go sulking off at night, and don't have any friends, and don't talk to anybody—of course he's worried sick about you."

"Nothing to worry about," I mumble.

"Anyway he doesn't want *me,* that's quite clear. Nobody's ever wanted me."

She looked so sad picking at her slipper that I felt I should say something bracing. "Everyone feels like that sometimes," I assure her. I personally didn't give a damn if anybody

159

wanted me at that particular moment. My object now was to put some starch into this girl. "We're all fond of you, you know. *Very* fond."

Ah, the ardors of the Chatworths, the Latin excesses. "Do *you* want me to go with you to America?" asked Priscilla.

Me? What difference did that make? "What about this chap that loves you? Adams?"

"I didn't say he loved me. I said I loved him." This was getting a little sticky for my taste. "He's too good a party member to *need* anybody. Oh God," she put her head in her hands, "why doesn't anyone just love me?"

Too much. "Don't you think you're being just a bit self-pitying?"

She looks up. "Yes, I daresay I am. How wise you are, Pen." Gets up briskly, walks out, shuts door.

My heart is pierced. I do love her, but this is a Marchbanks-like sickness, and must be fought. Our family cannot go on clinging to each other forever. The war is over. I have had the guts to fight free. Prissy must do the same. I am torn with an urge to run out and put my arms around her and sink my head in her hair and cry with her until dawn. I want to say, "I just love you," but I don't do it. I DON'T DO IT.

Waiter, fetch me the Pope. I think we've found serious matter this time.

15

~~~~~~

Being a mythical beast, I have to keep both my front and back ends in good working order. My front is the eternal tourist, with that look of goofy wonder painted on his face; my ass is the oldest settler, who's seen it all. I may turn them around from time to time, but that's who they are, and I heartily wish I could get rid of one or the other. Preferably the damn tourist.

Specifically, I wish I could phase out of one country or the other, but I've a hunch if I lose one I'll lose both—that's how closely they watch each other. I know there's a cabal of colonials at the BBC that can't stand English accents, but they can probably only put me over on the other team as a flourishing half-breed. I am nature's compromise candidate. As for America—ah, these things go deeper there. Americans play identity for keeps. They even keep reservations full of lapsed Englishmen in Hollywood and elsewhere as a warning: and late at night these miserable twilight characters are let out just as far as the nearest talk show, to remind Chatworth to keep on his toes. Mustaches drenched in tea. Ugh.

So I have to keep going out and coming in again, like a cast of three trying to play Ben-Hur, in order to seem like a fresh character. And miraculously it works. My new series, "Ourselves as Others See Us: The Outside World Looks at America," has opened to thumping reviews even by the young hardnoses who tell it like it is. Even allowing that this great country can't resist an excuse to look at itself one more time in any light whatever, the show must be considered a genuine personal triumph. So I must guard against wallowing again. Look at these damn clippings for instance. It is so degradingly easy to be called civilized in America. What sort of pig farms were they raised on themselves? And this, "It is such a pleasure to hear adult conversation"—why, in God's name? Who is keeping it from them?—"and not to be talked down to." That's what you think, Cyclops.

Mm, I love you all anyway, but I won't fall for you this time. The memory of Jersey is too real, and my civilized adultness has reasserted itself in time. Also, my compliments don't travel. Nobody in England ever called me civilized. Over there it is my transatlantic sparkle. Yeah, and my impishness. Get a load of that, Muldoon.

If going out and coming in again is the name of the game, I really got down to it in 1947. On my first two crossings I had been as innocent and reluctant as a tennis ball, but this time I'm going where I want to go and with my eyes, so far as I can tell, open.

Before returning to America that year, we dance a Chatworth fandango, with my will power playing softly on the tom-toms. Mother will stay with Priscilla and I will go with Father. Unthinkable? On the whole, yes. Peace has not shattered us *that* much. All right. Priscilla will marry her Ron in a Catholic Church, and Ron can keep his fingers crossed if he likes. No? Ron says we're a pack of bloody cynics? May have a point there. Father will change his mind then? No, no, no.

Mother capitulates. Her show of spirit is over. She seems very old, yet what is she? Middle forties? Unbelievable. Father is in his fifties, but he's never seemed fitter. Now that his mind is made up, he's lighthearted as a boy. A week passes, two. He will not break. So it turns out that Priscilla will come with us after all. It is not quite as weak a decision as it sounds. Ron Adams has insisted that she denounce her family. He wants a scene, and asks for an appointment. It is all too much.

"It's for the better, Prissy," says Father. "You'd have had to give up so much. Not just your clothes and books and comfort—at your age, one doesn't mind those things, I dare-say. And you'd probably find a cold-water flat positively exhilarating, and several rather moist infants would be a wonderful challenge. But you'd be giving up your *life,* in ways that you don't even know about. You'd be this man's slave."

"I already am a slave," says Priscilla. "And it's all *not* for the best. I just haven't the courage to go through with it."

Father shrugs. As long as she does the right thing, it doesn't matter why. He is free now from the burden of her love. Priscilla will hate him till the day she dies, and beyond. All for the best. His nerves are too fragile for love.

I talked to Priscilla about this years later and she assures me I'm quite mad. "I can't even remember what Ron looked like. But I'm sure it would have been a disaster. I didn't love him, you know. I was probably using him to get attention. And he certainly didn't love me: he just wanted to make a scene in an upper-class house. Anyway, I'd mind very much a cold-water flat by now." Priscilla will tease me till the day I die. I don't know if anyone else understands her, but she is hellbent that I never shall. Even on the great Daddy Question. She has a large picture of the old man on her bedside table, but never talks about him. She is cool, witty, and evasive like him, and her husband is a great fool, like Mother. Or perhaps he just does it for me.

That year in New York was what I would later be calling a period of transition, if not a downright watershed, in my college essays. New York was as bright as London was dark, and I remember a jumble of clear blue days and gleaming snowbanks and dazzling white teeth which, on the smithy of my soul, became a pop star with a difference.

The very first day, I asked a cop, "You got the time, Mac?" and he said, "British, huh? I was over in the war." Chatworth had no idea he'd sunk this low in a year and a half. St. Boniface had slightly unbalanced him in one respect: he assumed that all Americans despised the English, even when they were praising our beautiful accents. So I wrote the cop off as an oddity and set to work on the real problem, bending my accent back again. Talk about your fateful decisions. "Cuppa cawfee," I muttered to myself; but in public I asked for a glass of milk. (Phoneticists note: The broad *a*'s are a snap, but oh those short *o*'s.)

In the violence of his own anti-English recoil, Father enrolled me in a local Catholic college: by which accident my warped Anglophobia was sustained. The IRA was beginning to stir, and my new friends invited me to go downtown one night and picket Ernie Bevin, the British foreign minister. No Camus character was ever more existentially torn. Here I was playing the Irish game again as farce. My buddies and I had been drinking beer all afternoon and we set forth in the thoughtful spirit of a panty raid. I felt a little queasy picketing my own foreign minister, but I probably would have felt queasy anyway.

"Have yez got the dynamite, Gypo?" I whisper, to keep things light.

"No, I t'ought *yous* had the dynamite."

"Jaysus—ya know something, fellas? We forgot the dynamite."

We are laughing so hard we collapse on a pile of overcoats. There's no treason in that.

The teen-age mystic of London became giddy and harebrained in the spanking air of postwar New York. In 1947, pollution was only a speck on the horizon, and life was a dance, even for my old man, who had entered a religious phase himself. He began catching early Masses and late Masses and going on retreats where they sang obscure liturgies. Was he really enjoying America? If not, you could have fooled me. He bounded off to what he called his work at cockcrow, catching Masses as he went. In spare moments he talked to me gently but vaguely about my plans.

"Any thought to the future, Pen?"

"Not really."

"Plenty of time, I suppose."

"Yes, that's what I thought."

"Lord, it's such a different world. In my day, an old man could still talk to a young one and tell him *something* of use, but now . . ."

You don't have to, I wanted to tell him. I didn't wish to confine my greatness to a profession just yet.

"The law?"

"Possibly."

"Perhaps you should start thinking about it."

"Perhaps."

Then suddenly, "I want you to be first-rate, Pen. Think you can manage that?"

"I'll give it a try."

We smile. His duty done, he is off for Benediction with a spring in his step. He had never really been religious before, except in that jingoist way of counting Catholic heads and gloating, but now he'd found it was the only thing left a chap could count on. What did he think about as he bent in prayer? Old cricket matches? Superb breakfasts? An absolutely first-rate God?

I also wondered to what sort of work he bounced every day. He couldn't still be spying, could he? If so, on what? For some reason, I could not accept his import-export business —partly because I never met any witnesses. He brought home no business friends, and his briefcase looked empty. All I know is he just dressed neatly, swooped downtown, and disappeared.

By now I realized that most English gentlemen of his generation appeared brain-damaged; it meant nothing, they were simply covering for the others. But I couldn't shake the notion that Father was basically unemployable, and I decided that we must be living on Mother's money. That's what it was. The Chatworths had seen her coming and had taken the simple colleen to the cleaners. Now they sneered at her.

At any rate, there was something poisonous in the English air that had rusted their marriage and given it a harsh, peevish feel. I wondered if it had been like that before the war, too. Perhaps Mother had poured the tea upside down at a sensitive moment in 1931, and Aunt Maude had snickered, and Father had reddened, and the cat had fainted, and things had never been the same. How small and quaint it seemed from this great bright city twinkling on its bed of rocks. At times now Father and Mother were almost like lovers again, touching each other by mistake: as if they'd come here to save their marriage.

Anyway, Mother's little mutiny seemed to have folded completely. In exchange, she had become almost too dutiful a wife, and I was slightly disgusted at her lack of spunk. I mention this to show my fanatical attention to detail as a fuck-up. Astrologers tell me I'm a perfectionist, so maybe that's it.

Priscilla had obtained a part-time job in a library and in the evenings went out listlessly with large, smooth men of the stockbroker persuasion. I got a feeling she was going to make a wretched but socially suitable marriage, out of spite. I see this now as perhaps a self-mutilating unhappiness, but I thought at the time she was being rather silly. Thank God the American Catholic aristocracy never quite came up with the right combination of horrors. My father didn't think *any* of them were socially suitable.

I took only the remotest interest in all this myself. I was too busy singing the Whiffenpoof song in German beer cellars and steeping myself in America. Muldoon is here, or at least his type, but how he's changed in two years: quieter, more buttoned-down, raising hell in a rather ritualized way on Saturday nights: knocking off at twelve, hitting the books, going steady with Catholic girls who smile around the clock, but will not put out. At least not for Muldoon, who respects them for it. He's OK with me. Americans are not really people, like the English, with their niggling particularity, but ideas, spaces. Muldoon is, for instance, what is appropriately called a square. This is because he is really a killer and has to watch himself. I knew him as a kid, before he became an abstraction. This still gives me an edge over most foreign observers, who think Americans are born that way. It also gives me a disadvantage, as I wait for the killer to pounce.

Actually, American Catholics were rather a special subspecies back then, but they were all I knew. We all stopped drinking at twelve sharp on Saturday nights and we thought twice about saying "Jesus"—but didn't everybody? We had no non-Catholics to judge by, so that going around with soot on your forehead and a blessed throat seemed perfectly normal. Perhaps our weirdest practice, though, was the avoidance of uncharitable remarks. Guys would fall silent or in extreme cases leave the room if you talked behind someone's, anyone's, back. Friend, foe, it made no difference: he was precious in the eyes of God, so he'd better be good enough for you, buddy.

Has any remote tribe ever practiced anything so inhuman? Charity established a reserve among us as stern as any religious order's, and made close friendship almost impossible (which was perhaps the point); but to make up for it, comradeship abounded, since you could have an equally good time with any group—no more, no less. And the iron goodwill later turned out to be perfect for game shows and sales pitches. A priest's cold warmth remains the ideal for daytime TV.

The absence of friends also makes a dreamer of you, and my dream that year had consequences, because it was so astoundingly commonplace. And you can't be a public figure unless you've had at least one branding, blinding, 100 percent commonplace dream.

It usually started out with a long shot of me, bouncing my shanks in a jalopy, riding along ratty highways through towns of throbbing vulgarity—"Ma's Eats," "The Pink Pussy," "The Boom Boom Room"—and on into the void. One last Texaco pump manned by a Navajo, and then nothing. Land too bare to support cactus. Air so pure you can see a hundred empty miles. Close-up and dissolve. A man, either me or somebody else, standing in the middle of the widest Main Street you ever saw. The sidewalks deserted, except for the weeds in the cracks. A theater marquee hanging by its rust, a general store with the windows shot out, a tavern, a barbershop. Time to be moving on. I or somebody else starts walking slowly toward the great American emptiness. The quaint English village can go stuff itself.

You'll spot my sources, of course, and can probably name the exact movies. MGM gave me Mrs. Miniver and Universal took her away. Never mind. The films are only my pallet. I have to fill them with life or death myself. This man, me or somebody else, can change his name or his face at will. Mustaches come and go. At the same time he is a rock of integrity, of some sort. I am intoxicated by this vision. I can invent myself here, so long as I am first-rate. There is no book of rules in America, running to a million volumes, which they won't let you see anyway; there is no graveyard with my name already on it. The vultures will get me out there in the blue instead.

The funny thing is that it's all come true.

Priscilla, who is bored with the question, told me the last time I saw her that I began to amuse people around then with jokes and imitations. This is so far from my own memory of the period that I scarcely believe it possible. Knowing that I'd outgrown Muldoon by then, I ask her craftily, what was the nature of my comedy? Making fun of the *English,* she says. Which English? *All* the English. Everyone you ever met there. But most especially Gussie Marchbank. Your imitation of him was so cruel we began to think you were some sort of genius.

I tell her she must have the dates wrong. I was trying to get rid of the English at that point and I could not afford to touch the accent, even in fun. "Have it your way," says Prissy, yawning. "You theater people [she always calls me "theater people" in her wicked English way] do have to worry so much about yourselves, don't you? Your images and so forth." She's becoming more and more like Father. "Thank God," she goes on, "I have no such responsibilities to *my* image and am only too happy to forget the whole dreary business." Do I look hurt? There are wounds only an older sister can open. "I mean my part of it," she adds quickly. "I don't mind talking about you forever." I reach stiffly for my hat—or whatever one does when one hasn't got a hat. The horrible thought strikes that if I was making fun of the English then, I must have been doing it to please my new gang.

Enough of this morbid crapping around. The thing to remember about my dream is the two themes, emptiness and vulgarity, embraced with all the ardor and poetic force of adolescence. Yet even this dream I have betrayed at times.

Toward the end of the school year Father enters the hospital. He is dying. Isn't that just like him?

He did it like a gentleman. Multiple myeloma was the name of the inconvenience. He'd been taking treatments for months and now the jig was up. He packed his own bag and off he went with Mother to a hospital overlooking the East River. Mother kept us informed, easing us into the shock as gently as she could. Death was messy, and he clearly preferred to do it alone. So I didn't see much more of him.

When I did, he chatted amiably about this and that and I began to wonder if he knew.

"Oh yes, he knows," said Mother.

"For how long?"

"I don't know. Longer than I have."

She fell silent, and I sensed she wanted him for herself. Unfair, of course. It's just that one mustn't die in front of the children. It leaves a nasty taste. God, how they tried to protect us. Very un-Catholic of them, I think now. Good Catholics want you to look at Death early and often, so you get used to it. But for once, manners won out over religion.

For my part, I think I at least half wanted to talk to him about it, to ask how he'd discovered it and what it felt like. Conversation might take the curse off it. But his sense of privacy was fierce and cunning. He would not tell me, he would show me, how to die. His calmness began to terrify and infuriate me. I couldn't die like that in a million years. Crack, damn you. Weep. Don't go on about the promising crop of players at Wimbledon.

Did he cry when we left the room? I hope so. I cannot stand his damn superiority. I sense that he limits our visits because he cannot maintain the manner very long. Being perfect is a strain even for him. He is doing this for me. He is destroying me.

"Do be first-rate, won't you Pen?" My last visit with the old soldier, I know it for sure. He has shrunk to nothing. It is grotesque to go on talking about Wimbledon. Can't we talk turkey just once? He looks at me humorously. Decidedly not. Turkey, forsooth.

I feel cheated even now. Why didn't I force him to talk? Wouldn't it have been a relief for both of us? I couldn't, that's all. I didn't even cry or show my sorrow, but left on a jaunty note. I had bought his style without his content—something else for my bag of tricks. Never teach someone to hide his feelings until you've made sure he has any. But it was all so quick and deft, I had no time to feel. He was suddenly gone, like a conjurer's handkerchief.

I felt lonely and terrified when he died a week or so later, and took this for grief. I hope to God it was. The three of us clung together giddily—the Chatworths abroad and alone again. Priscilla had seemed, I recall, unconcerned during those last weeks, but now she devoted herself to consoling Mother, who was in a genuine flash flood of grief.

I had never realized how much I personally had depended on the old man's presence. It had nothing to do with liking him: I just needed him in order to perform. Without him I was nobody, a lost child. For a short while I even gave up my dream of the harsh empty plains and longed to huddle round an English fireplace in my jammies. Mummy and Prissy seemed to be excluding me now. They were always together, murmuring, murmuring. It wasn't fair. He was mine as much as theirs.

Actually, Mother was more than willing to talk to anyone after the first day or so. She was a gregarious mourner, now that Father wasn't there to keep an eye on her, and such friends as we had received an earful. "Your father was a remarkable man"; her grief became, and remains, rather formal and ceremonial, as if she were unveiling a plaque. "The doctors tell me he might have had warnings before we left for England two years ago. He only told *me* after he decided to return to the States last spring. It was his way of persuading me to come."

A flicker. Does she feel guilty about treating him so thoughtlessly in England? No. She is too tough and sane for that. If he didn't tell her he was dying it is no fault of hers. That sort of sniveling guilt is for the heartless and the sentimental, i.e., for me. It leads, when its time is up, to resentment. Father *made* us act unfeelingly by not telling us. And he left us this legacy of doubt about how long he knew: did we treat him callously for six months? Twelve? Longer? His personal present to me was simply the impossible, malicious example he set of virtue and love which ended my dreams of saintliness for keeps. My own grief has hardened into a different shape from Mother's. How dare anyone outlove me so? What unbeatable moral advantage has he taken into eternity?

Meanwhile, there were practical problems which Mother and I proved laughably unendowed to meet. By default Priscilla became the man of the family. She took care of the funeral arrangements, which I vaguely supposed somebody else did for you. (Father had said any piece of Catholic ground would do, so Prissy vengefully took him at his word, and he rests today in Yonkers. "Goodness what a name!!") She also dove into his finances and helped Mother make some sense of them. His business turned out to be quite real, and she told me he'd left us a good bit in trusts and insurance, damn him. Finally, Priscilla rehabilitated Mother, making her at least appear to be a functioning human being. (This imitation, by the way, is now complete. She is widely considered a remarkable human being.) Then Prissy announced she was returning to England.

Mother regressed on the spot. "Then we'll *all* go," she said brightly.

"What about me?" I piped.

"Yes, what about Pen?" said Mother.

"I give up. What about Pen?" said the masterful Priscilla.

"Suppose I don't want to go?"

"Then you can stay."

"Oh Priscilla," Mother whinnied. "He can't stay by himself."

"Well, why don't you stay with him?" Priscilla looked desperate. "Look, *I* am leaving. For once, I'm doing what I want. The rest of you can suit yourselves."

But the sight of Mother coming unstuck again was almost too much for her; and the thought of not doing something unselfish must have burned.

"I'm not leaving," I said helpfully.

Mother sobbed.

Prissy said, "Oh my God. This is impossible." For a change, *I* ran from the room.

Mother had always depended on someone else. Even her little burst of independence in England was under Daddy's shield; it was a kind of Irish play-acting. Or am I wrong about this? Was it *her* shield all along? Either way she is lost without him.

We all are. Suddenly we are sickened by our need for each

other. Being alone against the world is bad for one's health. Priscilla is now twenty-one and I am eighteen and we can't break away. Loathing is not far away.

"I gave in last time," said Priscilla, when we were alone. "It's your turn."

"Yes, but you see, I *hate* England."

"Well, I hate America with all my heart."

"You do?"

"Yes, and I have from the day we landed in 1940, if you must know. Now as a British citizen I would like to exercise my right of return."

"I'm not going back to that perfumed shithouse."

"Pen! What colorful argot you've picked up. Look—why don't you just stay here by yourself and I'll go back with Mummy."

I should have, of course, but then there would be no Monty Chatworth today, and we'd all be the losers. As it was, I said that Mummy could never agree to that, and Prissy said that *she* couldn't desert Mummy, and we generally punched Mummy about until she was shapeless. I wound up accepting a compromise. If Uncle Henry could wangle me into his old college at Oxford, I would go back just for the duration of that. "There are lots of super Americans over there and you can practice your idioms all day long," said Prissy. "I'll even buy you a subscription to the *Readers' Digest.*"

I didn't want to go to the damn place. It was just a face-saving device. Father's death had temporarily sapped my strength. I suddenly saw how little I owned of this world. I could always rent a country and an accent, but all I owned for sure was a mother and a sister and a funny name. I would hang onto those a bit longer. Uncle Henry set up an interview for me with the fellows of Paisley College (yeah, hey nonnie nonnie) and I meekly agreed to cooperate.

I had a church, too, of course, but that didn't seem quite as firm without Father's smugness to support it. In fact, though he was as ignorant as a peasant about it and even a

173

bit bored, it was Father's church, and was one of the things he took with him. After that Mother's devotion just seemed childish and wishful, and Prissy gave up believing altogether. For myself, I realized that I was not an American-Catholic and I was not an English-Catholic, and there is no such thing as just a plain Catholic. The English kind were too corrupt for my taste and the Americans were not corrupt enough. The air is thin in American churches: it lacks the gamy smell of England, the delicate sense of rot. Once you have sampled Rome as perversion, it's hard to go back to meat-and-potatoes Catholicism. Only in the box where the priest mumbles inaudibly in the dark do I still get the tang of it.

Did I tell you the Marchbanks were Catholics?

It occurred to me as I flew back toward Oxford that England had indeed planted a small germ of corruption in me. There was a physical eagerness to get back that made my heart pound. For what? I determine to stay as American as I can, and to meet nothing but Americans in Oxford. They might be dull but they are clean. And a homeless man cannot take chances. Left to his own devices, Chatworth might just turn into a dribbling, giggling peer, slugging the altar wine and screaming blasphemies in Latin. And we don't want that to happen, do we ol' buddy?

16

~~~~~~~~~~~~~~~~~~~~~~~~~~~~~~~~

Why can't I go to Africa the way I used to? Because you can't, that's all.

The Third World was my kind of place, though, while it lasted. In a rumpled white suit you could be anyone—a German explorer, an Italian adventurer, a burnt-out schoolboy. Talk about your melting pot. Then they put in skyscrapers and air conditioning and they grew their own announcers, little black Chatworths who looked and sounded just like me. From Nairobi to Kenyatta, I'd meet these smooth customers—only in gray suits now—on the lam from Johannesburg, Cairo, and the Sorbonne. Who needed me any more? My rumpled suit looked like a Victorian clown's outfit in the emerging nations. I'd gotten a jump on the postwar world, but that was all. Little did I know that even then Chatworth factories were being planned in the jungles and fever swamps. All you need is 165 pounds of bullshit and you can build one anywhere.

So keep moving, Transatlanticus. This is your pilot Virgil speaking. You're lucky they didn't make you a newsreader.

You didn't like Africa and you know it: except the way a model likes a sand dune or a snowman or whatever she looks good in front of. Africa was a great showcase for your style, and now you're sore at it. Because one of the killing things about our homeless person here is that deep down, he hates foreigners.

Paisley College, Oxford, is the lowest of the low, let's say twenty-fifth out of a possible twenty-six. It is not Uncle Henry's college or Father's or anyone's, but the biggies are out of reach for an old St. Boniface man and the Master of Paisley is an old Catholic pal of Uncle Henry's. So through heaven knows what chicanery, I am accepted there. I can tell the fix is in from the boozy unbuttoned tone of the interview, with the sherry fairly flying. And three more weeks at Jenkins are more than enough to shoot me through the entrance exam in history.

Uncle Henry is nice about it, as he would be to any obvious retardate. "It's a jolly good college. I believe Bishop Tulkinghorn went there and the poet Simpkins, and various others." It is clear that he would see his own son work in a whorehouse before he sent him to Paisley.

Never mind. There is something to be said for these third-rate institutions of mine. Paisley College would be a ludicrous place to get an education, but it was superb for launching a career. Unlike some of the other bad-breath colleges, Paisley did not strive to impress. It had been around for a long time, and it had the pride of a small tradesman with roots. It didn't need scholars and it didn't need athletes —though the Master was hung up on lacrosse, so the place teemed with lacrosse players, and we were widely respected in the lacrosse community. Paisley would be here after we were gone, and nothing we did could add much to that. After one of my recent English triumphs I ran across a note in the alumni magazine asking for the whereabouts of P. A. Chatworth and it almost made my cry.

It's a local joke, which they keep from you just long enough, that every Oxonian starts out belonging to every club in the place that will have him. Shivering in one's rooms, one is flattered to be solicited in turn by the salty tough from the Labour Club, the twenty-guinea blazer from the Tories, the hot-eyed fascist, the flat-earther: they all want *me*. How have they heard of me? Never mind. Two and six is a small price to pay this godlike fellow here. Only later does one recognize the great shakedown for what it is. The cards on the mantelpiece are sucker's trophies, a register of how much you yearned for acceptance that first week. Knowing hands destroy them before too many people get wind. By the second time round, the sleazy little con man from Labour, the flatulent hanger-on from the Tories are clearer to you. By the end you belong to nothing.

Not I, however. Everyone else leaves with a small precious relic of Oxford, a few friends and memories that make your eyes water forever; but I shall want an Allied van to back up for my memories; I wanted everything, like a good American.

Which means I got nothing, right? Wrong. None of your two-bit French wisdom around here, please. At that age you can do it all. You can drink and drop your pants with the rugger players, and you can burn incense (and drop your pants, with feeling) with the aesthetes; you can demonstrate with the reds, and sit behind the curtained windows of the Wolfenden deploring the hooliganism. You can even have principles—any number of principles. On Sundays I wallowed in the rich fruitiness of the Church; on weekdays I dismembered it for the synthetic a priori proposition that it was. What a fate for the whore of Rome, to be shrunk like a Papuan skull by scrawny Oxford logicians.

Everybody else was so preposterously sincere that I assumed it was a gag, and that they were all having as much fun as I. The Socialists were so madly socialist, tearing at lank strands of hair in their passion; and the Tories were such

177

perfect old gentlemen, wheezing through preternaturally aged nostrils—surely they had had operations? How was I to know that they meant every word of it? That the secret of English acting is that they are not acting at all? Even the phonies are absolutely real. But I didn't know this then, and I jumped in merrily, playing this part and that in the Oxford game, never guessing that I played alone.

I began as Chatworth the American. This can be further divided into the rich American, and the all-purpose American. By juggling the two, I could get into anything—even into intellectual circles, where I was treated like a Central African with bananas on his head. Everything I said was greeted with enormous respect: it talks! Since I knew the English tricks backwards, I became at once the Brilliant American—although all I was was an average Englishman.

I'm sorry. I couldn't resist it. At night, if I was sober, I reviewed my basic positions and found them unchanged. First, I am a Catholic; that was the word written on my heart. Then I am an American convert—so sure of myself that I could afford to fool around. Politically I am—what? A gap here. My father had once run for Parliament as a Tory, but this didn't mean he was remotely interested in politics. On my American side, I couldn't see Bogart or Cooper sitting on committees of either persuasion. I am free to create myself, my besetting sin.

I have no interests, no allegiances. I shall play the field while I'm still young, before settling down with some nice older ideology. Meanwhile, what am I bid for the clever American? I feel my father's lazy smile forming on my lips. Because I am a Catholic I can afford to be playful about worldly matters. Of course, I have since learned that Daddy worked himself into a collapse over that parliamentary candidacy in 1936—he took everything so damn hard—but right then I thought I was reliving his Oxford with an American accent, the ultimate dandy twist. The light fades and the tap

178

drips. I am a Catholic, I am a Catholic. I am a man saying he is a Catholic.

Tuesday night. The Socialists. A huff of duffel coats. The mood is truculent and they jostle you on the way in, although there are only twelve of them. We are rough, we are authentic. Superb. There will be no false politeness around here, only love. We will hold your dying head in our arms, but that's all we'll do for you. You'll have to fight for your cup of tea same as the rest of us.

Everyone present has a working-class accent except for me. I can do one, but it would seem to carry the joke too far. I don't know what will come out if I try to speak.

The talk turns to America, and turns ugly. I am the oppressor, it seems. My inherent contradictions will undo me eventually, but in the meanwhile I'll have raped the globe for markets. And what do I make of that?

I put up my hand.

"Let's hear it from the Yank."

Coarse working-class laughter from the young gentlemen.

"Let him speak, for Godsake."

"Thank you, brother," say I—"comrade" seems a bit much. "I guess I'd like to inquire right off which Americans the brothers are referrin' to? As a guy who's woiked [the "woiked" just slipped out, I swear it] since I was twelve myself, I'm not sure who I been oppressin' all this time. Could somebody straighten me out on that?"

Silence from the ninnies, as middle-class values reassert themselves. They have hurt my feelings! How puce-making. As one who has gone up to Balliol from the Klondike, I hasten to bury these cupcakes.

"And my old man woikin' at the Navy Yard durin' de Depreshun—[I am trapped with the accent and I can't even do it very well. Is there an American in the house?]—was he oppressin' people all that time? I'd really like to know."

"Unwittingly." A strangled mumble.

"It sure as hell was unwittin,' " I thunder.

My problem was not to sound too illiterate to be at Oxford in the foist place. I slyly drop the "dese" and "doze": what do *they* know? "We sure didn't wit it at home, over the caviar and truffles, and we didn't wit it as we piled into the Cadillac for our Sunday outin's. Jolly dense of us, I suppose."

An imitation imitating an imitation—Ah, Chatworth, you're killin' 'em.

In their desolation over the breach of manners they had lost their intellectual bearings, and you would actually suppose I was scoring points. I should have left it at that, I suppose, before I was found out for sure. But you know how it is with these things. Merlin probably overdid it the first time with the wand. The lessons of a lifetime came together and they worked. So now I just wanted to see if I could *unembarrass* them: "Just remember when you guys talk about American oppressors that there's millions like me, who're just as oppressed as you are, and who boin for justice like you do. Tank youse." Sits down testily.

The chairman does his best, like a ruffled dowager calming a drunken genius. "I think we'd all like to apologize for any misunderstanding and possible impoliteness. Shall it so be passed?"

"Aye, aye," gruff working-class sounds again.

"And to thank our transatlantic cousin for reminding us that there are indeed two Americas." Spattering of applause.

It is just a game, isn't it? Can I come out now?

"We don't get too many of your sort here," says a surly Yorkshireman of a kind who doesn't like to apologize and will make me pay if he can.

Damn right you don't. I am tempted to start again and tell them I was only speaking for all the Brooklyn boys they will never get to meet at Oxford, but decide against. The Yorkshireman conveys a physical menace rare in Englishmen, and touches an old nerve of prudence; he is a barbarian from the

North, a type I learn to respect on the spot. (Of course. He doesn't get the point up here: he is not acting.) But something more than that stills my tongue. There is a sense of awe among the others, as they circle a live American. I know what they mean; I have felt it myself. To be near one is to be near a great center of power, like a dam or a blast furnace. Even these Yank-baiters feel it, against their wishes (except the Yorkshireman.) This is 1948; it will never happen again. I, surrogate, imposter, am standing in for the American powerhouse. So I go on with my Brooklyn imitation, which is based on the same movies they have seen, and which they could probably do just as well.

Wednesday. Dinner at the Wolfenden with my new friend Tufnell. He is a great fool, but cunning. He is not impressed by Americans—quite the reverse. He considers them an utter calamity. Hear him first at the Oxford Union bar: "Worse than the Visigoths, worse than the Tartars. *They* would only have raped our women, not our language as well."

"Poor bastards," says a cheeky American down the bar.

"Eh? What's that?"

"I mean your language is pretty good."

Laughter. Tufnell bridles.

"It *was* pretty good until you people got hold of it and updated it vocabulary-wise into a rooting tooting balls-up. You don't care what words *mean,* as long as they have five syllables and sound important."

"Well, what can you expect from huddled masses?" says Chatworth (for it is I). "We should never have let the bastards land, in my opinion. But tell me, sir," ultrathick middle-American for this bloke, "what exactly do you masters of language mean when you say 'awfully decent' and 'frightfully nice'? And what *precisely* is the sense of 'terribly' in the phrase 'terribly good of you'? I'm here to learn, sir."

The crowd at the bar is having a jolly time. This being the Oxford Union, I suspect they're all South Africans. Tufnell is not as dumb as he looks. "I daresay you may have a point, Mac. What are you drinking?"

So I become his American and he takes me to dinner at his club and tells me all about it. "It's so rare to meet a gentleman from across the pond."

"And it's so vulgar to call it the pond."

He is delighted, as I knew he would be. I remember this man from a previous existence. He is fleshy and good-looking and he assumes comfortably that I take him for upper class. But that face and voice belong irrevocably to the better sort of businessman. That is why, for all his nonsense, he needs an American. I enjoy knowing that my class is actually better than his.

"I suppose you went to Yale, or some such?"

"Er—yes, Yale, that's it."

"Then you must know Tony Hotchkiss. Marvelous value, Tony."

Ohmygod, he's got two Americans. Chatworth, you're getting smug. "Well, I was sick a good deal of the time there." One question about Yale would strip me clean. "Also, I went sailing with Dad a lot. The Bahamas and so forth. What with that and the polo . . ."

I was laying it on wildly now, so that it would seem like a good joke when he caught on. But the silly bugger believed it all. So zany was their picture of America that one could tell them anything. Oh God, what a temptation for an innocent boy.

The talk drifts on over the suspect *pâté* and the thimble of roast beef. Difficulty of getting a decent meal. Quite. For a crazy moment I miss my father, quite overwhelmingly. Yonkers! It passes.

"I must say I envy you Americans in one respect. At least you haven't been taxed senseless by the bloody welfare state. I mean, you can still afford a decent tailor." He looks at me sharply: in my double-breasted wingding with the unfortu-

182

nate stripe, I clearly haven't afforded one yet. "Would you care to have the name of mine?"

"Goddamnit, that's decent of you, sir," say I. "You're a real white man."

Anyone who knew anything about America would see that I was dressed like a Broadway cowboy in my manic Americanness. But this simple fellow thought that even the best people dressed like that on the wrong side of the pond. Oh, I tell you, I was having a high time. This son of a manufacturer was undertaking to turn Pendrid Chatworth into a gentleman. Let us leave them both there heading for the deep armchairs, bearing large cigars and brandy glasses, and laughing their own laughs.

The tailoring question was just one of the hazards I was discovering in the Game. Of course I could afford his damn tailor. But how could I go to the Socialist Club in a forty-guinea blazer? Perhaps I could get a reversible one that turned into a duffel coat. What *was* the correct uniform for the Game?

It was not this, however, that ended my unbroken string of victories, but a lapse of understanding worthy of an earlier Chatworth. I grew a third face, which I frankly didn't think was in me, for the athletes of Paisley—not the best athletes in the world, but as coarse and unthinkingly joyful as good ones. At that age the knees and kidneys haven't gone, and they drink all night and whore as best they can (in my experience, no group tries harder to less effect) and sweat it all out next day in a cheerful stream. If they had been American I wouldn't even have tried. It was an article of prejudice with me that no Englishman was physically impressive, and no American intellectually. A good working prejudice, and no sillier than most.

As it was, I fell into this face by accident. I was standing at the college bar listening to the lacrosse players stumble, as

183

such dear fellows will, over the words of "The Good Ship Venus." Since I knew about twenty-five verses from St. Boniface days, I chimed in softly, and then louder as I noticed them encouraging me. Everything a Yank does surprises them over here, and is immediately misunderstood. I would as soon touch a live grenade as a ball or bat or mace or club, yet I am taken at once for a jock. The legend of reckless virility embraces us all, even the pointy-headed exchange students. I am one of the boys.

"What game do you play, Yank?"

This one. What I am playing right here. I can't help it. "American football," I say despairingly.

"Fancy you could learn rugger?"

"Trick knee."

"How about rowing? You're big enough."

Trick wrist. Dizziness. Fear of heights. "I hadn't thought about it."

Already the captain of rowing is at my side, practically holding out a contract. Everyone is watching: my tiny credit with these people is gone if I don't play *something*. My mind gropes for alternatives; almost all are ruled out by my putative trick knee. Damnit. I don't need this group. I've got Tufnell and the socialists, and other worlds unknown. Still, the bar is small and warm and friendly; there is an openness about these guys that is absolutely new to me. I don't want to lose them. So rowing it is.

God, what a miserable decision. The rowing men do not drink or carouse. The captain is a bluenose. He comes to the bar solely to recruit bodies. Even now, he is drinking a lemonade. He looks at the beer in my hand. Already I am breaking training.

"It looks as if you've found another rabbit, Roger," says a Hearty. "You fucking white slaver you." They do not like him. He grins a gap-toothed grin: he doesn't even look like them. Why hadn't I seen that?

"Start training, Yank," says a Hearty. "It's past your

bloody bedtime." The bar is suddenly chilly and indifferent.

Beware the openness of athletes. They are like big dogs that maim you in fun. Of all the subjects I interview, none makes me more nervous.

I will master them, you shall see. But for now it's a defeat, and it reminds me of others, and I leave the bar feeling weak and drained.

Fourth, fifth, and sixth faces to come. Perhaps my finest will be my man about town. This year's crop of Gussie Marchbankses are fresh out of school and have a lot to learn; I have been on the circuit, I have played the clubs. They look, little fledglings, for leadership. I bring them wobbling from the nest, to instruct them in elementary arrogance and teach them their own game. There is nothing so sophisticated as a sophisticated American.

Then there is the worm in the apple: my desire to have *everything*, even Englishness. I go to the London music halls and recognize another source of my wit. I am *au fond* a Cockney comedian. *Gott in Himmel,* I would be a French Apache and a Swiss yodeler if they'd let me. Once one has mastered the art of assimilation there is no stopping it. I enter everyone like the curse of the body snatchers. I had wandered the streets of London like a Dickens child, and was here to claim that too.

Finally, there will be Chatworth the actor, who puts all his shit together for the OUDS (Oxford U. Drama Soc.). Yet this Chatworth will be the unhappy one. Although I never see an actor without seeing myself doing it better, I shy from the actual attempt. Up there, with the lights melting my face, I really threaten to become somebody else and it frightens hell out of me. I play Alfred Doolittle in *Pygmalion* and am praised for my uncanny mastery of cockney; but this is what I don't want. I have done it too well. Let me try to explain this to myself, because it is important. The one thing that holds me together is that I am an *American* doing these things. I am not six different people, but one man doing six imitations. I must keep these artificial for the sake of my sanity. Chatworth the socialist and Chatworth the snob still have something in common: me. Real acting is a menace to this. I could lose myself in it forever. So I refuse to play anything but American parts, and get little work in this Shakespeare-sodden country. My bastard career is shaping up: Chatworth imitating Chatworth, accept no substitutes.

Let me see now. I am a Catholic. I am an American. My nightly litany has all the punch by now of a family rosary, and the effectiveness of a grace before English meals. "You know, you almost seem like an Englishman at times," says Tufnell. "If it weren't for that extra*ord*inary name of yours. Only Americans have pseudo-English names like that."

I remember my earlier resolve to frequent Americans and absorb their grace. Yet fate has granted me some strange Americans to frequent. The ones at Oxford are just the kind the English despise: their minds move like heavy machinery, and their tongues can barely keep up with their minds. They stare at you solemnly for a minute after you have spoken, and then the answer rumbles out as from a cave. They are *stoodents* and I am ashamed of them.

I know what the English are thinking. "They're not typical," I cry. "I'm typical." "Thank God for that," huffs Tufnell. But perhaps they are typical. I may have made a mistake. There is only one American who reassures me, and he is a menace in his own right: a fast-talking southern boy called Fletcher, who affects a down-home drawl and convulses the natives with such phrases as "rainin' lak a cow pissin' on a flat rock" or (for the buck-toothed Master of Paisley) "he could eat corn through a picket fence," which they imagine he makes up as he goes along. He is a hustler, watchful, on to these people. Can he be real? If so, my own authenticity pales before his souped-up ringding variety, and he would certainly be on to my game in no time: Yale,

Brooklyn, polo, and stickball. Fortunately, I am a menace to him too, and we keep our duchies separate.

Yale, Brooklyn—I have, God help me, even tried Texas and Winnipeg to remain an American, with all its privileges. I had better avoid Americans, the dimmest of whom could expose me. Yet without them, my accent falters and I find myself uttering little English cries. "Bugger it!" I yelp as the oar slips from my hands. "As you guys would say," I add.

The first term was a joy, for all that. Oxford is bigger than it looks, and I could always find new groups to baffle. For instance, I spent an afternoon mastering the New York school of art (and didn't know what to do with the last half-hour) and presented myself as an expert on that. I also studied John Cage, if such be possible, and his use of the two-toned shotgun, and for the groundlings, Bix Beiderbecke and Bessie Smith and Leadbelly—all, mind you, from their own libraries.

And after I had Jenkinsed the arts, I began occasionally to invent: Wishbone DiMaggio at the washboard and Moms Hargrove, the nonverbal poet, and Slats Pettigrew, the primitive without portfolio—so pure that he refuses to name his art form. What madness was this? Do I have a secret embarrassment wish? Or am I so in love with my own art that like the girl in the red shoes, I must dance myself to death?

All I know is that the tide began to turn in my second term. It started with a solemn Americanologist questioning my latest invention—Winthrop O'Toole and his chopsticks in blue; I babble of obscure Decca labels and silence him for now. But he will be laying for me next time. And in every group there now turns out to be at least one man who knows more about America than any other living person; the only thing that has saved me so far is their timidity in face of a live source.

As my accent slipped, the buzzards seemed to gain confidence. First, I felt my short *o*'s going. Then I began avoiding

187

words like *first* and *third*. My phrases were stilted and carefully planned. I was becoming a hunted man. When I asked a question at the Oxford Union in what I took to be my own accent (it was one A.M. and the joint was empty), the Yorkshireman was waiting for me outside:

"What happened to Brooklyn, you crafty booger?"

"It comes and goes," I murmured.

His face reddened (a rare thing in real life) and I thought he was going to hit me. But it must have been a trick he had, like wiggling his ears. Because he said, "Funny. So does mine, old chap," which gave me the heart to go on a little longer.

Then the trap closed from another direction. My sister came to visit. Where could I hide her? She had now become quite floridly and excessively English, gulping it down as I had my Americanness. People should not be allowed to choose these things. Even the English must have found her funny. She was saying everything but "pip, pip."

I smuggled her out of Paisley somehow, which wasn't easy, since some of the lacrosse players loutishly prowled the quad for woman visitors at all hours. "Hey Mac" (I might as well confess, I had buried Pendrid under this nickname). "Introduce me, won't you, Mac?" Panting like lap dogs: my best friends now, to an oaf.

"It's my sister Lulu," I muttered.

"What *are* you talking about, Pendrid?" Her voice pealed across Oxford.

"Yeah, sure, Lulu. Quit your kidding."

I said desperately, "Lulu's a great kidder."

The oafs were all at sea, fortunately. Prissy gave me a quizzical look. "Sorry, pardner," she said at last. "I was just putting on the dog for the folks."

Our old alliance had reasserted itself just in time. But outside on High Street she demanded explanations. "It's a game. They think I'm an American."

"Just those people? Or everyone?"

188

"Some people," I croaked. "Here and there."

"How desolately silly," she said.

"Why? It's what I want to be. You made me come back here. I *want* to be an American."

"Pen, don't be so sincere about it. Nobody made you come back. And you can't just be an American by wanting to."

"Why not?"

"It's unhealthy. You'll grow up all crooked like some sort of cripple. The Americans won't believe you, and the English won't care." She looked concerned. It was a cold day, and my eyes were watering. "Just be yourself, Pen, if you can manage it."

"And, pray, what is myself?" I said angrily. I didn't care to be called a cripple, though now I take it as my due. "Am I half-ass English? Or maybe something from Goose Bay or Labrador? You don't think *you're* English do you, Prissy? That imitation wouldn't fool a Harvard linguist."

Prissy suddenly looked doubtful. "Do you really think so?" She took my arm. "What a pair of freaks we both are. Let's have some tea."

She was the serious one then, and I was the child. Yet when we talk about it now she is all amusement. "What a lot of nonsense it all was. And do you remember the rest of that bally afternoon? Cousin Cynthia joining us for tea, and then your ghastly friend from the Midlands?" That was Tufnell, and I remember it all too well. He came over for some good Yankee palaver, chewing the fat as it were, and got, for his pains, an earful of rankest London tea-party chatter. Cynthia was at Somerville it turned out, and all her friends were at the House or Magdalen or some such.

"How did you ever wind up at a slum like Paisley?" she asked me brightly. Tufnell looked gloomily at his own Paisley tie. "Your pa-pah went to Balliol, didn't he? I know your grand-pa-pah did."

Oh, spare me this part. Tufnell's Yank is turning into a prince and I don't want to watch. But years later Prissy insists for once on picking through the bones. "Your commercial traveler friend was utterly poleaxed by Cynthia, wasn't he? His jaw flapped and his tiny eyes simply *swam.*" She goes too far. "It was all rather naughty of Cynthia. You remember what a flaming Red she was in those days? And she couldn't bear snobs. So when she spotted your man in Grain Futures, she fairly lit after him, and old-familied him to death."

I feign a smile. It is true enough in essentials. But Cynthia wasn't that good, and Tufnell wasn't that graceless. It is common for top people to assume they've routed bottom people and annihilated middle people. In fact, he behaved with more dignity than any of us.

"I thought you were American?"

"I am, sort of."

I stonewalled as long as I could, claiming not to have heard of Cousin Arbuthnot or of Farnsworth Hall, or of anything at all east of the Brooklyn Dodgers. But Cynthia was relentless; she had admired me once and was out to save me from the wrong sort of Englishman now. "Oh come off it, you old fraud. You're as English as I am. I know about your shooting box in Scotland. I know about the famous scene at White's."

My God, it was Millicent all over again. And I was suddenly one of them, tormenting an outsider. Was I enjoying it a little? Does a yogi enjoy his nails? I grinned apologetically at Tufnell but he chewed on stolidly as if nothing were happening. Please don't let him lick his fingers.

Before it ended, Prissy was loyal enough to try to help out. "Cynthia, don't be an ass. You know Pendrid hasn't got a shooting box, or anything ap*proaching* a shooting box." In that voice it didn't help much. "He really is an American by adoption, you know."

Cynthia laughed merrily. "That's like announcing you've become a Negro. Congratulations, Pen. I do mean the very warmest ones, on your new color." Dingle dangle. "So very

190

becoming," she lisped, sighed, gurgled. "It matches your tie."

Tufnell had had enough. I held my breath. He stood up OK, but then he said, "Pleased to meet you," and spoiled everything. I felt a sick delight, like a cop kicking a pervert in the balls. He deserved it, as we all do, I suppose, one way or another.

"I can't impress on you enough," said Cynthia, shaking his hand vigorously, "how incredibly English Pendrid really is. To the bone, Mr. Tufnell, to the *bone.*"

He made his way out without incident. Maybe he tripped on something, but I'm practically sure he didn't fall down the stairs.

"You shouldn't have done that," said Prissy.

"Why not? He was *awful,*" said Cynthia. "And now. Pendrid. Tell me. Why haven't you come to see me? I'm very cross."

"I didn't know you were here."

"Ah, so *that's* why you cross the street whenever you see me coming. You think I'm somebody else. Possibly a typhoid carrier." So that was it. An act of blind vengeance had been executed on poor Tufnell simply because I'd cut poor Cousin Cynthia.

"Why don't you come to the Socialist party meetings?" I counter weakly.

"Socialist?" she squeaks. "I'm far to the left of all that bourgeois muck. *I'm* with the Marxist-Leninists, the, 'ow' you say in your country? Big Banana. Yes, I'm down air wivver real workers, ducks."

Mr. Smooth fairly writhed. And enjoyed.

17

~~~~~~

I felt rotten the next day. Tufnell favored me with what was to become his standard grunt when I saw him later in the quad, until by now his sad porcine face comes to me as a mute, suffering Jesus, to add to my collection; but at the time, I didn't worry that much about Tufnell. I worried about me.

What the hell was I doing? I hadn't set out to be a fraud. Fraudulence had been thrust upon me by history. When I was a small boy, the dimmest cousins could tease and hoodwink me; I needed my aunts' jokes explained; dulled-eyed errand boys scoffed. "They're only pulling your leg, Pendrid." Who, where? My sister's meaningless laughter follows me down the years. I am still humorless, under the tinsel. Yet here I was, capering fiendishly in the world's fraud capital, reducing fat men to tears.

Well, I'd put a stop to it right now. Make a clean breast of it. Tell a few key people. Nail my pedigree to the church door. However, it isn't always so easy to phase out of fraudulence, even at Oxford. I did tell a few people who I really was, and they either didn't care (the captain of rowing most conspicuously) or they thought I was trying on a smashing new identity. Though mind you: "Chatworth, it won't really wash. Englishmen are born and not made. Besides why would you *want* to be one, and give up all your lovely dollars?" "Have it your way," said the captain of rowing. "It means balls-all to me."

Where had I heard this before? Somewhere back in the St. Boniface murk it came to me: "Still a limey prick to us." They're still pulling your leg, Pendrid. In my heavy, literal way, I was trying to get too much out of nationality, sucking at it till my face was blue. And I thought the joke was on *them*.

The clubs were empty by this time of year, as everyone had rushed for the river, where they crouched like Hindus during a plague, but the confessional fever was on me and I went to the Socialist Club anyway and poured out my mind to five or six chaps in ragged sportscoats who stared back at me blankly. The hard-nosed masochists who hung in there through the sweet May nights keeping the place open didn't remember that I came from Brooklyn, didn't care. "Suit yourself," said the president in response to my wailing retraction. "It really doesn't matter."

"But I lied about my *class*," I cried.

"Well, I daresay you wouldn't be our first member to do that." I looked around for my Yorkshireman, but he was long gone. To the ballet society, no doubt. "Now if you don't mind, we'd like to get on with something just a little meatier."

"But isn't this meaty enough for you? All the chaps who come in here juggling their pasts, their accents, their very selves? How can you have a politics of meat if people do that?"

Yes, well, very awkward this. "I must say that this would seem to be a rather personal problem of your own. The sort of thing one has leisure for in America perhaps. Most of us here are too poor to worry about our identities."

There is a gruff burble of agreement from the chaps. Even on this warm night they pull their scarves tighter against the dank air of the coal mine. Actually, they have spent all their lives in lonely libraries, being weaned away from their class and being thought sissies for their pains, but up here they are *workers*. And their accents will grow thicker every week that Oxford pulls them further from home. (See Chatworth, *Oxbridge and the Revolt Against Rising Expectations* [*The Listener,* Oct., 1968.]) I can only say they seemed fearfully authentic at the time. Everyone seemed authentic. I accepted their judgment, and anyone else's who cared to make one.

Not an American! One of my crutches is missing. I furl myself round the other. But not yet. My first reaction is to wallow in phoniness, to exaggerate it, to become the hollowest, emptiest, most alienated kid on the block. In short, to keep acting. Later I shall meet a girl at the Catholic chaplaincy. Which is awkward because I already have a girl.

But this is getting tangled and I don't see why I should straighten it out for you, you nasty little tape recorder. I've had better drinking companions than you, my friend—better listeners too. Yes, I had a little drink tonight in the safety of my hotel room. Claridge's won't snitch. Owing to some opening to the West I find myself on the Queen's goddamned honors list. How do you like them apples, Tufnell old bean? Back to England to pick up my garter or whatever. You'd drink too, you beastly little object. In fact, I'm turning you off RIGHT NOW.

Click. We return you to our studios. No one to talk to, so on we go again. I've really come to depend on you, you know that, Father? Pah! The only Father will be me, when I play the tape back and absolve myself handsomely. In fact, I plan to plunge through the screen and congratulate myself on a life well spent. But for now—you say I should do the thing with the girls, Father? Oh, all right. But let's wait till the morning, when I can remember their names and won't cry so loudly. OK, little buddy?

An MBE—Christ what an insult for a Chatworth. It's an honor just above dogcatcher and below common hangman;

194

but any honor would be an insult from those born-again Krauts. You understand, of course, that the real Queen Elizabeth used to hang Chatworths like dogs for not joining her piss-ant religion? Yeah, the Crown crapped nonstop on my people for three solid centuries, but I'll teach them. I'll *take* their damned award. I can't afford not to.

Yeah, and I know how drunks talk too. Don't I do it right, old buddy pal, huh? Upon my word, yes. Phrases for all occasions. Can also cry real tears in two languages and wet himself. Now how would you like it if I disconnected your batteries, you goddamn spy?

And a good good morning to you. I wasn't that drunk, I think; I was just trying to shake something loose: what it was escapes me. Anyway, it seems that Mr. Snead is back in town. The MBE has attracted his squinty attention. He can't wait to stand in line with all those jockeys. I only hope he doesn't do one of his mad dances and sprinkle the Queen with holy water. And it isn't just Snead, it's all of them. For instance, I thought I'd buried the quiet American, the lonely plainsman by moonlight, on the way home from the Socialist Club that night. Yet here he is again, homesteading my skull and spitting on my honors. An award from the Queen? Hot shit. Does that mean you get to lay her? Oh, just some letters after your name. I get it. That's real cute. So what with my father sneering at my *American* praises, there is really no award I can comfortably enjoy—although the Nobel Peace Prize might be OK.

Can I send a messenger? "One MBE, just sign here, mum." No, NBC wants me there in quivering person. They want to ask me afterwards what it *felt* like. Jesus. I hope they don't get Snead by mistake.

But now, two hours to countdown, we'll do the girls, the girls. In my manic phase before the unmasking, I had met my first big-league Englishwoman, an undergraduate from Lady Margaret Hall, whose great brown eyes alone could command me like a dog trainer. In those days at Oxford, the men outnumbered the women by about nine to one, and the good-looking women by infinity. So Diana was a trophy, and I only beat the competition because I thought Yankees had magic powers.

"Do you like Americans?" I ask her once just to confirm this.

"Not especially."

"Then you must at least hate them, loathe them, envy them, no?"

"Not especially," she smiles. "I think I like you, but that's rather different. It doesn't commit one to a whole continent."

Oh well, my bigotry had done the trick for me by then. My rivals, counting the odds, had dropped away in despair. To me, the best of them looked malnourished, nervous, ill-coordinated; the big ones had outgrown their bones, and such good teeth as occurred were only a front. So I went busting through like O. J. Simpson (nice chap, by the way). This was the American century, and the woolliest Rhodes scholars were making out like thunder.

So with my Yankee virility and limey know-how, there was no stopping me. I started out in the traditional Oxford way by rescuing Diana from a party. (Everybody in England wants to be rescued from parties: it's what makes the system work.) In this case, the native oafs were obviously planning to surge around her the moment she stood up, offering their clumsy services in a great roar. So I beat them to it by perching on her armchair and crooning, "Would you like to take a walk?"

She looked up calmly, appraising me at leisure, perhaps actually thinking. "Why not?" she said at last.

The oafs fell back stunned as I whisked her past them.

"That was a boring party, wasn't it?" I said, as we clattered down somebody's staircase.

"Was it? What was boring about it?"

Eh? What was this? Everybody knew that parties were

196

boring. Safest remark in the world. Was she a foreigner of some kind?

"Well, if it *wasn't* boring, why did you leave with me?"

Pause. "Curiosity, I suppose. I wondered what masterful thing you'd do next."

Nothing actually. I had no plan. Chatworth's urbanity occasionally sprang these leaks. "Pub?" I said.

"All right," she said without interest.

Silent clip-clop along Turl Street. "Can *you* think of something masterful for me to do?" I said.

"Not a blessed thing. But then, it's not my game."

We went to the Queen's Arms, where my friends stared like wolves and clamored for introductions, and she drank cider and was very sweet with them. I was quite proud of the little Sabine woman I'd thrown over my shoulder and brought here, but ashamed of my hairy-nostriled brothers.

"God knows, they're not much," I muttered.

"What's wrong with them?" she said.

"Oh, come on. Not again. Tolerance must stop some place."

"Well, perhaps, perhaps."

After that we had tea and fried tomatoes, or whatever they were serving those days, in a café on High Street, and then more clip-clop to Lady Margaret Hall where she had to be home by twelve o'clock. It seemed to be against university regulations to be masterful. Until I had my own rooms, this was the only kind of date I could have, and one passed gloomy undergraduates crisscrossing after identical evenings.

"Can I see you again?" I said at the gate.

"I think so," she said.

"What does that mean?"

"What it says. It generally does with me," she said rather tartly. "Look, I hate to be a bore, but there are complications. Do you mind? I'll let you know." She kissed my cheek and was gone like a dream. As she disappeared, I thought,

God that girl trots beautifully. It was the most ardent thought I'd had all evening, I suppose because I was watching *her* for a change.

As I raced for my own deadline at Paisley, I thought, "Did I sparkle? What did she make of Chatworth?" I assumed the complications were another guy. Some English smart-ass who chattered like a magpie. Well, I'd take him. I'd outchatter him if necessary. As I broad-jumped the cracks in the pavement, I felt some of the old St. Boniface blood pounding. "Let's get 'em, gang." You see, I wasn't always a little old man. I could be young on special occasions. You'll see, Queen.

It was typical of Diana that whatever the complications were, she disposed of them quickly and neatly. If they were another chap, she didn't leave him dangling: down he came with one snip, and up went Chatworth. There were no tear-stained ex-lovers in our wake, no sunken wrecks with half a hope. Whatever she said she must have said clearly. I did my caveman act a couple more times, dragging her into tea shops on sight or going on bracing walks (ah, Oxford), and one day she said, "Why not?"—our code phrase. The third time she said it, about two weeks later, left my knees trembling to this day.

But my confessor wants no part of smutty talk. It upsets his judgment. And he doesn't want to hear the good news either, about how innocently happy we were. There can be no defendant in the confessional, deflecting God's mercy with his puling rationalizations. There is only accusation, stripping the subject bare for the rays of Grace to strike. This is as it should be. I am a black belt at making myself look good. It is my profession. However, it's quite in order to make your *victims* sound good, as saintly as possible in fact, to highlight your own nastiness. In the Catholic world view each of us is a wharf rat surrounded by snow.

So I shall tell the story in terms of Diana's virtues, which I may exaggerate outlandishly. I am not under oath, you know.

Proceeding in this spirit: Diana was so incorruptible that I thought for a while it was a trick. She passed through the jungle book of Oxford life untouched, as if she were really being tutored the while on her father's lawn by saintly bishops. Of course, I wanted to show her off a few more times to the troglodytes who swore in their beer that you couldn't get a good woman up here, but she said, "Pendrid! You don't even like them."

I was stuck. "There's no such thing as a bore," I murmured.

"Oh yes there is, and you know it. The planet teams with them."

"Even at Axford Cahlege *England?*"

"Here's where it all begins, yes. And fans out. This isn't exactly Flahrence Idaly, you know."

"But was Florence itself really Florence?" says Chatworth, who knows his donnish prattle by now.

"Of course not," she says. "That's what literature is for."

One last try. "I thought that since you found our hosts interesting the other night, you would put up with anything," I croaked amusingly.

"Isn't that rotten luck? They *were* interesting. Do you want your money back?"

Could we be punting again? Or are we strolling through Christ Church meadows? I have developed a picture postcard mind about it. She is invariably dressed like a Henry James heroine, while I prance by her side in various regalia —cowboy hats, boaters, side whiskers, whatever seems appropriate. Why are my bad dreams so clear and sure of themselves and the good ones so thin and silly?

Anyway, I am now stuck with a beautiful girl and no one to show her to, and must make the best of it. It seems she has come to Oxford out of intellectual excitement, something that hadn't occurred to me, so I decide to try that, with grave misgivings.

Diana puts me onto literature and painting for the first time in my life (I think my father thought they were middle class)—although, again typically, she says if I want to talk music I'll have to look elsewhere. Since I had half-consciously thought of culture as a means of getting ahead, I assumed that it didn't matter which art you talked about. You either knew them all or you posed as a genial Philistine like my father and scored points that way.

A light flashes briefly into my sewer. My *mother* liked the arts—the worst examples of each. Strauss waltzes, Kipling, Murillo. That was what happened if you listened to your instincts. Disgrace. Better to fence, as I fenced now with Diana. Although she could not even understand lying, and was game for the plucking, I could only bluff so far with Proust ("I liked the part in the middle") and James or Tolstoy, so I came on as a raw youth eager to learn. It was understood I had an unspoken interest in frontier literature and the Adams family, but we didn't press it.

Remember, I am still mad and trembling with my imitations. The scene with Tufnell hasn't happened yet and I am trying on hats faster and faster. After my noble afternoons with Diana (tea at her place, tea at my place. Oxford!), I dash off to parties with new lists of atonal composers from prairie and factory (the likes of Luigi Seltzer, who actually hired a bottling plant in Kearny, New Jersey, and just let it blast away) and painters who only used white and all the pulsing excitement of America. I exaggerate the names but not the fever. I am throwing a whole lifetime of dislocation into the performance. Luigi Seltzer, *c'est moi.*

And the next day I return to my cloister, as one joins a minuet, and once again Gary Cooper takes milady's small volume in his big raw hands and says something unbelievably sensitive about it.

"I really think you have the essence, the root of the matter, Mac." (She thinks the name Mac sounds delicious in such sentences.)

"Well, shucks, ma'am, I ain't much for book learning."

We laugh and snuggle. "But seriously, Pendrid, it's exciting to see someone come to books a bit late, with some real experience of life behind him. It shows bits of the books to *me* for the first time."

"And talking of experience of life" . . . at this time I am more American than Catholic, and her acceptance of sex is so open and obvious that my moral qualms haven't time to warm up. What had been intended as an obligatory salesman's pass over the teacups glides without a snag into lovemaking. No wait a bit while I change, turn out the light, unhook this, get more comfy; no checkpoints for the inspectors, but a ski run into clear blue air. And so it remains. Either that, or a "not today," said so quickly it hasn't time to hurt. My moral defenses were bypassed like the Maginot Line; or at least I think they were. Again, I cannot remember my virtues.

Only a fellow schizoid will understand how these aesthetically purifying sessions, far from purging my heart, gave me more strength for the evening bouts of fraud. Perhaps I felt in some twisted way that I was doing it for her sake. But an alcoholic can always find an excuse for a drink. I showed off because they let me; and because lying was the *truth* about me, the performance I offered to God, and the lady.

And, of course, it was meant to be funny.

So that was my life, a fairly typical Oxford one you may say, until the Tufnell incident, at which point my passion to confess took that great incongruous leap forward. I suppose it would have happened anyway, and was for the best, but all the starch had gone out of Tufnell. No more swagger, no more colored waistcoats. Even his voice had stopped sounding like a hunting call. Shrink, shrink, shrink, like a Lewis Carroll character. In my modest way, I took total responsibility for this, and felt I must atone to someone. It was as if Tufnell had invested in the South Sea bubble. But I couldn't tell Diana. As a veteran liar, I recognized a truth virgin when I saw one, and I knew their blind horror, their sheer incomprehension upon hearing their first lie from a loved one. I learned it from Mother, as a matter of fact, when I was about six, and it had something to do with cake. I might as well have mugged the poor woman. But I must tell someone now precisely what I've been up to, to insure that there will be no more Tufnells.

Obviously the captain of rowing was a poor choice: I had counted on his morbid contempt, but not on his jeering indifference (however, it did give me an excuse to resign my oar and leave them a man short, ha ha), and the Socialist Club was not much better. Here I was, showing them a real cancer eating their society, and they preferred to talk about nationalizing marmalade. Oh well, their choice.

My last throw of the dice is an actual confession to the Catholic chaplain, a dim but courteous old fellow renowned for his meandering advice. Penitents have been known to dash off before his absolution so as not to miss tutorials.

"You say you're American, eh? Oh, you say you're *not* American."

"No, I said I'm *sort* of American." This is going to be hard to explain in whispers.

"I see. *Sort* of American. Well, that's very interesting in its way. But you know, you don't *have* to state your nationality in confession."

"No, I understand. But the thing is, I lied about it."

"Lied about *what?* Being American? That isn't so terribly serious, is it?" He realized he was guilty of levity with a troubled, possibly deranged soul. "Well, I suppose it's wrong to lie about anything at all, but honestly, I shouldn't disturb yourself *too* much over this comparatively minor offense." He sounded dazed.

"It's not that," I hiss through the wire. "It's all the lies that followed. One lie leads to another, you know, until there's really nothing else. One's whole life is a lie."

Silence, as the good man tries to cope. "It does sound complicated," he mutters. I can tell he has no mental picture, so I blunder on, using simple examples. "I mean, suppose they ask what part of America you come from and you say 'Texas.'"

"What was that?"

"Texas."

"Texas. Ah, I see."

"And they say what did you *do* in Texas." . . . ah, this is hopeless. To accommodate the old fool, I have simplified the problem out of existence.

"Look." I raise my voice. "I *became somebody else.* I lied about the soul God gave me. That's a sin, isn't it?"

The raised voice gave him the clue he needed. "That isn't Chatworth, is it? I'd know your father's voice anywhere."

Blood freezes. Great Moments in the box. My real voice when angry is my father's. All the rest are fakes. "Oh yes, yes. Knew him well. Upon my soul, haven't seen much of you, Chatworth. Yes yes, well well." I kneel, crushed, barely breathing. "Must try a bit more of the sacraments, you know. Minds sometimes get muddled up here, oh yes they do. But a little of His healing grace can do wonders . . . yes, yes, knew your father well. Marvelous man, marvelous *Cath*olic. Used to make retreats with him. He actually talked about becoming a priest. Just as well he didn't, eh? Just as well for you at any rate. Yes, next thing to a saint." I block my ears, until it's all over. When I unplug them there is silence again. Has he gone? He says, "That was a very good confession, my son. Pray for me." The fluty upper-class voice sounds impatient. I have outstayed my welcome. If Daddy had become a priest, the chaplain would have been spared this, at least. In the black stillness, God laughs till the tears come.

I wandered around town wondering whether I was forgiven, or whether my case had even been heard. I bumped viciously into some people in scarves and belted raincoats. Get your teeth fixed, all of you. This is my father speaking. Being untrue to yourself is not a sin. It is not even serious. I can get no help in the confessional, though I shall never cease trying. It is the only place I can tell the truth, but they won't listen. It's a small boy's sin at best, good for a chuckle. There's nothing for it—I shall have to try Diana. She seems in memory to have been waiting all along, and I start right in, "Bless me, Diana, for I have sinned." No, surely not. She

203

is as usual sitting by the teapot, hand raised to pour. I have always wanted to confess to a woman; it would be a more complete act. My sister would be perfect, but she'd laugh louder than anyone.

So I shoot the penitential works that night, gushing like all the fountains at Versailles, even making up new frauds involuntarily as they flash through my mind. God knows how, and by what subterranean tricks of technique, but I must have managed to sound funny and adventurous about it, because at the end she said, "How romantic, Pen. You *are* an artist."

"But I've hurt people."

"Of course."

I rallied slightly. Artist, eh? That wasn't so bad. My hands trembled over a new toy.

"And have you lied to *me?*" she asked.

"No," I lied.

That was the one that did it. But my mind wanders. Artist, by George. Why hadn't I thought of that? Roaming the streets just now, a thin mask of pain. Was that or was that not an artist? But one mustn't spoil it now by cheering up too quickly.

"I feel driven and exhilarated at the time and then sick with shame afterwards."

Her eyes glittered. My God, she was buying it. If an Englishman had talked like this, she'd have known he got it from a book. But this was Gary Cooper, the raw material of books, and he was proving the books were true.

"You're a dear," she said, hugging me to her cardigan. "My dear sweet artist." I cannot go straight if I want to.

"You don't mind lying?" I croaked.

"Not if it's done beautifully enough. Most lies are so clumsy and ugly. The others we call Art."

So now, nothing remained but to find an art for me to practice—as one picks a beau for an heiress. Tomorrow we shall go out shopping. But first, let me introduce you properly to Diana, whom I am just meeting for the first time myself. Up to now, she has been the prettiest girl in the room; and, of course, my teacher, of which I can never have enough. But today she is all I've got, so I must pay attention. Every mask in my garbage can represents a lost friend, or at least an escape. Now I am down near the skin.

Diana Godwin is fearfully bright. She will undoubtedly get a first in modern languages without breaking a sweat. In fact, she is so good she spends most of her time reading other subjects. She is also totally without vanity, which is as baffling to Chatworth as a missing feature. Perhaps women don't need vanity.

She is at least to my taste nerve-rackingly beautiful. Small, with dark eyes—oh, what's the use. Pin on the face of your choice. Outside of a fine English chest, she does not look particularly English, an excellent thing in a woman. (Plunkett jests that his partner will not cry. Snead for all his vileness is the better man.) She is really a Roman garden at dusk with a voice like bells, and that's all there is to it.

Rocked in her arms, flooded with the sense of another person, Chatworth could have sworn he had grown up. And so he had, so he had. But the world is full of ways to reverse that. Now if Chatworth the newly born artist had thrown away *that* mask too, before it hardened, and then the skintight one underneath—ah, but you're asking him to throw away his face and that's a bit much. But he is close enough tonight. He is almost real. Hail and farewell. And now I'm off to pick up my little tin star from Her Majesty.

18

I've met them all, of course: the king of Basutoland, the Dalai Lama, Tricky Dick. So don't imagine that this Hanoverian interloper cuts any ice with me. Her ancestors were grunting around the forest in Germany while mine were backing the wrong Rose; I know they later cleaned up their act and became the Windsors, but I'd know that crowd anywhere—the funniest aggregation since the Marx Brothers. "Ah Emily, let's get married. All three of us." Say, let's give her a hotfoot, Muldoon.

So why are you grinning again, Chatworth? "Well, I suppose any Englishman has to feel a little bit proud, Jack. It's one of the few remaining symbols that still means something, isn't it?" The Americans will kill me if I don't say this. I am a hostage of NBC. "Oh yes, very gracious, very gracious indeed. And *unpretentious,* of course. That's the main thing, isn't it?" I am led away babbling. "Unpretentious, oh Lord yes, unpretentious and unassuming, too." Diana's work of art has come to a pretty pass. But that was long ago and in the same country.

The rest of the summer term would bore you frightfully, Father. Nothing but conversation and innocent lovemaking and punting to magic pubs up the Cherwell. Not your sort of thing at all. Not while you're on duty anyway, squatting there in your little tape recorder. *Innocent* lovemaking? Yes, I'll swear it. She once actually commanded me to read some Henry James before meeting her, so that the two of them are still improbably entwined and I hear the bells of San Marco as I wait for my lover. And if that isn't innocent, I'll eat my cassock.

But don't worry, the snake will be along shortly and old James will be banished to his tea set. An integrated Chatworth cannot hold for long: other Chatworths stir and demand to be heard from.

"I am American, I am a Catholic"—the phrases had dropped away like "God bless Mummy and Daddy," or like the rosaries I used to say with O'Connor to the sounds of Jimmy Durante. But they had only gone underground to work up more sophisticated routines.

Omen: "You must stay in Europe forever," says Diana. "It's so deliciously decadent."

"You really go for that, huh?"

"Only when there's someone terribly nice to be decadent with. A rugged, uncorrupted American, say."

"Sorry. That sounds just too damn cute."

"Does it? I suppose that's just what a rugged, uncorrupted American *would* say. What a pity!"

The man-about-Mayfair winces. Buzz off, you tiresome plainsman. Yet I had meant it when I said it, and still do. I hate cuteness and revel in it. Lord hear my prayer.

Omen: Chatworth: "You wouldn't happen to be religious, would you?"

"I don't know yet." She always writhes earnestly in the presence of ideas. "Is that something you are or just something you'd like to be? I mean is it like blue eyes, or more like," she kissed my lids, "this."

207

I also writhe in the presence of ideas, though no one knows. "The second sounds warmer. But its chancy. I mean, supposing you don't meet the right church?"

"And how do I know when the right church comes along?"

"Stars fall on St. Peter's and you smell incense everywhere. No, you see, that's what the Catholic Church objects to. Romantic individualism. But I'm sounding pompous."

"Go on. I love it when you're pompous."

I'd been hoping, almost praying, to avoid this. It was a sin to leave someone in darkness. Yet I'd somehow worked the conversation around to a point where I had to do something. For now, I brushed it aside like a leaf. The love between us was still so intense that I could bury my head in it and forget anything I wanted to—Rome, America, the rusty voice in the box.

Finding an art for me proved more difficult than we'd expected. Classical music put my feet to sleep and museums were like torture chambers. I began to feel that, like my father, I grandly didn't see the *point* of music and painting. They seemed like vulgar middle-class additions to the main thing—life itself. "That sounds very Protestant of you," said Diana, who for all her art history never really understood aristocracy. The Chatworths were above culture. Or rather, they *were* culture. Drawings and tunes were for the servants.

I'm not a snob, but blue blood can cheer you up when all else is gone, and right now I'm reeling from a man-killing blow to my pride. We are up river in a bower of willows that would enhance even Rod McKuen, and I have played my ace, a brace of rugged verses written specially for Diana. I am confident that their stark simplicity puts them outside literary judgment; but now as I watch her struggle with her disappointment, I realize that there are standards even for stark simplicity.

"Of course, it's not my sort of thing," she says.

"I guess not."

208

She frowns as my poetic persona, No-man (some call him "Johnny Eagle") sets out West in his jalopy.

"But you're not really *like* this, you know," she says at last in raw agony. "You're not primitive at all, you're—something else."

What, what? Throw me a bone, a fragment of compliment.

"Perhaps you're something new and there isn't a voice for you yet. Perhaps you're trying to borrow one." Nurse presses my hand soothingly—"*You're* so much better than your poems," she says, leading me grinning into a fresh tiger trap. If I am so much better than my work, there must be some inherent quality in me. And since my rotten cousin Cynthia has just reminded me of my ancestry, I reach blindly for that.

Well, I had to do something. Diana was infinitely brighter than I, and she had culture by the throat. She could have paralyzed a less resourceful man. The louts at the college bar frequently snarled their opinions about these brainy girls, who obviously terrified them. For all their own intelligence, half the guys at Paisley were paralyzed by the female kind and so talked with brutal swagger of subduing it with "a yard of this." "They'd rather read about it anyway." "That's because they never had it," etc. I at least did not do that. I was already on to these pale-faced clerics who talked like coal miners and Latin lovers in their sanctuaries. My acts were always better than that.

But a man must fill himself with something, and ineffable worth lay to hand. If Diana the art-goddess worshiped me, I must be in some sense an art object myself. So while I take my time finding my voice (please, her eyes begged, no more poems), I will make my life my art. Well, OK.

I swear it was not calculation but mere good chance that made this my most useful decision to date. Up to now, I had been dashing off broad parodies of myself like a street cartoonist, but Diana taught me to plane and smooth them all and blend them into a single Self that I could take anywhere. Thus my raw American had been a gag for English consumption, but there was a real Americanness in back of it that *just* might work. Not a lonesome man on a horse, that couldn't even fool an Englishman for long, but something perhaps from the New York area. Over here, Manhattan sophistication seemed as tough and crackling as Chicago machine guns, so I didn't have to give up my hard-man image, just dress it in a dinner jacket. And then my innate Englishness, in dry ice since the twenties and thirties, could complement it perfectly like a splash of handkerchief or the right cuff links. As such, I was a prewar luxury item that could almost be advertised in the *New Yorker*. While, beneath all that, she saw sturdy and plain an English recusant family, immune to fashions, playing with them, transcending them. God, she thought *I* was an artist.

Diana, with her literary sensibilities on fire, set to work like a tailor making this new fellow real. She did not do it explicitly, but more as one would guide a deaf person through a maze. She signaled with little smiles and nods when I was on the right track, or with the most delicate disappointment when I slipped into one of my old routines. Her eye for the genuine would have opened a safe, and by the end of summer term I was so genuine that I was a *complete* fake, a restoration, a fraud of world class.

But I was real to her, her lovely work of art, and I was real to me, and at the end of term we went to all the college balls we could manage and drank toasts to George Eliot and the Tradition and danced the Charleston (God knows how, but she even did that well) and floated with luminous fatigue through floodlit gardens. Again the good is interred in picture postcards. All my selves came together with a bang in my first tailcoat. Leaning against a mantelpiece, glass in hand, cracking wise—this was my definitive statement. A free spirit at ease in the family uniform. Not the best Englishman nor yet the best American, but the two together, *voilà*.

At some point, almost too groggy to speak, I muttered the word "love" for the first time and she said, "Why yes, of course." As we embraced, she said, "You Americans are so slow." And this was true. The word "love" had great weight for me then; it was like saying God's name out loud.

"You really mean it, don't you, Pen?"

"Oh yes."

"My precious humbug." She squeezed me. "My darling fraud. You'll never know how real you really are."

This was true too. I never will. A day or two after that we were standing together on the platform of crushed dreams on the down side of Oxford station and she said, "I suppose by next term it will all be different. Never mind."

"Why do women always say things like that?"

"It's our insurance policy. Our painkiller. But I won't regret anything, ever. I promise."

Ah, you little stoic. Her eyes didn't even mist over, mine did. Bless these women for their toughness. They will need it against Chatworth. I'm sure I mumbled "never" and "darling." But I couldn't shake a tear out of her any which way.

The point was, we were not going to meet during the summer. She was going to Germany on some student thing, and I had promised to go to Italy with my mother and sister. Why didn't I chuck that? Something passive and cautious in me perhaps. In the Black Forest, my flabby personality, which was all highlights, would have been rearranged in some new way by Diana. She knew the language and Europe was her playground. I must go off somewhere first and become an equal.

But with my mother and sister? It couldn't be helped. After a brief round of jaunty widowhood, "doing the things I always wanted to," Mother had lapsed back into a leaky helplessness. Like me, she had been propped up invisibly by my father and now flopped like a cushion without him. And she always seemed to land on Prissy, who had once again been forced to postpone her dream of living alone. "You *must* come," Prissy had wired. "I can't stand it by myself."

I passed this on to Diana, and she didn't answer, except

211

for that slight tensing of the lips that said, "You're wrong." For the sake of love, mothers and sisters must die. A man of quality would know that. That's why she knew that next term would be different. If Pendrid the art object planned to spend the summer as housemaid, it was no defect in him: he just didn't love her, that's all. He had used the word under duress of booze and moonlight; but if he had really meant it, he would come with her, now.

How did I know all that? Because she had taught me so well. I knew the ways of the heart inside out by now. So picture Chatworth, eyes streaming, waving through the window at his dry-eyed sweetheart as the train lurches out.

Forget her, eh? I might be flabby, but I'm stubborn. I made a vow that I would still love her in October. And I kept it in my fashion.

But first, down to Rome with Mum and Sis, cursing myself for a big baby, and sullen with the two of them as only a baby can be.

"You might as well have stayed home," said Prissy as I pouted around the *pensione* the first night. But Mother seemed glad to have me in whatever form I took, and she kept throwing me shy little smiles until my nerves screamed afresh. She would do anything right now to keep us both around—crawl, beg, whimper. For this I had given up my love.

Oh well. I remembered the fine mature person I'd become in Diana's arms, and tried to think instinctively what he would do. Well, he would certainly not let his family make him childish again. And he would not mistake being a brat for being a stormy romantic. In fact (and this was the hard part), he would not even have to think what he would do— he would know. So I knew.

It's only now that I see the fiendish acrobatics of all this. And only now that I realize how much I needed to impress Prissy. I wanted to show her I was learning things about life that she would never learn, outgrowing her and outdeepen-

212

ing her: not realizing that we were jumping together in the same sack.

So I told Prissy I was sorry to be a pill, but that I'd left someone behind. And she said, "You too? Ah, what we Chatworths sacrifice on the altar of family love. Only it's a bloody great pyre in our case, isn't it?"

We became sort of friends again on that, though I was committed to the idea that she was superficial. We tried to do Rome together, leaving Mum to knit endless scarves and blankets (she couldn't turn corners, but simply abandoned things after a while and gave them names). But Priscilla was indeed superficial. She thought the old churches were monuments of superstition.

"But they're beautiful," I pipe.

"Oh yes, that," says she. "How many people died to build them?"

"If you really cared, you'd know," I said. (My history tutor, Mr. Short, used arguments like that a lot; he felt they were invaluable in examinations.)

"Starved and toiled for a God who was planning to boil them in hell for not coming here every Sunday."

Where to begin? Her view of the late Middle Ages wasn't worthy of a crackpot Marxist on a streetcorner.

"It's like Daddy's funeral," she went on. "I don't know if you followed all the rigmarole, but do you realize they spent half the time apologizing for the poor man's sins? Daddy!" She sobbed. "The kindest man who ever lived."

"*He* would have understood," I said. And suddenly, so did I. My perfect father went to confession every week of his life. He knew the score. Here in St. John Lateran feelings swell and soar grandly. My father—almost a saint, except that it would have been pushy—knew that envy and spite and malice were the air we breathed, and that you had to confess them again and again like washing your hands. But how to explain this to a part-time second-hand rationalist?

"You can have these rotten places," said Prissy, her feel-

213

ings also soaring. "I'm going back to keep Mummy company. While she's still alive and sinning."

After that I did Rome by myself, tramping till my feet bled, or so it felt, from church to church, in love with God again in each shattering rendezvous. The thought of Diana fit this mood symphonically: she had opened my heart and made a spiritual life possible. I wrote and told her so, and she wrote back to say she was glad she'd given me that at least, and to be sure to get to Florence. The letter was cooler than I'd hoped, but my mood promptly exalted it like organ music. "I'm glad I've given you that." Shazam. "I've given you that." Blablam. Her face appeared in every fresco, as virgin and mother and angel.

Well, that would be a problem. We had been sinners, there was no getting round it. We'd have to work out something about that. I felt in my heart that God would forgive something so beautiful, but the priest I made the mistake of confessing it to sure as hell didn't. I hadn't hit the box since Oxford, where the chaplain affected not to hear sexual sins out of sheer good manners, so I had a false sense of security. By ill chance, I spotted a confessional that said "English spoken" and I plunged in on one of my ungovernable pious surges. "English spoken" probably just meant "How mucha time, how mucha sorry? That'll be ten lire." But no, it seemed to be an American in there to judge from the glasses. Ouch. Purity, the Blessed Mother, The Book. Too late to get out.

He listened silently, while I broke the rules and said it was really love this time (fancy telling that to an American!) and that in my heart I didn't feel guilty and all the stuff Clarence Darrow would have said on my behalf. When he finally spoke it was in a quiet, educated voice (probably some damn Bible student) and he spared me hellfire and the Blessed Virgin and went straight to the point.

"Do you intend to stop?"

"I don't know."

214

"Well, I'm afraid I can't give you absolution until you make up your mind." We paused as if I could do this on the spot. "Do you want to try to stop?" he asked helpfully.

"Yes and no."

"Of course. That's right. But I'm afraid I can't give you a 'yes and no' absolution, can I?" As one tourist to another he was more expansive than I'd bargained for. "Cruel as it sounds, you will simply have to choose between your love of Christ and your love of this girl. You must also decide whether your love of this girl is as pure as you think it is, and whether it will remain so after you cut yourself off from Christ and His sacraments. The greatest human loves are indeed beautiful, a gift from God, but the worm is usually in them from the start." I peered in at the pale face, not much older than mine. What did *he* know? "And you must ask yourself if you're acting in the girl's best interests even now. Consider what happens if your love weakens for even a moment, say a year from now. And then one day you walk into a beautiful church such as this one and you find God still waiting, and you say, 'Now, now I must end it.' " By George, he was dramatizing. His neutral scholar's voice had even taken a slight Irish turn. Had he once been in such a situation himself? "You'll say, 'Now that it isn't quite so difficult, I'll do it,' and then where will she be, my friend? A year older and a year wiser." Ah, he'd only heard about it. They must get a lot of soap operas in the seminary. And novels about nurses.

"I'll think it over," I said stiffly.

"And I'll pray for your soul," he shot back.

Well, Diana certainly deserved better than that. St. Peter's seems for a moment cold and hostile, an Oriental bazaar full of gewgaws for the Big Potentate upstairs. Diana is small and alive and not some big slab of gold offered to the Grand Vizier and his eunuchs. I will put my faith in her, and trust God's famous mercy.

A spark of rebellion, eh? Just part of my well-rounded

character. While I'm shaking one fist, the other is calculating. In twenty years Diana will be fat and living in Capri, or skinny and living in Venice, and God will still be here. I don't know what to think. There must be some way to bring all this beauty together.

Naturally, I wrote this in full to Diana, and she answered, "I'm not your conscience, darling, and I'm not your mother. Why don't you and Father Goodbody decide my fate between you?"

Oh God, this was going too fast. I was not being a person of quality in these letters, and I had been refused absolution. I was losing in both worlds; I was twenty years old and sinking.

Meanwhile, Prissy has taken to sitting on the Via Veneto with my mother, looking at the movie stars and wallowing in superficiality. "Come out of the morgue, Pen, and join the land of the living. Isn't that some gorgeous hunk of Spam?" she says of some passing lizard in dark glasses. Her vengeance licks me like a whip. "This is the real Rome, Pen. It's all there is." My mother smiles appealingly through the sacrilege. It's so nice to have you with us again, Pen.

I do the churches once more and they tear at my guts. God can't see you today. He has a perfectly splitting headache. You seem to have offended Him in some way. Although I walk from front to back, I seem to be outside. Doors are closed on me. They won't let me in my own home.

I write to Diana to say I must have her, bad Catholic or no, and she answers, "Please don't do that. I still love you, dearest, but I refuse to be somebody's crisis of conscience. You know, I loved another Catholic once [not a pale priest with glasses?] and it's just too exhausting. So why don't we forget each other for now, and you make your confessions and enjoy your Rome (and I'm *so* glad you enjoy it) and we'll see if there's anything left to talk about in the autumn." The postscript, written later to judge from the ink, said, "Believe it or not, I admire your great cruel Church, and I even once

216

thought of joining it. So I'll respect your decision whatever it is. But don't ask me to sit still on my rack while you make it. Actually, I'm having a rather super summer myself."

Still no tears. Cry, damn you. And how dare you ask me to be a grownup at my age?

So I kneel and pray and curse and love my churches and my love. Looking back, I believe that either decision would have been virtuous. The only sin was the one in the middle. So Chatworth steers straight for that.

"I'm glad you love Rome so much," says my mother. "Your father and I had some wonderful times here."

Her heart reaches out to me, and I'm old enough to know it, but I feel nothing. Later, when she's truly old and impregnable, I would do anything for her. But she doesn't want anything now. As the Good Book says, you only get one shot at these things. "I was sick and you visited me not." That summer when her wound reopened was the summer she needed me, but I had other fish to fry. I had a great big broken heart of my own.

Well—Prissy wasn't much better. In her fury at being here at all, she grew more and more blasphemous about the flocks of pie-faced priests and nuns in the streets, and her mockery became gross and provincial, as if she'd never had a day's instruction. "A Church of the dagos, by the dagos, and for the dagos," she'd say, presumably to madden Mother. But Mum didn't seem to care so long as she had company. And Prissy at least provided that, day after long day.

Naturally Prissy is now back in the Church as part of her lifelong retreat from life, but that's strictly between her and Daddy. It's no affair of mine. When I ask her about that summer, she is slyly reticent in the family manner. "I suppose I was awful, I generally was. But you were pious enough for two. And you did go on about the art work. You! Art work!" she laughs.

She is right. I took the super soul that Diana had given me and forged it into a hammer with which to smash her skull.

217

But she expected that. "Rome has a terrible effect on Catholics. They're never the same." Did she say that, or do I read it in her dark eyes as the train pulls eternally out of Oxford?

Anyway, I Jenkinsed Italy like mad and was an aesthete to the fingertips as we rolled through Tuscany and Umbria. Only, my real art remained life itself, whether in the green terraced hills, shaped for the sacrament of wine, or in the churches where a piece of bread sat shrined in gold. I remember a luminous ardor as I stared at those hills, my heart fairly bursting from my chest—but it's better to put this down to animal spirits than to think it meant anything. Otherwise the betrayal would be too frightful.

In Assisi, my religious glands slopped over, and my heart hopped across the cobblestones with St. Francis and quivered to the simplicities of Giotto, before art got so damn smart. Surely, I thought, art was worship, nothing more nor less; otherwise it was idolatry. Maybe Diana had this all wrong. Making a God of art was precisely the decadence she admired so much about Europe and which made her a small glass figure, a perfect reproduction of a miniature. But I had found life itself, right here in this old Church, fresh and eternal. I love it when I'm pompous.

Tararaboomdyay. If I had found it, why didn't I keep it? The Dianas of this world still totter to their museums. But the boy mystic has not been heard from since.

Sincerity is no excuse. Ignore those throbbing wattles. What I was really doing was covering up my aesthetic deficiencies with top-notch super-soul tactics. It was the perfect Jenkins approach to catching up on the art world. I had something even Diana would never have: an instinct for the *whole* truth. Which is a terrific thing to have if you don't know anything in particular and are too lazy to learn.

By the time we reached Florence, I was getting quite severe with poor absent Diana. She had insisted too much on this town, but I saw in a twinkling that it was nothing but Beauty. It didn't have the rich, profligate heart of Rome or the purity of Assisi but was slick and heartless and ready for Ronald Firbank. Diana was paying dear for dominating me and making me over in her image. To ward her off, I would even adopt the peasant rags of my mother. I was closer to God that way. The gutter rat knows a lot of ways to beat you.

At that, the Uffizi almost did me in. The religious paintings were so gorgeous that I had to remind myself repeatedly that they were just a convention: this was cash art now, commissioned by sleek patrons in the wool trade, and not the fresh outpourings of some unspoiled heart.

Sentimentality is my most repulsive feature, and as my ratings show, I've made a bundle from it. If this were some puling twenty-year-old we were considering, we might forgive him. But, unfortunately, it is vintage Chatworth. I can still do it. My voice sobs at famines and injustice and purity of heart. I cry over Ulster and Bangladesh and Grandma Moses. In that mood, I have even threatened to destroy these tapes, for the lying trash they are.

But I have to keep the tapes in order that the real Chatworth, who is a pretty good egg, may live and flourish. If I couldn't do this dirty little thing, his mind would crack. That is why one preserves tapes.

After a week in Florence, I found that Diana's aspect had changed quite drastically in my mind. She had withered and become old; she was my art teacher now, my crone. I almost dreaded seeing her again. Yet I couldn't let her smug prophecy about the summer come true. Again and again I took her picture from my wallet: she was as young as ever and lovely and not trying to dominate me in the least, merely to pass on her own joy. Her only crime, like my father's, was wanting me to be first-rate. Hah! We'd see about that!

Oxford looked different when I got back: an old Catholic city under the skin, Rome in English clothes, a suave hybrid like myself. It was mine as much as anyone's to claim if I wanted it. There was no need for games. I postponed Diana a few days and plunged into Catholic activities, on the grounds that I was praying to make a decision about her. The chaplaincy was an outpost of "my people," where we flung our defiant credos at the sky. The Reformation hadn't beaten us; the Church of England had come and gone, and rationalism had reasoned its skinny self to death, and here we were fresh as a May morning bellowing the same songs (I assumed they were the same) as the monks who built the place.

I hadn't looked too closely at my fellow "people" yet. If I had, their pale good sense might have shaken me some. But Chatworth with a new image is like a blind man. My people could have been stuffed and mounted for all I cared.

Even sex may be suspended for a Catholic in this state. Unbelievers will never understand this—how a lifetime of holy exultation can make chastity a pleasure. Under the sly urging of Oxford, with its hundred atmospheres and voices, I even gave some thought to a celibate vocation. It would certainly be up to Diana's standards of first-rateness. And besides, this was no world to bring Chatworths into. My father could barely stand the sight of *his* world, and it was getting worse. I was here to close the shop and put out the lights.

I am driven to thinking beautiful thoughts in churches, which makes them particularly dangerous. A vocation to intermittent chastity can be a public nuisance, and after about a week, I got a note from Diana saying, "Well?" I had no particular plans for her at present. My prayers for a decision had not been answered, for the good reason that I didn't want a decision. I was having too much fun praying for one.

"I told you it wouldn't last," she said when we met at last in some damn café after pub closing. "Summer term is basically unfair. It's like the Riviera. Or shipboard. Love affairs really don't count. One has the most awful hangover."

"It's not that," I said, stung. It was I who had cried on the train platform four months ago, if only to get *her* to cry

Leaving her now made me look like a perfect fool. "It's something else."

"Yes, it usually is."

"No, it's what I wrote you about. God and all that." Feeble.

She looked annoyed. "Yes, well, if it really is 'that,' and 'that' means more to you than my love, then I can only honor you as a spiritual giant and beseech you to get out of my life immediately." My glass miniature sounded tougher than I remembered. But they came. Tears at last. A little something for the sadist. Why didn't I just leave her at that moment?

Because of the tears, of course. I loved her suddenly as much as ever, and there was a happy flooding of my own heart at the thought of my rottenness. I couldn't very well let her cry alone.

"Make believe we're drunk," I mutter. Her face is against mine, drenching it and being drenched right back. She hiccoughs and giggles. "My dear, sweet, spiritual giant," she whispers. There is something vulgar and wanton about her, as if wine were dripping down her chin. Doll Tearsheet. She knows who's on the side of life around here.

A cracked chapel bell goes off in the distance and an old abbot swears for the thousandth time he's going to fix it. I'm hers, for the time being.

19

Mother just phoned to congratulate me on my MBE. "I never know where you are," she said, making two of us, "until I read the papers."

I know where Mother is, but I don't trade on the information.

"Of course," she went on, "you know that your father was offered a KBE for his work in World War II, but he refused it. He said it wasn't his style—didn't match his tie or something of the sort. You know how he was."

Quite. Chatworth RC should be good enough if you *must* have letters after your name. Rum Protestant practice, to make up for not having saints, I suppose. . . . But does Mother know that she's making things worse? A KBE is something *worth* turning down: it's built to the scale of a gentleman. An MBE is something you find in a cereal package. Look—is there anywhere I can dispose of this thing? NBC, BBC, *help* me. Meanwhile, let it be said that Mother lives triumphantly by herself in London now, while the rest of us beat our heads against her façade. And Chatworth RC,

MBE, faces life, and the succulent ghost of Diana, drifting spectrally back to her digs on a misty October night in 1949.

These battles are not so easy to win, whatever St. Augustine tells you. But for a time that night it did all seem to flow together—the pent-up juice of our summers, Art and God, Germany and Italy, our own little axis. We dined off each other as if what each had learned was exactly what the other needed. Diana wanted Rome to warm up her Siegfried and her Lorelei; and I needed the Black Forest to blow a cold clean wind through my churches, rattling my monsignors. Done and done. We said it with our bodies and our minds and we wrote it on the windowpane, yes yes yes, *si* and *ja*

"Wanna become a Catholic?" I drawled.

"If you promise it won't be *too* much like school."

"I'll do my best."

She had changed. There was a wild dirty grin that hadn't been there before, like a Bavarian barmaid's; and as she rolled and plunged over me, she *talked* dirty for the first time. Super summer indeed: she must have spent it with the boiler crew of the *Bremerhaven*.

However, that was just for sex. Afterwards, she was as demure as ever, the only woman I've ever known who could look as modest in her nakedness as a little girl dressed to the chin.

"I realized when I got your letters—and I know there's no way of saying this that won't annoy you; forgive me, dearest —that you were much younger than I had thought." I am annoyed, of course. Embarrassed to be found out. Relieved to be found out.

"I mean you're so incredibly poised in person, but your letters were so adolescently earnest, the way Americans are *supposed* to be. Now I *am* annoying you, aren't I?"

"Mother told me never to be serious around English people. I won't make that mistake again."

"I mean, showing me around your latest feelings like a

223

freshman showing off his rooms. Asking my advice. Next year all the furniture will be rearranged, I daresay."

There was the bitterness again, coming and going like a radio wave band. I had obviously disappointed her terribly. Even my handwriting was too childish for a great man.

"Why didn't you just give me up?" I asked. "And put me back in my cradle."

"Believe me, I thought of it." She was rocking my head gently, as if to say, don't take this too seriously, it just has to be said. "But I decided I'd been approaching you all wrong. I'm quite young myself, really, and I'd been looking for a hero. Wasn't that silly of me?"

I believe I groaned. Surely I was just the thing for someone looking for a hero?

"So I read your letters again and decided to treat you just like the other men I've known. You're still pretty good on those terms." She reached down and patted. What pagan nonsense was this? I was tired now, and fretful.

"Was there someone in Germany?" I croaked.

"None of your business, I'm afraid." She stood up, and even her bottom had a knowing sway that I hadn't seen before. "I shouldn't have proposed myself as a China doll. We were both very silly."

Old Nanny Oxford took a hand at this point. Diana had to dress fast and get back to her college; and I had to explain her to my new landlady. The walls of the kindergarten were closing around us once more.

"I'm sorry I disappointed you," I said, as she ducked for the door.

"It's all right. I'll get over it." She gave me a broad, coarse kiss and said, "I must dash."

I was the one who wanted to dash, but I had to sit there on my tousled bed in a clump of poisonous thoughts. I saw now, with all the wisdom of St. Thomas Aquinas and Dr. Watson combined, how my pompous letters had broken the heart of a child. I pictured her crying for days (all my women

224

cry behind my back) before reaching desolately for some skiing instructor, and learning to smirk and curse in flawless German. She had been too delicate to last, I guess—but why did I have to be the one to spoil it? Chatworth had corrupted the most perfect thing he would ever meet, by dint of sheer mediocrity. The same damp little self-importance that had made a fool of him at St. Boniface and points east had done it again.

But a cad has no business feeling sheepish. If I was such a destructive force, why did I seem so small to myself now? Face it. Because I had made a fool of myself with those letters, and the overeducated slut had witnessed it. An ego regrouping itself is a horrible thing to see. What had I done that was so wrong? I had exposed my innocence to the English again. And what had she done? My body was sore from our lovemaking, and hanging from it, my soul. I was appalled and terrified by certain initiatives she had taken with her silver tongue. They could keep their stinking maturity over here.

Homesick for God knows where, I fell on my knees and prayed. Diana was not a bad girl. I had made her think I had wanted lust; I *had* wanted lust. The evil was in me, no mistake. I prayed for her to reclaim her naked modesty. I would help her with my own sheer will power. In my current whacked-out condition, this did not seem impossible. I slept in that position, my tail toward heaven for the angels to mock.

Time, of course, heals these things at comical speed when you're twenty, and in a couple of days my dreams dripped sweetness and I was ready for more. I went to Sunday Mass, the worst possible place in my condition. With a slight twist, religion becomes again an occasion of sex. The bell at the consecration is like a fire alarm. The word is made flesh—no, no, go back. Be a word again. Desperately I call for help but Beelzebub answers the phone and breathes into it heavily.

225

I rushed for the fresh air, bowling over ghostly communicants, and raced for Diana's college in a trance. I was in hell and she was the fire exit.

By chance, this was one of the magic hours when women were allowed to receive men in their rooms, and I burst into Diana's bower with all its books and its prints and I kissed her savagely and said, "We've got to stop doing this."

No, I couldn't have been that silly, even then. I mean, I didn't kiss her savagely, I'm sure, but more like a football coach. Then I held her at arm's length with a sad smile, and saw that she was blazing. "What do you mean 'we'? Who are you to make these decisions for me?" Had I aroused her somehow?

"Suppose *I* like doing this?" she said. "Suppose I say we've got to *continue?*" Her brown hair swung like a bell. "Am I allowed even one vote in this?"

"I don't know what to say. Do as you like."

She reached for one of her rare cigarettes and sucked it in half. "Why did I have to find another Catholic? You're all quite mad." She drew again and the cigarette was gone, or so it seems. "All right," she said, "we won't do this. I can live without it. In fact, if you're going to call this 'this,' I'm not even sure I want to do it. *But please stop torturing me.*"

Again my notes are confused. I had been sent on a grownup's errand and felt I should try to talk like one. So I murmured, incredibly and meaninglessly, "Marriage?"

She shook her head again. "You're really too much for me, Pen. That's the way you propose to a shopgirl who wants an abortion. Please just go away now and leave me alone."

Note how the masterful techniques I've acquired over the years come to a head in this scene. Grotesquely, I am riven by lust at her anger. Her body is electric. And one powerful emotion is much like another.

The Devil is working on his masterpiece, the ultimate Chatworth fiasco, clearly Old Nick's life dream, but Diana

226

must sense this, because she screams, "Just get out!" and I jerk my way through the door like a silent-screen comedian.

Chatworth can take it. I decide to sublimate with greatness. Theater, politics, wherever a great man is needed. But what's this? It doesn't seem as easy as it did last year. My loss of status in Diana's eyes has sapped my strength. The English twits that I once despised seem like overpowering rivals—intelligent, virile, viciously charming. Last year, as a vain child, I handled them with ease; but as an embryonic adult, I pad the streets like a dwarf, peering up at everybody.

One night I sign on to speak at the Oxford Union and find my palms sweating before I reach my seat: the level of wit is intolerably high, with all those future prime ministers Father had told me about blasting from the hip; but that isn't the problem. It suddenly comes to me in this palatial beer garden that I don't have a style anymore. As I wait my turn, I can't find a voice to go with my jokes. American or English, fast or slow, fat man or thin—I can't place myself in any category at all. What sort of height am I, for instance? I mean, deep down?

On all sides, the English have sharp, fixed faces like characters in old political cartoons, and voices to match. I have a face like bubble gum and no voice at all. I have washed away the blueprint by painting over it too often. Mercifully, the joint empties, as if everyone is moved by my embarrassment, and I have no one left to please but the last glassy-eyed patrons and a few talent scouts looking for yet more prime ministers and lords of the woolsack in the night.

My styleless voice bounces off the empty rows and comes back to me; and I choke with terror. It is the most godawful sound I have ever heard. This is not the no-voice I'd been hearing in my head; rather, it is every voice I've ever encountered: Philadelphia and Jersey Irish and county English and East End whore, like a thousand mimics screaming into one

227

tube. Since I am too weak to play tricks, I assume this is my real voice at last, crawling splayfooted from its cave. I must hide it somehow. I can't expose other people to this. I hurry on and somebody out there groans. I understand perfectly, sir. It must be awful for you.

I know what it is to feel foreign, but I have never felt inhuman before, trapped like this in an animal language all my own, too loathsome for civilized company. Even my few jokes sound evil and insincere like jokes in hell. Clearly the owner of this voice has never really been amused by anything.

I left the building in silence, avoiding people like a leper and lurching home by back roads with my cloak over my face. Perhaps Snead was born that night, called forth by the sound of his own voice. Perhaps all my people were. Of course, I've since learned that many of us have the same reaction the first time we hear ourselves speak and it's nothing to fuss about; but few of us can have more than one level of deceit to get used to; I had a symphony that night.

I hadn't realized how much I had lived by voices and how much I had counted on my own to be perfect, and not this guttersnipe amalgam. Shattered, I knelt by my bed again like a Giotto figure and prayed to have my sores blessed and my voice forgiven. I couldn't even confess to anyone, because no priest spoke my language. I could only point to my throat and grunt, "Here, here's my sin."

The next day I got a note from Diana saying she couldn't get me out of her system, which almost started me off again. "Welcome to Cancer City, my good woman," said the great false voice, Muldoon and Daddy down in the sewer together. "Everything's up to date here, as the song says." Yes, I would just do voices from now on, more and worse ones; I'd get my own transmission set and spew them over the landscape like king's vomit. If all else failed, I'd write novels.

But then, the Lord heard my prayer and sent a messenger in the form of a solemn, familiar-looking fellow with a gold

228

mustache, who stood at the foot of my stairs and spoke as follows: "I'm Hoskins from the Labour Club. We were wondering if you'd like to speak for us." I stared down at him as he stumbled eternally toward me, tripping on each stair, over and over. "I heard you the other night and you were really quite good, you know. At any rate, the Tories didn't much like it." Tories? Had I attacked the Tories? My jokes were so garbled, they might have attacked anybody.

Hoskins stood panting at my level. "May I come in a moment? Yes, we need good strong speakers like you. And we need *funny* speakers like you. Not facetious ones, mind you—Lord spare us any more lightweights. There was real honest-to-God irony in your speech, and I sus*pect* [delicate pause] real feeling, too."

I fumbled with my little silver teapot. I had never known what to do with it. Being totally beyond speech, I threw him a strong-looking nod.

"You'll excuse my asking," he said, "but are you by any chance Canadian?"

Strong-looking headshake. I wasn't going to add Canada to my portfolio. "Spent time in the States," I muttered.

"Ah, that's it. That's why your humor has so much more force than ours." He fingered his mustache. "God, how I loathe *whimsy.*"

I was still fumbling with my teapot when he left. Between clenched gums, I'd agreed to think it over. But he couldn't fool me. Even for flaying the Tories my voice was a fake—a library of fakes, in fact. Every pose, every shrill act of faith had stuck there, until it was my own portrait of Dorian Gray. I couldn't say "hello" without filling the air with lies and exposing myself beyond repair.

And yet, and yet. Liked it, did he?

Not right away, I swear to God. I didn't come round to my voice without a struggle, but attempted to talk for a while in such a quiet neutral tone that when Diana came round demanding a showdown, she thought I'd hurt my jaw.

"Have you had a tooth pulled, or what?"

I hadn't meant it to be that neutral. "I guess I don't like my voice much," I said apologetically.

"Pen, you're quite mad," Diana laughed. "So I suppose you've decided to trade it in for a new one, like a good American. Do you mind telling me what's wrong with it? Personally, I think it's one of the few unquestionably nice things about you. In fact, it's probably the principal reason I let you take me home that ill-fated night."

You'll note that her style with me is harsh now, almost contemptuous. She has come here because she can't help it, but that is all. There is no respect left, no admiration. This, as a French aphorist might say, is not unflattering.

But the cheap crack about Americans showed a vulgar streak I hadn't noticed before. It runs through some English people like anti-Semitism, and even after prodigious displays of tolerance, it squeaks out like a fart. So—perhaps *I* had overrated *her* last year; out of mutual misunderstanding, we had created a god and goddess. Which, *mon ami,* is why people travel, no?

Where did that leave us? No question of love, of course. There was nothing left to love. I could see ugly hints of intelligence in her mouth, defacing the old loveliness. Her thoughts were not angelic illuminations, but just those of a smart little skirt going about her business. We were, in fact, two clever people on the make, among hundreds of such at Oxford. Well?

She wasn't really that either, but perhaps she thought it was what I wanted. Or all I deserved. *Who knows?* I do know that she said she loved my voice, and started me on the awkward road to loving it myself. It so happened that she knew somebody in a recording studio, and in no time I was standing there listening to the monster again, gagging over it like a kid with his first whiskey, trying, trying to like it.

It was still horrible, but perhaps not *quite* as horrible as before. Imagine David Frost and Norman Mailer put to-

gether, and you still haven't got it. "Lovely and original and
sexy," purred my temptress, Diana. "How did such a dreadful man acquire such a divine instrument?"

Hold my hand, dearest. I can never make it without your
help. "Sexy, intelligent." Yes, yes. She means it; she is not
like Millicent. I am green, I can tell, and trembling. The little
prig at St. Boniface is in there. I can hear him distinctly, and
behind him the other little prig who wants to fight the Germans single-handed, and laid on top are all the swaggering
tough guys and smoothies of my lying heart—and they are
still in there, by the way. Because the voice I am hearing is
pretty much the voice you all know and love, the one that's
talking now. Monty Chatworth, your host for the evening.

That's it. My voice *is* my confession, Father. It's all there.
What need have I of sins? That must be why I'm doing this.
Talking it all away. Now what I have to do is join a Trappist
monastery and take a vow of silence. . . .

"Darling, I think George would like to close now," says
Diana. How long have I been here? Days and days. A lifetime. Twenty minutes? "You certainly are a glutton for punishment if you really hate it so much," she says, echoing
O'Connor and the mirror. Echoes and mirrors, my life story.
Could even Narcissus have coped with a second interest like
that?

"The sheer horror fascinates me," I say weakly. For I have
taken the first faltering steps. Yes, there's something in there
I like. Even Dorian Gray would have found something kind
of cute in his picture given time. My love affair with my voice
is about to begin.

Slowly and blindly. The heart is stealthy, even in matters
of autoeroticism. Diana is again my procurer, lasciviously
devising a new hero for me out of my dirty old pipes, all else
having failed. Amazing woman, destroying and creating. But
they all did that in those days. We called them devils and
saints quite arbitrarily.

231

Why did *she* do it, in particular? Because, to get my attention, she had to hold up mirrors. This one arrived in the nick of time, just as her magic had gone. I simply had to love the first girl who loved my voice. The look of intelligence vanished, she had no more need to calculate, and we were once more two grinning lovers in a looking glass shaped like a heart. Note the improvement, the growth in Chatworth. I had loved the gawky Millicent for one vague compliment. Now I demanded precision. State your reasons for loving this person. State them over and over.

And now, as I talk, no reasons seem good enough. My wastebasket brims over with fan letters and I live alone. My heart can only be fueled by compliments and it has flooded. What can a woman see in me that hasn't been seen a thousand times before? What gem of character remains hidden? "My kindness, my courage, my English wit in America, my American wit in England. My fucking voice everywhere." Laboring at thirty, praised out by forty, poor devil. If you start out as God with a woman, it has to be downhill after that.

All Diana actually did was encourage my little dash at politics, and even take an interest herself for the first time. Fate had cast me with the Labourites—well, that was where my heart really lay anyway, didn't it? No, seriously. I remembered my relatives' sighing over their damn west wings, and also how they had made fun of my mother, and all the shit I could muster on that side. As with any well-balanced person, left and right both appeal to me enormously.

I was not—it's time for a little heartbreak here—quite the success I'd hoped to be at the union. Perhaps I was too sincere for them. I don't know. Although I was from the first a better than average titter-provoker, the talent scouts somehow knew that I wasn't prime minister material, and I couldn't rise in the party and get to sit on the platform where the public could memorize me. Politics is not *quite* the same

232

as acting. You can't pretend to be a politician any more than you can pretend to have sex appeal. There's a quality in there deeper than mannerism. Ambition, power—I could make the faces, and I knew what to do with my hands, but I could never fool a pro.

"But you're so good at demolition work," said Hoskins, when I asked him for a major speaking assignment. "And we need people to hold up the tail." Some sporting phrase that can't be as bad as it sounds. That's what they'd signed me for, and that's all they'd signed me for: as an entertainer to beef up the bottom of the lineup and bring in the last-minute vote from the flippant elements.

I now believe the power elite of the Labour party would have been hard to crack that year, even for a master. It was a snug little machine long since set in its ways. I assumed that it had already parceled out future cabinet posts and was not looking for any new mouths at the trough. Tough, stagnant men: they were not playing, could not afford to play. Their own grip on English power was not so secure that they could afford to share it with me.

I missed this at the time, partly because the whole grim business proceeded so facetiously. These men debating for their lives were obliged to do it with jokes and languor. Little bursts of indignation were OK, and even obligatory for top leadership, but they had to be perfectly timed and precisely right. The listener was supposed to feel a sober shock at the back of his neck. "That's right. It's time somebody said that. The joking's gone far enough." Perfect. I learned a lot from those boys; but I wasn't debating for my life, and they knew it.

So my patchwork career continued, in a manner indigenous to Oxford. I became a "figure" at the union: part clown, part charmer, and all heart, obviously using the place for my own ends. Fair enough. The politicians had sewn up one corner for themselves, leaving the rest for adventurers, puppy eccentrics, and people who just wanted to establish their indifference. Later we would move in a body to the BBC and continue uninterrupted. Or if not us, people just like us. (The Labour elite barreled over to the Bank of England or someplace, but I'm sure the machine is still intact.)

A bit of acting, a bit of nuclear protesting, a funny interview with *Isis*—one puts the juggler on automatic pilot, and *voilà,* a career. It seemed as careless and amateur as in my father's day but, as I say, most of my generation were playing for blood. Even I, with my private income, knew that my elbow was hitting someone else on the way up. Even when you're going nowhere, there's only so much room at the top.

That was the counterpoint to the life of the heart, and should be kept in mind. Because it could be powerfully distracting. E.g., when Diana came back to me, she was deadly serious about Catholicism. "I was," she said, "impressed against my better judgment by the torment you honestly seemed to be going through. Any religion that caused so much pain must have something to it." Oh, *I* don't know. "So if I'm going to go on suffering from Catholics, I might as well get the good of it. So please tell me something, anything, about it."

It is a vicious lie, circulated by my memory, that I had ceased caring about the Church just like that. But my ardor was fitful now, as the excitement of speaking at the union battered me in torrents. I summoned my religious feelings for Diana, and sometimes they were real and sometimes they weren't (they'd been asked to do so much). But whatever they were, they seemed to move Diana almost frighteningly. My God, she's turning into a saint, I thought. Please don't. I'm faking some of this. Keep your sense of proportion, I beg you.

The worst of it was, she took absolutely seriously my old paroxysms of celibacy. "I know how hard it is for someone like you, a passionate man in love with life." Who, me? "God how I admired you and how I hated you. But I won't give you any more trouble. I'll try to make it as easy as possible."

234

And she certainly did. No Spanish duenna ever arranged more demure or desolate trysts than our next batch. We went to the Catholic chaplaincy together and had buns with the old fruitcake in charge, and at last the terrible day came and she asked to take instructions.

I'd brought it on myself. There would be no getting her in the sack now. I had hoped after a suitable interval to break down and admit that my love of life had become too great and how about it, huh? God works with broken reeds— enjoys the challenge, in fact. But now, that was out. *I* must help *her*. We must fortify each other. You've done it this time, Chatworth, you and your crazy acting.

I swear I tried. I prayed for strength and I guess I got it. At least, the voluptuous memories of our lovemaking began to fade. I almost forgot what her body looked like, though, strangely, I can see it now, dancing in firelight. Maybe it's somebody else's. And I found that the very act of praying strengthened my faith. In fact, now that faith was such an albatross, I couldn't seem to lose it.

But the one thing that praying couldn't do was keep me from getting bored. Holy women were old hat with me. Diana had been different, because she'd flattered my under-nourished artistic side. But being loved for my sterling character was so stale. Even if it had been true, I'd have received no pleasure from it. As a rancid lie, it was intolerable. All my virtue amounted to was that I was too vain to back down from a pose of virtue.

All I could do to buy time was speak and act and show off —like a middle-aged man sublimating a bad marriage. Con-cerning which, yes, that subject was now serenely in the air. Where else could we go? A virtuous marriage to a holy woman—it was too much. I was too young. I had to make my way in the world. What's that? You say you'll wait forever, Diana? No, please don't do that. I can't ask you to make the sacrifice. . . . No sacrifice at all, you say? *Please don't.*

235

It was in this mood that I met Letitia O'Reilly at the chaplaincy, a veteran Catholic with streaming gold hair who understood about God's mercy to sinners and other tricks of the trade. Which usually means a bad Catholic on the way out, but I didn't stop to ask questions.

A double life is the most unbearable memory known to man, and I'd really rather not dwell on it. What is the least one can say in confession? Diana was my muse of speaking, of showing off. A little relief on the side would make this arrangement possible. A man has needs.

"You old humbug." Letitia was a laughing bawd and she found my scruples uproarious. "Don't come the old priest with me, my good man."

She was damned if she was going to be a little relief on the side for anyone. "Where's saint Diana today? Out doing good?" she said, feathering me with her breasts. When I took Diana to the chaplaincy, Letitia would grin and wink at us, until Diana got quite bothered.

"Who is that girl, and what's the matter with her?"

"Search me."

But even that wasn't enough for Letitia. "Introduce me to your friend," she says one Sunday after Mass.

I mumble an introduction like an altar boy and try to tug Diana away. "Oh, *you're* the one who's going to become a Catholic," says Letitia. "Just as everyone else is leaving."

"Yes, I thought you could stand some new faces," says Diana pleasantly.

Sacred and profane love stare at each other. Everything in Letitia's face and body says, "We've done it. Pen and I have done it." The honesty of women will be the death of me. All my games, my dances, my peacock feathers, wither in their gaze. Letitia doesn't have to say any more. Diana nods, smiles at her.

"What about her?" Diana asks me calmly afterwards.

Chatworth gestures. He can't field them all.

"How funny. How very funny," she says. "You know you really are a *dangerous* child."

I pause. There is still time for a desperate avowal and a howl for mercy. But do I still want her? I have been offered a way out. "You're too *good* for me Diana," I mutter.

"Oh, that's too rich. Too priceless."

We are either walking or drinking tea or both. I don't want her, but *I still want her good opinion.* "You've got the Church now," I say. "Perhaps you don't need me anymore."

"Oh that. Now that you mention it, I don't suppose I shall ever go near a bloody church again, as long as I live."

For a wild moment I think, oh great, then we can go back to where we were. A man is not responsible for his reflexes. She is small and shrunken from trying to please me, and the least I can do is let her.

"Please, take your hand off my arm," she says, "and keep it off. I don't want to see you again and I mean it."

She walks away in the flat winter light. Her back screams, "All I wanted was *you,* on any terms you liked. Wasn't that silly of me?" I hitch my duffel coat around me. I have turned a soul away from my beloved Church. I am alone in a silent street. I didn't mean it, oh Lord. I didn't mean anything.

20

~~~~~~

Now I'd like to be declared a grand marshal of Texas, just to balance things. I also want my golden-gun award, and a tiny star to protect my heart from silver bullets. And a white sheet, while you're up.

But I'm learning to live with my MBE, whatever Mother says. Devalued though it may be, it matches my Jenkins tie very nicely. And my Paisley shawl.

As Diana loped away carrying her load of adulthood on each shoulder, a devalued Chatworth faced a devalued Oxford, and found it was just his meat. This illusion is common to second-year men, and is never seen again. Thanks to Diana's lessons, I had become the perfect undergraduate. And, as a moral imbecile, I was free as a loon.

I didn't face it right off, but threshed around the old way, confessing and moving heaven for guidance. My speaking and acting took on a new depth. This man has suffered. I didn't need my muse anymore now that my feet were on the ledge. My moral collapse coincided with an incandescent burst of talent.

But I sensed that this depended on being "serious" in some

way. And religion was still my other dimension, my secret, the reason people felt there was something behind my jokes.

So I still went through the motions of feeling guilty about sleeping with Letitia, to her amused irritation. "Come off it, Pen. You know we were both sold a bill of goods about all that."

Well, it was bad enough going back to Tish at all after a hurry-up bout of remorse; but to lose another Catholic soul as well was more than my overloaded conscience could bear. So I said, "I happen to believe it, damn it."

"Pooey, it's just that you Americans don't know what to do with yourselves when you're not feeling guilty. You think you must be wasting your time. I'll bet your first little words were, 'Father, I picked my nose three times and I kinda enjoyed it.' "

"I never heard a sentence that began 'you Americans' that was either funny or even normally intelligent."

"But it's true. You people should never have been told about the Catholic Church. You were simply bound to take it too seriously. Look, Pen, why do you suppose they print the dirty parts in Latin? So that people won't worry about them, that's why. And then some officious Yank comes along and says, 'Hey, Padre, what's all this *masturbatio* and *fornicatio* stuff, huh? Does it endanger my immortal soul or what's the story on that?' "

"And spare me American accents done by the English. You're just trying to excuse your own wantonness by calling it Old World."

"As you wish," she said, stroking me. "As you wish."

I have done my duty by my beliefs, by stating them, and I have paid my dues to seriousness. On the other hand, I'm not about to talk any more girls out of my bed. So I set to with a vengeance, reflecting as I pump that poor Diana had worn herself out being a saint for me and a sinner for me, but that Tish will never do anything as schoolgirlish as that. She is, in memory at least, the spirit of sheer bawdiness, take it or leave it.

239

I shall, in fact, leave these girls with infinite regret, because no one will look like that again, although I've seen a thousand just like them. Whatever has happened to my inner works has made romantic love all but impossible from now on. Tish was the transition point. "Love?" she said once. "What's that? A rumor spread by some pansy troubadours." She refuses flatly to stop seeing other men, can't even see the point of the request. "What earthly difference does it make?" I forget.

We spent a blowsy boozy summer term, a parody of last year's Jamesian delights, and signed up for a student tour of Denmark, where Tish seemed immediately restless without the mild constraints of Oxford. On our second night in Copenhagen she got roaring drunk and tried to have sex with me in a café. "Come on, no one can see it." There was anxiety in her eyes. She *must* do something bad tonight. As I fought for my honor under the tablecloth, she turned and commenced soul-kissing another student. Too bloody much. I'd tell her I was leaving. "Well, good for you," she said between sucks. "You'll find a Bible in your room."

Sometime around Denmark's early dawn she turned up in my room drunk and hysterical. "Have you got anything to drink, Pen? God, I wish I was dead."

"Where have you been?"

"None of your fucking business, you puritan prig. I'll go where I like. And with *whom* I like." She was suddenly a trull at the Abbey Theatre flinging her shawl this way and that.

"Sure you will. That's great."

She suddenly sagged against me. "Oh Pen, I'm so worthless. *Have* you got anything to drink?" I have a little schnapps and she pours it over her chin and grimaces. "Christ, I'm no good. They tried to make me good, you know, but I outfoxed them. Ah hah!" She sagged again. "Now I'm frightened. I can't seem to control myself. The brakes are gone. Down and down and whoosh, we go. Help me, Pen. *You're* good, aren't you?"

"Yeah, I'm a bloody marvel. Come to bed now."

"Down and down and whoosh!" She hiccoughed a couple of laughs as I guided her to my scrawny hostel mattress. She tried politely to make love on the way down but collapsed in a damp heap and began to snore and cry simultaneously. "My God. Oh, my God," she said a few times.

I made myself some coffee and felt like a death's-head as I gazed out the window. Did I have another reform case on my hands? Would Scout-Commander Chatworth have to lead another fallen sister to daylight? I'm afraid it looked like it. Tish seemed to have dissolved into tears and beer and piss, until her very soul was a puddle. I know it sounds crazy, but I've never had such a sense of *liquid* about anybody.

But when she finally awoke, she was hung over but organized. "I'm sorry about last night. You seemed embarrassed."

"I did? And you remember it?"

"Oh yes, oh yes. I remember everything. Always."

"I guess we'd better take it easy today, huh? Make like tourists, and all that."

"Are you joking? Right now I can't wait to get my jowls round some more of that lovely beer."

"You mean after last night?"

"Yes. And not one minute before." She sat up on the mattress with a jerk and seemed to catch her head with her hands before it flew off. "Look Pen, if you don't like last night I shall try not to bother you again. But don't preach to me about it. Or look concerned. Or rub your chin. Or anything at all. Last night is the price I pay for the way I live, and I pay it with my eyes open."

"But isn't it going to get worse?"

"So they tell me."

"A thousand headaches and a painful death and all that?"

"I wouldn't be a bit surprised." Her cup beat a tattoo on the saucer. "If your good moments are as good as my good moments, it's worth it. As for you . . ."

Quite. It wouldn't be worth it for my good moments. It

strikes me that Diana would understand Tish infinitely better than I do. People over here, even ones named O'Reilly, seem to take the measure of life early on and decide precisely what's best for them. They choose between sensuality and thought as one might between cricket and rowing, math and languages. The country is one big aptitude test, administered by a fag tailor. "Vice wouldn't suit you, sir; you have entirely the wrong build for it. Have you considered God, sir?" There is no good or bad about it: so-and-so's a lecher—that's his thing. His friend Charles is a monk.

Chatworth is an American. He will never take the measure of life because he refuses to admit it has limits. He will keep his options open. He has no face yet (in the sense that the English do) because a face would limit him. He can never have a good time (in the sense that Tish does) but he can never give up hope either. He is laughable, but he keeps coming at you.

In the wearying Scandinavian daylight, I felt again the rigorous puritan emptiness that had settled in me in my teens. Travel can play these tricks with time. These are definitely Viking thoughts as opposed to Latin ones: I am a martyr to geography. Tish can already see to the end of her life and has counted costs; this entitles her to a face, but leaves her pathetic, small, finite. I am damned if I am going to see to the end of my life. I can still be anybody I want to. I will choose a face when the time comes.

"Don't look so stern, Pen. I'm a fearful poseur, like all the O'Reillys. This week I'm doing the Fallen Woman."

As she shakily applied her lipstick, she said, "Well, at any rate, I won't commit suicide. Oddly enough, that's one teaching of Mother Church I accept with all my heart."

So much for romantic love. Tish had decided it cramped her style and slowed her libido to a crawl. And she drained it out of me. For the rest of the tour, I fed her beer and let her sleep where she might. I got no more and no less of her than if I'd locked her in her room.

All right, it wasn't that easy. Envy is hard to kick, and at first I bit the bejesus out of my lower lip. But once envy is kicked it stays kicked. And since if you can't envy you can't love, I was free in one more way. I entered the world of indiscriminate sex where there are no men and women, just heads and tails alternating. And I can still be found bobbing about out there with the gang.

With so much freedom, I will never get a face now. As I look in the last of my mirrors, I see I've left it far too late. Still, the public seems to like what they see. Perhaps it's themselves.

Back to Oxford for my third and last year. Suddenly the signs were up everywhere: "The party's over," "All aboard the *Titanic.*" Funny I hadn't noticed them before. The air now crackled with talk of careers, and I guessed I'd better talk careers too, just to keep in the swim. But my heart wasn't in it. I still wanted to do everything, but that didn't seem possible over here. English careers were more like walling yourself up in a monastery. The starting pay in all walks of life seemed downright ludicrous, but my friends were willing to hang in and wait forever. The timid buggers. Why didn't they go to Australia or somewhere? Even last year's lords were scrambling for crumbs, like sparrows. Pah! Me Chatworth!

"I suppose you'll want some sort of degree?" asked my tutor, Mr. Short. "I mean any sort at all?"

"I guess so," I said.

"Well you're not going to get one at this rate. And I do mean, *any* sort."

Ah well, that sounded quite distinguished in its way—the kind of thing great men tell you after dinner. Went down without a degree, egad, belch.

Mr. Short had chosen the ever-popular insouciant route through Oxford, which plays hell with the lower spine, and he had shown no interest in me at all up to now. However, as he lay there on the sofa with a bottle of beer balanced on his chest, I realized that even he must have his anxieties in this tense little country. He had also, as you will see, spent five years in the merchant navy, which had destroyed his mind and prepared him for Paisley.

"Think, if you will, of England as a madly overcrowded refugee ship that is sinking *ever* so slowly in the North Atlantic. Not one of my best metaphors, but if you're not going to get a degree, what does it matter? It is imperative on this ship that everyone keep calm, and that nobody raise his voice. In the circumstances, passengers like me can be quite good value. Our apparent laziness is soothing, and our understated humor is just the thing for a sinking ship. We also do our little bit and don't take up much space. But passengers like *you,*" he opened an eye and cocked a finger, "are another matter. Passengers who don't have to be here in the first place and who can leave at will, and who flaunt their wealth in the ship's bar."

He didn't sound angry: he talked exactly the same way about Cromwell and the rise of the middle class. It was his Method, and I didn't take it to heart.

"You see, most of the chaps here had to claw their way on board—well, perhaps this metaphor has gone as far as it will go. It doesn't pay to buy cheap. Anyhow, they had to struggle to get here, and a degree is a matter of life and death to them. So you can perhaps see that such a figure as yourself, however dashing, might be a pestilence to certain nostrils."

If he kept on talking, I might not have to read my meager, unresearched essay at all. So I said, "I believe I've gotten, got, *something* out of Oxford, Jonathan—the sort of thing my father got, and wanted me to get. Civilization, if that isn't too pretentious."

"Your father, ah yes. You had a father up here. Mine was a grocer in Stepney. That might account for our different perspectives. Now, I suppose we'd better get on with your essay—if you've brought one this week?"

The essay was so small and bad that it was read and demolished in no time at all. And this seemed to nettle him again, although he retained his bored drawl as before.

"Perhaps as a vocal member of our Labour party, bringing us valuable insights from abroad, you can see that in your father's day Oxford was a species of leisure cruise in the Aegean, where one could still pick up scraps of civilization for the mantelpiece; but that now it, along with England, is *crowded* and *sinking.*"

Lordy, how that man could talk. But my conscience wasn't used to this kind of material. In my obsession with one-on-one sinning, I didn't realize he was telling me roughly the same thing my women were: that you can sin in crowds or all alone, if your heart is really in it.

"I see your point, Jonathan," I said. "But I'm here, and I don't need a degree as badly as I need other things. Maybe even the working guys could use a holiday from the sinking ship instead of three more years of worry and competition. But anyway, *all* of them *already* have more culture than I. They've *been* through the Aegean before they got here. This is my first time." What is all this shit about the Aegean? Why am I talking like him?

"Well, you've learned a little something about arguing, at least. And specious arguing is better than no arguing at all, I suppose. If it really is the Aegean you're sailing through and not Mayfair, perhaps your time here has not been entirely profitless."

He didn't really want to convert me, just to prove I was wrong. Anti-American resentment took funny forms in those days. He'd have given his back teeth to be rich enough to cruise through Oxford; in fact, failing that, he now acted as if he *were* cruising through Oxford, with his drawling and his beer bottles. What a parody of the lordly dons my father used to talk about! Because what it came down to was that this hand-me-down dandy could not afford to have one of his customers fail an exam!

Still, I was sorry for the little tyke, and I decided to do a spot of work. Everybody else was doing it anyway; it was the only game left. And I'd tried everything else up here. I knew that the real education is locked away in little coteries and societies with funny names and it was much too late to crack those. But I did borrow another chap's notes and set forth to Jenkins my finals.

And just as well I did. Because when I got home for Candlemas or whatever, Prissy said, "You'd better get a good degree, Pen, because we're broke."

Prissy loves to shock. "Well, not literally broke," she said. "We can still get free teeth and glasses."

"Well, how broke are we, and how the hell did it happen?"

She and my mother sat on the sofa smirking like conspirators, as if something simply wonderful had happened.

"*If* you'd been paying attention . . ." said Prissy, and laughed. "You didn't really think Daddy was rich, did you? Rich enough to support you forever?"

"Not forever," I said, "just long enough to get started."

"Well, consider yourself started now, old bean. Daddy would have."

"What do you mean by that?"

"When he made me his executor, he said, 'I'd like Pen to have a really good Oxford, in the old-fashioned sense. Free from care, free to grow. So tell him not to worry. He's so absentminded these days, he probably doesn't know what an estate of this size looks like when the abominable tax man is done with it.' "

"You're making this up."

"Merely paraphrasing. What he really said is, 'That twit is so vague he won't know what hit him.' Anyway, he wanted you to have as much as possible in a lump sum, while Mummy and I got ours in dribbles."

So that's what they were smirking about. Nothing better sums up our family than this Victorian scene. "He told both of you this?"

They nodded happily.

"Behind my back?"

"Where else?" said Prissy.

"It was for your own good," said Mother.

Oh, I knew that all right. The gallant old fellow had out-virtued me again. And look what he'd got for it. A burned-out cynic, a rich passenger.

"You've done just the sort of thing he wanted," rambled Mother. "Speaking at the union, traveling, though I'll never *really* understand Denmark."

My eyes, I fancy, bulged furiously. This last act of Daddy's kindness had added the finishing touches to my rotten character by cutting me off from the real life of my generation. In fact, with the best will in the world, he'd always done that, hadn't he? But one couldn't get mad at Father now: the family would crash in ruins.

"I don't much like having my life planned for me," I said.

"Well, it won't happen anymore," said Prissy. "We won't plan another thing for you, will we Mummy?"

"And do you have to gloat like that?"

"Yes, I do. Nobody ever planned anything for me, Pendrid. Three scrummy years at Oxford without a care. Daddy felt you'd missed so much because of the war, you poor dear. And now you have the gall to be angry about it."

"I'm not angry," I said reflexively, "just penniless."

"Not completely," squeaked Mother.

"Anyway, you must have bags of juicy connections by now. The old-boy network will begin to hum and you'll be in clover. Daddy felt," I shut my eyes: Oh God-like Daddy, always right, "that you would go further if you relaxed and made friends than if you worried and worked too hard."

"Daddy," I said, through my tight little mouth, "was undoubtedly right in his day. But he never really came to grips with the postwar world."

"He believed that the facts of power in England were changeless."

My soul tossed in fever. "He seems to have talked an awful lot to you," I said. "Why didn't he tell these things to me?"

"Just shy, I suppose. He thought a man should discover the world for himself. Women have to be told."

"You," my mother said, rubbing salt gently into the wound, "were constantly on his mind; you were to be his legacy."

"And he took it for granted we felt the same." Prissy looked at Mother and winked at me. "And we do, of course, don't we?"

Having nothing better to do, I smiled. "Don't let them see you're bleeding," Daddy used to say. Aye, aye, sir.

When I returned to Oxford, it was the same grim institution it had been for the others all along. I was into the real life of my generation at last, clawing and scratching to stay afloat. The little creases around Mr. Short's eyes subsided. He took entire credit for my sudden burst of application. "You should get *something,*" he said. "Lord knows what." He didn't care; he had never cared.

But the juice had gone out of Oxford for me. This last crushing act of paternalism had turned the place hopelessly sour. I'd been given *his* Oxford; but without *his* income that Oxford disappeared like a magic village. I've since learned that that was a Golden Age and that Oxford has really become dreary since. Perhaps. We had a couple of suicides in my year, but that can happen in a Golden Age.

What ate at my liver was that technically I couldn't get angry at him. He had done me a kindness in his foggy way. I still had a big fat allowance and could buy drinks for everybody. I could purchase new friends in every bar. But I had dropped a class in my mind. "We didn't want to tell you," Prissy said before I left home, "but we thought we'd better before it was too late."

Who the hell are you to have this power?

"I really am sorry," said Priss. "King for a day. If you ask me, I think Daddy was a bit cracked."

Cracked? He was power-crazy. He even thought he was my father.

"He manipulated both of us," said Prissy. "But I suppose that's saints for you."

248

For half a moment I was deflected from my own concerns. "What did he ever do for you?"

"Kept me from having smelly communist babies. Remember that? Also, he offered me a jolly good job in the import-export business. Which I refused. And he offered to give me a coming-out season. Which I refused. I *fought* him, you know—for all the good it did me."

Fought him? By George, that's just the thing. I'll do it. But how could I fight him now? By not being first-rate. By being an unworthy Chatworth. By dropping my pants in church. Believe me, I've done it all.

You can't exactly Jenkins Oxford, because Oxford invented Jenkins. The whole system is a web of shortcuts so intricate they constitute an education. Only the greatest of scholars don't use them. So, although I'll only say it once and in the secrecy of the confessional, I worked like hell for two terms.

(Did you know, Father, that you are bound to secrecy? Otherwise, I'll remove your batteries and kill you.)

I got a good second and received an amused note from Mr. Short. "I don't think you're an American at all," it said.

Even Alcatraz must look lovely by sunlight. For the last couple of weeks Oxford looked achingly beautiful and I realized, now that it was too late to help, that I would never be so happy again. Suffer? Oh yes, I'd suffered all right. Young Werther never suffered as I did. Despair? You bet. Reveled in it. Swam in it bare-ass. Walking down the High in May, bursting with *angst;* lying under the willows, burbling with sadness. I'd give my soul to have it back for five minutes.

21

~~~~~~

That last tremolo is Plunkett at his fruitiest. Given time, he would have gone on to describe the brilliance of his generation—all Oxford generations are brilliant, and the members spend their interminable dotage gurgling over this. Plunkett cannot resist these colorful customs. But luckily he goes to sleep soon after I do, and as we face the lemon-colored dawn together, I'm in charge. The voice of hangover and truth.

We (MBEs are always we, which suits us very well) got a letter from cousin Cynthia today, rubbing it in all the way. To wit: "Somebody showed me your name on the Quaggers' Hoggers list the other day. I must say, how super for you, Pen. It's funny what happens to us old lefties, isn't it? Here I am fighting fiercely to keep Entwistle open, and I know the help you've been to Egbert in keeping *his* old stones up. We have to, don't you think? We did so much to knock them down at Oxford.

"Anyhow, ideology and arthritis don't mix, and Dicky and I are much too poor to have opinions on anything at the moment. By the way, does this mean you'll be paying English taxes now?" . . . and so on.

Rough stuff, in the best family tradition. Translated into Human it means: "Dicky and I want a handout, so we can have opinions again and I can have my arthritis fixed. As for you, you jammy sod, you became a turncoat to avoid the taxes that you and your Labour friends were so keen on raising." It was this steady rain of kidney punches that depressed Father so much after the war. Cynthia is now as old as her aunt Maude was then. Nothing changes.

I do, of course, pay some English taxes and some mighty American ones, too, but it still leaves me with much too much for my relatives to stomach. "I'm afraid we're not very magnificent these days," they'll say, tugging at their shawls and their cheap sherry bottles. Father's trip to America in 1940 has never been paid for.

I actually had lots of reasons to go to America besides taxes. But English taxation has cast a shadow over all us émigrés. Are we *sure* we would have left if it weren't for that? Did I, in particular, see America in a slightly fairer light because of the surtax? I prefer not to think so, but the doubt is always there, to be tickled by the likes of Cynthia forever and ever.

As I say, I had lots of reasons to leave before I'd earned a penny or paid a tax to anybody. I left Oxford in a muddled fury. It had all been a contemptible trick. Tish was knocked up and suggested a raffle. (For the morbid: she is now a headmistress at a good girls' school, and appears on talk shows about education. Pretending to go to seed is one more item in the Isle of Games.) But already I was sick of irony, the Oxford drug.

Chatworth faces adult life. I had been backed onto the stage unknowing, while the crowd roared. The obvious solution to this was the BBC, which sucks talent like bits of fluff into that big white building, where it's safe forever. But I had my tattered pride. In fact, my whole array of virtues was intact; only the man behind them was missing. I didn't really give a damn anymore whether I was English or American, but the U.S. was still the prairie of record, the place where the garbled soul of Chatworth could re-create itself. Or failing that, become famous.

Because, let's face it, an Englishman in America was more impressive in those days than his clockwise counterpart. Before the cattle boats began' disgorging secretaries, English voices were unheard between New York and the Gold Coast and I had the best. So the old ladies who used to gush over my cute accent would now be made to pay through the nose for it. Young Chatworth gave a bitter laugh as he remembered how he used to flinch and try to hide that accent. Pah. Does the bearded lady shave? Does Tom Thumb lie about his height? Use it, boy. Sell anything you've got.

I also had a little green card and a social security number which were magic passes clamoring for use; I even had a draft board that wanted to rope me into the Korean unpleasantness. I was supposed to report back to the doctors that summer and parade my lung tissue once more or lose my privileges forever. But that's not entirely why I left, is it? No, not entirely. There is always an element of running away in Chatworth's advances.

The three of us had just whirled into one of our mysterious grand tours of the Chatworth bestiary: Uncles Henry and George and the Scottish branch.

One look told me, as it was meant to, that Henry's son Egbert, my old madrigal pal, had gone round the bend. He came down to dinner in a green dressing gown festooned with peacocks; his face was white as a clown's, with two red spots on the cheeks and a blood-red mouth. Oh shit, Eggie, nobody does it that way anymore. Today's fag is up and doing. Drives an MG and dates older women. Eggie tried drawling amusingly about how he would have gone to Oxford except for the fearful effort of going up and down to it. "If only one could go there *sideways,*" he said. (Had English Catholics kept this dreadful style alive? Was there nothing they wouldn't preserve?) But then he got onto the ugliness of modern living and his voice shook like an old man's. The

252

poor bugger didn't know who the hell he was, and was doing his ancestors one by one.

Afterwards, he invited me to his room for a chat, and I dragged myself reluctantly up to the bell tower where he lived, as to a tryst with the Wolf Man. I wasn't a bit surprised to find the place drenched in incense. He turned up a gaslight and flopped onto his bed; there was no electricity, and in fact no book or picture or glass animal made later than 1900.

"Don't you find all this rather banal?" say I.

"Oh yes, yes. I have no imagination at all. After Oxford, the decor must be quite sick-making."

"Not at all." I feel Muldoon coming back: he haunts these houses. "A little fart-making maybe, but no worse than that. Tell me, do you spend much time here?"

"Oh, *all* my time. Except for brief trips to the refectory. This is my cell."

"And you intend to go on living like this?"

"Forever." He stared at the ceiling. "What else is there?"

"I don't know, come to think of it."

"I mean, I don't *look* like a businessman, do I? And of course I was turned down by the army. Their merry laughter still sounds in my ears. As for the law, I find it just makes me cough uncontrollably. No, worse, it disgusts me. It's so remorselessly Dickensian. Conveyancing, indeed. Escrow. The solicitors are downstairs with the bills of lading. Egbert breaks out some more incense to make them go away."

"You sound like an artist, at least."

"Yes, don't I? But I'm not, you know. That's the hell of it. Deep down, I have the coarse soul of a Chatworth. Courtesy of Mama."

Ah yes, Aunt Maude. The one who persecutes my mother like an eighteenth-century bully boy. "So why do you live like this?"

"Somebody has to do it," he said. "It's just a shame I'm so bad at it. If you look around, you'll notice that this is not an artist's room at all, but the room of a rich middlebrow, circa 1880. That is your basic Chatworth. There's no other kind. You'd do well to get away from it, Pen. Go somewhere where you can be vulgar and up to date at the same time.' He raised his voice, "Go, obviously, to America."

Yes, I think I will.

"But, of course, you've done that. And look at the difference. A bustling clean-limbed young fellow staring at a sunken ruin. Suppose our positions had been reversed. I'm sure I'd be dashing about in a zoot suit while you'd be decaying boringly. I envied you, you know."

He's mad. I could never have been like him.

"The point is, my dear cousin, there is no satisfactory way to be a Chatworth anymore, so you might as well drop it. Uncle George's estate may be good for one more generation, but who wants to wait around for that? Besides, guns make me faint. And a squire must be a mighty hunter or lose face with the natives. Do you know," he jumped from his bed with sudden energy, "what I *really* wanted? . . . This."

He flung open his closet and there, hanging like a corpse, were a priest's vestments.

I want to go to America right now.

"But I failed the physical," he went on chatting. "They seem to be much fussier about these things nowadays. I promised I'd be a good boy in the seminary and not keep the others awake at night, but the head chap hemmed and hawed and said it wasn't exactly that . . . but, well, high-strung, sensitive, the usual drill. In short, buzz off, you pansy. So there it is. Even the dear old Church has become all tough and modern. It's a beastly world, Pen, for the likes of me. I daresay I nauseate even you."

"Not at all," I said, gagging. "Because I don't believe you really exist."

"That's the nicest thing anyone's ever said to me."

I staggered to my own room, where they still kept a jug and a basin so you had to brush your teeth in your shaving water or vice versa, and I thought, Christ, England! The funny thing was that Egbert had talked to me like a brother warning me, through his clown's mask, to get out before something dreadful happened.

Nightmares come and go, but only a few have your name and family shield on them. After all I'd seen, I could handle affectation in suffocating quantities, but this wasn't affectation. It was something somber and old—much older than Oxford. Old and tough. And he assumed I'd understand perfectly, as I did. After all, it was really me talking to me. Run, Pendrid, run, while I keep the ghosts occupied.

Or at least his version of them, his bitter, raging parody. Egbert *is* an artist in the only way possible to him. Uncle George, whom we visited next, took a much sunnier view. "Ah, the Chatworths, yes the Chatworths." He rubbed his hands with delight at the word. "Not a bad lot, by and large."

We were pacing the lawn at Chatworth Manor again; I can scarcely remember doing anything else with old George. Unless it was pacing the corridors, pointing out priests' hiding holes. He may have ripped off a wing, but there was still plenty left. I remembered for the first time in years trotting alongside tweed legs of both sexes trying to keep up. What was I, five? Running, running, at the ever-receding tweed. Now I was a tweed leg myself, striding along grandly with Squire George, lamenting the absence of gardeners and drinking to the past.

"Of course you know about your ancestor Pendrid, the Elizabethan martyr."

"I've heard talk."

George smiled thinly. Blood is thicker than wisecracks.

"This was his private chapel. They arrested him here during the Consecration. I suppose that was the part of the ceremony when the Mass became technically illegal." George plunked onto his knees, just like that, and began absentmindedly to pray, although it wasn't a chapel anymore. I did so too, facing the same way, though there was no trace of an altar. Incongruously, we prayed together in this shabby old sitting room, two Chatworths doing their thing.

George crossed himself and stood up. "It's been an expensive hobby, if that's what you call it." We were pacing the corridors again. "Perhaps we should send the Papacy a bill someday. The amount of wasted talent on these walls could positively make one weep. David here, cleverest man in England . . . George . . . Henry . . . George again." After three years of studying English history, I'd heard of none of them. "They were all so busy keeping the faith they didn't have time for history. Perhaps if your namesake hadn't been so stubborn, the rest of us would have fallen in line and entered public life as good little Protestants. But a martyrdom puts one's back up. It became a matter of family pride to stay Roman Catholic; and then, gradually, it became the whole point and purpose of the family. I suppose," he said, pausing at a picture of my father in World War I uniform, "it was worth it?"

"What about *him?*" I pointed.

"Yes, well. Of course, by our time the old wars were over, and a Catholic could be almost anything he liked short of prime minister or king, which are basically service professions anyhow. But wartime habits are hard to break—observe, for instance, how tight I pull the curtains at blackout time—and your father and Maude and I grew up under siege, though the siege had been lifted. Which meant that the Church was everything to us; if it wasn't the most important thing in the world, we would have looked like awful fools, crouched in our bunker, so to speak."

We take another turn on the lawn, and ghostly tennis players in long white dresses scurry from sight. "I don't know whether your father would have been a religious man in any other setting, but he certainly was in this one. All the talent and energy that other families pour into life we funnel toward Rome. And David, being the best of us, was also the Churchiest. If Rome was the family 'thing,' then he would master it like a trade. Even as a child, he practiced saying Mass and Benediction on a soapbox—although fortunately he drew the line at hearing confessions. And of course it went without saying that he would be a priest."

One look at George's settled face told you that he was not

normally a talkative man; but with a fellow Chatworth, however debased, he would say anything. We were, after four hundred years, still alone, and one of a kind.

"Then various things happened. Your favorite subject, history, caught up with us, and we've never really recovered. David and I went to war and came back a little dazed. We were more a part of England than we knew. At least the Protestant ruling class had permitted us to die with the others, and might easily do so again if we weren't careful. So, reluctantly and against all his instincts, your father took a stab at what they, for some queer reason, call 'real life.' "

He blew a sigh through his mustache, which was thin and sandy like my father's. "Then again, we were both getting on and neither of us had married, and the family seemed in imminent danger of disappearing. Even Maude, the sexiest of us, if you'll excuse the Americanism, was hanging back. So we couldn't even wobble along on the female line. David began to fret. He would stand out here and gaze at these pictures for hours and shake his head. He hated waste. So one day he said, 'Not a very good time to become a priest, it seems. I suppose I'd better marry someone.' I suggested he'd need a little more enthusiasm than that even to propose, and he said, 'Don't worry, I'll manage the enthusiasm. I'll do the whole thing well.' The war had somewhat blown us apart, and though we were as intimate as ever, I never *quite* understood what he was saying in later years. He seemed to have a vague sense of mission, but—like today's veterans, too, I suspect—he didn't know quite where he was or precisely what was expected of him. He did try the seminary, you know, in 1919, but I think it bored him."

George stopped to fill his lungs: he was one of those puffers who need an awful lot of air to talk.

"My own feeling," he had filled up another paragraph's worth, "was that David was too, well, clerical for marriage, and that his life would be much too pious and dull to share with children. So you can imagine my delight when you and your esteemed sister turned up here after the war, a couple of gum-chewing, ready-for-anything young Yanks. Perhaps the first contemporary Chatworths since 1570—yet with the old virtues there too. What a relief! He *had* done it well after all."

Will he stop and give me some peace? No. He is sitting by the fireplace in the big drawing room where old books on market gardening rise like canyons around us, and we are drinking port. "So now you've had Oxford, too. How splendid. Your papa broke the ice, and he tried so hard to enjoy it, but he was a bit old by then, and the war hadn't done his nerves any good, and he wasn't quite sure how far a Catholic should go. There wasn't much precedent, you know. But he kept telling us what a jolly time he was having, and perhaps he was. I had lost touch with his real feelings; and so had he by then, I daresay. War drives them back into a man like penny nails.

"Anyhow, what a party it must have been for you, in spite of the austerity. Your mama tells me that you sampled everything, from the union on down. And your sister tells me that you had friends of all classes."

Dear Priscilla and her wistful malice. I presume I must have said *something* during George's seamless harangue, but the gaps are missing. George seems to be talking to an empty room.

"So you are probably as well equipped as a man can be to face the fourth-rate abomination that England has become. Politics, the arts, what is it to be?"

Eh? Time to speak up. "Dunno," I said.

George nodded as if this were very wise of me. "Chatworths like to take their time. We tend to be late bloomers." I was beginning to feel as if George had already painted me and hung me on the wall: just another Chatworth. Anything else I'd done or been up to now was just a preparation for that.

I'm an *early* bloomer, I wanted to shout. But George would have found some sense in which that, too, was typically Chatworth. I began to cringe at the very name as it closed over me: "You are a priest forever, of the order of Chatworth." "Bloody hell I am." "A very good answer. You can start your duties immediately."

It is next morning and we are walking among the headstones in the village church, the final part of my course. Nameless villagers lie at the outskirts; but the center is reserved for me. The only name in town. After I've been painted I shall lie down with the others and merge.

"Whatever you decide about your life," said George, "and you're quite right to take your time, I should like to propose something that would go very well with almost any career—politics, the bar, whatever. In a word, I should like you to help me manage the estate, with a view to eventual ownership."

View to eventual . . . My nerves jumped in the stillness and my jaw locked.

"Your father and I discussed it . . ."

The hell you did. My rage boiled over so suddenly that it must have been there all along. Was there anyone, other than me, that my father hadn't discussed me with? Some stranger in the street he'd overlooked? Shit, this was intolerable.

"And he fairly glowed at the prospect. But he insisted that it be a free choice. After all, *he* had gone to Oxford and *I'd* stayed home to mind the place." There was the old whiplick of rancor again: *he'd* gone to America, *I'd* caught the war. "And now he's buried in New York . . ."

"Yonkers."

"As you wish. He was such a good Catholic that I sometimes think he overdid things of that sort. He believed that a Christian should be buried with his neighbors, however scruffy. But that's by the way. More apropos, he felt that sending you to Oxford in the old style would prepare you for the family tradition."

I am about to strike my father in earnest but my hand is suspended. Did the saintly fool actually believe that scruffy postwar Oxford would prepare me for this graveyard and the deathhouse on the hill? Bless his poor, muddled, romantic

259

soul. My hand caresses his cheek, but it's cold as stone. "Not to fuss," says his corpse.

"What about Egbert?" I croaked. "He's used to this sort of thing."

"Egbert is going through a difficult time at the moment. It's nothing to be alarmed about. The famous Chatworth nerves seem to strike roughly one in three. You, for instance, seem to have escaped them entirely [hah!]. Anyhow, one outgrows them in time. In fact, we all tend to end up quite stolid."

I looked at George and saw him for the first time as a young man with anxious eyes, who had to fight to become a pudding. He and my father must have passed the family nerves back and forth like a grenade.

"In any event, I don't think it's Egbert's sort of thing, even at his best. You, on the other hand, would obviously be ideal for it: mature, level-headed, sufficiently brainy."

Another jolt rattles my skull. Is he talking about the raddled schizoid of Oxford, the faceless wonder and dangerous child that Diana had described so well? My God, are all appearances as deceiving as this, or am I alone again?

"I'm not even a good Catholic," I mutter desperately.

He purses his lips under the mustache ("where else?" as Prissy would say). "No? That would certainly sadden your papa, although it may be just a phase, you know. Chatworths often . . ." He looks at me and backs off slyly, abandoning the thought. "Where was I? Yes, sadden your papa, but of no real consequence. You don't suppose that *all* your ancestors were good Catholics, do you? It's just not like that with us. It's more like a badge or a coat of arms. Some believe and some don't, but we all wear the uniform. Otherwise, we'd be nobodies."

There is a ferret cunning in George's face that I hadn't noticed. Does *he* believe or doesn't he? Ah hah. It's part of the code not to tell. That's why he had pursed his lips. A member of the brash younger generation had broken the rules. He'll learn.

We are standing again by the old house, not one of your great beauties, but a mishmash of styles, rendered lopsided by its torn wing, and we are looking down the slope at the rank garden which will never regain its loveliness until gardeners bloom once more. It's like inheriting bomb damage.

Still, perhaps my strange mixture of gifts can carry the place through this period, give it a new direction, even stamp it with my own personality—some weird Anglo-American Catholic development with jazz bands and chapels and croquet courts. My heart leaps with this little rush of childishness, a feeling I thought I'd lost forever, and I am grinning as Uncle George talks about so many quid a year at first and a percentage of the rents and what not.

We turn toward the shade of the back door. "At least it will keep you on your feet while you look around."

Yes, it'll do that all right. Not to mention my arse. As we clunk across the cold stone floor of the hallway, I realize that by cutting off my income at this point my father has practically flung me into accepting the job. George is watching me as he must have watched my father, trying to read our collective face. Meanwhile, he babbles like a conjurer about that good old American vitality which, harnessed to an English education . . . I scarcely listen, because I'm so busy fighting the undertow. An old family can accumulate enough force to break your arms and legs; and right here under the old staircase is the very heart of the magnet.

Uncle George has maneuvered me here. He is not dull at all. He is a ferret, fast on his feet. He has kept our flag flying through a difficult generation. What about me? We stand in the damp dimness surrounded by suits of armor, swords, cannon balls—the last survivors in the final confrontation. He is naked, I can say anything to him.

"Christ, I'd rather die," are the words I remember now.

261

22

~~~~~~

My agent is a scream. He flew in to London this morning, instead of phoning like a rational man, to talk about the Big One, and the enchilada de luxe: he would have talked in code if I'd let him. But for once he may be right. It seems I am in the running for an assignment that makes even these iron knees tremble a little. "Not a word to anyone, Pen baby: planes are bugged these days, toilets are bugged, even bugs are bugged." He glared at my tape recorder. Has he guessed our relationship?

So he flies in and I fly out, like a pair of demented shuttlecocks. Marty wants me to go into training for this one like a prizefighter, and I'll probably need to. I shall have to get my soul in order as never before. Just the two of us and Telstar—with every crevice of character showing, every lying vowel, every false smile and hand movement. You can't rehearse these things. You can only be as good as you are on that particular night. Oh God, what a prospect.

Marty also says the negotiations could be lightning fast: they have their own problems of timing. Their boy is a master of the afterthought and the cautious backdown, and they

262

themselves study world impact like astrologers. So it's off to Jersey for a week or two to wait and set. I might as well rush through the rest of this story so I'll have time to forget it. And then, perhaps, pray, meditate, levitate—the usual tricks of the trade.

Fade back in to the front hall, where gumboots and old umbrellas rub elbows with suits of armor and picture of Bonnie Prince Charlie.

"Christ, I'd rather die."

Uncle George turned away politely, as if to say, the chap obviously hasn't made up his mind. Mustn't rush him. I scooped up my mother and sister and fled. Just like that.

So I won my precious freedom and have wandered the earth ever since, tapping on windows and inserting my face and voice into living rooms, while my soul shivers outside. Does that satisfy you, Father? I have to go to the bathroom.

No. Not yet. We need just a little more, to make sure it wasn't the taxes that made you fly the coop, and it helps if you're uncomfortable.

England had laid out a face for me after all, and a style, like a butler laying out dinner clothes: the only ones that were *me*. I would have done it well, too, like Daddy. Instead, I ran screaming into the void. George's offer made leaving England seem absolutely imperative. I couldn't bear to sit around while he pulled down his other wing, and then his insides, and then his lawn. We would plan little holding actions together, fighting grimly for the greenhouse and the birdbath, but the patient would die and I'd be middle-aged. "Leave it to Egbert," I told myself; but in my heart I knew better. Egbert would not bounce back from the Chatworth nerves; he might try, he was a ballsy guy in his way, but enough is enough. So there was no one to save the place *for*, and George would proceed to liquidate with dignity.

I insisted on the point till my head burst, as my bladder is bursting now. The Labour party that I'd helped along in my small way would dismember the Chatworth estate gleefully. The last priests' hiding hole would come down and the invisible chapel where George and I had knelt, and everything but the old graveyard, which was at least functional. One of the most gloriously pointless families in history would vanish in a cloud of rubble. It *had* to be so; otherwise I couldn't have left England with a clear conscience. And now I'm sick of taking orders from this damned seat belt.

. . . Easy, my son. This isn't Krapp's last flight, you know. Of course you have a lot on your mind today. But try to tell your story calmly, without disturbing the other passengers.

Very well. [low voice] With the family definitely dead, I could do anything I liked, even down to holding up boxes of detergent on TV and applying my Oxford brain to their washability—well, I don't have to do that now, of course; I'm much "too grand," as my relatives would say.

But to become grand on television, you must first be humiliated and broken. If you're lucky you get to do honest work like game shows and roller derbies and crawling-on-your-belly-with-the-contestants shows. But God help you if you have "class." For then they will stuff you with straw and wheel you around like Guy Fawkes; they will stick a reed in your hand and a tin crown on your head and point, "Look at our class guy." In short, they will force you to parade the one thing a gentleman never shows; namely, his gentlemanliness. Thus do aristocracies perish, peddling first their jewels and finally their manners. On the other hand, class guys are only brought to you by contributing grants from oil companies or, at the very least, Benrus watches.

I didn't mean to have class. I started out as a disc jockey on the West Coast, because in the East I could still hear the house of Chatworth falling down. My first need was to bleach out England and its claims and its pain. I wanted to forget Egbert in his bell tower, and George gallantly puttering, and the whole damned freak show. I had a right to that, I thought. Give a fellow marvelous American vitality and don't expect him to come back as an estate manager in

Dripping-on-the-Mold, hey hey. Get off your ass, Egbert. Conquer that fear of guns.

In passing, I also left my mother and Prissy for dead. What could I have done for them? I suppose our sickly little unit could have lurched on somehow, choking and strangling on its own dust; but I wasn't strong enough to guide it anywhere. They have both found their places in the English mausoleum and they grin and nod like dolls when I visit. I can do them no more harm.

Prissy is always asking me to stay over, but I don't know. Fifty English miles still equal two hundred of anyone else's, and I don't like her husband much. He makes rather a thing out of not watching my shows, which might be refreshing if he weren't *quite* so heavy about it. At least, to my mind, keeping a set which barely works in an upstairs closet strikes me as heavy. And so do his hollow cries of "What brings you over here?" every time we meet.

Priscilla's polite interest hardly makes up for Charlie's leaden ways. In fact, I can't help feeling she eggs him on and is amused by the result. Brothers and sisters assume their wrestling holds early in life, and nothing much changes after that. Although Prissy appears to treat me like a grownup, I know better. The cool amusement is like a deep well down there that only an aborigine can hear.

So I settle this time for a breakfast phone call, trying hard to remember the names and character defects of her five kids, and hearing the well at least do its gurgling at a respectful distance. Yet, it does bring her back, most uncomfortably. To hell with her oafish Tory husband; I don't want Priscilla brought back. That's why I see her so seldom. So get out of my confession, Prissy, you toad. You, too, Mother.

Radio was just a way station, a chance to look around before proceeding to greatness. I could see *them* from behind the mike but they couldn't see *me*.

Yet *they* spotted me somehow, even on this skid row of the business. Somebody heard the Voice. "What are you, British? Don't I know you from Oxford? [Yeah, the old-boy network stretches easily to the lower depths of Fresno.] And the face looks kind of British too. You know, distinguished." Vile little men in Hawaiian shirts thrust me into my purple robes and my top hat. "Class, real class."

Not so fast, Plunkett, or you lose the flavor. If this had all happened in one day, I might have been fooled into agreeing with them about my class. But in slow motion one observes the staggers and facial contortions behind the graceful leap. I did not find it so easy to rise to the top in California after all. Glib young men grow like oranges out there, and finer, juicier than our own. Rich baritones with trip-hammer tongues, laconic bassos who could go for twelve hours without feedback—and all of them former kindergarten radio majors. At an over-the-hill twenty-two, I needed a trademark badly, and guess which one I used.

It wasn't planned, I swear it. For days I had traipsed around Los Angeles, using the voice that had thrilled the Oxford Union and revolted me in equal parts, and received no reaction whatever. This was the one thing that had never occurred to me. I not only flunked Los Angeles, I wasn't even noticed there. By the time I got to Fresno, I was desperate: hot, sweaty, and no doubt sobbing soundlessly, a grim cartoon of my poem about Johnny No-man riding West. The station manager was the poorest grade of fat man I had seen so far. To be turned down by this blob would be the final disgrace. Yet, I needed work. I wasn't used to fear, and I botched it. It was really much too soon for a man of my pretensions to crack, but this was California, and I curled in my chair like a homesick child.

A sweet taste flooded my mouth. I recognized my old friend at once: foreignness, gone berserk like a drunken mouse. I stared at the fat man's bow tie, just to locate myself somewhere. Anything went now, anything that would anchor my sanity. In this state, I emitted the rankest imitation of an Englishman ever heard. I wasn't going to get the job anyway—what the hell. "That's kind of cute," said the station manager. "What is it, British?"

So I was hired, on the understanding that that was my real voice. How silly. I'd be gone in no time, of course.

For days and days I continued to re-create myself punctiliously in the blank California sun, swimming and driving and stopping for orange juice. But at night, I unraveled and did my performing Englishman. For pennies. "I say, this is rather a good one," I'd burble over some groovy platter. "Shall we give it a spin, chaps?" All right. *You* try auditioning in Fresno sometime.

I realize, though, that Fresno is no excuse. Even in L.A. I'd been reaching slyly for my meal ticket, my no. 2 accent. At each interview I had come on a little more English, but a little more isn't good enough in Tinsel City: they wanted, in those days, the whole hog. And finally, in Fresno, they got it, down to the monocle and spats.

Just a temporary phase. "Still feeling your way," wrote Uncle George, confirming this. "Gathering experience. *Admirable.*" He wrote to me as a full partner now, discussing short cuts, economies, and a rumpus room for the gamekeeper. Mysteriously, Chatworth Manor stayed afloat like Lord Jim's old ship, mocking me as I piffled into my microphone.

I say—must we go into all this? It's like asking where did you touch her and how many times. A sin performed by a disc jockey is performed again and again. My joke became my style. "A jolly one, what?" Delirious, alone in my booth, I committed my solitary act again and again. No one was listening as I blasphemed against the voice I loved. "This is Pendrid Chatworth, doncha know." Is it any wonder I have to confess to a tape recorder? The outside world was removed like stage scenery years ago.

Nobody listening? "You sounded American last night," said the first of my fat men. "We're getting complaints."

"From whom, for Godsake."

"Never mind 'from whom.' Look, Penny baby, the woods are full of Americans, and face it, as an American you're mediocre. As a limey, you're all we've got."

So my career was built on travel restrictions. In England they could probably get better Americans too. But better Englishmen could not obtain work papers over here. So I won by default.

My dream of being whatever one liked over here had to be modified slightly: one was free to be whatever the traffic would bear. Time to find honest work, I suppose, in some other line. But my precious voice said, me me. Or perhaps I could have hung on a bit longer and forced my own style on the public. But what was my own style? If I'd mislaid it in Oxford, you can imagine me in California. So what with one thing and another, I wound up singing the national song, "I did it their way."

Why is Snead still here? He can't still be sniveling about the MBE. It wasn't a crown of thorns and he knows it. Something else is eating him. God, I'm jittery. If I don't get through JFK soon, Snead will call a press conference and spill the beans.

Let me insist for the last time: I was not running away from anything back in '52. California was obviously going to be the home of television, and one had to get a foot in the door somehow. It was an exhilarating scramble, and we did some crazy things. If my English accent was so outrageous, what about the chap who played the piano all day in a store window? And threw salamis into cabs? Is he scourging himself for that now? Snead has no sense of humor.

And note how one distortion leads to another to balance the picture. I did not panic in Fresno, and my accent was not all that far-fetched. Why can't Snead be content with small offenses? What is this megalomania of sin? Similarly, I don't remember thinking twice about Chatworth Manor, unless it was to vow to send George some money when I had some. Which I have done. In large quantitites. Until his recent death. I have saved the effing place the only way it could be saved. What, precisely, does Snead want?

Whatever it is, I hope he finds it soon. I hate these tapes, but now that he's back he insists on playing them over and over, and even editing them to make them worse. I wish I'd never started this damn game, but now he won't let me stop. I begin to fear for his sanity, as he perhaps fears for mine.

Jersey, and not a second too soon. Snead is actually several people, all born on radio. One night I foolishly invented a partner to talk to on my disc jockey show. Schizophrenia was an occupational disease on radio, as we bounced unseen from voice to voice; but for an all-night disc jockey it was almost a necessary health measure. I needed a surly, what-the-shit fellow to check Chatworth's rush to fruitiness. So I dug up a Brooklyn friend, who actually came from Jersey and sounded suspiciously like Muldoon—but who could tell out here?—and I allowed him to heckle me like a ventriloquist's doll. Mo Rosselini, I called him, and we fought like cats till dawn.

He didn't last long.

"The guy's too nasty," said the station manager. "People out here don't dig that negative stuff. And besides, Brooklyn guys are goofy and warm-hearted, period."

"OK, I'll warm him up for you," but I couldn't. Mo was a mean son-of-a-bitch or nothing. When I tried to clean him up, my accent wobbled. Since it was still the sunny fifties, my producers retired him—only to replace him with a flesh-and-blood Mo Rosselini, a kid from Pasadena who did a standard Brooklyn imitation, goofy, lovable, and even phonier than my Englishman. Later, they turned him into a Chicano, and nowadays he's an aging coffee taster. Does *he* cry about it?

Once a voice has been launched on the air it never goes completely away. Mo is still in there with the rest of my menagerie: Snead's research team. Funny, I'd forgotten him. "You let dem kill me, you moidering creep." "Hush, now." The original Snead was a phantom phone caller one further remove from reality, who griped good-naturedly about things that happened to be bothering me, until he got unaccountably abusive and I had to retire him. Why has he alone survived?

Look—the series on old English families was honest and constructive and paid any remaining debts. I had to fight the house Maoists to have it put on at all. And Squire Egbert sent me a nice note about how the late Uncle George would have loved it. "First-class. It showed that for all our faults, we *do* have hearts; we are *not* all monsters." What, I repeat, does Snead want?

Oh shit, where do I begin? Egbert was writing me from a mental home, where he spends half the year recovering from his imitation of landed gentry. And from his iron-willed wife. And from having to write letters like the above. But let it pass. Chatworth Manor has been saved. By good American money that Daddy sent me here to get, for all I know.

What truly dumbfounds me is Plunkett's account of the California years. Exhilarating, crazy, foot-in-the-door—who is he kidding? Sell that shit to the press, buddy boy, and the Godforsaken public, but not to a priest, not to my little black friend here.

Those were bitter, humiliating years for a man with dreams of greatness. To give Plunkett his weaseling due, he is indeed right about one thing: I had gone to California to find real glory. But what he leaves out, or cunningly forgets, is that I simply gave up. Not right away or all at once—that would have been superficial—but inch by inch, until indifference bored through to the bone. By the time glory came, I had eaten too much dirt to take real pride in it. Instead, I had these little bursts of vanity followed even then by bouts of remorse. Make no mistake, that was real dirt and it's still in there. Up there in my sweaty little bower, I would say anything for money, in any voice, under any name. I had long since ceased gazing out to sea and was fighting for my swimming pool like everyone else. Like a rat in a maze, I didn't realize that salvation was only a foot or so away, and I just lay down and died.

As for my famous inner life, I flogged that along a little further. I decided that fame was overrated anyway and quite possibly middle class. Even the best kind was built on compromises, though these got fancier the higher you went. My present ones are collector's items, as small as diamonds. But the principle is the same.

California at the time was even more abuzz than usual with religion, as we all faced, with the same sick disgust, the work we had to do in the fifties. And among religions, the quality one right then was my own. Catholicism was both cosmopolitan and unworldly, a rich enough diet for the tawdriest sellout. Protestants seemed to think that religion should have something to do with your life, and this was simply impossible in Southern California. But certain of us Catholics, who believed that our kingdom was not of this world, managed to sneer at Hollywood and play along with it, the way popes do with princes or priests with golf-mad fat cats. And, for practice, we sneered and played along with the American Church itself, that dealer in cotton candy and real estate.

I, of course, was an English Catholic, virtually incorporeal in my fineness. This in turn got me in with a rather good set: the Hollywood converts, scavenging for scraps of class in their new home. A cultivated Catholic needed only to make known his availability to be surrounded by Goldwyn girls who'd seen the light, exotic French Jesuits, the whole Hollywood motley, jangling their bells. And the higher you rose, the better the Catholics: $1,000 a week, $2,000, right to the top. Chatworth jumped a class immediately. Oxford *and* Catholic? Do come to our Greek Mass. Or here—meet Père Pamplemousse: he's a saint, you can smell him anywhere. And you can speak to him in *French*.

I didn't want to exploit this—but try not exploiting something in Hollywood. Everything about you but the squeal is exploited, if it isn't neglected. But between these party games of religion I still prayed real prayers. Or I hoped they were real. Because only thus could I face the necessary degradations of my work. Religion gave me the strength to go on. (When you see the dreadful movies of the fifties you will understand the massive doses of private religion it took to make them possible.)

The disc jockey job lasted just long enough to soften me up. By now I could chatter like a mynah bird in my funny voice and I had a nice gibbering persona to go with it. Letters in deranged handwriting began to roll in. So it was time for the people who listen to such things to get in touch with me and offer me the next step up—a local TV job back in the city. An Oxonian talent scout whiling away his nights in Purgatory was the one who recommended me, and I signed a contract, large enough to float a swimming pool, which entitled them to all my services, day and night. "A technicality," they explained, lying. In fact, no obstetrician ever worked stranger hours than I did for the first year, doing news, weather, and just stuff to fill in the cracks. But it was one of my innocent periods. I went nowhere and betrayed no one. I told my beads and married a Catholic beach girl and prepared my soul for the ultimate treachery.

Welcome to Maureen. But not now, honey. I'll get back to you in a little while, OK? Swell. Where was I? Ah, the big one, the Sin you've all been waiting for. I wish I could say it was difficult. But if the termites have done their job properly, it's no big deal when the roof falls in. After my freshman hazing, the fat men sent for me and nodded their approval. "We're getting a good response. You've got class." A thin man nods and leaves, too revolted to go on. This is Ian Comstock, the resident Oxonian and fashion adviser, who has gotten me into this. A real class guy, slowly dying of the same disease I've got.

"How would you like to take a crack at an interview show?"

Wow, sir. My big break. I compose my features into a look

of wild enthusiasm—the least that's expected out here, even of reserved Englishmen. "Mm-mm," I murmur warmly.

"Right. Great. There's only one catch."

Pause. "Yes?"

"We don't think the name Pendrid quite plays over here."

"It doesn't?"

"No. We need something more Englishy."

I squeak, "Pendrid isn't Englishy?"

"Nah. It's just a funny sound."

"Thanks."

"Don't get mad. How would *you* like to be called Emmanuel?" I really have no idea. Nothing in my varied training has prepared me for the Hollywood mind.

Their idea of Englishy brings me back full circle to MGM in the forties; they are asking me to play Master Miniver.

"Monty isn't English at all," I say wildly.

"Over here, it's English," they tell me.

"Well, I won't do it."

"You won't, huh? Not even if it's in your contract?"

"No . . . What do you mean it's in my contract?"

"You intellectual guys slay me. You always think contracts are too utterly boring to read, so you'll sign anything. Yeah, it's in there all right, along with your balls and an option on your circulatory system."

"OK, I'll simply break it."

"Hey! How about that British spirit, guys?" My genial host winks around. It is a primitive time in history. "A real fighter. They'll love him. With the initials MC and all."

Little Sir Winston rides again. But he's just going through the motions of riding. Shortly thereafter ads appear in the local paper for the new Monty Chatworth interview show. Son-of-a-bitch, I'll take care of that. Deny it on the air. Test of character. My voice quivers as I confront my first starlet.

"My name isn't really Monty, you know." My voice has never sounded more juicily English.

"It isn't?" says the starlet. "Huh. That's funny."

There is a foolish pause. Then a comedian next to her says, "Yeah, that's funny. Neither is mine."

Well, er, so much for that. The next listing has me down as Monty Chatworth, and the next. I can't see myself telling an endless stream of bored guests the real truth about my name. Like all sins, it seems less important every time around. At least it will never get outside California. Thus, a legend is born.

Your little face looks sad. You don't think that's much of a sin, Father Sony? How would you like it if I made you change your name to "Tojo"? No, it's got to be sex or violence for you. Well, we'll see what we can do about that. Meanwhile, I felt as I signed "Monty Chatworth" to my next contract that I was completing a Faustian negotiation worthy of six Hollywood agents. The sin was in the Bureau of Records now, and the Devil pays up fast before you can renege. I was suddenly allowed to slide back toward my own voice, as my victims grew better and more intelligent. In fact, I became more or less myself again now that it was too late. It was like moving into a corpse.

If you can get your head above the swamp of brute talent in Hollywood, you suddenly stand alone. Success there has to be overnight, it can't move any slower. Like a Christian, you must keep watch day and night for its coming. Then go, man, go. Off like the wind. Don't turn back for your coat—or your wife.

My religious background had prepared my heart perfectly for my new idol, success-as-defilement: all the key things like dedication, sacrifice, and knowing when to kneel and where to kiss were second nature by now. My apprentice years had simply streamlined me, scraping off excess culture and regret and pointing my nose toward the moon.

The interview show was a hit. I Jenkinsed my victims well and got a name for stupefying erudition. In the land of the one-inch forehead, the two-inch forehead is king. (Real intelligence would have caused mass panic.) Daring experiments

274

with insolence had been tried on the East Coast, and I adapted these to the softer climate, mixing them with boyish respect. Hollywood contains real killers, and killers must be polite with each other. And the effect was more deadly and sinister than brashness could ever be.

Above all, I was onto my guests' tricks, as one conjurer is onto another's; and as I traced their techniques, I found more and more that there was no source to them, only more technique. Of course, this was especially true of my brothers the actors. I felt a quite morbid pleasure when they got onto their favorite causes, from muscular dystrophy to communism, because their sincerity was technique at its rawest and most flagrant. It was down near the base, the uncaused cause and the formless matter, of technique. They never acted worse than when they thought they meant it.

And I followed them all the way, like the ghostly ferryman: I had made this journey many times myself. No wonder people praised the power and empathy of my interviews. I was peeling people down to my own size; which meant no onion at all.

When it began to happen with religious leaders and living saints, I got a little frightened. With some it was a pleasure; but with a few, I rushed to cover them. My little taunting-truckling device was ripping up too much black cloth, and I began to long for a real saint. The whole world couldn't be in my condition, could it? The damned are prey to these visions.

Perhaps a saint was simply good technique, a sinner bad. God was excellent technique. My father? Leave him out of this.

The Moment came when one of my very best Catholics ($5,000 and up) recommended my show to a network president. She was a famous actress who had withstood my Grand Inquisitor tactics as only a fellow Catholic can. For good professional reasons she had to sound scatterbrained, but she knew exactly what I was doing. "Of course I feel empty sometimes, Monty," she said on the air. "That's space for

God to fill." Only in Hollywood could anyone be so fluffy and theologically correct at the same time.

She assumed from the questions that my work had some veiled missionary purpose. "You're doing a lot of good," she said afterwards. "That was sort of like going to confession." Oh no, please. "Only someone who had been there a lot himself could have done it," she said, driving the nails into my hands. "It's funny, if the people won't go to confession, perhaps we must bring confession to them. That might be the interviewer's calling these days."

I mumbled something about psychiatry's doing the same and she shook her head violently. "No, no, *that's* all about approval. You withhold approval, in some way. Forgiveness, yes. Approval, no."

Plunkett preened, he cannot help it. And he and the woman are still fast friends. But, as usual, it was based on a lie. If I had picked up some tricks in the box, it was only a habit; just as she had fallen into the penitent's posture out of habit. Whatever it was, she thought she was doing the Lord's work in bringing my mission to the networks. Which meant, in those days, going to New York to meet the boats. Quick, Chatworth, move. I talked before about leaving my wife, and that's what I did. She refused to go East because you couldn't wear a bathing suit all day in the East. I do not wish to discuss this girl. She was an incident. She moved up the Coast to prepare for the sixties, and I never saw her again.

What's this? A broken marriage isn't a serious matter? And you don't want to discuss it? Father Sony is all ears again. He is mad about poontang, it seems. He is not the first priest to disappoint me.

23

Jersey, all is Jersey from now on. Let's have this out here and now, Snead—we don't have all the time in the world. You know why we're here, don't you? Right. It is a deeply humbling assignment, and we've got to get ready for it.

Now you and Father Sony both seem to think I'm barking up the wrong sin, that it's something in the private sector, that it's animal, and not a goods or service at all. And that, mysteriously, all the victims have been women. Well, I'm onto Sony's lascivious interests by now, but there's no excuse for Snead. Take Maureen, for instance. Why do you always take her side, Snead? You know that she left me, I didn't leave her, and that I was heartbroken about it and I spent years trying to get in touch with her. I concede that she was not a beach bum, but a psychology major at UCLA, but I can't see what difference that makes.

My only crime with Maureen was my usual one—mistaken identity—and I couldn't do anything about that by then, could I? It was committed years ago.

To begin with, Maureen was a mystic before her time, and

I looked kind of mystical. And she was fearless and wanted to give it all up and live the beach life; maybe even form a religious community. And didn't I look about right for that, too? Even a lifetime of thinking about one's self can make one look kind of spiritual; and I sometimes threw in God for good measure. Look out the window at that slapping sea. I am still half-monk and half-goat. The only difference between me and Egbert is that I carry a mike.

But mainly she liked me because I was un-American, and any un-American was better than none. It was assumed that I hated tin cans and electricity and phoniness, and I do, I do. I hate them and love them. I mean, I still cry when I think of my first pop-up toaster. But I might have been worse: I might have been West German.

And I had fallen for her for the same basic reason— difference: in L.A. you fall on difference like a dying man. Little did I know that even then Maureen was a copy. I had been misinformed. She was also significantly different from Diana and Tish, with their personalities with the herbaceous borders. Maureen was open and undefined, the perfect counterpart to my old dream self; so I galloped along with her, openly and spontaneously, like an old man dancing the tango. We slept out and had no fixed meals, which gave me simultaneously insomnia and indigestion. We took unplanned trips to the mountains and subsisted on berries and edible grasses. The Good Fairy was putting me through the ringer for my silly wish: the plainsman was a buttoned-up Englishman after all.

Yet, there is good in everything, as Father Mulcahy used to say back in Tewksbury days. I became tanned and fit and versed in the kinks of nature, so that I was more than ready for the flower children when they came along. In fact, my special on the generation gap won my first Emmy; it showed me eating my way up a mountain as a gaggle of slack-jawed teen-agers looked on. "It isn't so hard," I lectured the parents. "They're calling you back to something—something you've forgotten to your cost." Maureen, wherever you are, I hope you didn't catch that one.

Oddly enough, she did not particularly mind my English impersonation, nor my silly name; as a good radical, she saw it as a metaphor for the job market in general and felt that, if anything, I was ripping off the system. Or at least I *think* this is what she felt. Because, unlike Diana and Tish, she did not accept the limits of language, but expressed herself in modulations of silence and body heat as delicate as Henry James, once you knew the language. (The English seemed hopelessly flat and blunt in comparison.)

She may have sensed before I did that I was devouring her for future use; that I was, in fact, a machine for devouring people which had run amok. Because she seemed to shade herself against me: "I don't want you to know what I'm feeling," she seemed to say. "You'd cheapen it." At the same time, she'd try to surprise me into her own kind of candor. "Quick. What do you really think of that old man over there? Before words like 'underprivileged' and 'caring' come and spoil it." But the words came so quickly that even when I didn't speak they showed in my face. I'd lived by my tongue too long. She would shake her head and drop the subject.

For a while she tried to silence me with Zen and inner peace, but the tongue still moved like a dumb man's larynx. And perhaps she could already see the future specials forming there. My three-parter on Oriental wisdom would indeed give me a huge jump on the sixties and make me something of a cult hero. Imagine—five minutes of complete silence on prime time. So even not speaking, she could not hide from me and my machine.

Still, she loved me for a while, perhaps because of all this. Being quarried like a natural resource has its fascinations even for mystics. Especially for mystics. My verbalization pleased and amused her. I eagerly agreed that words were far inferior to intuition and tended to weaken it. I told her I could never penetrate her inwardness but could only skim its lovely surface. All very flattering, for a while.

Then the interviews started, and she saw that I had my own vile kind of intuition. I could penetrate inwardness like a safecracker, though I had no use for the jewels inside. "You're the Devil," she said. "You're a different person for every show."

I was still enough of a Catholic to be shaken by this. "I'm not the Devil. It's a trick."

"That's what I mean," she said lucidly.

There is sometimes a bond between old Catholics, as between brother and sister, that should prevent them from marrying. She looked almost sympathetic over my affliction. Devil possession is no joke.

So what seemed to the secular public a rather adroit interviewer, and to my actress friend a priest for our times, struck my young wife as an abomination. She knew me better than they did and knew that I was unmasking people for my own sweet sake. I was using the spiritual illumination of our tradition to get ahead in the world.

"I'm only ripping off the system," I suggested, caressing her stringy hair, which was her one doomed attempt to look plain.

"Is that it?" She rolled closer. "You don't do it to me too?"

"Good grief, no."

She began then, slowly, curiously, to make love, as for the first time, kissing my neck and chest like a stethoscope. Try being spontaneous in those circumstances, Snead. I felt my skin turn to prickly cardboard and my fingers lose their touch: they squeezed too hard and stroked too feathery.

"Yes, you do do it to me," she said. "Mr. Gable."

The next day she was gone, and Snead had lost his best friend. He still thinks that was a perfectly fair test, and there should be more like it.

But wait a damn minute, Snead—nothing in life happens like that. On a bad day, Maureen was capable of thinking that Smokey the Bear was the Devil. The kid was flaky and paranoid. And as I became better known, my intrusions on her dream world became intolerable. She wouldn't go out and meet people, but preferred to stay home and bake brownies; or, if I brought them to the house, she went *out* and baked brownies, for all I knew. How the hell could I have held on to her? Be reasonable, Snead.

Sure, the interviews bothered her. The simple fact is the kid didn't talk herself because she couldn't and was sore at those who could. As long as I pretended speech was a crippling deformity, she went along. But when she found that I could use it to see through *Marlon Brando,* she knew I could see to hell and back through her and she moved on out. I tell you, it was just an incident. Let's get this show moving. My Golden Age is about to begin.

What, no children? Absolutely not. That was a contemptible trick on her part, and I think it wraps up the case against her. She sent me a note some months later from an unmarked post office somewhere in Drug City. "I always wanted to have a child by the Devil, but I wouldn't want the Devil to raise him," it said simply.

Quite impossible. She could not have been pregnant when she left. But the mere possibility of the last Chatworth waddling around Haight-Ashbury looking for his daddy in the ruins has haunted me ever since. Even Snead cannot face it.

I really did try to trace her, but by then her type, lankhaired and large-eyed, had faded into the landscape. I know for a fact she is not a Manson girl (I checked personally), so that's a relief.

I finally got a Catholic nullity, than which there is nothing more null. It means that *nothing happened,* despite appearances, and I wish you'd try to remember that, Snead. Sure, I loved her. But I will not accept Snead's thesis that she was right about me, and had given me a million signals, a trillion chances to change and that I would have saved my soul if I'd paid attention. You don't save your soul shooting up in an ashram, my friend. And if it comes to beaches, why I've always got New Jersey here.

It is true, I have not married again, at first for good Catholic reasons but later for the real reasons. Maureen had frightened me. The delicate equilibrium that keeps a Chatworth tottering above the snakepit cannot stand a woman's stare. My father married a poor blind one, yet he was struggling by the end. And I have a further difficulty: What *I'm* doing seems so close to what *women* are doing, and they seem to do it better. They get too close, know too much. Snead's clumsy heckling is a joy by comparison. At least I can control him; and deep down, he sees no more than I do. He needs women to give him ammunition.

My last serious attempt was Lisa Montez, and that worked for a good long time. Lisa was so extroverted, and her command of the language so shaky, that it took her forever to see through me—and in a sense she never did. She was a minor actress who had what she took to be a passion for Englishmen, although with her ear, she thought all sorts of people were English, including Burt Lancaster, so she'd cut quite a cheerful swath before we met.

Lisa suited me perfectly. She loved men with a generosity that absorbed small weaknesses like crumbs off a rug, and simply bypassed large ones. Her two favorite pastimes were laughing and changing the subject. The threat of seriousness bothered her like a rumor of disease. One felt that if it ever came it would carry her away, she would be so good at it. But Englishmen were a splendid antidote: they made her laugh on sight and continuously. Even with me, I could never tell whether it was my jokes or just the general idea of me that set her off, and I didn't care. She had, in fact, a very sophisticated sense of humor, but it never kept her from laughing anyway.

Lisa carried me through the carpentry years, where you

282

nail a career together carefully, like a coffin, and she kept me from those ghastly charades with women that I could barely face anymore; and I thought we'd stay together till the *ignis fatuus* was at least manageable. But seriousness did come at last, and I was right—she got a terrible case of it. Her seriousness was lovelier than anything I'd ever seen of its kind, not just theatrical but somber and definitive as the Escorial. I had wiped the smile off her face for good. Don't ever do this to a Spaniard.

But that was only two years ago, when I landed kicking and squalling in midlife, and I haven't figured what to do with myself since. Father Sony, with his strange passion for chronology and filth, wants to know first if anything bad happened when I left Hollywood for New York.

Nothing that bothers me much, I'm afraid. I was on the magic carpet where you can do no wrong, the servants do it for you. My agent took over the greed, the publicity director handled the vanity, and so forth. I was as carefree as a eunuch.

For all her transparent wackiness, Maureen had also frightened me a little about the interviews, and the ones I did in the East were like fake surgery: all white gowns and rubber knives. Candor was already in its decadence, and a display of flying elbows was all you needed. But beyond that, I would, for all my sins, rather be second-rate than damned. (That is one of my sins.) Besides, the networks preferred it that way. As usual, they had hired me for something they didn't really want: namely, my power to discomfit people. On the other hand, what they got was a disappointment to people who remembered, or looked forward to, the old California killer. And then suddenly everyone got tired of watching celebrities filleted, and the show came off after one season. But even failure on coast-to-coast network makes you a household word.

My rare interviews these days tend to be senile celebrations of toothless superstars, or else thoughtful exchanges with statesmen. The killer lives on, of course, but he only interviews himself now; it is all that's permitted to a Christian. And with nowhere else to go, he keeps probing long after he's reached the truth. My career from now on is objectively blameless, but I've got to keep occupied.

My last linchpin, the Catholic Church, chooses this unfortunate moment to go out of business, taking confession with it, so my need to unbutton myself goes flapping around the barnyard with no one to talk to. Oh, I know it didn't really go out of business, but only pretended to. One of my first major assignments was the Vatican Council, and I recognized it for the sly affair it was. Like the New Deal, it preserved the old order by making modern noises. Very little was really changed.

Yet, a religion lives by its noises. People picked up the new tone, and to hell with the substance. Sunday Mass might still be important, but it didn't *sound* important. So we didn't go anymore. Confession? Who would endure that ordeal if it weren't a question of life and death? The Church had lost its gravity. By expressing ancient beliefs in modern terms it had removed all their weight. That is the whole point with modern terms.

My first feeling was one of relief. I was off the hook. If the Church wasn't serious, I'd be a damned fool to be so myself. Rephrased in modern terms, I wasn't such a bad fellow. In abandoning all my traditions, I was only following Vatican guidelines. Chatworth Manor need not outlive the Latin Mass. Flushed with *aggiornamento,* Uncle George could now move to Hollywood and become a stage Englishman. Egbert could wear his bishop's robes in public—he'd soon be the only one anyway. And I could go on as I was, frolicking in the winds of change.

For a few giddy years, the guilt cleared. As I got classier and classier, I was allowed not to do commercials—the one task that had seemed unarguably sinful for a Chatworth. My father once went into a paroxysm of contempt when he heard that the Duke of Argyll autographed his socks for the American market ("I'm surprised he doesn't sign his bum," said Father with rare vulgarity), and I could still see his eyes bulging out there every time I held up a carton of cottage cheese.

Now that that was cleared up, my career seemed downright praiseworthy. From inane dignity stuff, royal weddings and such, I had gone on to global responsibilities, and I defy Snead to find fault with my handling of these. To be sure, I was fearlessly anticommunist in the dregs of the McCarthy years, briefly dazzled by Camelot, shocked by Kennedy's assassination, took a firm line with Castro, but welcomed détente—what the hell do you expect? You think a network is a soapbox in Union Square?

I was on the side of *people,* wherever I found them: starving in Biafra, dying in Ulster—all the people one would normally be against.

. . . So what the fuck have you accomplished, Plunkett? Depth, vividness—one newsreel camera does more than you in all important respects. In fact, your job is to neutralize the cameras with their crazy discoveries by running them through a totally conventional mind. Christ, you even think like a network.

. . . I don't care. I'm the best. I am fearless and enterprising. It says so right here. Sure, I was disappointed to find that even when I'd reached the top, I still wasn't completely free. And Snead has a point in his twisted way: I do think a little like a network, in the sense of knowing there are a lot of people out there and that I can't beat them over the head with my personal opinions. So? I move them a little in the right direction. Snead doesn't move them at all.

. . . Did you ever hear a network talking? Well, I did. Was there ever such scalding horse piss as the above? This milk-fed anonymity actually thinks he's moving the public in its rush to the sea. If it weren't Chatworth, it would be somebody else just like him riding herd over them. The sum total of his achievement is that he speaks passable English; and even this is canceled out by the sheer mischief of rephrasing clichés. People think they're hearing something fresh and brilliant every time their prejudices come bouncing back at them. Why don't you read your praises onto the record, Plunkett? They'd be a touch of vinegar for a thirsty man. In fact, they might even complete my work.

. . . OK, you nihilistic bugger. I don't know how much remorse you expect of me. I could cry myself to death and you'd say I faked it. I could feel heartbroken over hunger and poverty, and have, and you'd say, where'd you learn that little trick? You're a disease.

I must hear an outside voice; I need another opinion. And then perhaps, pulling myself together as best I can, I'll be the judge.

24

I have been asked not to describe this new assignment to anybody, even you, Father Sony, in case you should fall into the wrong hands. Do you think you wouldn't break? Pah. Some ruthless person would shoot a few hot volts through you and you'd tell everything. Don't feel bad about it. You're only electric.

Frankly, I don't think it will happen at all, but I'm still on standby: if anyone gets it, it'll be me. Dealing with that gang would drive a jellyfish up the wall. Sources close to sources think it *might* be arranged if the price is right, etc. The famous Chatworth nerves must think this is a dance marathon. Inactivity is worse for them than exhaustion: I've got to keep practicing, but my own thoughts get viler all the time. I am losing the art of talking to myself decently. I am like an old marriage.

So, yes, let's read something else into the record, only not, for Godsake, my praises. That will only bring Snead yowling to the back door. Let's pick a reasonably hostile interview, so I can rehearse the basic Chatworth sentence in the worst possible setting.

This particular one also conveys my avuncular relationship to the sixties—a time of turmoil for most people, but of unearthly serenity for me. I heard no voices then, my ancient blood hadn't begun to stir and growl, my family and then my Church were decently buried in tasteful ceremonies—above all, my talent sang, a little more English in America, a touch more Yank for England, nothing more. In youth an artifice can spin along without asking questions. And I thought it would last forever. You laugh. But if your prime happens to coincide with the Black Death, it is still your prime, damnit, and you're entitled to enjoy it.

"I've never been able to stand Monty Chatworth because he's so utterly perfect."

The writer is an English kid living in San Francisco making hairy pseudo-American noises from the underground. His face is boily with resentment, the kind that makes England the proud seat of festering gossip.

"I can take the witty and civilized bit. Barely. Phonies have to eat like everyone else. But the man of virtue is just a bit goddamn much. The patron of Biafra and Bangladesh, and the greatest fund raiser since the invention of leprosy, was found the other day in a suite that could house an Indian village, or at least a cancer ward. He is currently helping humanity in the Beverly Hills area. So let's take a closer look at the chap.

"In the flesh he resembles an English army officer of the old school. The famous mustache is groomed like the Queen's horses, the smoking jacket gleams like regimentals, and the posture makes you want to clear your throat on entering. In other words, he's a screaming antique.

" 'I say, Monty, are you there?'

" 'Speaking.'

" 'I say, Monty. I'd like you to tell our readers how you do it. I mean, save the world week after week.'

"Monty doesn't blink. 'Come off it, cocky,' he says mildly.

"What's this, what's this? 'Monty? Are you still there?' "

" 'You heard me,' he says. 'I know your type. You are the latest breed of English hustler. One of my children.' "

This, as you will guess, is a little-known interview from the *San Mateo Mole*. Circulation, 300, readership, nil. A chance to enjoy myself. I am improvising as I read, but the gist is there, and it's a useful impression from a fellow con man. I figured that my best bet was to be even ruder than he was: celebrities are so fixed in people's minds that any variation takes them off stride. And being tough with a celebrity has to be rehearsed bravely; it cannot handle the unexpected. Back to him.

" 'Now do you want an interview, or do you just want to show off?' Chatworth asked me. I didn't seem to have much choice. It's a long walk from the Beverly Wilshire to San Francisco. 'Can I do both?'

" 'No.'

" 'Oh, all right. Where were you born?'

"It was a funny kind of interview. Before I had learned anything at all about him, he had learned that I came from Manchester, had been a private in the army, and hated the ruling class. 'Which includes you,' I said.

" 'Yes, I quite understand,' he said.

" 'What are you doing in the sixties, anyway?' I pursued. 'I thought your type died at the Battle of the Somme.'

" 'Oh, we did, we did. Like most of our countrymen, I'm a complete imitation. Like you, for instance.'

" 'Like *me*?'

" 'Yes. You're an uncanny replica of a fifties rebel. Still hating the ruling class. How quaint.' "

Me: But I do hate them.

M.C.: I'm sure you do. And it does you credit. It's one of the pleasures of an old civilization that there are so many types to choose from. Then we can come over here and sell them to the Yanks. But you don't honestly think you could get an audience for that angry stuff back home, do you?

Me: Is that all you think about? Audiences. Believe it or not, I have real concern.

M.C.: I should certainly hope so. It wouldn't work even over here if you didn't have that.

Me: You cynical bastard.

M.C.: It's what you wanted, isn't it? I hate to disappoint. Besides, if one died at the Somme, it relieves one of certain responsibilities.

Me: OK, if you want to crap around. But when you come on as a member of the kiddie culture, eating wild berries and demonstrating yoga positions, don't even you feel ridiculous? Not to mention, a traitor to your damn class?

M.C.: You'll never understand my damn class, will you? That's just the kind of thing we've always done. Wild berries, yoga—who the hell else would do anything as silly as that? Let me tell you something, cocky. I'll be here long after you've gone. Five years from now, there won't be a hippie in sight. If you keep your integrity, which I doubt, you will probably wind up working for Underground Papers, Inc., a branch of General Electric. I shall still be a triumphant oddity. The truth is, your class doesn't know beans about survival. Now tell me about real concern.

It's funny—I'd forgotten that last part. It's the only time I was ever smoked out on the class question, and my answers were like automatic writing—or like jousting with my Oxford tutor. What I learned was that the vein of snobbery was still there. It runs quiet and deep, having lost all biological purpose, but it's also weatherproof under the skin and feathers. Depressing and elating. What I was saying was that my class would stick its head in a coconut shy to survive.

I have absentmindedly pulled rank and condescension on the guy and he knows it. Up to now he may have been going through the motions of class resentment, but suddenly it all comes back to him, and he really rips me with a series of insulting and largely pointless questions, about my family and who the fuck were they anyway (Who indeed?), and winds up with the house special, which is whether or not I'm a fag.

M.C.: [smiling] Maybe that's it.

Me: It's what people say.

M.C.: Quite all right. It's entirely possible.

Me: I'm gay myself, you know.

M.C.: Yes, I know.

Me: The only sin is hiding it.

M.C.: Is that so? [Smiles politely. Pause. Never say too much.]

Me: You know, most people would be sore as hell if I asked that about them.

M.C.: Would they? Yes, I suppose they would.

Me: But you're not?

M.C.: No. It's always hard to tell with Englishmen, isn't it?

Well, that's about enough of Cocky. The last part gets a little far-fetched. Some sympathetic talk about the hard life of a fag in our society, followed by my giving him advice on how to get a writing job in television. He didn't really give a damn about Vietnam, let alone the African nations, which I roguishly asked him to name and place. The only real concern he felt for anything was gay liberation; and even the sores of class stopped itching briefly when that came into view. So by being vaguely sympathetic about that, I neutralized him, and he left the worst bits of tape out of his story. There are worse fates than being called a harmless old fart.

. . . Now hold on a minute, Plunkett [Oh God, who let him in?]. Let me refresh the bubbles in your memory. What happened in the blank space there? I'll tell you. This kid Higgins (yes—he has a name too, Gorgeous) implored you to come out of the closet, in which case he would follow you anywhere. He saw you as a great moral leader. You know very well that nobody can take celebrities calmly. He came in hating you and walked out loving you. You allowed him to do that.

I don't know who was the more degraded by the whole thing. He bought your shit because he thought you were a brother, *and that's the only reason.* Like Diana buying the Church. Like everyone in this love-starved world. And you

291

—you'll admit to anything to win them: fag, transvestite, communist. Once you found it didn't matter which you were, you've been a full-time whore. Once upon a time you and I cared so much about being this or that, Irish, Catholic, Eskimo, what the shit. Now you prey on the people who still care. That's how it is with whores. "Do try to be first-rate, Pen." Is this what you think Daddy meant?

... All right, Snead. Maybe I should have said I wasn't homosexual, but I didn't think it mattered. I am that man's brother whether he knows it or not. If he thinks I have to wear his club tie—OK, I'll wear it. If that's his only idea of a brother, consider it done. And someday perhaps you'll tell me how an intelligent man can do anything for anyone in a mass society. By keeping up old estates, I suppose, and hearing Mass in private chapels. You're still a Catholic, aren't you, you useless son-of-a-bitch? And a snob and a fourteen-carat semiprecious perfectionist. You've changed, Snead. You used to be an American, and you got adopted by an old English family, and now you're worse than any of us. Just tell me one thing the Chatworths have done, up to and including Saint Daddy, to equal the money I've raised for cancer research alone. What do you want of me? Why do you drag on my soul like this?

... To keep you humble, Plunkett, that's why. Talking of which—how about doing the one you've been avoiding. The one with the nun.

... Who? You mean Sister Trivia of the Suffering Succulents?

... No, the one I liked so much. Veronica. *Don't* be so lordly about names.

... In fact, the following article was written, though for obvious reasons not published, by an unfrocked nun of some academic standards. I don't know why Snead likes it so much, but doubtless he has his reasons.

25

〰〰〰〰〰〰〰〰〰〰〰〰〰

I met Pendrid Chatworth, as he prefers to be called, at his hideaway on the Jersey coast. He has been coming here, or somewhere just like it, for twenty years now. His conditions are that the place be plain as a monk's cell, overlook the sea, and be connected to some small, unconcerned village. I promised not to divulge its whereabouts, or to describe the ridiculously simple disguise that hides the well-known face from the disinterested villagers. [*Sic.* Nuns don't learn English, they only teach it.]

"I have never given an interview here," he announced, "because I am not a public person here." However, since I write for a small religious publication, he felt that talking to me would fit well enough into his retreat. "No public talk, though, no celebrity talk. I am not, nor have I ever been, Monty Chatworth in this house."

We were sitting in the kitchen with a jug of wine and a wheel of cheese, his diet for the two or three weeks he manages to squeeze in here. The house is startlingly bare, and so, in a manner of speaking, is he: white shirt, black seminarian pants, and sandals. And with the disguise added, he might pass for the Unknown Priest.

"Do you consider this a *religious* retreat?" I asked.

"Yes, precisely. In a secular world, it is the best I can do."

"No crucifix on the wall, no skull on the table?"

"Right. Only bread and wine. My mother cured me of crucifixes, and I was never really into skulls, as the kids say. A crucifix would be flashy. Simplicity, *nothingness,* is the only honest way for me. I'm known as a loner in the business, but out here I double it."

"And what do you do during your retreat?"

"Well, to begin with, I try not to meditate. I do enough of that in real life, you know. And I try not to be too spiritual. For a Catholic, being spiritual is pushy. I decided all that at sixteen, gave it up for twenty-odd years, and have since returned full cycle. And having a spiritual crisis is intolerably pushy. Do you understand me at all?"

I should certainly hope so. Even the smartest of men cannot accept women as spiritual professionals.

"All of that is a way of saying, 'Me, me—look, God, I'm over here.' Whenever I hear of people finding Christ I shudder. What convulsions of vanity they must be going through. And then, *losing* themselves in Christ. Who are *they* to lose themselves? It's all ego, finding new games for itself to play."

I hate to tell him how elementary all this stuff is. After all, he is a layman, doing his best, and I don't want to discourage him. "But what else is there?" I ask, like a straight man.

"Nothing. Which is what I practice here."

"How do you do that?"

"By going to the village every day," he was taking the question literally, "and buying my stuff there. By having some drinks with the locals and talking about the weather. By going to church and playing bingo. By attending to the action of walking, the fact of breathing, the sound of talking. Paying close attention to textures, but drawing no conclusions. Anything added to that is flashy and unnecessary, don't you think?"

"I don't honestly know."

"Come *on*, you're a nun. You understand these things. Only a saint can do more than walk and breathe and talk to his neighbors, and hope he's doing it right. And a saint is taking an awful chance."

"Tell me—are you putting me on, Mr. Chatworth?"

"Ah, they don't make nuns the way they used to. All right, I'll talk to you like a regular reporter. In my business, the ego overheats, and I come here to cool off. In my case, my spiritual life also overheats when I'm working. But I won't alarm your readers by describing that."

"But do you still believe in God and religion?"

"That isn't the point."

"What do you mean, it isn't the point?"

"If I tell you, you'll only write that Monty Chatworth goes bananas in the off-season. Send me a real nun and I'll explain. I suppose you joined up to do good, did you? Most Americans do. Being brides of Christ isn't good enough anymore."

Monty Chatworth goes bananas in the off-season.

"But if belief isn't the point, what is?" I press on.

"All right, I'll tell you. Worrying about whether you believe in God is impertinent. Can you imagine the Angel Gabriel rushing up to the Throne to say, 'I hear that Monty Chatworth believes in you, sir.' or 'I'm afraid we're losing Monty'? "

"I can imagine that."

"You can? Hey, you're better than I thought."

Well, I was glad to hear that from such a great man. It confirmed my own feeling entirely.

"I hate to ask you, but everybody wants to know whether you're, you know, celibate on purpose."

"Ah, purpose, purpose. How does one know when one is *on* it? I guess insofar as celibacy is an act of negation, of refusal, I chose it, yes. To put it bluntly, I don't want children. And for a Catholic of whatever condition, marriage is nothing without children, it doesn't exist. I don't need a steady roommate and I don't see any point in marching into a legal tangle. Though I almost did it, you know, with Lisa Montez. Do you remember her? *Blood Along the Nile?* Or didn't that make the convents? But we were always fighting over the bathroom. Marriage without children comes down to that—low comedy. I'm too rich and famous to need it."

"But why don't you want children?"

"Off the record? Fear. Guilt. Despair. For one thing, I don't want to be a father and live on in some child's mind as a prehistoric monster. I don't want some psychiatrist digging me out of there year after year. And, I don't want a son *inventing* me, as I invented my father, and tormenting himself over his invention. I'd rather distribute my favors evenly. Millions of people have faint pictures of me, but I don't *bother* anybody."

"That's what you think."

"Well, perhaps I bother some lonely women who are looking to be bothered—but this is not a patch on what a father can do to a son. At least in my family."

"Your family? What's so special about them?"

"A very good question. I wish I could tell you. I mean, they are special, but I honestly don't know why. Anyhow, whatever it is, they can't go on like this. Another Chatworth would be simply ridiculous. The curtain is down for good (I know, because I pulled it myself) and the play is over. So there you have it. The English don't like children anyway; they only have them out of duty, and my duty has been lifted. There is nothing for the next generation of Chatworths to do."

"Do you really mean that?"

"Oh—*I* don't. But someone inside me does. Someone who lives near the action and runs the machinery. You see, he won't let me discharge into a woman and start the whole

296

perilous business in motion. He has a million excuses and they may all be, as you say over here, malarkey, but at least his performance is sincere. After a long blissful period, Lisa Montez suddenly asked me for a baby, and I said well, OK, if you must, but *he* wouldn't do it. Pigheaded, you might call him. You're not going to print this, are you?"

"I don't think they'd take it, do you? Maybe I'll just circulate it privately, to you."

I hadn't meant it, but my own words had an erotic effect on me. Well, you know that, Pendrid, so we won't go into it here.

"Yes," he said, "the old boy just quit on me. Lay down on the job, so to speak. So I couldn't very well get married, could I? Poor Lisa said she would raise the child herself, practically out of sight, that I wouldn't be disturbed for a moment; but this wasn't right, either, and she knew it. 'Maricón,' she wound up calling me. 'That's what that's about —children, not women at all. You're a fag because you fear my fertility.' A very Latin point of view, I suppose. I don't quite go along with it, but I do agree that to a Catholic, in whatever state of repair, marriage doesn't just mean children, it means children *at the center.* The mother dying for them, the father giving his life to them. I would have to do it that way myself. I would have to do it well.

"My God, that phrase. Anyway, I would have raised hell out of any child I had, and left him battered and bleeding for my pains. But Lord Henry wouldn't let me do it. Impetuous fellow though he usually is."

"Is he? Still?"

"Decidedly so, yes."

That's enough of that. My interviewer kindly typed up the story and sent it the next day, but I can't read the last part in my own voice. It would be obscene. She had left the recorder running, and perhaps she was performing for it. At any rate, she was noisy enough, making all the sighs and moans she must have imagined lovers making as she tossed on her bony convent mattress. She enclosed with the piece a note of further invitation but I refused. My self-disgust was cleaner than usual and uncomplicated. I have allowed no reporters to my nest at Toms River since.

. . . Since? You make it sound like a long time ago. Like all your sins. You have distanced yourself from them like an old man, even the recent ones. But here we have something piping hot. Come on, now. Confess while the body is warm for a change.

. . . Don't disturb me right now, I'm grabbing a winter nap. Seaside resorts should only be visited in the winter, don't you think?—when the gloss is off them. We've built a big fire and are looking into the flames like a child, watching them paint faces. This is quite a talented fire in that respect. Plunkett found this particular hellhole and is more or less in charge here. For instance, that was his epicene philosophy quoted above—as useless as Egbert in his bell tower; as precious and useless as the blue veins on a dowager's hand. But he insists on it every now and then, so for a few weeks, just to humor him, I consent to be a Chatworth. What the hell, it enriches my style.

. . . The hell it does, you mellifluous turd. It only means that Snead has to reduce the sugar content again later on.

. . . That's very eloquent, the stuff about resorts in the winter and the big fireplace; it's almost enough to make my grease paint run. But the real reason I'm here out of season is that I'm still waiting for word on the assignment. Can it be that they're trying to get rid of me? The assignment always seemed unlikely, and now it's beginning to seem impossible. And if I don't get it, it occurs to me here in the silence that when I get back I may find that my fifteen minutes of fame are just about up. You get no warning until the clock strikes. But recently I appeared on a list of splendid anachronisms, and in the same month was nominated for the High Camp Hall of Fame. The networks are alert to all rumors of leprosy, and NBC has cut me back to four puffy specials this season, so dignified they could pass for funerals.

In England life lingers longer, but in grotesque forms. The Queen's honors list may have signaled the end and I didn't know it. Again, dignity is the tip-off: for the last three months I've been rededicating cathedrals, laying cornerstones, taking a long, hard look at the crofting industry. Stuffy events are being concocted just for me by the world's grand masters. When I told my hippie interviewer that I would outlast him, I may have been right by about a year.

Oh, I would have the tricks to start over again—a new life, a new style—but I'm not sure they'd want that either. A monument is supposed to sit still where the pigeons can find it. I've suggested changes to my masters and none of them seems quite right; for all my eminence, it turns out that my straitjacket hasn't grown an inch since my first year in Fresno. It's as natty as a bishop's robes by now, but I'm still trussed up in it. The congregation doesn't know that their leader is a prisoner, too, that's all.

So any comebacks I make (and I expect to make exactly two when the time comes) will be the mixture as before. The Good Fairy, bored to distraction, rolls your last forty years' worth of dice at once. As I understand it, I shall be well known for ten, remembered as well known for another ten, then a trivia question; and if I still haven't taken the hint and died, nothing at all.

All this will be, of course, very crushing and liberating. The worst will have happened. I shall be laughed at definitively—the thing I have fended off so desperately will land and splatter me good. After which, life perhaps can begin. It's all that's left. I can even go insane if I choose without disrupting my schedule. I think I'd rather like that.

Now, about the nun. I insist you tell the rest about the nun, if you want absolution. And tell it straight.

All right, slanteyes. She slept with me, yes; not because I'm famous, the usual reason, but because I looked like a priest. She said as much, through hysterical tears. She also said she was the worst woman in the world, because she had always burned to sleep with a priest. So I said, "Well, now you can do it and not do it at the same time," and she stopped crying just like that, as if this made sense and she had been forgiven on the spot. By a make-believe priest.

"I'm worse than you are," I said, "because you really *are* a nun." And just saying it made me feel absolutely ill. I did *not* burn to sleep with a nun—far from it. The idea revolted me like incest. Yet, for me to be desired for that particular reason was suddenly overwhelming. Looking down at my clothes, I saw that they were indeed priests' clothes, priests' hands: my own confessor was standing above her.

The tape reveals a strange strangled growl on my part that I barely recognize, though I know my voice like a lover. And talk about noises: it wasn't the nun at all, but the urbane Monty Chatworth who banged away like a herd of bulls that afternoon in his madness. In fact, I was briefly reminded of my parents in the old days. A Chatworth through and through.

And then, in the midst of the uproar, her voice: "You see, you *can* have a baby with me," as if that's all she'd been trying to prove to complete her interview. It was true from my end of it. I had asked nothing about precautions, although I am usually meticulous on that. Perhaps I felt it was impolite to mention birth control to a nun. Anyhow, something in the circumstances made me feel profligately potent. "You *are* having a baby with me. I know it. I feel it." I wanted to fling myself out as from a burning room, but I somehow didn't, but settled in deep and warm and wet. And she cradled me like a child and wept with me over what we had done. And left without speaking.

In her note the next day, she concluded, "If it happens, don't worry. It's strictly between me and the Holy Ghost. A child does not have to be at the center. I don't know what gave you the idea. Your life is much too important to give up; but your sperm, my darling, is much too precious to waste. Love, Veronica."

The words make me cringe. Her lips had been formed around sacred words and now they were used for my vile product. I don't deserve such ardor and shouldn't be asked to. I shouldn't be subjected to good people. It's too cruel. I want to get out of here right now and back to my one-night bunnies, who think my sperm is a dandy souvenir. No more religious poets, ever again. They take sperm altogether too seriously.

. . . But supposing she is having a child. Isn't at least part of you pleased?

. . . No! And even if there were, it would be no match for the part that's horrified. You know my reasons. Throw in the population explosion for good measure. And my citation as non-father of the year. Throw in anything you can think of. I don't want a child.

Yes, I recognize what that means. I am not an idiot. Without a child, all else is hustle. And all the causes I fight for mean nothing, if I'm not prepared to launch one child into them. Even the cause of population control. Don't I know that the world will need intelligent children to look after even that?

But on the other hand, and for the last time, a man should be allowed to choose superficiality if he wants to. It's not my fault that I know too much to do it naturally. I've paid my dues to the world by raising money for it, and now I want to be left alone. Look, it's like the women who cannot face childbearing. Some quality of imagination makes it realer to them than to others, so that they suffer birth pangs for the whole nine months. You don't blame *them,* do you?

Well, that's how I feel about the father-son drama. I play every stage of it in my head: the look of trust when he's small and the hand in mine (yes, I can feel that easily); the withdrawn look in adolescence; and then, in a brief flash that lasts forever, the wounded-deer look, as if I've done something

301

terrible to him that he can't remember, some unforgivable crime; and then the blank-faced adult with all that locked away where only a shrink can find it. *I* did all that and *he'll* do it too, whoever he is.

And please—don't give me the good part, the joy in his company when he's young, the growing comradeship and finally the manly friendship. That's the *worst* part, the part that makes the rest so horrible. The good things are so fragile. I couldn't bear them. The clouds would come up and I couldn't protect him. Don't you see that? Life would bruise him mortally, as it does everybody, and I would just stand by helplessly, and he'd know it was my fault.

. . . Have you ever considered it might be a girl?

. . . Even worse. I know about that too, remember? My father didn't even mean to be a killer, and look at poor Prissy. I *would* mean it; I'm a professional. Imagine me with my know-how faced with a daughter's love. My charm is a deadly weapon like a fighter's fists. And I'd be too weak not to use it. I'd eat her alive like an aging courtesan by the time she was four.

. . . You're talking like a child yourself, Plunkett. Every father who ever lifted the burden knows what you know. It just has to be done again and again. A man your age has no business being so goddamn fragile. And hiding out behind the Chatworth nerves. You're as strong as a horse, and you know it. Your whole life is callous and coarse-grained, so you're splendidly equipped to be a father.

. . . Well, it's what Egbert said. The Chatworths have mastered the art of being sensitive and coarse-grained at the same time. We have the nerves of prima donnas and the souls of bank managers. Lots of old families are like that.

. . . They should never have told you about the nerves. You can imitate anything, even mumps. But if you didn't have nerves of iron you wouldn't have reached the top of your lousy profession, Plunkett. And you wouldn't be able to carry me on your payroll. A normal man would crack under the weight of a Snead. Yet no one out there has ever questioned your sanity, you know. Why? Because I am not, believe it or not, a nervous disorder. I am a conscience.

. . . Ah, go fuck yourself. You're just giving yourself airs, Snead. A conscience! Aren't we being fancy!

. . . Look, I wasn't born yesterday. How dare you use irony on me? A moment ago you were sobbing about your fears of growing up. Now you're swaggering again. And in a moment you'll be boasting about your professionalism, and how your work justifies your empty life. Please God you won't be able to wave that excuse at me much longer.

. . . Empty to you means childless?

. . . One way or another, yes. You don't have to have a baby if it's going to make you faint. But you've got to have something! As far as the kid is concerned, it's my opinion you're just scared he won't like you. He'll get to know you too well; and you won't let anyone do that, man, woman or child. Even when the public starts laughing at you, they won't know what they're laughing at. They've never met *you*. But what bothers me right now isn't the kid, it's how you treated the nun, how you talk and think about her.

. . . She bit me.

. . . That's too bad. Please don't try to make me laugh. You talked about Lisa that way, and all of them. Remember when the light went out in Lisa? She stopped loving you almost between blinks. The respect went out of her eyes, and you went berserk. Threw furniture . . .

. . . One small ashtray, when she called me a fag. Even Emily Post allows that, I believe.

. . . Because you couldn't have a bambino. Latins are funny that way. You loved her because she was so *católica,* so rich in life—and then you couldn't join her there. The sterile Englishman took over, as he has right now.

. . . Racist pig. After all these years, still using the tourist clichés. I say, this fire *is* good. It can do every face we've mentioned. What next, oh swami?

. . . Call the nun.

. . . What's the use of that? It would just be a celebrity calling a nun.

. . . No it wouldn't. She's never taken advantage of that. She's a bride of Christ, remember? She doesn't need celebrities. She loved something deeper in you than that. Call it priesthood. Call it class. And it frightened hell out of you. You *wanted* her to love the celebrity, so you could slip away unnoticed. You want the whole world to love the celebrity, so you'll be safe forever.

. . . I have that right. I don't want to be loved for myself; it's too disgusting. I'd lose *that* kind of love for sure. Veronica would look at me one day and see what I see. You're right, I couldn't bear that. It belongs in the confessional, and nowhere else.

. . . Call the nun.

. . . Christ, has it come to this? I never thought my moral duty would be to propose to a nun.

. . . Well, these are strange times. And it's a new Church. But I didn't say anything about proposing. It's just that your moral duty must come down to *something specific.* Some task laid out by your friend, the Good Fairy. How can I give you absolution, if you don't *do* something?

. . . You can't give me absolution, you blasphemous bastard. Somebody else has to. Somebody who doesn't exist anymore.

. . . What about the nun? I loved the way she put down your spiritual pretensions. You haven't even reached the first Mansion of the Soul, old buddy. You'll never have to worry about spiritual pride again with that broad around.

. . . The fire's going out. Should I just let it? Do I dare to eat a peach?

. . . That's it. Play your confession to the nun and see what she thinks.

. . . Shall I wear my trousers rolled? Well, why the fuck not, T.S.?

. . . Watch the love die out fast. Or not. Either way, it would settle things.

. . . Would you go away if I did?

. . . I can't promise anything. But it seems likely, doesn't it?

I can see Snead, me, in the dying fire. I would miss the little bugger. Or is that Plunkett in there? One of us would die, and it would be very lonely. Like a little boy with an imaginary friend. God won't play with me anymore or walk with me in the garden. I've been alone for a long time, ever since 1940, perhaps, when we sailed from England.

. . . I can't do it. I don't want to change. I want to stay the way I am.

. . . Then you're damned.

. . . So be it.

Snead seems to be leaving at last, if his little straw suitcase means anything. It is as if I'd made my decision and there was no more for him to do. So I might as well wrap up these tapes, then. I guess they've done their work. Let's just label them "What I did during my mid-life crisis" and forget about them. I don't expect to sound so old again for years.

Just to close the show properly, and prove how thoroughly I've been cured of this last vestige of Rome, this mystique of confession that had stuck in my teeth like a grapenut, I shall now absolve myself, using my best priest's voice for the occasion.

"That was a thoroughly mediocre confession, my son. [Laughter] As far as I can tell, your sins sound depressingly average. Perhaps that's the worst of it. Stringing a few girls along, as men have been doing since the dawn of time. Lying, faking, pretending. All one sin, really. Denying your heritage. Selling soap. Defrauding the public. Abandoning your mother and sister. Spitting on your own faith. Not being first-*rate*, Pen."

My God, is that my father's voice again? "What you are

305

doing now is perhaps the worst of all. Pretending to be a priest. Blaspheming your own bone and sinew. Making a mockery of all our lives. Perhaps it had to end this way. Egbert wanted to do it, too, you know—become a priest and end it all that way. But at least he wouldn't have been so smug about it, so bouncy. He'd have done it like a Chatworth of sorts. To have a cheap television announcer, a Yankee salesman, wind up our affairs in jest is a bit thick, don't you agree?"

"Father, forgive me."

"Out of the question, old chap. Impertinent of you even to ask. You haven't been first-rate, you know."

I should never have started this game. Sweating, groaning, I kneel my way across the wooden floor to the telephone. My hand soaks the black plastic and rattles it on its moorings. I shall call the nun.

26

~~~~~~

She sounded as startled as a small girl when she answered the phone; and I realized that among the many experiences she had sacrificed for those years was the humble telephone. My heart jumped at this like a frightened rabbit. I was talking to a grown-up child, a monstrosity. To illustrate—let me read the rest of that note into the record, while we're waiting.

Dear Pendrid,
   It seems to be as hard for you to find God as for me to find the world. I guess we both deserve *A* for effort so far. While you were learning all those clever things about people and places, I was looking only for God. And that was fine, except that one day the word got out that He wasn't in the convent anymore. I asked the other sisters about this, and they looked even blanker than usual. Some of them were already packing. The others said that they'd wait and see. Sister Superior was wearing a horrible new suit, so I didn't even bother to ask her. I was afraid God might have left the Church altogether.
   So I came out to look for Him, in the faces of the poor, where they always said He'd be, and I've been doing some work along that line in Harlem. But I don't know when I'm seeing it. You see, I don't know the world at all, and I don't

know who's putting me on. Probably being Christ-like is the first thing a bum learns, if he wants to make a hit with social workers. So I thought maybe if you don't mind we could pool our resources a little bit. They didn't teach me how to say more than that, so I'll stop here. But I would like to see you again.

Oh, and if . . .

Well, you know the rest.

Rereading it, I find that the naïveté gives me the shakes—it seems almost decadent in a woman of thirty. It's like finding an old man still looking for the Easter Bunny.

Maybe that's why nuns have always frightened people: they are one of the Church's strangest perversions. Yet, whatever it is, I want it. I felt an excitement with Veronica that I haven't felt since I was a boy. In fact, she is like myself coming round again. Her skin is fresh as a baby's, her eyes are so sea-blue clear you can almost see white sand behind them, and the brown hair growing tentatively back reminds me of spring planting.

Another victim for you? Perhaps. Yet, she is probably tougher than the others. It takes the guts of a burglar to be a bride of Christ. I don't think I could hurt her after that. And what do I know about the New Nun anyway? Out there on the spiritual frontier, they must develop some weird kinks of their own. Though it's funny, she told me right off that she'd been released from her vow of chastity—as a teen-ager might show his driver's license to a bartender.

I must have it. A second chance. With her I can be *vibrantly* superficial. It will be like leading a child through the forest—a joy and a terror. Well, at least she must have no delusions about who the Big Bad Wolf is. If I describe myself in the usual way, I'll dress myself in ribbons and bows of evil and look divine. But these tapes are just between me and God, or the closest I can come to that in my farcical forties. It's hard if you don't believe anymore, but I've done my best. And Veronica is the only judge I'll accept now, the only one within a prayer of having the proper credentials.

27

~~~~~~

Now, about that precious assignment: it turned out to be just another Italian joke. Some of the clowns at the Curia must have been hoping to turn a fast lira. But everyone knows the Pope doesn't do talk shows.

Meanwhile, the real enchilada went to the other fellow, the one with the funny voice. Ominous. And rumor has it that NBC is hiring another Englishman. Rumor also has it that it doesn't matter. The two countries have been growing closer, flattening me like Spam. Get back, both of you, while there's still time.

So although it's a sunny year, the storm warnings are always out; old mariners know when even bright sunshine looks wrong. In view of which, Veronica and I have decided to issue the following joint announcement:

Reverend sponsors, NBC executives, members of the public. I have been advised that the only God left is you, and that I must apply to you for forgiveness. You can signify your approval by showering me with ratings, unto seventy times seven; or you may punish me by switching to CBS. Either

309

way, it will be a merciful release. My confession must end somewhere.

Heaven knows, you are not much of a God: a sickening comedown, in fact, from my dreams. Hermits wasted away in the desert and saints were crucified upside down for something slightly better than this. But my new spiritual director insists that God is in you somewhere, deep down in your dull eyes and wandering minds, and that absolution can only come from you.

In other words, Veronica has instructed me to publish the tapes, so that you will know once and for all who I am. I'm afraid she is not that unworldly. She belonged to a fund-raising order. Besides *nobody* these days is naïve about money. So I think I can safely speak for Snead, Plunkett, *and* Veronica when I say I hope we make a bundle on it, and launch that new career as Mr. Honesty.

She has never said it in so many words, but I was afraid at moments that she found the tapes funny. This, of course, is what I feared and hoped for, the perfect punishment for my particular case. But it's hard to tell with nuns: their polite smiles cover so many possibilities. They would be perfect for criminal lunatics, for instance. In that case, pray God, Prissy will find them funny, too. Mother won't read them at all, of course—she won't read the comics if they threaten to turn ugly. As for Father Sony, he has been retired to the retreat house in Jersey, and serves him right. His replacement, Father Magnavox, is a big, healthy fellow who hears no evil: a muscular Christian of the best sort. Snead is so in love he keeps pulling out chairs when there's no one there. I believe Veronica will assume his sterner duties once she gets the know-how.

I've never been taught by nuns before—the one essential I've missed. She has already sent out for some friends for me, a very big thing in the new Church. Perhaps the only thing so far. All I can say up to now is that ex-Jesuits seem very hearty.

Sister Rip Van Winkle is still excited by almost everything

she sees. For instance, she was dying to visit Las Vegas, so I took her, with all the grim warnings decency demands, and she loved it seraphically. "All those lights going day and night; only there is no day and night, is there?" All this before we'd left the airport, mind you.

And so it went in Caesar's Palace and all the blazing infernos we passed through. "The people seem so vivid. They're either crushed, or raging, or exalted—anyway, they're totally alive. What we used to try to make them do in churches." She laughed at the comparison. "And we achieved the exact opposite, didn't we?" If she could see good in these places, there is hope for all of us. Of course, she believed, like a pious Catholic, that gambling was a good thing for people to be doing: it brought their souls to the boil, she said, and freed them from their crabbed, calculating dailiness. "Do you realize these people may be insurance salesmen in real life? They've been *saved.*" To her, everyone in the outside world is in the insurance business. But she wouldn't gamble herself; the clasp on her little purse opened rarely and reluctantly, and a tiny folded bill would emerge. A little crabbed dailiness herself, perhaps. She also used words like "teriff" and was poignantly, heartbreakingly close to being silly. I won't deny I've thought of doing a program on a nun in Las Vegas, but I swear I haven't approached anybody.

As for hotel rooms, I won't say she plays with the faucets in the bathtubs, but she does ask for quarters to make the bed vibrate. I don't know how much of this I can stand; but right now there's a freshness and bustle about it, like a medieval kitchen, that makes me realize how dark one's life had become, and how dangerous these games of mine have been. Veronica tells me with that fixed smile that I have been venturing with diabolism. Shades of Maureen; but Veronica seems to welcome it, like a nurse rolling up her sleeves for a really good epidemic. Meanwhile, I solemnly promise never to talk to myself again.

Next week, we'll be visiting what's left of Chatworth

311

Manor, and I only hope she doesn't fall in love with it like an American. I will not go back there, even for her. American ghosts are more outgoing, more fun; or to put it another way, the place scares me to the marrow, from the stone floor in the hall to the motionless velvet curtains to the me that awaits me there, smiling: knowing all along that I'd come to my senses some day and return for good.

Beyond that, my life with Veronica is none of your business, although there's no concealing the fact that she's expecting a baby in the fall. I fear for the little bastard and I hope I don't hurt him too much. But in the clean, muscular air around Veronica, these night fears grow temporarily faint.

Otherwise, I think that about cleans it out; the nastiest words in my heart. There's nothing underneath them—nothing now between the nerve and the drill. Forgive me, Father. And get off my back.

A neon light shines through my stained-glass window. "Consider it done, old boy. You know, of course, that I never made any such claims to importance in my life. In fact, I distinctly remember bending over backwards *not* to seem like God, and I trust you'll do the same. But nomadic peoples will make a fuss over their leaders, you know. Look at Moses. And so it was with us. The thing to remember," he screws a monocle in viciously and his mustache bursts into flower, "is that wherever you go and whatever you do, you're sure to wind up cryin' those transatlantic blues."

Thanks, Pop. Jackson. Solid. Ripping. I knew you weren't God, but it's good to hear it in your own words. And now, down the steps and into the sunshine, until next time.